An Oath and a Promise

The Riehse Eshan Series, Book Four

ADELAIDE BLAIKE

Copyright © 2023 Adelaide Blaike

All rights reserved.

ISBN: 9798864341230

Chapter Twenty-Eight	251
Chapter Twenty-Nine	258
Chapter Thirty	271
Chapter Thirty-One	276
Chapter Thirty-Two	282
Chapter Thirty-Three	294
Chapter Thirty-Four	300
Chapter Thirty-Five	305
Chapter Thirty-Six	311
Chapter Thirty-Seven	315
Chapter Thirty-Eight	319
Chapter Thirty-Nine	323
Chapter Forty	326
Chapter Forty-One	329
Chapter Forty-Two	332
Chapter Forty-Three	336
Chapter Forty-Four	340
Chapter Forty-Five	343
Chapter Forty-Six	346
Chapter Forty-Seven	350
Chapter Forty-Eight	355
Chapter Forty-Nine	358
Chapter Fifty	361
Chapter Fifty-One	364
Chapter Fifty-Two	370
Chapter Fifty-Three	375
Chapter Fifty-Four	383
Chapter Fifty-Five	391
Chapter Fifty-Six	396
Chapter Fifty-Seven	400
Chapter Fifty-Eight	405
Chapter Fifty-Nine	407
Acknowledgements	413

AN OATH AND A PROMISE

CONTENTS

Author's Note	i
Map	iii
Genograms	v
Translations of common words	vii
Recap of the series so far	ix
Chapter One	1
Chapter Two	7
Chapter Three	15
Chapter Four	25
Chapter Five	31
Chapter Six	43
Chapter Seven	53
Chapter Eight	68
Chapter Nine	82
Chapter Ten	89
Chapter Eleven	95
Chapter Twelve	100
Chapter Thirteen	106
Chapter Fourteen	118
Chapter Fifteen	124
Chapter Sixteen	128
Chapter Seventeen	131
Chapter Eighteen	144
Chapter Nineteen	154
Chapter Twenty	167
Chapter Twenty-One	177
Chapter Twenty-Two	181
Chapter Twenty-Three	192
Chapter Twenty-Four	203
Chapter Twenty-Five	217
Chapter Twenty-Six	236
Chapter Twenty-Seven	246

AUTHOR'S NOTE

While some of the practices and languages in this book share similarities to real cultures, this is for fictional entertainment purposes only and (many) changes have been made to suit the story told. As such, nothing in this book is intended to be a reflection or commentary on any real culture or person, alive or deceased.

> This book has a major trigger warning for on-page sexual assault (which is also referred to by the characters as rape, consistent with the applicable law in the author's state) involving the magical equivalent of drugging. Please note that this book also contains externalised homophobia (including on religious grounds), misogyny and gendered abuse, BDSM, anxiety/panic attacks, and discussion about suicidal and self-harm inclinations. It's darker in a lot of ways than the previous books, but as the last in the series, does have its (hard-won) HEA. This book is intended for mature readers only, and reader discretion is advised.

AN OATH AND A PROMISE

MAP

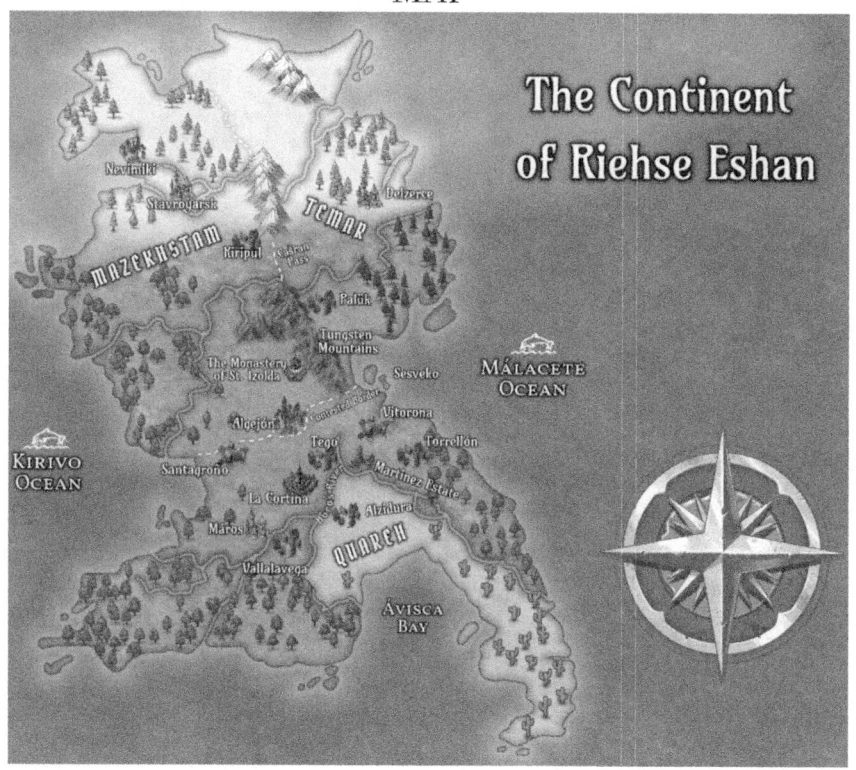

AN OATH AND A PROMISE

GENOGRAMS

Quarehian Royal Family
Iván Aratorre
m
Consuela Aratorre
Laurita Aratorre
m
Horacio Aratorre
King
Zidhan Welzes
m
Alondra Welzes
Mariana Janssen
m
Pieter Janssen
?
Renato Aratorre
Basilio Aratorre
Félix Aratorre
Nohr Janssen
Mazekhstani Royal Family
Ksenia Sluchevskaya
m
Stepan Sluchevsky
King
Oleg Panarin
m
Freja Panarina
Lilya Sluchevskaya
Pavel Sluchevsky
Oleg Panarin
Regent
Astrid Panarina
Kolya Panarin
Temarian Royal Family
Anton Velichkov
m
Queen
Zora Velichkova
m
Dafo Velichkov
Petra Velichkova
m
Valeri Velichkov
Mila Velichkova
Aleksi Velichkov
m
Bovana Velichkova
Nathanael Velichkov
Yiorgos Velichkov
Dafo Velichkov
Ana Velichkova
Zahari Velichkov

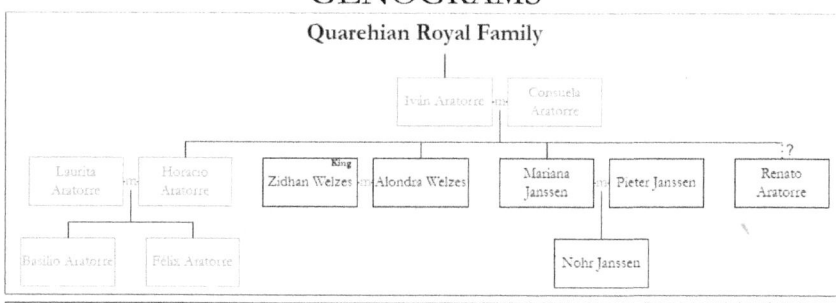

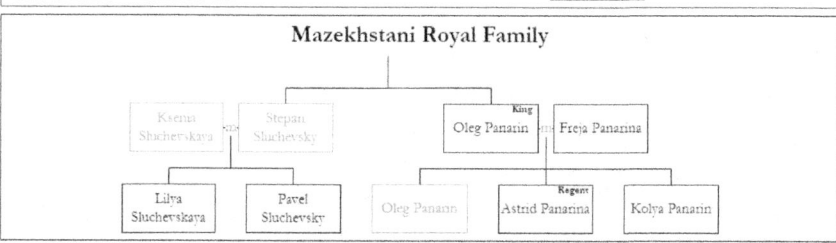

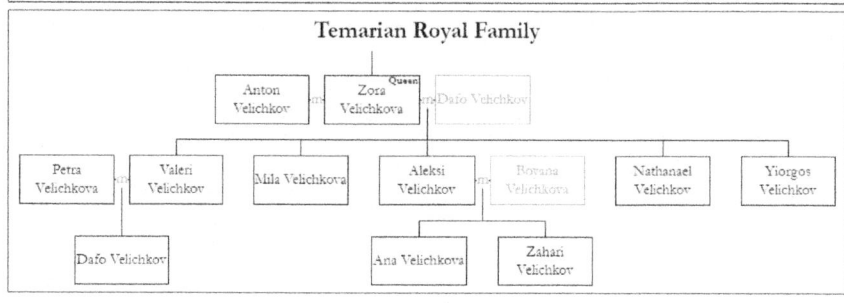

AN OATH AND A PROMISE

TRANSLATIONS OF COMMON WORDS

<u>Quarehian</u>
Bárbaro – Barbarian
Buenos días – Good morning
Dios – God (por Dios is oh my God/for God's sake, while Dios mío is my God)
Lo siento – I'm sorry
Mi amor/cielo/corazón/gato montés/sol – My love/sky/heart/wildcat/sun
Mi querida/querido – My dear or my darling
Mierda – Shit
Por favor – Please
Sí – Yes
Señor/señora/señorita – Mr/Mrs/Miss

<u>Mazekhstani</u>
Blyat – Fuck
Da – Yes
Moy dorogoi/knyaz – My darling/prince
Nyet – No
Otlichnyy – Excellent
Poshel na khuy – Go fuck yourself
Svoloch – Bastard (plural: svolochi)

<u>Temarian</u>
Blagodarya – Thank you
Da – Yes
Dobar den – Good day
Ebasi – Fuck
Leka nosht – Goodnight
Vednaga – Now

Please note that occasional foreign words which are used when the characters are permanently speaking that same language are included solely for creative impact. Any errors in translation are the author's own and are apologised for in advance.

AN OATH AND A PROMISE

AN OATH AND A PROMISE

Recap of the series so far

Mat: Please, *please,* tell me that this is the last of these damn things we have to do.

Ren: You're a right ray of fucking sunshine, you know that?

Mat: If you wanted cheerful, you should have found someone other than me to annoy and harass. I mean…*court.*

Ren: *(laughs)* I'll start us off, then. So there was our first time when I fucked him over a table, and then we got frisky in this tiny-ass bed but his brother walked in on us, and *then* I got Mathias on his knees and-

Mat: Is your recap seriously going to only cover the times we had sex?

Ren: It's meant to include the important parts, so…yeah.

Mat: Fine. *Fine!* I'll do it.

Ren: *(hopefully)* And I'll do you?

Mat: Um, *(flustered)* …so after the horrendous events of the Morenos' coup that left Iván Aratorre dead and Ren inheriting the Quarehian throne, we made plans to meet up outside of the palace for some time alone before he was crowned.

Ren: Time alone, which is spelt S-E-X. I told you that was the only matter of import.

Mat: And yet there must be more, because otherwise we'd have had a nice romantic night at the hacienda in the hills…and yet instead, we both ended up abducted by my family when they led Temar's army to Quareh.

Ren: Urgh. At least yours was a mercy kidnapping where they thought they were *saving* you from some dastardly fate. Mine was humiliating, time-wasting, and quite frankly, irritating. Your brother Valeri and sister Mila tried to ransom me back to my dead father, for fuck's sake.

Mat: Only because we hadn't told them he was dead for fear they'd decide to kill you instead.

Ren: That's true. But it still doesn't excuse all the maltreatment I was rudely

and thoughtlessly subjected to, does it?

Mat: Maybe if you hadn't pissed my brother off quite so much, he wouldn't have been so keen to hit you.

Ren: Maybe if your brother got laid once in a while, he wouldn't need an excuse to get his hands all over me.

Mat: Oh yes, the fact that Val completely freaked out when he found out I preferred men meant he was *absolutely* trying to feel you up by repeatedly punching you in the fucking face.

Ren: It's not my fault I'm irresistible.

Mat: Most things *are* your fault.

Ren: Not the part where, after leveraging my freedom from your family with the assistance of Temar's royal seer, what's-her-name…

Mat: Aksinia.

Ren: Yeah, the señorita who said if I was ransomed back to Quareh it would be horrendously bad for the whole continent, which was ominous as fuck but I wasn't going to complain if it meant she helped me escape. Which she did. After *that*, you may recall that you openly kissed me in front of thousands of your people and caused a riot in response to our public display of – alleged – illegality.

Mat: That too.

Ren: *How*, Mathias? How is that possibly *my fault*?

Mat: For being irresistible.

Ren: *(temporarily lost for words – but only temporarily)* Oh.

Mat: I didn't want to hide anymore, Ren. I didn't want to sneak around pretending we were still enemies when we'd confessed our love to each other literally only hours before. I didn't want you to think I was ashamed of you.

Ren: Oh Mat, I never thought…I know it was difficult for you. With the north condemning sodomy as sinful and illegal, what you did risked you a likely fatal flogging or worse. I couldn't bear it if you suffered because of me.

Mat: Right. Which is why you were an absolute prick in an attempt to drive me away…because *that* was a solid and not at all ridiculously stupid plan.

AN OATH AND A PROMISE

Ren: It didn't work, remember?

Mat: Because it was a ridiculously stupid plan. You're such an idiot at times.

Ren: And you're a reckless fool. You almost died after inciting that mob when your brother refused to hand you over to face their *justice*.

Mat: Then it was lucky I had a dashing prince willing to whisk me away to his palace and protect me from my people's fucked up bigotry, right?

Ren: Hmm. Very lucky. As long as you're talking about me and not Prince Kolya Panarin, who wanted to do something extremely similar, if I recall correctly.

Mat: Kolya is...*(sighs)*

Ren: Hopelessly obsessed with you?

Mat: He's only-

Ren: A complete prick of a Mazekhstani prince who tried to steal what is mine? That's you, by the way.

Mat: It's just-

Ren: A murderous bastard who ignited black powder during the tournament we were hosting, killing dozens of people so that our attempts at achieving peace would be ruined...and to take me out so he could have you for himself?

Mat: I'm finding it difficult to argue.

Ren: Yeah. Because when you rejected him, Panarin got particularly nasty, torturing and trying to kill us both with the anti-healing magic of his Touch. I really should thank Valeri for saving us from him.

Mat: *(waits patiently. Waits some more. And more, now quite impatiently)* Well?

Ren: I said I *should* thank him. Not that I'm going to. He didn't manage to finish Panarin off, so he gets points deducted from his heroism for that.

Mat: As gracious as ever.

Ren: Meh. Velichkov deserves it for trying to denounce you as a prince of Temar and taking away your right to ever ascend to its throne.

Mat: Are you just inventing reasons not to like my brother because you've realised he's – in your words – *not terrible*? Because you seem to have forgotten

AN OATH AND A PROMISE

that the denouncement was *my* idea, Ren, to try and soothe my people's anger at me and restore confidence in my family as their rulers. Besides, it never went ahead.

Ren: I'm not thanking Panarin for that, even if his explosions did distract them long enough for me to sneak you off to Máros while our peoples were still recovering from the chaos he caused.

Mat: *(quietly)* And busy building peace. Because we did that, Ren, you and me. And Val and Mila. We showed the continent that the north and south can co-exist without violence.

Ren: That was all you, *mi sol*. You believed in what we all thought impossible. And what *I* thought impossible was Valeri fucking Velichkov voluntarily riding into Quareh's capital city to attend my coronation.

Mat: Only you weren't crowned, because one of your father's former councillors, Navar, was so afraid of losing power that he accused you of being your mother's bastard son without any claim to the Aratorre name or the throne. Then he tried to have you arrested.

Ren: Convenient how the next in line to the crown was my oldest sister's husband, Zidhan Welzes, a misogynistic prick who matches Councillor Navar's interests quite nicely, wasn't it?

Mat: Very. Less convenient was how we were cornered trying to escape the palace and had to leave your guards behind.

Ren: Dios. I hope they're....I hope they're okay.

Mat: Please worry about yourself first, Ren.

Ren: I'm fine.

Mat: You're not fine. You ended up with a fucking arrow in your shoulder, or have you forgotten?

Ren: Oh. Yeah. That... *(in a faint voice)* hurt.

Chapter One

"Here's your bastard prince."

I choked out a cry as my brother forced Ren down to his knees in front of Welzes, keeping hold of his collar. My lover had his hands bound behind his back and he shot a hateful glare up at Valeri before turning that same pissed off expression onto the Quarehians standing before him.

There was something dark smeared around his mouth, staining his chin and the front of his shirt. He didn't even *try* to speak, and perhaps that was when I should have known something terrible had happened.

"Renato," Zidhan Welzes purred, looking delighted. The Lukian man adjusted the gold crown on his head for no reason other than to draw attention to it, his fingers lingering over the jewels embedded in its surface. "You've led us on a merry chase, dear boy."

Then he winced, glancing at the nobles gathered around the room. "And yet, considering what he can *do*, Prince Valeri, I find it disturbing that you've brought him here."

My calves were bathed in hot agony, and I couldn't put any weight on my legs at all. Someone was holding me upright, their grip firm on both my upper arms, but I wasn't looking at them. All I could see was Ren, and the man pretending to be Quareh's king as he leered at him on the floor.

"You needn't fear," my brother assured Welzes, looking down at Ren disdainfully as though he was dirt under his boot. "The little snake cannot weave his manipulations while he's missing his tongue."

No.

I stared at the thick mass of blood around my prince's mouth, chilled to the core.

In turn, he glared silently at a smug Welzes, his bloodied lips pressed defiantly together. Val reached down to pry open his jaw, ignoring his furious efforts to shake him off, and the gasp that echoed through the gathered court reflected my own.

"Ren!"

Brown eyes found mine across the room, angry and hurting.

I blinked and…

"Ren?"

The same eyes stared back at me through the dusky gloom, only these were a lot closer. Mere inches away.

And while there was pain buried in their depths, there was none of the fury that he'd worn in…in…

It had been a vision.

"Thank fuck," I said, nearly sobbing as I reached for the man lying next to me. Ren gave me a bemused smile, his fingers dancing across my skin as if assuring himself that I was real.

I rubbed a hand over my eyes and tried to shake off the remnants of my prescient magic that so often felt more like a curse than a gift. I had *not* needed to be shown my lover bound, captured, and mutilated like that, especially not so soon after the reality of almost having to watch him die from the arrow that had pierced his shoulder when we escaped the Márosian palace a few days ago. "You still have your tongue?"

Ren batted his eyelashes at me, brimming with mischief and not at all put off by the oddness of the question. His tongue darted over his bottom lip: enticing, sensual, and promising to inflict a whole host of wicked things on me.

His *unsevered* tongue.

"*Sí.* Want me to prove it to you?"

He dipped his head to my bare chest and captured my nipple in his mouth before I could stop him, grazing his teeth daringly against the skin. While it helped to chase away the lingering fogginess caused by the horrific vision, I was under instructions to keep the prince as still as possible.

So I gently – and reluctantly – pushed him back down onto the blankets that served as our bed down in this draughty basement, sheets billowing around us where they hung from lines stretched between the walls. "As thankful as

AN OATH AND A PROMISE

I am that you're not really in the hands of my fucking traitor of a brother, you're still healing."

Ren tensed under my touch. "Your brother? Mat, what did you See?"

"He delivers you back to Welzes," I said bitterly, hearing my voice breaking on the words. "After everything that happened with the tournament and Kolya…I really thought Val was on your side."

My prince was quiet for a long moment. "You said yourself that the Sight isn't absolute. What you Saw might never happen."

"But it might." I shook my head. "I'd thought about reaching out to him to ask for help, but we can't take that chance. Not if he's working with that fucker claiming to be Quareh's king."

"That…doesn't seem like your brother."

"As a person? No," I admitted, absently tracing shapes on the blanket between us. "But as the heir of Temar? He'll do whatever he thinks is best for his people."

I was positive there would be a reason for why Valeri had done what he'd done…what he *might* do. He wasn't a monster. Yet to not only hand Ren over to his enemy, but to fucking *mutilate* him first by cutting out his tongue? What could possibly justify that?

Then I remembered the vice-like grip on my arms, the pain in my legs. If Val believed that by damning Ren he could save me…my brother had acted out of desperation before when it came to my safety. What if this was no different?

"Urgh," Ren groaned, gingerly peeling back the bandage wrapped across his chest and left shoulder so he could peer at the wound beneath. "Whoever you asked to tend to this was a fucking butcher."

"*Well*," I said, drawing the word out. "He was."

"I'm glad you agree, because…" Ren paused and stared at me. "You mean *literally* a butcher, don't you, Mathias?"

I gave him a bright, comforting smile that he didn't buy for an instant. "I didn't exactly have many options when you were inconsiderately bleeding out all over me."

"About that. Why do I still hurt?" he asked, tugging back the bandage further to reveal ugly stitches. He prodded at them until I smacked his hand away. "You know magic exists, right?"

"Healers don't grow on trees," I retorted, pulling a face at his patronising yet playful tone. "You try finding someone with the Touch who doesn't work for the crown or is on its watch list."

And then I frowned at him. "You don't remember me telling you this already? You woke up yesterday after scaring the shit out of me for being unconscious for over a *day*."

"Not a word," Ren said cheerfully. "Although I vaguely remember you crying."

"I wasn't crying. I don't *cry*."

He patted my hand condescendingly. "Of course you don't."

"What do you actually remember?" I asked.

"Pain. A lot of it. Someone saying I'd pull through. Then some nonsense about not engaging in any *strenuous physical activity* for at least a week, at which point I thought I must be having a nightmare and went back to sleep."

"Ren," I began slowly, not wanting to relive those terrifying moments where I'd thought he was going to die. "You were shot as we fled the palace into the city, and you fell from the horse. You dragged me off with you, so you kind of landed on me instead."

"It's good to know even my unconscious self wants to get you beneath me," Ren commented slyly, and then quietened as I shot him a dark look.

"A lot of your people saw it happen. And obviously the rumours about your illegitimacy hadn't reached the city yet: all they saw was their prince injured, and they helped get you away from the men pursuing us. By the time order was restored – apparently Councillor Navar himself had to come down from the palace to validate the demand for our arrest – I'd managed to hide you." I gestured to the dim room around us, although little could be seen past the sheets that surrounded the makeshift bed. "But as it was known you were wounded, the city's healers were the first to receive a visit from the guards. The butcher was the only one we could trust who had any experience with…flesh."

AN OATH AND A PROMISE

Ren wrinkled his nose. "Animal flesh, Nat. *Dead. Animal. Flesh.*"

"Yeah, you complained about that yesterday, too."

He thought about that. "If we did already have a conversation while I was delirious, then I've missed the rest of it. Give it to me now."

"The rest of what?" I asked, suspecting a trap from the way his eyes had begun to sparkle with mirth.

"The part where you flung yourself at me in overwrought relief as to my heroic survival, *mi amor*," Ren said with a shit-eating grin. "The part where the distraught and certainly *crying* northern prince breaks down out of fear that he might have lost his one true love forever, and then he wails in gratitude as he pulls through, having promised to do anything – *anything, Mathias* – if he would just live."

"You've read too many books," I said dismissively. "There was none of that."

There had, in fact, been a *lot* of that, but if Ren didn't remember rousing to consciousness before now, I certainly wasn't going to be repeating such an embarrassing performance.

"I think you're-"

Footsteps echoed in the basement with us; close, heavy treads on stone that strode towards us with purpose and made him falter.

Mat, Ren mouthed. *We're not alone.*

The noises drew closer, but their maker was hidden by the linen sheets gently fluttering around us.

The prince's fingers found mine and squeezed tightly.

"Señor?" our visitor called out.

"Morning," I said easily, and one of the sheets was tugged aside to reveal a short Quarehian woman with her hair plaited and pinned around the crown of her head. She had a chipped jug in her hands, which she almost dropped when she lowered herself into a hasty curtsy at the sight of Ren.

"Your Highness! You're awake!"

His eyes flickered to mine, uncertain.

"Señora Hernández," I greeted her by name for his sake, and reached up to

5

take the jug from her limp hands before it splashed more water over the floor. "The Hernándezes have been very kind in allowing us to take shelter in their home," I explained, helping Ren to sit up when it became clear that he was going to do so either with or without my assistance.

"You have my gratitude," he said sincerely, with a graciousness that held none of the prince's usual sarcasm or flirtation. The woman gave a shy smile and withdrew, letting the sheets fall back into place to enclose us once more.

The room was too cold at night and swelteringly humid during the day when the basement became the laundry it was primarily used for, but we'd be sleeping on the streets if Señora Hernández hadn't found us. She and her wife risked a hanging – or worse – for offering us aid.

Sequestered away like this, with nothing but white cloth surrounding us, it almost made it seem like we were cloistered among the clouds. Somewhere peaceful and serene, and not a dank basement that now, thanks to our presence, reeked of sweat and the iron tang of blood. Where Ren wasn't recovering from a hole in his fucking shoulder after being driven from his palace by malicious lies.

He swayed against me, eyelashes and breath fluttering, and I took his weight.

"Rest," I murmured, helping him to lie back down on the floor and untwisting the sheets that were tangled around our legs. I could see him struggling to keep his eyes open now that the brief surge of excitement had faded.

I stroked his hair in the way I knew he liked until his body surrendered to sleep once more.

With a warrant out for my arrest alongside the prince's, and looking as distinctly foreign as I did, it would be unwise for me to leave the basement. But even if that hadn't been the case, there was nowhere I would choose to be other than here, listening to Ren's shallow, pained breathing, keeping him cool with a wet cloth draped across his brow, and holding his hand in mine.

*

Chapter Two

"*No*," I said, pissed off. "The man may have taken my sister, my crown, and my country, but I draw the line at my fucking *bed*. Welzes actually had the audacity to move into the king's chambers?"

Lord de la Vega nodded sombrely from the carriage seat opposite us, where his significant bulk took up most of the space. The nobleman, who had made his fortune in trade, had travelled with us from *la Cortina* to Máros to attend my coronation, and was now one of our only allies in the city. "Although I *may* have mentioned to him what you'd been up to in it only a few nights ago, my prince. I fear I upset his enjoyment of his new abode somewhat, as I've never seen anyone pale quite so quickly." He looked at Mat and chuckled, a glimmer of amusement flickering in his beady eyes. "You have a beautiful singing voice, Your Highness."

My northerner cocked his head, frowning in confusion. Then his eyes went wide with horror as he registered the lord's meaning and he promptly buried his face in my uninjured shoulder. "Oh!"

"Now you have," I said, cackling.

"How?" Mathias wailed, his voice muffled by the itchy fabric of the commoner clothes I was wearing.

"The guest rooms I was assigned in the palace are below those of the king," de la Vega told him, sharing a conspiratorial wink with me. "Certain...*sounds* travel rather well."

"We're changing that, Ren," Mat snarled into my shoulder. "The moment you get your crown back, we're removing everything from that entire wing."

"Certainly, *mi cielo*," I said amicably, patting his hair. "I shall of course defer all those pesky amendments to the gender laws and focus my attentions solely on palace renovations designed to allow you to scream even louder when I fuck you."

He peeled his face away and glared up at me with murder in those blue-grey eyes of his I adored so much.

But because I loved courting danger and wasn't done teasing him, I glanced at de la Vega. "I hope you also encouraged Welzes to take a look in my bedside drawers? My toys should keep him reminded of whose rooms he's sleeping in."

"Naturally, my prince," the man said smoothly, and Mat choked, glancing between me and the lord with a clear question in his eyes. I blinked back innocently.

"Can we fucking *focus?*" he snapped, now peering worriedly at the curtained windows of the carriage as if expecting to see soldiers staring back from the other side. "We're being hunted like Blessed dogs through the city, and the net is tightening every day. Sooner or later they're going to catch us – catch *you,* Ren – and Welzes isn't going to give a fuck about having to change the sheets on his bed when him and Councillor Navar have your head on a spike."

"Hmm," I said, doubtful. "Decapitation isn't the way they'll go. Considering they have no intention of letting me live long enough to stand trial for my alleged treason – because it's complete bullshit – they'll have to make my end look like an accident or a suicide. Losing one's head tends to suggest foul play…unless you think anyone would buy that I accidentally tripped and fell neck first onto a *really* sharp axe?"

Mathias shot me a disdainful look. "I don't care *how* they're planning to kill you, just that they are."

"It's terribly sweet of you to care at all." I beamed at him, nudging my elbow against his. Unfortunately, de la Vega's carriage turned a corner at the same time, and the nudge became a rather hard prod to his ribs as I fell against him. He smacked my thigh sharply in response.

"I care," Mat hissed. "To the extent that if anyone gets to finish your irritating ass off, it better be me."

I snorted at the interesting wording. "We're dissecting *that* sentence later, *mi sol.*"

De la Vega wore a mildly bemused expression as he watched us both from the rear-facing seat, swaying gently from side to side as the carriage continued to trundle down the street. It was a risk for us to be here, but these days it was a risk for us to be *anywhere,* with the whole population of Máros looking for us thanks to Welzes and Navar declaring me a traitor. If only my people knew how damn ironic that was, but the universal truth remained: the man with the soldiers got to define the narrative, and I didn't have a single person at my back except Mathias.

And Lord de la Vega, apparently, although trusting him was a risk too. He'd always been loyal to me, but so had many others who had now seemingly thrown in their lot with Welzes as the 'true' king, because that was how it worked. A ruler was only as good as recognition of their legitimacy, and while my father had taken the crown twenty-five years ago through bloodshed rather than birthright, now that he had, as long as an Aratorre remained breathing we were owed Quareh. It was why Comandante Moreno had tried to force me to formally cede the throne to him rather than having me killed as he had my brother and my father: with my sisters still alive, they would have had more of a legitimate claim to it than he. Unless he'd sent assassins to the mainland to execute them and their children, no Quarehian would have supported Moreno's claim without the legitimacy offered by my cession.

Which is exactly why Navar had sought to discredit my lineage. If I wasn't Iván's son, then the crown passed to the next Aratorre in line, being my oldest sister Alondra. And because Quareh was, in my darling Mathias' eloquent words, *a misogynistic fucking shithole,* that meant the real power would be held by her Lukian husband, Duke Zidhan Welzes.

Who, because he'd rudely inserted himself into my coronation ceremony after we'd been forced to flee the palace six days ago, was now *King* Welzes.

Urgh. All the Dios-damned celebrating we'd encountered in Máros over this past week had been draining, not just for the reminder that someone else was sitting on *my* throne, holding court in *my* palace, and eating *my* fucking coronation cake – the three-tiered orange and almond one I'd specifically commissioned as a private joke for Mat – but because it put twice as many people on the streets at night than usual. Sneaking around the city was fucking difficult, especially with a pale-skinned Temarian in tow, and we'd had too many close escapes already, many of which had only been evaded by the benefit of my lover's Sight.

As Mat had said, we were running out of time and places to hide. Which was why we'd had to trust that de la Vega wouldn't sell us out the moment we accepted his coded invitation to meet, although those seconds after we'd joined him in his carriage while it paused in a deserted alleyway, wondering if we'd find ourselves surrounded by palace guards in the next street...or the next, or the next, had been some of the most tense moments of my life.

Yet here we were, ten minutes later and still not clapped in irons, so I figured the trust thing was going as well as could be hoped. Mathias had tried his darndest to get me to stay behind in the Hernándezes' laundry, but if we were taking the risk of meeting with Lord de la Vega face to face, I wanted to be there to hear what he had to say.

Besides, as I'd pointed out to Mat, if he was captured then there was really no hope for me either, because I'd give myself up the moment they threatened him. That had apparently not been as romantic a thing to say as I'd expected, because he just proceeded to look pissed off for the next half hour.

I'd spent the same half hour carefully constructing a series of subtle questions and evocatory expressions designed to tease out Lord de la Vega's true intentions and learn his underlying motivations, each word scrupulously calculated to not alert or alarm him while I assessed his trustworthiness. I opened my mouth now to commence the planned eleven-minute artful interrogation, only for Mathias to speak first.

"Why the fuck are you helping us?" he asked bluntly, rudely, and with as much sophistication as a dead pigeon. I cursed him under my breath, and then again, out loud.

De la Vega chuckled. "My dear boy, I don't need your seer's gift to recognise what's good for business," he said, "and that's a united Riehse Eshan with open trade between all three countries. Something our new king has already shown he's not interested in pursuing."

Or rather, Councillor Navar wasn't. I wondered how much influence each of the men held in this new arrangement of theirs, and which of them would break first when pushed.

"So that's it?" Mat demanded, indignant. He straightened in his seat, his shoulders practically vibrating with fury. "You only want Ren back on the throne because it will earn you more *money*?"

"That's good enough for me," I said, and it was. We weren't all so magnanimous and selfless as my lover – in fact, it was highly doubtful *any* of us were – and a man looking to protect the gold in his pocket could be relied on to act consistently with that goal. Except…

"Although if it is riches you're seeking," I added casually, "wouldn't turning us in for the reward be in your best interest? I hear there's a significant bounty on my head."

It was hard not to preen at that, because it really was an enormous sum of money that had been offered to any citizen who handed me over. That was another thing that had made it too dangerous to stay in the city, but with Máros encircled by high, guarded walls on all sides, we weren't getting out without assistance.

"There is," Lord de la Vega agreed with a suspicious amount of cheer. "Especially now Prince Valeri has doubled the amount."

Mat stiffened at the mention of his brother. It had been a sore subject for him since he'd told me about the vision he'd had, and one I hadn't dared to broach. But it seemed we couldn't escape the Velichkov-sized awkwardness any longer.

"Doubled it?" he asked, baring his teeth. "What the fuck is he playing at?"

The lord seated across from us merely shrugged, yet Mathias wasn't done with him.

"Answer Ren's question," he snapped. "If it's so profitable to sell him out, why should we believe you won't?"

"I don't deal in *people,* Your Highness." The nobleman's expression was uncharacteristically fierce, his usual jovial smile replaced by a steely hardness. "My mother was a slave before Onn abolished the practice, and I vowed that no matter the reason, I would never buy or sell another human being."

Mathias deflated at the vehemence in his tone, and Lord de la Vega offered a weak smile in an attempt to restore his good humour. "Besides," he added, patting his massive stomach with a pudgy hand, "food can't have you executed if they ever return to power."

I snorted. "Depends on how many oranges you bribe me with," I said, but before I'd finished speaking he'd already reached into a pocket and pulled out two of them, barely disrupting the lines of his silk clothes. By the Blessed

Five, my people knew me too well. I pounced on the fruit, reaching down to slide Mat's knife from his boot where I knew he was keeping it and avoiding his half-hearted attempts to bat me away.

"So, my lord," I asked, slicing one of the oranges open and reluctantly offering one of the segments to Mathias, immensely relieved when he smirked and shook his head in refusal, "what evidence was put to the nobles to convince them that I'm not of my father's line? I assume there had to be something for the coronation ceremony to have gone ahead with Welzes in my place."

"All lies, my prince, I'm sure-"

"Tell me."

De la Vega gave a heavy sigh. "Do you remember Yanev?"

"My father's personal healer," I responded with my mouth full, accidentally spraying orange juice onto the cushions of the carriage and covering the mess guiltily with my hand. Mat raised an eyebrow. "An elderly Temarian granted refuge in Quareh a couple of decades ago in return for his service. Decently gifted with the Touch, but never particularly talkative."

"Well he is now," the lord said wryly. "He was only too eager to tell the court the tale of how the late king Iván Aratorre was happy with his first-born son, Horacio, but then his wife bore him too many girls."

"Two girls," Mathias said scornfully. "That's *too many*?"

"Six, Your Highness."

We both stared at him.

"Yanev said that Queen Consort Consuela became pregnant four more times after she gave birth to your sisters Alondra and Mariana, my prince. That through his Touch, he was able to determine their gender within only a few weeks of conception."

Mat scoffed. "Bullshit. That can't be possible."

De la Vega shrugged. "The average healer could not do such a thing, but Yanev has the most powerful Touch ever recorded."

Mat and I looked at each other, and I knew he was thinking exactly the same as me. But we had no idea how to go about finding Starling, if she was even still alive.

"In any event," the lord continued, "he said that upon learning that each subsequent child would be female, the king ordered him to terminate the pregnancies so they could conceive again without needing to bring a daughter to term."

Fuck. I thought it; Mat said it.

"There's more," de la Vega said grimly. "His Majesty decided that it was his wife at fault, as men are prone to do. He confided to Yanev that she would not be allowed to see the year's end."

I was silent; angry and sick, and my hands hurt. I glanced down to find my fingers so tightly clenched that my nails were cutting into my palms. I had no idea where the half-eaten oranges had gone.

"Apparently Consuela, who was alerted to the king's intentions by those faithful to her, sought a desperate solution to save her own life. And it seems it was the king who had a propensity to seed girls, for her next child was a boy."

Lord de la Vega paused, wincing. "You, Your Highness."

Mathias' hand found mine, and he pried open my sticky fingers to wrap them around his.

"Who?" I asked quietly. "Who does Yanev say is supposedly my real father?"

"That, the old healer did not know, although whether he had his suspicions or not is unclear. What he *is* clear on is that he knew you weren't the king's, and yet kept it from him – he says out of fear, *I* say as a result of bribery – even after the queen consort's death."

A death that took on another motive, as did Iván's hatred for me as his youngest *son*. Had he suspected that I wasn't his?

No. It was too convenient. For this to be the first time such a rumour had ever been raised – on the same day as my coronation, nearly twenty years later – surely meant it was nothing more than a desperate conspiracy between a councillor fearing the loss of luxuries he'd grown accustomed to, a foreigner seeking more power than the Dukedom he held, and an old healer who had nothing to lose.

"It's not true," I said curtly. "None of it."

Lord de la Vega lifted a hand and knocked sharply on the front panel of the carriage. A moment later, I felt us slow and then come to a stop.

"Then prove it, my prince," he said as Mat ducked his head through the door to check we wouldn't be seen leaving. "And then no one will be able to dispute your claim to the throne."

Chapter Three

"This is not how I wanted to show you the city," Ren said with audible disgust as we crouched in a filthy alleyway waiting for a boisterous group of Quarehians to pass. The clink of glass and raucous cheers told me they were probably too drunk to notice us even if we directly crossed their path, yet we couldn't take the risk. We both had our hoods up but even that wouldn't completely conceal my distinctive complexion, and who knew how many citizens of Máros would recognise their should-be king?

"Oh, I don't know," I whispered, rocking back onto my heels to wait the inebriated men out. "With all the running and hiding we've done through it, we've probably seen a lot more of the city than we would have surrounded by…in a royal procession."

I silently cursed my carelessness in almost mentioning Ren's guards. He went deadly silent whenever I did, adopting a countenance of self-loathing that made me feel sick.

"Well, we will have to remedy that," the prince said lightly, but his face was in shadows and I didn't know if the casualness was feigned or not. "Piss-drenched alleyways and spider-strewn cellars must be added to the royal tours immediately. How can one truly appreciate Máros without the unique…*scent* of such places?"

I snorted softly. "You're not one to talk."

When I gave an exaggerated sniff in his direction, Ren's eyes narrowed and he shoved at my shoulder.

"And why exactly is that, Mathias? Could it have something to do with the fucking *rags* we're wearing, perhaps? Clothing so foul that you could have only found it discarded under a pile of dog shit?"

Rolling my eyes, I peered around the corner of the alleyway to watch as the last of the drunkards staggered out of sight.

"Because our coronation outfits wouldn't have drawn attention to us when slumming it out here? Besides, at least *this* shirt isn't soaked in your Blessed blood," I hissed, catching a fistful of that same shirt and dragging him with me across the road where we ducked into the shadows of yet another alleyway, depressingly similar to the last in both appearance and stench.

Ren hummed his disapproval. "I'd rather blood than fleas."

"It doesn't have fleas," I said in exasperation, although I was hiding a smile at his dramatics. Those first couple of days while he'd been recuperating from the arrow wound had been terrifying in their sombreness. A quiet, sincere Ren was not one I ever wanted to meet again, not if such characteristics only came with him nearly dying.

"Yours certainly does," he murmured as we hurried through the back streets that had become so familiar to us recently, careful to keep our faces averted from any windows and doorways in case anyone was looking our way. "I went to kiss you this morning and found every inch of your skin *covered* in bite marks."

"Funny how those bites look less like the work of insects and more like some ridiculously horny prince crawling his way over me last night."

"That horny prince had to satisfy himself somehow," he whispered back, although the attempt at being quiet was entirely ruined by the loud slap he landed on my ass. "Considering you wouldn't let him fuck you."

"You're still healing!"

"I'm *fine*," Ren said blithely, only to give a sharp inhale of pain when I grabbed at his arm that told of how dishonest he was being. Mouthing out an apology, I gestured for him to back up, tucking us both into a crouch behind a pile of discarded crates.

"What is it?" he breathed in my ear, and then stiffened as he heard it too.

The very distinctive, accented voice of my brother speaking Quarehian.

"We know you've offered Aratorre aid," Valeri said sharply. I peered cautiously around the crates, spotting him handing over the reins of his horse to one of his guards and closing in on the couple who had been sheltering and feeding us for the last week.

The shorter señora Hernández wiped her hands on her apron and shooed her wife behind her, glaring up at my brother with an admirable amount of scorn considering the difference in their height and status. And as this was Quareh, their genders also put her both socially and legally below that of the male prince standing before her, even if he was a foreigner.

"And we have absolutely no idea what you're talking about," she snapped.

Val stretched, rolling his neck from side to side. I knew him well enough to recognise the movement as a sign of stress rather than deliberate intimidation, but it made both Hernándezes stiffen, their expressions drawing tight.

"Let us not feign ignorance," he said. "One of your customers made the palace guard aware that you are harbouring a pair of rather distinct guests. Where are they?"

"Our customers? Asleep in their beds, I would imagine, considering the hour." Señora Hernández's words were pointed, accusatory, and I watched them rile up the Quarehian guards standing with Val's own. "We run a laundry, Your Highness, nothing more sinister than that."

At Valeri's nod, two of his guards brushed past the couple and entered the tiny building that was both their home and business. The taller of the two Hernándezes shot them a sour look but made no move to prevent their search. Faces had begun to peer out of nearby windows, curious yet not brave enough to venture out on the street for a closer look at the exchange.

"*You* run it?" jeered one of the Márosian palace guards, his face contorting into an ugly snarl. I clenched my fists, my nails cutting into my palms. "Where the fuck are your husbands?"

"Getting drunk off their asses in a place called Why Do We Need Them?" señora Hernández shot back, and her wife clutched her hand in warning. "It's down the road from It's None of Your Business and just past Go Fuck Yourself."

All of the Quarehian guards lurched forward at that, and my heart rushed into my mouth as two of them drew their swords.

"Stand down," Val commanded, his voice terse.

"You don't get to order us-"

"You were given to me by King Welzes to assist me in *my* search," he snapped. At his feet, Wolf's ears flattened against his skull as he let out a low growl. "I outrank you no matter my nationality, and if you can't follow a simple order, I don't expect your master will have any concern with me rewarding your disobedience with a flogging."

That quietened them, at least until his own men emerged back into the street with a silent shake of their heads. Then the palace guards clamoured for the Hernándezes to be arrested for treason.

Ren hissed out a furious breath in my ear. If we let ourselves be seen, surely they'd chase us rather than waiting around to arrest our alleged accomplices? But with the guards so close and numerous – with my brother *right fucking there* – would we be able to escape if we did?

"No," Valeri said, narrowing his eyes as he surveyed the couple refusing to cower before him. Fuck him for being a good enough person to let them keep their freedom while also planning to throw Ren to the wolves like he was nothing. "I need them to pass a message onto my little brother. You will tell Nathanael that Aratorre's days are numbered. Tell him that with the hundreds of men we now have combing the city, he has no choice but to surrender his prince. Tell him," he growled, leaning in as if to utter a secret despite his words being loud enough for the whole street to hear, "that there's no fucking way they will leave Máros alive."

And with that, he marched sharply back to his horse, mounted it in one elegant movement, and led the procession of guards back to the palace.

I turned to look at Ren, who was watching me with wide eyes.

"We're leaving Máros," I snarled. *"Tonight."*

—

A couple of hours later we had reached the eastern gate of the city, forced to scuttle and slink our way through the streets while remaining hidden from the late revellers and early risers, which made for slow progress. We hadn't dared to say goodbye to the Hernándezes – as much as I wanted to thank them for their courageous hospitality, it was too much of a risk for all of us. Val or Welzes might have had someone watching the laundry awaiting our return, and the best we could do for the couple was not expose them to any further danger. Still, I imagined them fretting when their prince didn't return, wondering what had happened to him. I knew that feeling well.

"That's him. The red-headed guard Lord de la Vega said was open to bribes,"

Ren murmured, and I followed his assessing gaze to the man stationed in front of the heavy gate. The city walls towered over us, blocking out the stars and making climbing them an impossibility. Which, I imagined, was the whole point.

"Is that red though?" I asked dubiously, eyeing the guard's hair in the light of a nearby lantern swaying gently on its hook. "It's more like...an interesting brown."

"Dull auburn, at least," said Ren. "Come on, my knees are killing me! I can't stay squished up like this a moment longer."

"I'm fairly sure cramp isn't a valid reason for risking our lives if you're wrong."

He waved an impatient hand. "I'm never wrong."

"Ah," I said dryly. "That fact had eluded my notice because of all the times that you were-"

I was silenced by a hand clamped tightly over my mouth. It smelled of oranges.

"*Mathias*," the prince whispered, his face an inch from mine in the gloom. "Now is not the time to start spreading lies about completely imaginary moments in which I didn't quite get things right."

When he dropped his hand, I nodded, chastised. "Of course. Because we need to stay focused."

"No," said Ren. "Because I have a cramp. Move your ass before I'm tempted to bite it."

I considered that. "And if I want you to?"

"Then I shall magnanimously oblige," he conceded, offering me a grin. I felt a little giddy at the sight of it; he had barely smiled these last few days, and it must have been the knowledge that we'd soon be out of Máros and putting distance between us and those who hunted us that allowed him to do so now. It even made me shift aside to let him out of the hiding place we'd been crouched in – this time, a small gap between two rows of empty crates that stank of rotting seafood.

"Señor, a moment of your time," Ren called loudly, approaching the guard with all the subtlety of...well, an entitled prince used to getting whatever he wanted. "I believe you can help us?"

The man narrowed his eyes. "*Us?*"

"Oh," said Ren, clearly remembering too late that good upstanding citizens of Máros did not generally keep company with enemy northerners, which is why we'd fucking *agreed* that I'd stay out of sight while he handled the delicate negotiations for the bribe. "No, just me. I need to leave the city."

"Come back at daybreak like everyone else." He narrowed his eyes. "Or do you have something that won't pass the checkpoint inspection?"

"I do," Ren said cheerily. "And I heard you take money in exchange for opening up that gate back there for a minute or two without any inspection required?"

Oh, for fuck's sake. I let my forehead smack forward into the crates, silently cursing his sudden inability to be diplomatic.

The man's eyes widened, and his mouth gaped comically.

"Are you...are you attempting to illegally bribe a member of the city watch?" he finally bit out, the words nearly exploding from his mouth.

"Well," my prince said, shrugging, "I'm certainly not attempting to *legally* bribe you. Do you want the money or not?"

A drawn sword was the only answer he received.

I pulled out my knife, tiny in comparison to the gleaming two feet of metal pointed at my lover's throat, and prepared to die horribly and pointlessly in his defence.

"An imprisonable offence," a new voice said from the street, and I inadvertently shrank back into the shadows of my hiding place. "Yet not a fatal one, so I suggest you sheath that sword, Cortez. I'll see him to the gaol."

The original guard gave a sharp salute to the stranger and a nasty parting look at Ren, but it was only when the second man grabbed my prince's arm and yanked him away from the gate that I got a good look at what he was wearing: the uniform of another city guard. Only this one was marked with the rank of captain.

I sighed.

The captain dragged a sullen Ren past the pile of crates I was hiding within, but I didn't dare move with the gate guard Cortez still watching them go. When he finally lost interest, I gave it another half minute before darting across the road to lose myself in the shadows lurking at the base of the huge city wall.

Several hundred yards later, just far enough to be out of sight and earshot of the gate, I caught up to Ren where he was depositing a fistful of coins into the captain's hand. The man counted them out carefully, raking the fingers of his free hand through his hair. His decidedly red, and not Blessed *dull auburn* hair.

"I've just remembered a time when you were wrong," I said to Ren as I joined them.

He tsked. "Cease your delusional ramblings," the prince shot back at me. "I found him eventually, didn't I?"

"More like I found you," said the captain, eyeing me suspiciously. "What the fuck were you thinking, approaching Cortez back there? He's straighter than a fucking flagpole!"

"That's what this one once claimed," Ren drawled, draping an arm over my shoulder and plastering himself to my side. "And now look at him, unable to keep his love-sick, smitten self off me."

"We're not looking to cause trouble," I said in a low voice, my back straining under Ren's weight. "We just want out." I nodded at the gold in the guard's hand.

He cocked his head and licked his lips. "This doesn't even come close."

Bullshit. It was twice what Lord de la Vega had told us he usually paid this man for letting entire carts of stock pass unchecked.

"It's more than compensatory for opening a gate."

"Ah, but where's the extra fee for my silence?" the captain asked, leering at us. "Difficult to live in Máros for this past week and not know who you both are. I imagine Cortez will also cotton on shortly once he gathers his wits. If I'm to sell a story in which His Highness escaped back into the city instead of ending up in a cell, I'll need more...*incentive* to remind me of which story's the correct one."

I blew out an irritated breath. "This is your fucking king you're talking to!"

"Then he can afford it, can't he?"

Ren gave a broad smile, one of the false ones he offered those who wasted his time but knew he had to pander to. "Of course," he said smoothly, reaching into his coat and pulling out the small pouch of gold we'd been given by de la Vega – with the strong suggestion that he'd be wanting it repaid with interest when Ren returned to power. The prince counted out another three coins and held them out, but the captain smacked his lips and reached for the pouch instead.

"*Nyet*," I hissed, slapping his hand away. It immediately dropped to the hilt of his sword and I froze. Fuck, he didn't even need a weapon to screw us over: a loud yell would do the job just as well, with the gate guard close by and us trapped at the edge of the city with nowhere to run. His cold smirk said he knew it as well as I did.

"Mat," Ren cooed soothingly, increasing the brilliant intensity of his smile. "This fine gentleman is just doing his job and deserves appropriate compensation for all the perils that come with such a position. The money is yours, señor."

The captain's greed clearly blinded him to the implied threat in the prince's words, for he eagerly accepted the pouch and slipped it into his own pocket, leaving Ren with only the three coins he'd removed from its depths. Surely the man wasn't stupid enough to think he'd be forgiven for such a thing when Ren recovered his rightful place as king? And then he sneered at us, and my blood ran cold at the realisation that his confidence was based on a belief it would never come to pass. Did all citizens of Quareh have as little faith in Ren as this one?

"This way," he said, and when he turned, I caught sight of Ren's lip curling in distaste as he finally dropped the fake amicable expression. We shared a dark look but said nothing, hurrying after the captain as he led us into a shadowed alcove tucked between a guard post and the outer walls. There was a small door there, a service exit in the city wall that was a tenth of the size of the formal eastern gate and clearly designed to be only used by those on foot. After it was unlocked for us, we ducked through in silence, and while I was all too willing to let that continue, Ren turned to the captain with a furrowed brow.

"Which way is south?"

The guard raised an eyebrow. "You're at the eastern gate."

Ren nodded eagerly. "We sure are."

"So south is *right*," he said slowly, with the condescension of a man who believed he was talking to an idiot.

The prince turned to look in that direction, squinting over the open plains that lay beyond the walls. "Are you certain?"

"Of course he's fucking certain," I said with a note of fake irritation in my voice when I realised what he intended. "The sun's starting to rise over there, which means over *there* is south. How have you survived two decades on this continent without a basic sense of direction?"

"Surrounded by people who worried about such nonsense for me," Ren said airily. "And you can't talk. You didn't even know where Naledo *was*, Mathias."

"Oh do forgive me for not memorising every last coastal port in your stupid fucking country. I'm sure my ignorance of Quarehian geography will be terribly inconveniencing to us when we're hundreds of miles away in Onn. However will we survive?"

"See what I have to put up with?" demanded Ren indignantly, looking to the captain as if for support. The man just shook his head, wisely choosing not to get involved in our argument.

"Get the fuck out of here," he growled. "And you never saw me, okay?"

With that, he slammed the door in our faces and left us alone in the open countryside beyond the towering city wall that made me feel like an insect.

We shrugged at each other and headed for the road that led out of the eastern gate, following it to the south.

"That bastard stole all of our money," I seethed, scowling over my shoulder at the city as it slowly began to shrink behind us.

"Not all of it," Ren said quietly. When I looked at him in surprise, he grinned and withdrew his hand from his other pocket, half a dozen gold coins clutched between his fingers. They glinted in the early morning sunlight. "I set some aside in case he got greedy. I just...didn't expect it to be *that* greedy."

"Good thinking," I muttered, annoyed I hadn't thought to suggest taking such precautions.

"A slightly better idea than trying to pick a fight with the man who was our only hope of getting out of Máros," Ren retorted wryly, but his expression was amused. Maybe he'd finally given up on being exasperated at what he liked to call my *reckless, impulsive, so-called decision making, Mathias.*

And then he sighed. "But this isn't going to get us far," he added, hefting the coins in his hand once more before dropping them back into the pocket of his thin coat. "Certainly not enough to charter a ship at Naledo."

"A terribly good thing we're not going to Onn then, isn't it?" I said, and my lover winked at me. "Think this is far enough?"

"Reckon it is," Ren said, and we turned left from the road, ducking into the undergrowth and veering back to the east. When the captain inevitably talked, either as a brag after one too many ales or under interrogation when Navar and Welzes realised we'd left the city, they'd hopefully waste some time following a false trail to the south coast. And as tempting as fleeing across the ocean to Onn and the sanctuary that Ren's other sister may have been able to offer was, it wasn't an option either of us had considered.

While Riehse Eshan had fucked us both over, it was still our home, and we'd be damned if we'd be leaving it without a fight.

*

Chapter Four

Ren

When we'd set off from Máros, full of the high from having the last laugh over the corrupt captain, I'd been feeling rather optimistic about it all. Out of the confines of the capital, taking a jaunty stroll across the best country in the world, and able to fuck Mathias whenever I liked, free of any interruptions? Even the looming worry of Welzes on my throne felt distant, banished by the gentle rays of the rising sun and the lyrical birdsong around us. I'd threaded my fingers through Mat's, declared *all* of the filthy things I planned to do to him before night fell once more, and proceeded to drag him over to investigate every mildly interesting tree or patch of moss until he was cursing my name in three languages and I couldn't see from laughing so hard.

Yet half a day later, all of that felt like a decades-old memory, and the fun had long worn off. I was hot, sweaty, and tired, suffering the pain of a dozen blisters which had formed in my cheaply made shoes, and near about *dying* of thirst. I couldn't even play with my boy, because it required a level of mental and physical flexibility to jerk him off while we were both traversing uneven terrain that unfortunately even I couldn't achieve.

Mat was clearly as uncomfortable as I was, scratching incessantly at the mosquito bites that lined his neck and wrists – fucking thieves – and walking with a limp that belied similar ankle blisters, but the resilient bastard hadn't whined about it once. I'd compensated for it by complaining each and every step of the last twelve hours, naturally, and my northerner had ferociously bitched about me bitching, yet hadn't said a word about the excursion I'd dragged him on.

"For fuck's sake, Ren," he said now, when I repeated my comment about my parched throat in case he hadn't heard it the first eighteen times. "Don't make me find something to gag you with."

"That's not fair," I objected, even though it was unequivocally, indisputably, fair. "I haven't threatened to tie your hands behind your back to stop you scratching, even though that would also be for your benefit, have I?"

"No," he agreed. "Other than the four times before now. Do those not count?"

I sighed, not having the energy to continue our banter. "What are we doing, Mat?"

"Returning to *la Cortina*," he said instantly, nudging his shoulder against mine as he parroted the lie we'd frequently told ourselves merely so we'd have a vague direction to walk in. "Where we can pick up money, horses, and hopefully some allies."

"We both know that's bullshit. Neither of us are going to get within ten miles of the place: Navar and Welzes likely had men posted there the day we went missing. We need a plan."

"No," I said, stopping in the middle of the path. It had been too risky travelling on the main road from Máros, and the cost was having to pick through the bordering undergrowth and farmland instead. "*I* need a plan. You need to go home: what the fuck are you still doing here, anyway?"

I'd been completely blind, so addicted to his reassuring presence that I hadn't even *considered* that it wasn't necessary...other than keeping my heart and soul from breaking into a hundred thousand painful shards, of course.

"Eh, someone made me realise I'm a masochist," Mathias drawled, shooting me an accusing look tinged with fondness. "So passing up the chance to torture myself with his insufferable company and being hunted down by a whole country for treason just seemed like a waste."

"Ren," he added gently when I screwed up my face, not impressed with the reminder of what he risked. "We're in it together to the end. You told me that, remember?"

I tried to swallow past the lump that had formed in my throat, but the damn thing refused to cooperate. Temar wasn't the wisest place for my lover either, considering he'd outed himself in front of its entire army, but there had to be *somewhere* he could go that would be safer than at my side.

Mathias swatted me on the arm. "Try sending me away again, and the grovelling you had to do last time will seem like a pleasant dream, you prick."

I winced, remembering how hard he'd made me work for it in the ruins that night after I'd attempted to break us apart. My knees and jaw had ached for two days straight.

A flash of light had us both glancing skywards, and a few seconds later the accompanying thunder rumbled through the air. We continued to stumble through the darkening field, but Mat blew out a breath as raindrops began to pelt our shoulders minutes later. It didn't even have the decency to cool us down, the humidity only worsening as we bowed our heads to the weather and ploughed forward.

"We need to find shelter," he muttered. "I don't much fancy trying to sleep in the rain."

"How about the convenient village just over the next hill?" I offered, and was met with a narrow glare.

"You can fuck off with that dry sarcasm, Ren, I know we're not-"

"It may be hard to believe," I interrupted, beaming back to show him just how fucking grumpy he was being, "but I am occasionally capable of speaking without being facetious. Look."

He followed my outstretched arm and squinted at the hazy orange glow emanating over the curve of the hill in front of us.

"Fuck me," Mathias said, surprised, and then beat me to the punchline by sulkily adding, "yeah, I know. Invitation issued and accepted, right?"

"Damn straight, *mi cielo*."

I was already imagining the food that awaited us. The bed. The fantasy of lashing Mathias' wrists to his ankles tomorrow morning before he was properly awake to growl at me, and then once he was, fucking him like that, bent in half for me and unable to move as he was forced to take whatever I choose to give him.

I opened my mouth to describe those plans in detail, and then decided to save my breath for the wild dash we made towards the settlement, pleasantly surprised to find it was in fact a village and not just a hamlet. *Vallalavega*, the sign read as we re-joined what passed for a road in these parts, and although it wasn't familiar to me, the wooden board swinging on creaking chains outside of the largest of the buildings sure was.

"An inn," I murmured with relish, tugging Mat's hood down low over his face before anyone could catch sight of my northerner and decide he was as tasty as he looked. Or that he deserved to be stoned for being the enemy...either reason, really.

The rain or the recent nightfall had driven the whole village's occupants inside the inn, it seemed, for while the street and square were empty, the taproom was a lively, humid atmosphere of music, enticing smells, and raucous chatter. Ensuring Mathias kept his head bowed, I pushed my way through the throng of people to reach the worn bar, only just catching myself before I could make the mistake of resting my hands on its sticky-looking surface.

When I met the eye of the bartender, a short man with a balding head and wide smile, I started to request a room when I was spoken over by a man who had pulled up to the bar a few seconds after me. I opened my mouth to snarl out a curse to the queue-pusher and then snapped it closed again, letting the asshole order his drinks before trying again. The meekness grated on me, but I could easily picture Mat's disapproval at causing a scene and drawing attention to us, as satisfying as it would have been to put the drunken villager back in his place.

The bartender looked me up and down, wiping his hands on a rag. I could see the moment he took in my shabby coat because his lip curled, obviously reassessing whatever value he'd assigned for my custom in his head.

"We need a private room, hot food, and a bath," I said, flashing a gold coin before he could turn us back out into the rain. "And discretion – my parents and I are in a little disagreement about who I'm to marry, so I'd prefer to keep them off mine and my lover's tail should they come around these parts."

That had been Mat's idea. We knew that story wouldn't hold up if soldiers were to arrive asking about people matching our descriptions, but the lie and small bribe were less about actually keeping the man's mouth shut and more to give the village a plausible reason for our suspicious behaviour in turning up without horses or baggage and keeping to ourselves despite the open revelry in the taproom. We'd rather have the locals gossiping about a pair of naïve elopers who thought love would be as easy to live on as daddy's coin, than speculating about what we were trying to hide from.

The bartender's tongue roved over his teeth. "Four gold."

"Two," I said. I might have been a prince drowning in wealth – usually, anyway – but I wasn't an idiot. I knew the market value of everyday goods and services used by my people, for how else could I manage my country's finances without it? And even with the bribe and the lack of other nearby inns driving up the price, four gold was extortion and we both knew it.

The man shrugged, the demands of his other patrons clearly lessening his desire to haggle. "Fine."

He whistled to a serving girl and barked out orders to draw us a bath, and the surprising efficiency of the place had me and Mat seated in the corner of the taproom with a jug of ale and two plates of overcooked rice and vegetables within a bare minute.

We ate as quickly as we could, hungry enough to stomach the unappealing dinner, and only had to fend off one too-interested local who decided to join us without waiting for an invitation that was clearly never coming. The red-faced man faltered as his proximity at the table allowed him to catch sight of Mathias' pale features under his hood, but even the presence of a northerner this far south didn't interest him enough to withstand the tedious droning I piled upon our unwanted visitor, and I talked enough shit about basalt quarrying extraction methods that he soon excused himself to find more interesting company.

My lover let out a soft whistle. "I didn't realise you knew so much about the properties of stone."

"I don't," I told Mathias. "I repeated the same sentence a dozen times using different words."

"You could have just told him to fuck off," Mat commented darkly, chasing a rubbery bean with a fork that was missing a prong.

"Confrontation would be too memorable," I said, eyeing the rest of the room to see if anyone else would be stupid enough to bother us. "Dullness wipes itself from the memory easily enough." I'd been exposed to enough of it from the courtiers back in *la Cortina* to make the statement with nothing less than certainty.

He gave a low laugh. "No one could ever accuse you of being dull, Renato."

"Hmm," I said, although I knew he was just being kind. With my loss of royal status, my face unmade, and my clothes not having a splash of colour – let alone *style* – I was no more interesting than my latest joke, and I was feeling decidedly short on those since leaving my three guards to die in the capital.

Yet Mathias' smile was earnest, even shadowed under his hood as it was, and it softened something deep in my heart as he was so often prone to doing. My lover didn't give false compliments.

I swallowed, and then stole the elusive green bean from his plate to distract us both.

"Asshole."

I chewed with audible relish, not because it was at all tasty but because it had been the last mouthful on his plate. Unseen beneath the table, his boot found my shin.

I sought his gaze, indignant. "Did you just kick me?"

"Did you just eat my dinner?"

"Barely."

"Then...barely."

"Oh, no," I told him. "That's not going to work."

I dropped my voice. "It's been a week since my injury. You know what that means."

I only received a casual shrug in response, but I saw the way his fingers tightened around his fork.

"Upstairs, Nathanael. *Now*."

Mathias gave me a slow, teasing smirk as he leisurely uncurled from his chair and sauntered up the staircase behind the bar.

I'd like to say I had sufficient self-restraint and composure to wait until we reached our rented room before trying to strip his clothes from him.

But that would have been a lie.

*

Chapter Five

Mat

Ren was tucked up against my shoulder, his dark hair splayed across my chest featherlight and slightly ticklish. When I ran my fingers down his arm he shifted in his sleep, curling his knee around mine and locking our legs together. I smiled at the effortless affection.

"*Buenos días*," he murmured after a moment, sleepiness making his accent thicker. He cracked an eye and glanced at the pale outline of the window before groaning and twisting around in the creaky bed to face me.

"In what world are you awake before me?" Ren rasped and I chuckled, landing kisses on whatever parts of him I could reach with my mouth. He may have normally been a horribly cheerful morning person – the type I most despised, so it was no wonder we'd once been enemies – but our fun the night before had clearly exhausted him, considering he'd been doing most of the work while I ended up with my face shoved into the pillow.

The prince sighed and rolled gracefully out of bed, squinting into the pre-dawn grey haze beyond the scratched and mildewed inn window. Stretching and regretting the loss of him in my arms already, I pushed back the blankets to follow him, but he immediately spun around on his heel with a wicked grin carved across his face.

"Where do you think you're going?"

"To get dressed. Wash up. You." I gestured around the room.

"Let's skip to that last one, shall we?" he purred, stalking closer and looking every inch the predator.

It seemed he was no longer tired.

I got to my feet and shivered in the chill of the room, wishing we could indulge but knowing it wasn't sensible. "We should get going."

"It's still raining," he told me, as if he had actually seen anything through the window other than grime and dust. "We'll only make the innkeeper and the rest of the Vallalavega suspicious if we set off in that rather than waiting for the weather to clear and the sun to actually, you know, *rise*."

"Then we should talk about where we're going."

Ren cocked his head, considering me. "There's really only one place."

I frowned. "There is?"

"*Sí.* Back to bed."

I gave a put-upon sigh even as I revelled in the playfulness in his voice. "Or maybe we should find something to eat?" I teased.

His abrupt laughter startled me. "Oh, I intend to, Mathias. But seeing as you got to lie there last night and enjoy what I gave you, I think it's only fair that I put you to task now. Kneel."

His eyes were bright and his gaze adoring, and fuck, I loved being looked at like that.

"Down on your knees, Nat, or I will force you to them and you will *like it*."

Although I'd been about to obligingly drop to the floor, I caught the edge in the prince's tone and realised what he wanted.

So instead I stood my ground, grinned, and drawled lazily, "will I?"

He struck like a snake. I grunted as my bare knees hit the rough floorboards harder than expected, but I had no time to protest before he'd gathered a fistful of my hair and pressed my face into his groin. I breathed in the scent of him, of his natural musk mixed with the cheap soap we'd bathed with after our exertions last night, and felt his cock stir against my lips.

Ren ignored my efforts to push him away, knowing they weren't sincere, and cradled my head in his hands. "Look at you," he murmured, his voice thick with lust. "You can tap out if you need."

I turned my head to carve out air for myself, as it seemed he wasn't going to offer me any. "I'm not going to give you the satisfaction," I assured him through my heaving breaths.

"Then you can fucking take it, can't you?"

"Maybe I won't give you the satisfaction of that either, *knyaz*."

The prince hummed thoughtfully.

AN OATH AND A PROMISE

I wondered if he'd ask to tie me up in the way he liked: tight binds with a deliberately built in escape. I wondered if I'd be brave enough this time to tell him he could forget the slipknot, if he wanted. I found it and the out it offered to be distracting.

But there was another type of hunger on Ren's face now, one that was no less terrifyingly thrilling.

"Mathias? I'd like you to be good for me now."

It was a request for obedience, not a demand, because me behaving for him wasn't something we were always in the mood for. Last night had been hard and brutal, a quick, rough fuck being exactly what we'd both needed to expel the day's frustrations. Little talk, even less foreplay.

But this morning held a different air. A different craving. The sweet caresses Ren was now administering to my neck were satisfying in a manner all of their own; a gentle, yet possessive touch that roamed over my skin and marked me as his.

I nodded, slow and considered so he knew I wasn't just mocking him. "I can do that."

"I know you can."

I glanced up at him and did my best to look compliant, rewarded by his sharp intake of breath. My words were soft. "Where do you want me, Your Highness?"

"Shush," Ren said silkily, dragging his fingertips down my face. "All my brat needs to worry about is how he's going to swallow my cock until he chokes on it."

My prince was as good as his word, prying open my mouth and feeding me every inch of himself until I felt the fat head of his cock bumping against the back of my throat. When I gagged, he allowed me only a single hastily drawn-in breath before forcing himself deep once more, viciously using my mouth for his own pleasure.

"You're doing so well," he whispered, his voice soft and affectionate again, although he didn't let up on the punishing thrusts between my lips. "You're so fucking beautiful, Mathias."

I wrapped my arms around the back of his thighs and pulled him closer, trying to convey everything I felt for him through touch alone, and for a moment his grip in my hair eased. His breath hitched. I could tell my lover was getting close.

Tears streamed from my eyes, and although I was unsure if it was from emotion or the ruthless way he was fucking my face, I knew better than to wipe them away. I'd learned that lesson the afternoon we'd arrived at the Márosian palace, and could still feel the sting of his palm coming down across my ass if I thought about it.

Which I liked to do. Often.

"Oh, you're so good," he purred, making my heart race with happiness and pride.

Yet less than a minute later Ren's praise lost its coherency and he gasped out half formed words, tugging painfully on my hair a moment before the hot, salty taste of him flooded my mouth. I closed my eyes and drank him down, loving the feeling of him losing control.

"Dios," he murmured when he eventually pulled out, brushing a finger over my bottom lip to catch the cum that had spilled out of my mouth and feeding it back to me. I sucked on his finger eagerly, lost in a headspace that only he could invoke, one which made me feel like I was soaring among the clouds.

Ren pulled me to my feet, licked the tears from my cheeks with a pleased smile, and pressed his mouth to mine.

"Now, for breakfast," he said when he was done tasting himself on my tongue, and I swallowed down my disappointment when my own neglected cock twitched in protest. The prince must have noticed, for he offered a dark chuckle that sent a wicked thrill down my spine and then shoved at my chest, pushing me down onto the bed. My back had barely hit the scratchy blankets before he was crawling over me, running his tongue up my neck and pressing my hands firmly down by my side.

"These stay here," he commanded. "This, here." I blinked as he reached out to force something between my teeth, tasting the cold hardness of glass and realising it was a small vial of oil. Ren grinned and yanked the cork carelessly from its neck, and I hurriedly bit down on the bottle to stop it from tipping over into my mouth.

"And these-" He took hold of my ankles and moved my legs apart, exposing me to him, before pushing my knees up and hooking his elbows underneath. "-aren't going anywhere either."

Ren groaned. "By the Blessed Five, you look so fucking hot like this, darling."

He lowered his head, but instead of taking my cock into his mouth, he merely nosed at it for a long while, the tease of his warm breath showering me in desperate need. I tried to thrust against him to convey what I wanted, but he held my hips in place, and with my mouth full all I could do was grunt incomprehensible curses at the impossible man and his damned sadism.

"What was that? You're profusely and eternally grateful to me for taking such good care of you?"

He stroked a finger up behind my balls, drawing a whine from my throat. Not wanting to disappoint him by moving them, my hands fisted in the blankets, and I bit down so hard on the glass I feared it might break.

"That's what I thought," Ren said, and he sounded so smugly satisfied that I scowled and attempted to tell him exactly what *I* thought, my tongue flickering awkwardly around the vial.

He just laughed. "I imagine you're trying to insult me right now. Feel free to keep uttering those delightful noises, *mi corazón*, while I amuse myself by pretending they're compliments you're moaning at me instead."

I huffed out an incensed breath. I was not making *delightful noises*. And anything that stroked the prince's ego, particularly at a time like this, was to be avoided like an addict-filled *molchaniye* den.

But it was hard to be quiet when I felt his tongue lap around my hole, hot and forceful, before spearing inside.

Fuck me. That was…I hadn't even known that was…and oh, *fuck!* Absolutely delightful, was what this was. Why had we never done this before?

There was something about Ren that brought out a wild side I hadn't known I had, far from the vanilla sex I'd enjoyed back with women back in Mazekhstam. My prince was exotic and fun and daring, and he made me want to be all that too.

I wriggled against him and he obliged my silent request, dragging his tongue over me again before pushing it deeper. I could quite honestly have died happy in that moment, dizzy elation flooding my soul as my lover proceeded to laver attention on me with a dedicated reverence akin to worship.

"The best kind of breakfast," he murmured, before humming happily and returning to eating me out. He alternated between nipping at the sensitive skin and tracing lazy circles around my opening with his tongue, before driving it so deep I was practically sobbing, my vision going white and my muscles weak.

I was so lost in pleasure that I didn't notice my grip on the bottle had gone slack, spluttering when it caused some of the oil to spill over its rim. Ren paused, plucked the glass vial from my mouth, and watched patiently with his head cocked until I'd managed to spit out the unpleasant mouthful. Then he lifted it to the light and gave it a swirl, eyeing the contents dubiously.

"I'm going to fuck you with what's left in this, Mathias, no matter what," he promised me, his eyes sparkling with delight. "So unless you want to take me dry, I suggest you be more careful."

It clinked against my teeth as he placed it back in my mouth, my oil-coated lips slipping around the glass. Asshole.

Ren gave a dark chuckle and lowered his head back between my legs. He pressed a gentle, open-mouthed kiss to my thigh and then playfully ran his stubbled chin against it.

This time, when he lifted my knees higher and bit down on the flesh of my left ass cheek, I managed not to even wince, quivering with the effort of holding still. My fingers had seized into claws as I clutched at the blankets to keep them in place and my cock leaked a steady stream of pre-cum onto my stomach, betraying how much being ordered not to move and entirely at his mercy was turning me on.

The prince retracted his teeth and pressed gentle kisses to the skin before drawing back. He always did that, as if the rough treatment had to be balanced out with the tender. But as he didn't usually inflict pain on the same place twice in such quick succession, it caught me by surprise when his hand came down hard on my ass, engulfing the bite mark in a wave of aching heat.

Oh, fuck.

Luckily, enough oil had spilled before that I was saved from a similar fate when my back arched involuntarily from the bed.

AN OATH AND A PROMISE

Yet he wasn't done, repeating his attentions on the right and then continuing to tease my poor cock with frustrating, featherlight kisses before he finally pulled the vial from my mouth and smeared the remaining oil over his fingers. I was thankful that there had been any left at all when Ren ignored any semblance of courtesy and immediately shoved two fingers as deep inside as he could get, stretching me ruthlessly as I simultaneously praised and cursed him out.

But he didn't torment me with his fingers for long, soon replacing them with his cock and driving into me with quick, hard thrusts that made me see stars. It was uncanny how he seemed to know exactly what I needed at any given time, even if he only *sometimes* gave it to me, cruel prick that he was.

The light in *moy dorogoi's* eyes as he whispered filthy suggestions down at me was impossible to resist, and I'd lifted a hand to my aching cock before I realised what I was doing.

Ren tsked. "Keep your hands on the bed, Mat," he chided, "or I'll stop completely."

I immediately slammed my palms back down onto the blankets, but he pulled out anyway.

"What are you doing?"

"Stopping completely."

I hissed out a complaint. "But you just said-"

He swatted the top of my thigh, amused. "Who makes the rules here, brat?"

"*Rules?*" I rolled my eyes, still feeling the slickness of oil on my tongue. "More like whimsical fancies that change without any fucking notice."

Ren grinned and flicked my forehead before swooping down to kiss it. "You're learning."

He climbed off the bed and rummaged in his clothes that he hadn't bothered to fold last night – or even pick up off the floor, the lazy shit. When he miraculously produced a second vial of oil from their depths, I peered at him with unfettered suspicion. It wasn't in my lover's nature to be *nice* to me at times like this, and promising to fuck me with limited oil only to later offer me more did not add up at all.

"I don't suppose I'll be getting the benefit of that?" I guessed, and Ren shot me a playful grin.

"In a way."

He returned to straddle my hips, making sure to kneel on my hands where they were still pressed to the bed. Perhaps to keep me in place and perhaps to inflict discomfort on me, but knowing him, most likely both. Intrigued, I watched as he poured half of the bottle's contents on his fingers and slicked up my cock where it waited between us, impatient and erect.

Oh.

I remembered the wide-eyed look the prince had once given me on the floor of the bathing room that time when we were half-drowned in wine. I hadn't pressed him for an answer on the matter since, knowing how terrifying the prospect was for him. "Are you-"

"Ordering you to top?" Ren asked, emptying the rest of the oil onto his hands and reaching behind himself. He wouldn't meet my eye. "Yes, I...yes."

By the Blessed Five, he was *trembling*.

"Do you need me to help?" My mouth was dry with the mere anticipation of being inside him.

Ren shrugged, trying to act nonchalant even though I could hear the harsh catch in his breath as he hovered over me. "I've been planning this since you...for a while," he amended with a half smirk. "So if you're asking if I need as much preparation as your tight little ass did, the answer is no."

I blew out an amused breath, wondering *when* exactly he'd found the time to finger himself while he'd been accused of treason and on the run for his life.

"Mathias," he added, the dominance in his voice no less present than when I was spreading my legs for *him*. "If you think this is your chance to repay me for every rough, degrading, controlling act I've ever inflicted on you, think again. You're still mine to do with as I wish."

The words may have been thrown out with confidence but his touch as he stroked me to full hardness once more was tentative. Ren never did anything hesitatingly in bed: he was fearless and bold, every kiss and movement steeped in certainty like he'd practiced them a thousand times. But this was...this was new. New, and ever so fucking precious, as I was well aware of the number of times he'd ever suggested another man take him, let alone allowed it to happen.

The thought of being his first, as he had been mine, was intoxicating.

"Yours, Your Highness," I said obediently. He leaned down to press his chest to mine, closing his mouth over my shoulder and nibbling on my flesh, and then whispered his demand into my skin as if it was easier for him to voice that way.

"Fuck me, Nathanael."

I grinned up past him to the ceiling of our rented room. "You could try saying *please* once in a while."

A low growl sounded from the prince atop me, and I yelped as he pinched my side.

"*Ahora,* Mathias, before I decide not to let you come at all tonight. As it is, you're not allowed to do so until you've finished me off."

"I already finished you off," I pointed out, but when those ruthless fingers of his moved to rather more sensitive spots, I decided hasty agreement was the better option. Then I paused, realising the dilemma he'd intentionally put me in. "Can I please move my hands to touch you?"

Ren lifted his head, his hair cascading down around his face and his lips twitching in wicked satisfaction. "Good boy. You may."

I wrapped one of my hands around the base of my cock and tugged him forward to line us up, barely able to breathe. He felt too tight as I nudged the head of my cock against his opening, and I was worried I wouldn't be able to fit, opening my mouth to call it off before I hurt him. But the prince slowly sank down onto me with effortless grace. I didn't dare move until he told me to – not because of how he might punish me for it, but in the fear that I might scare him. I could see the visible tension in each of the prince's muscles, the way his body quivered in the gloom and how his mouth was set in an anxious line, and wondered if I should have insisted on checking he was really ready before agreeing to it. Because *fucking hell,* he felt amazing wrapped around me, and it was almost surreal that I was being allowed to do this, but was he capable of enjoying himself this way?

Ren swallowed, glancing down at me as he slid his hands across my chest to brace himself. It was difficult to keep my hips from meeting him in response.

I felt tightness. Resistance. And then I was fully inside, and fuck, that was good. Superb. Blissful. Many other words I never thought I'd use but were spilling into my head now, wrapped up in how gorgeously perfect he felt.

"Okay," he said uncertainly, starting to move with that same unfamiliar timidness as before, and I took that as permission to stop holding back. Our breaths shallowed as he hit a rhythm in riding me, his tight heat bearing down on each one of my eager thrusts. "That's not…bad."

I snorted.

"No, it's really good," he assured me, looking earnest enough that I couldn't find it in me to be offended. "I just don't understand the appeal-"

I shifted my angle to the one I always liked to feel when in his position, and he choked, his nails scratching at my skin.

"¡Dios mío!"

"Now you do," I said, grinning, and Ren's wide, shocked eyes connected with mine.

"Fuck, Mat! That's…"

"Yeah."

"Do it again," he ordered, and for once I didn't hesitate to obey, relishing every sensation far too much to even consider protesting.

This wasn't *anything* like fucking a woman. The feeling of stretching my prince open, watching my cock disappear into him, hearing him murmur how good I felt inside him, made my head swim. My toes curled as heat spread through my body, and remembering how to breathe became the most difficult task of all.

As we moved together on the bed, my hands clutched at Ren's hips while the bed creaked obscenely in either protest or encouragement. When the prince began to dig his fingernails into my chest, I used the sharp pain to drive deeper and faster against that spot inside him until I wasn't sure where I ended and he began. I was quickly becoming addicted to how I could drive the breath from his body, and the intoxicating way each one of my thrusts pulled an involuntary gasp from him.

And when my slick fingers found his length, he couldn't hold on any longer, my name tumbling from his lips as he came over my hand. I felt his muscles tighten around me while he rode out his climax, his head thrown back and his hands clenching into fists where they rested on my chest.

"I love you," I whispered, and Ren returned the sentiment in a hoarse, broken voice. We were slick with sweat and cum and yet neither of us cared, pulling each other close in that draughty, dirty room as he continued to rock his hips against mine.

I stared up at him as the prince's lashes fluttered closed and his mouth parted slightly. But the sheer pleasure his body was gifting me soon turned my thrusts into short, shallow snaps of my hips, and I forced a breathless curse from Ren's mouth as I came inside him, ecstasy clouding my vision.

"Mathias!" His voice was strained and my answering cry was no better.

Damn, he's perfect.

My prince shuddered when he finally pulled himself off me, still coming down from his high, and the blissed-out look on his face made me want to do it to him all over again. I rubbed my fingers together, coating them with his seed and marvelling how hard he'd come for me.

Ren gave me a coy smile and then grabbed my hand, forcing my fingers into my mouth.

"Payment for a job well done," he teased, making me suck them clean before leaning down to replace my hand with his lips and sinking us into a long, deep kiss tinged with oil and cum that bore me a million miles away…before reality inconveniently returned in the form of drying stickiness all over my stomach and chest.

A vivaciously humming Ren helped me wash up first and then slid into bed behind me a few minutes later, gathering me into his arms as we waited for the sunrise. Whether the cuddles were from affection or to warm his cold skin on mine was debatable, but he apparently hadn't had the same foresight as I had to dress before returning to bed because I could feel he was naked, his already half-hard cock pressing insistently against my tail bone.

He gave an aggravated sigh directly into my ear.

"The next time you dare bring anything but your beautiful self to bed, I'll spank your ass raw," the prince growled, sparing no time in dragging my newly donned clothes off me and subjecting me to the same cold sheets and thin blanket as him. "You're being *inconvenient*, Velichkov."

I hid my smile in my pillow, letting my lover strip me with all the patience of hurricane.

"I'm going to sleep now," Ren declared when he'd successfully torn every scrap of clothing from me.

"Okay," I mumbled, letting myself drift off too, and then yelped as Ren spread my cheeks and slipped a finger inside. I might have fallen from the bed in surprise had he not had his leg wrapped around mine, keeping me pinned.

"I thought you said *sleep*, you asshole!"

"Mmhmm," he agreed, even as he pushed the finger deeper and stole my ability to breathe. "This is just in case I decide my bed warmer needs to be put to better use."

"Oh, fuck off."

"If you weren't moaning in pleasure when you said that, maybe I'd take you seriously."

"Two rounds weren't enough for you, prince?" I asked, trying to block those same moans and failing quite miserably. I was in awe of his almost supernatural libido: it was a miracle he ever managed to get anything done other than me.

"Mathias," he murmured. "Nothing's ever enough when it comes to you. I want to experience every fucking thing this continent has to offer with you at my side. Or beneath me," he added, and I could hear the damn smirk in his voice.

And then: "Mat? Can I be the little spoon? Just this once?"

I rolled over and wrapped my arms around him, settling into the same position we'd woken up in nearly every morning since we started sleeping together.

"Alright," I agreed, grinning into his hair as he wriggled back against me and let out a purring sigh. "Just this once."

*

Chapter Six

Ren

Four days' travel from Máros, another slightly slimy meal at another slightly slimy table in another *very* slimy inn in a place called Alzidura, and I'd garnered a new appreciation for all the leg muscles I hadn't known I had. I hadn't previously considered myself unfit, what with all my horse riding and practicing looking hot as fuck when ascending the five steps up the dais to the throne at *la Cortina*...and the other stamina-based activities that were best enjoyed without clothes, but walking across the Blessed country exercised a whole new range of muscles that were absolutely aching from the miles we'd put behind us.

Mathias picked dubiously at whatever sludge we'd been served this evening, evidently trying to work out whether it was actually food or just a plateful of mud someone had scooped up from the road. Having long given up on my own not-dinner with far less optimism, I was busy thinking about Very Important Things like whether we had enough money left to order a bath tonight so I could spend another session licking and nibbling at that sweet little rim of his and sending my wildcat into a sobbing, desperate mess.

"Ren," he snapped now. "You're not listening."

I narrowed my eyes at him. We had enough money: I'd make sure of it. And when he was stretched around my tongue, pleading for me to release him after enduring multiple rapid-fire orgasms, I'd take great pleasure in forcing another from him with this exact moment in mind.

"I always listen to you," I said, offering up a broad smile so he wouldn't guess my intentions too early and try to wheedle out of the torment I had planned for him.

"Then what was I saying?"

"The usual." I shrugged. "'I'm too fucking sexy to be wearing clothes right now, Ren, and as even breathing makes you want to jump my bones, I'm thinking of stripping and bending over this table in a very suggestive manner.' My answer was going to be a wholehearted approval for the idea, by the way."

AN OATH AND A PROMISE

The answering glare I earned could have melted steel.

"Ren-"

I rolled my eyes. "You were saying you can't believe Quareh's trackers haven't yet caught up to us. I gave a vague 'mmm', if I recall correctly, because I have no more fucking clue than you do why those with the Scent aren't on our tail already. You repeated what you'd just heard that group over there say," – I waved a hand at the cluster of patrons in the middle of the taproom who were eagerly tucking into their food with an unhealthy disregard for their digestive systems and very lives – "which was that the border assaults between Mazekhstam and Quareh have started up again since Welzes' crowning. I'm fairly sure I swore at that, so you could be sure I was paying attention. And then you asked if I was alright, but before I could respond, you'd detailed all the ways I wasn't looking well, so I decided to ignore you because I look *magnificent*, fuck you very much." I drew my fingers through my knotted hair, grimacing. It hadn't fared well being away from a brush for so long.

"You *then* got a morose look in your eye that told me you were experiencing everything from self-pity to anger to completely unfounded guilt for not Seeing all of this, which you should know is ridiculous." I smirked, scooped up a forkful of food to punctuate the end of my speech, and then promptly dropped it again because being poisoned wasn't worth the flourish. "So ask me again if I was *listening*."

Mat didn't look nearly as impressed as he was supposed to be. "So what were you thinking about while I was doing all that?"

"Fucking you," I said.

"Deep," he shot back sarcastically.

I shook my head at him and his sloppy phrasing. "It's like you don't even care what you're saying anymore, *mi sol*."

There it was. That little smile, not quite hidden but certainly attempted to be, as he fought his amusement in favour of the sulky scowl he preferred to gift me with.

"...Velichkov," someone said, and we both flinched before forcing our stiff poses back into nonchalance, pricking our ears to hear more. The inn's taproom was quickly filling with people who obviously didn't know they could get their meals for free by eating the dirt outside, and it was making it hard to catch the words of the boisterous group who had been discussing the border before.

"...the king won't agree to...while his younger brother is abetting the false prince...he thinks... fucking peace?...good riddance to the whole lot of those bastard northerners, is what I say..."

Shit. Welzes was refusing to honour the move towards peace we'd managed to cement with the Velichkovs because Nathanael stood at my side in my alleged treachery? Not only did that give Valeri Velichkov a damn good reason for wanting to hand me over, but it put thousands of lives – Temarian and Quarehian – at risk if tensions between our countries escalated like they clearly already had with Mazekhstam.

Mat frowned where he was seated across from me, closing his eyes as if to hear better, but he was forced to keep his hood up and his back to the room in order to stay inconspicuous. "What are they saying?"

"Can't make it out," I lied. There was no fucking way I was going to add to his guilt by telling him that his very presence at our table threatened the entire continent. It might have been enough to get him to leave and publicly denounce any association with me, but after nearly a week of misery on the road and knowing I wouldn't have made it half a mile without him, I'd lost that streak of selflessness that wanted him to – or would fucking *let* him – go anywhere further than three feet away from me. I hitched my chair closer to the table so I could make it a generous two and a half feet, and immediately felt much better.

Mathias, when at my side, was an impulsive, wild, hot-headed mess of a man more prone to attracting danger and destruction than a hundred kegs of black powder.

Mathias, when not at my side, was all those things and more, and worse, might not have anyone to pull his ass out of the fire when he inevitably turned the mildest of situations into a tumultuous clusterfuck. At least this way, I could keep an eye on him, I reasoned, ignoring that irritating voice in my head that nagged me to acknowledge that it was really because I was a clingy, possessive fool who needed him more than oxygen.

Someone jostled Mat as they pushed past and he clutched his cloak to keep the hood from falling. "It's getting too crowded in here. We should retire to our room," he muttered, pressing his hands to the table to stand, and then froze in place as a knife flashed at his throat.

Icy horror passed through me at the sight of the blade and the faint indentation it made in his fair skin. I snapped my gaze up to catch the eye of the man holding it. He was broad shouldered, with bushy eyebrows, and his hair was twisted into a thick plait that hung over his shoulder.

"Stay there," he said mildly.

I made to rise, preparing to break his fingers for daring to touch my Mathias, yet a second pair of heavy hands fell on my shoulders from behind and shoved me back down into my chair with a clang of wood on stone that was lost in the chatter of the taproom.

The man with the knife gave a disappointed tut. "I see you follow orders as well as you blend in among us commoners," he said, an amused tilt to his lips.

"If we've done something to offend you, señor," Mat began, evidently attempting to bluff them out, but the knife silenced him mid-sentence with the drawing of a thin line of blood across his neck.

I stilled. "Go ahead. Keep hurting him."

The man scoffed. "You think you can pretend he doesn't mean anything to you? The whole fucking country has heard about your attachment to this barbarian." He glanced down and gave the top of Mathias' head a disgusted look.

"Go ahead. Keep hurting him," I repeated in the exact same tone as before, as if he had not spoken at all. "And I will *ensure* your death will be as painful as it is protracted."

The man behind me laughed, a deep rumbling chortle of genuine humour. "Oh, I like this one, Filiberto," he said, wrapping a hand in my hair and yanking it back so I was forced to look up at him. He was an older man with streaks of white running through his otherwise black beard, and ancient scars crossing his cheeks. The face of a mercenary.

"So feisty," he said fondly to me. When I offered only silence, the man grabbed my chin and steered my jaw up to meet his. His lips were rough, and he tasted like leather and smoke.

"José," Filiberto protested, but rather half-heartedly, I thought. "Stop molesting our king."

They knew who I was. Shit. This wasn't a random mugging.

"What do you want with Ren?" Mat asked in a low growl, his throat barely moving as he spoke against the restraint of the knife's blade.

"Nothing special," Filiberto drawled, unexpectedly indulging the question. His next words confirmed what I'd feared. "Just an enormous bounty on the easiest job we've ever done. Seriously, were you two even trying to hide?"

Mat's scowl mirrored my own. Sure, neither of us had ever actually been on the run before, or indeed been left unsupervised without guards for very long, but we'd made it this far, hadn't we?

How these two had found us before any of the Márosian guards was answered when Filiberto winked at the innkeeper, and the man tipped an imaginary hat to him in turn. Bad luck, then, that we'd been recognised by the locals and that there had been mercenaries close enough to capitalise on our misfortune. It perhaps meant Welzes and Navar were still ignorant of our location, but that wouldn't mean shit once we were thrown back to them like offal tossed to a pack of starving wolves.

"Behave for us, boys," Filiberto continued, "and we'll treat you both like royalty. Which I suppose you are," he added with a pleased grin, as if he considered himself hilarious.

Mat, who evidently didn't think the same, swore viciously at him in Mazekhstani. Filiberto leant down to speak into his ear, fingers digging into my lover's shoulder and making him wince.

"If you don't, we'll be forced to take precautions," he warned. "Yet I would expect that you would prefer to face your fates with a little dignity, and not be presented before King Welzes hogtied and blindfolded?"

"Fine," I said amicably, flashing him a grin. "We'll be good. I swear it."

Mat stared at me in disbelief.

And then he seemed to remember who I was and nodded fervently, falling effortlessly into his own lies.

"Of course," he agreed with feigned meekness, his eyes going wide in that expression of innocence he did so well and which couldn't be further from his true nature. "Please don't hurt us? We'll do whatever you say."

"Then we really should be going," Filiberto said, his grip on Mathias' shoulder turning into a friendly pat.

"It's already dark," José complained. "And I bet they've already paid for a room." He tugged my hair again, this time a little gentler. "What do you think about you and I making full use of it, ay?"

"*José*," Filiberto protested.

"*¿Qué?* This is an opportunity of a lifetime. How many men can say they got to fuck a royal?"

"If we're talking about that particular royal, probably more than you think. Settle down," he snapped, as Mat's shoulders heaved in anger. "You're going to end up slitting your own throat."

"Yeah, but they say Prince Ren has never taken it before," José pointed out, and grinned down at me. "Your call, gorgeous. What do you say to buying yourself an extra night on this continent – you, me, and whatever mind-blowing final acts you'd like to try before you're executed? There will be no judgment from me."

I was spared from answering by my wildcat's snarl.

"*Nyet!* Don't touch him!"

I tipped my head back and gave José and his crestfallen look a sympathetic shrug. I'd also be disappointed to not get to fuck me. I had been reliably told by Mathias that it was phenomenal. Exquisite. Something along those lines. I hadn't really been listening at the time, too full and satiated in my own bliss to pay attention to the exact compliments being paid.

"You really are an idiot, you know that?" Filiberto commented as he finally sheathed that damn knife and hauled Mathias bodily from his chair. "While you were busy riding below the crupper, what the fuck was I supposed to do? Stand outside in the cold with the rest of the men?"

Mat caught my eye, his expression reflecting exactly what I was thinking.

Rest of the men. Damn it. Hogtied or not, we'd have little chance to escape from a group of well-armed mercenaries.

"I want my share," the innkeeper called in our direction as Mathias and I were shoved towards the door, all of the room's occupants staring at us without any attempt at subtlety whatsoever. "Don't you pretend to forget it this time, you Blessed bastards!"

"Wouldn't dream of it!" José tossed back cheerily, before lowering his voice. "Greedy git," he muttered. "We do all the work and he gets gold for nothing but keeping his eyes open for the bloody obvious."

"Speaking of gold," I said, "you know I can pay you far more than Welzes for letting us go, right?"

José patted my back almost sympathetically. "Not now you're no longer an Aratorre, you can't. And we ain't taking the chance on you getting your hands on any money in the future, when we can get paid just fine for delivering your pretty ass to Máros right now."

"I'm glad you think it pretty," I replied, and jerked my chin at Mat ahead of us, "considering that one prefers to insult it instead of admiring it. I mean, does this *look* like an arrogant, cruel, spoiled ass to you?" I twisted around to pretend to look at it over my shoulder, while really directing my gaze to the mercenary's belt to see if he was wearing any easily accessible weapons. Unfortunately, the one knife I could spot was tucked too far around his waist to reach and there was no way I'd be able to grab it before he stopped me.

José shoved me forward when I paused for too long.

The night air bore an unexpected chill, and I shivered as I was pushed out of the crowded, fire-warmed inn onto the road. Two carriage horses stamped their hooves and breathed visible puffs of air from where they were harnessed to a canvas-wrapped wagon, and I swallowed as I took in the three armed men watching us with gleeful anticipation.

Mierda.

"You got them," one said with audible relief. "They put up much of a fight?"

Filiberto snorted out his amusement. I saw Mat's shoulders tense and knew it meant he was now offering one of his fiercest scowls to anyone with the misfortune to be looking in his direction.

Another of the mercenaries let out a low whistle, raking his eyes over me with disdain. "I can get my cock wet every day for a year with the money *this* one will bring."

"Noble aspirations," Mathias snapped as he was guided by the nape of his neck to the back of the wagon, which unlike the sides was open to the air. There were two rough-hewn wooden benches inside, lining the outer canvas walls, with a large metal ring secured in the centre of each one. A pair of shackles was threaded through the rings, but while the set on the left lay empty, the right held the wrists of a young Quarehian girl no older than fourteen, her dark hair tumbling over her face to reveal little more than a crooked nose and two jet black eyes glittering through the oily strands. She was straining at her restraints, sprawled ungainly on the floor between the benches.

"Dump her," one of the men said immediately. "These two are a thousand times her worth."

"After all the shit the little thief put us through to catch her?" Filiberto asked scornfully, letting go of Mat to shove the girl back up onto her bench and give her a hard kick to the thigh for inconveniencing him so. She hissed at him and he casually backhanded her across the face. "Not fucking likely. We'll collect the bounties for all three."

"But there's no room-"

"The boys can share," he said. "I'm not giving up gold because of your whining, fuckwit, so shut the hell up."

José hummed in my ear. "Another kiss for the road, gorgeous?"

"That's a definite no."

But he'd already turned my face towards him, so I decided to let it happen. My mouth had been in many worse places than on a stranger's, and a single kiss wasn't worth-

The man jerked away from me as Mathias' fist slammed into his jaw. The way José went instantly down into the dirt was satisfying, but I found it decidedly less so when Mat was forced to follow him there a moment later, ruthlessly descended upon by two of the mercenaries. The other grabbed me as I tried to stop them from laying into my lover, snarling curses at them as he was repeatedly hit and kicked.

"Fucking hold!" Filiberto growled, wading through the mess to haul Mat to his feet. He grabbed the collar of his coat and shook him hard before throwing him into the wagon. "You're Blessed lucky the king is willing to pay for you, too," he snarled as he shackled my northerner's right wrist, stopping him from pulling through the slack on the chain by grabbing the other end and gesturing for me to be brought forward as well. When I'd been similarly secured by my left hand, Filiberto spat on Mathias' face and gave us both a shove to keep us in our seats before hopping off the wagon and barking orders at his men.

José wiped the blood from his lip and gave a rueful chuckle, before disappearing around the side where the canvas walls hid him from view.

"Oh, *mi sol*," I said sadly, reaching up to clean Mathias' face with my sleeve. I was pretty sure I smeared dirt over the bridge of his nose as a result of how filthy our clothes had become, but at least he didn't have another man's saliva on him anymore. "If you're going to misbehave, could I suggest that you choose a time when we could actually escape? Or, and I know this is a huge ask, maybe more than ten seconds after we promised we wouldn't? It makes it difficult to lie to them convincingly when you do shit like that."

He just glowered, shooting a bitter look at the manacles, the floor, and the poor girl across from us. I tugged my wrist closer to me, forcing his to follow as a result of the short length of the chain, and he immediately yanked it back with the automatic type of fuck-you insolence he always gave me.

"Sorry," he muttered quietly after a moment. "I just...I couldn't watch him pawing at you."

"Defender of my unsullied virtue and irreproachable honour," I teased, pretending to swoon into his arms so I could feel him up without the girl seeing. Yet a raised eyebrow peering through the mane of her dark hair suggested I hadn't been nearly as subtle as I'd hoped, and my lover soon shoved me back onto my own side of the rickety, splinter-ridden piece of wood that didn't deserve to have my ass on it.

"We'll ride through the night," Filiberto called from outside, and while there were low groans from the others, they quickly disappeared when he added, "for the payout we'll receive when we deliver these three to Máros will mean we won't have to work for a month!"

"Ren..." Mat began, his expression dark, and I heaved out a weary breath. There was a click of hooves and then the wagon began to move, jolting unsteadily as it traversed the uneven road. Echoing hoofbeats and the leathery rustle of tack told me the other men were on horseback around us.

"I know," I murmured. There was little else to say: we were bound, surrounded, and being dragged back to our enemies.

Or, to put it more succinctly, we were *fucked*.

*

Chapter Seven

Mat

"No more inns."

"No more inns," I repeated after my lover, feeling shitty and terrified but mostly angry. At myself. I clawed at the rough metal of the cuff around Ren's wrist, each fingertip already raw and bleeding from my desperation to free him. "We were Blessed stupid to go anywhere we could be recognised...to *stay* there."

An assenting snort drew our attention to the girl seated opposite us.

"Oh, fuck off," Ren said to her, but without much bite. "Like you'd do any better."

Remembering what Filiberto had said about her being difficult to catch, I sighed. "She probably did. We were...that was fucking humiliating. We're not letting them take us back to Welzes, Ren. This will *not* be how we go down."

I returned my attention to where I had his hand in my lap, scratching and tugging at each link of chain in the hope of finding a weakness in the manacles that had somehow eluded the dozens of prisoners they had undoubtedly held before us.

"Mathias," Ren warned as he caught sight of the state of my hands, his voice low and furious. "Stop. You're hurting yourself!"

I ignored him. None of it mattered if he died; not the blood, not the pain, not the consternation of knowing how badly we'd screwed up.

"Mat. *Fucking stop*," he said in *that* voice, and my hands stilled of their own accord. He pried my bloody fingers from the metal, lacing them through his instead.

"I can't give up," I said, although it came out as more of a whisper. "I won't."

"We won't."

But he wasn't *doing* anything! How could he sit there so calmly, with every rotation of the wheels below us delivering him closer to his death? How could he let those power-hungry pricks win, after everything he'd fought so hard for? How could he-

"I said no more inns," Ren remarked, his lips twitching in amusement as he took in my expression. He leaned in and kissed the tip of my nose. "Future tense, little wildcat. I have no intention of going meekly into the afterlife, but rather than breaking all of my fingernails on re-proving the unmalleability of metal, I'm planning to hit a rather more tractable target. People."

The prince offered me a wry smile, lazing back on the bench and stretching his feet out so they rested next to the girl. She gave his boots a scathing look but said nothing.

"We know that my execution will have to be quiet and as innocent-looking as possible. That means Welzes and Navar won't risk being caught near me when it happens. And *that* means the involvement of other people...people whom we may be able to convince into helping us."

May. It was far from a guarantee, but it was *something*. A possible glimmer of hope that didn't see Ren's lifeless corpse being thrown into the river in the dead of night.

"I'm also," Ren continued casually, trailing a suggestive finger up my thigh, "trying to work out if we have enough time between our chatty companion here being dropped off at the city gaol and us arriving at the palace for me to give you one hell of a goodbye, *mi cielo*." Ren held up a vial of oil between two fingers of his free hand.

I stared at it. "How many of those fucking things do you have?"

"This is, regrettably and devastatingly, the last one. If you're hoping for a second round, we might just have to get creati-"

I snatched for it with my right hand but he jerked his left back, halting me in mid-air as the chain snapped taut. I growled out my frustration.

"Fuck, I know you love my cock, *mi corazón*, but I draw the line at getting it on in front of a child."

"Ren," I snarled. "Give me the Blessed oil."

He shot me a wicked grin. "You're going to have to beg harder than that."

"How's this?" I asked, elbowing him sharply in the side. He crumpled, his boots slamming back down onto the wooden floorboards, but still managed to keep the bottle just out of my reach. "We can use it to slide our hands through the cuffs, asshole."

Ren gathered his breath and dubiously inspected his shackled wrist. "I doubt it. I think they're too tight."

"We can at least fucking try!"

Chastised, he nodded and made to hand me the vial. "You're right. We should-"

One of the girl's chained hands shot out, snatching the bottle from Ren's grip. We both gaped at her in shock for a second and then Ren hissed out his irritation, trying to wrench it back. She kicked him away and pressed herself against the canvas out of reach of his straining fingers.

"By the Blessed, you're quick," he reluctantly admitted, and then dropped his voice back into that deliciously dominant tone that sent shivers up my spine and brought my cock to immediate attention. "*Give it back*."

But even though I was ready to hand him anything he wanted, dignity and all, she merely rolled her eyes and popped the cork, drizzling the entire precious contents of the vial over her slender wrists.

We both muttered angry curses as we watched her drain what was likely our final chance for getting ourselves loose prior to arriving in Máros, although the difficulty she had in freeing herself told the rational part of my brain that it hadn't been much of a chance at all. Her hands were half the size of either of ours, and it still cost most of her skin in working them through the ruthless bite of the cuffs.

"You're out for yourself, I can respect that," Ren said grudgingly. "But now you're free, you could at least…"

She shot him a rude gesture, staggered to the back of the swaying wagon, and swung herself around the side of it like a Blessed cat.

We stared, indignant and a little impressed, at the indentations in the canvas wall which marked her progress along the outside of the wagon towards its driver.

Ren blew out a breath. "Well, *fuck*. Wonder when she'll be spotted?"

He didn't have to wonder for long, for it was then that the surprised shouts began from the men around us.

"How the fuck did you-"

"Get the hell down from-"

"What in Dios' name-"

"You little bitch, don't even think about-"

There was a surprised shriek, several frightened whinnies, and the wagon lurched around us. My stomach flew up into my mouth as we fell backwards...and continued to fall, further than it should have been if the wagon had merely rolled onto its side.

I didn't have breath enough to curse or call out Ren's name, but the words flitted around my head along with the screams of someone outside. Man or horse, I didn't know: it was just a high-pitched noise of *terror* that vibrated through my skull, worsening my own panic as the world turned on its head over and over, something hard catching me in the shin, the temple, the back, and the chain jerking harshly against my wrist as we fell.

And then it all came to a halt.

The movement, the noise...but not the nausea, and I immediately retched, hoping to every one of the Five Blessed that I was the right way up and wouldn't vomit over myself. It turned out I wasn't – I was twisted with my knees above my head and my face in my arms – but it also became evident that not having eaten that terrible inn food had been an excellent idea, for nothing came up but bile. Both of my wrists hurt, and I could feel an unpleasant warmth on my forehead that told me I was bleeding.

But my first thought was for the man at my side...or wherever he'd found himself, and this time I prayed to anyone who would fucking listen that he hadn't broken his neck in our fall.

"Ren," I croaked, wrenching my head around to follow his faint groans. He was half splayed over me, half beneath me, and as he cracked an eye, I heaved out a breath of relief that cut off when he winced.

"*Dorogoi?*"

"My...shoulder," he gasped out, his free hand clutching at the same spot he'd been pierced with the arrow. Blood was seeping through his clothing and I swore, torn between haste and care as I wriggled out from the tangle of limbs and wood we'd found ourselves in to reach for him. It was made more difficult by being unable to move my right hand very far, as I was afraid to pull on the chain that bound it to his injured left side.

My hands and knees plunged into something cold and I blinked, alarmed, to see moonlight reflecting off water. It was already a foot deep and more was gushing in through the canvas and the huge gashes torn in it.

Shit.

Ren was almost submerged where he lay on his back. He'd started to shiver, but the cold didn't stop him from berating me when I tugged him upright to lean him against the now vertical floor of the wagon.

"Gently, asshole," he growled, flinching as I peeled his shirt back to peer at his injury. The butcher's stitches had torn, but the bleeding wasn't nearly as bad as it had been that first time and the entrance wound on his back hadn't re-opened. That was…as good as could be hoped for?

"Hold that there," I ordered as I pressed a handful of cleanish – at least, not bloodied and still dry for now – shirt to the front of the prince's shoulder, and his eyebrows shot up in mischievous delight at the command. Clearly, the fucker was fine.

"Yes, sir," he mocked, but obediently held the cloth in place as I splashed around in the gloom to locate the chain between us. Dismayed, I traced each link as I had done before, only to find them still intact, the cuffs around our wrists as secure as ever.

I let out a noise of frustration and the dirty water began to rush in faster as if to demonstrate its eager agreement with the sentiment.

"Mathias?" Ren asked, his tone casual.

"Da?"

"You may not have noticed. I'm aware it's hard to focus on anything other than me when you're in my presence. But if you *haven't* noticed, I feel it's my responsible duty to inform you that we're less than a minute from a painful and waterlogged death."

I gritted my teeth and rolled my eyes as I again yanked fruitlessly on the ring of metal hammered into the wooden bench below the surface of the water, my numb fingers slipping on the chain it was pinning down.

But snapping at him wouldn't help. Engaging in our usual banter at least settled my mind somewhat as I desperately ran my hands across the surface of the bench where the wood had split slightly from the impact of our fall. "Painful? Have you drowned before?"

"I have not," he said conversationally as I looked around in despair for something I could use to help us. "I imagine it would be a memorable experience."

"I'd be happy to let that be the one experience you try alone," I said, hissing out a breath as the cold rose to my thighs. Ren lifted his chin to keep his face out of the water.

"Oh! But there was that one time you attempted to drown me in the basin, remember? I'd feel a little cheated if my death wasn't by something completely new."

I heaved at his arm and he made a pained sound.

"Fuck, little wildcat! What part of 'ow, my shoulder' did you not understand? Basic anatomy, perhaps?"

"Begging your forgiveness, Your Highness," I shot back, "but I figured it was less important than letting the water rise above your head. That's generally how one drowns."

Keeping him upright with one hand while trying to free us with the other was not working. All my strength was going into holding his weight, and my boots were slipping on whatever mud or silt the wagon was rapidly sinking into.

"While I appreciate your efforts to ensure I can continue to harass you to the very end," said Ren, "I know we're not going to die here."

My gaze shot to his. "How can you possibly know that?"

He smiled, soft and beautiful. "Because you won't let us," he told me, and those words wrapped around my heart.

I struggled to breathe as I stared into the familiar brown eyes which were crinkled in fondness and pain, the water now lapping at our necks.

There was no slack left on the chain from where it was held down to the bench. And it wasn't long enough to allow us to stand, so we were both awkwardly crouched in the cold, wet darkness, waiting for our utterly miserable ends. Unless one of us dropped down below the water to let the other rise higher with the hope that the wagon would stop sinking soon, we'd both be submerged in seconds, and dead within a couple of minutes.

"Right," I said, and then let go of the man who had captured every fibre of my being. Ren immediately sank below the surface, his hair cascading around his head in an eerie halo before disappearing from view.

I took up the slack on the chain which it gave me, rising to my feet and bringing my foot down hard on the bench. It delivered nothing but a jarring in my ankle, but with the next blow I felt the wood give below my boot where it had been split, even soaked as it was. I adjusted my stance and continued to stomp on it, yanking at the restraints and trying to ignore the bubbles rising to my right even though this was taking too long, he'd been down there for too-

I stumbled backwards as the metal ring that had been holding us down by our wrists was tugged free from the crack in the wood, my arms flying out to keep my balance. And then I took a breath from the tiny pocket of remaining air and ducked down to gather Ren into my arms, relief flooding my soul as he grabbed hold of me.

The water resistance made our escape frustratingly slow and I snarled out a precious bubble of air when I discovered the back of the wagon had collapsed. I dragged the heavy canvas aside from where it had come loose and was wafting in the water, manoeuvring us both through the tight space just as my lungs began to burn.

When we broke the surface of the water, Ren immediately coughed, spluttered, and then mewled out a pained sob, clutching at his shoulder as I began to half-wade, half-swim to the shore of the river we'd found ourselves in. Thick mud, the heavy metal of the manacles, and a vehemently complaining prince all did their best to weigh me down, but I didn't stop – *couldn't* stop – until I'd heaved us both to the edge and we'd used the tough grasses that grew there to pull ourselves out. I rolled onto my back, staring unseeingly at the night sky, while Ren remained on his hands and knees and coughed up more dirty river water.

"That was something," he said eventually, trying to stand. Still shackled to each other as we were, the movement yanked ruthlessly on my outstretched wrist, but I forgave him for not remembering we were bound together as a result of him almost drowning.

Then he tugged again, the cocky grin telling me he clearly hadn't forgotten any such thing. I sighed and reluctantly climbed to my feet so that he could do the same.

Dripping and shivering, we both glanced around at the moonlight-drenched riverbank that had almost been our grave.

One of the mercenaries lay a few feet up the steep hill we'd presumably tumbled down, his body gruesomely contorted and his neck at an impossible angle to his shoulders. He must have been thrown from his horse, as the beast was nowhere to be seen. We'd been fucking lucky to have been inside the wagon itself, where the wooden struts that held up the canvas walls and roof had acted like a protective rib cage...although they'd certainly borne the brunt of such protection, with the wagon little more than a deformed, splintery mess where it was still sinking below the surface into the muddy riverbed. Ren muttered breathy gratitude to his god, crossing himself fervently, and I glanced up to the top of the hill where I assumed the road lay. Multiple lantern lights flickered up on the distant crest, telling me that either some of the mercenaries were still alive, or a bunch of helpful locals would soon be investigating our fall. Neither type of attention was good for us.

"Where did that little nuisance get to?" Ren grumbled, pulling at my wrist again as he turned in an unnecessarily brisk circle to look for the girl.

"Stop fucking doing that. And if your god is merciful, she got clear before the wagon went off the road."

"Merciful? She made me bleed!" he protested, gesturing at his shoulder.

"An arrow did that. She saved our lives in whatever she did to spook the horses."

"She also messed up my hair, Mat. That is unforgivable."

"We'll double her bounty when you take back your throne," I promised, "and then I can thank her for it properly when she's found. But to do that, we need to get out of here before they" – I pointed up at the bobbing lanterns – "find a way down here. I'll take a look at your shoulder when we're far enough away."

Ren narrowed his eyes, clearly wondering whether I intended to thank the mysterious thief for our unintended rescue or the hair thing, and then satisfied himself by jerking me forward by the chain once more. This time it was abrupt enough to cause me to stumble.

"I said, stop-"

"I like the idea of you on a leash, Mat," he said lightly, a slyness in his voice that was entirely inappropriate for the situation and yet I wouldn't have expected any different from the mercurial asshole.

"We're both on the same Blessed leash, *svoloch*," I reminded him, "and you'll note I haven't taken advantage of it like you have."

"Because I'm gravely injured," the prince retorted, but he did fall into step beside me as we began to limp our way along the bank, moving upriver and away from Máros.

"That wouldn't stop me."

"Or because you're the sub, not me."

"Am I, though? Still not the reason," I said.

"And you know that if you even try, I'll find a way to make you regret it."

"Nope."

"Then it's because you're boring?"

I glanced at him with suspicion. "Is that an attempt to provoke me so you have an excuse to punish me?"

"Maybe." His teeth shone in the moonlight, fixed in a broad grin even as he shivered. "*Mi amor?*"

"Yes?"

"You fucking did it," he whispered, the backs of his cold fingers brushing mine. "You saved us."

-

"I...think that looks right," I said, doubt hitting hard even as I spoke, and we both surveyed the crooked pile of sticks on the ground before us. Half of it promptly collapsed in on itself as we stared.

"Close enough," Ren agreed cheerfully. "How do we do the part where it bursts into flames?"

We glanced at each other uncertainly. We'd kept moving through the forest that bordered the river all Blessed night, exhausted and aching — and in Ren's case, occasionally bleeding from his shoulder whenever his tired feet caused him to stumble or fall — but too afraid to stop for more than a few minutes at a time in case our pursuers caught up to us. But we'd seen their own campfire flare up a dozen miles back, and the knowledge that they were taking the time to rest had lent us confidence to do the same now that the sun had risen and the flames wouldn't be visible from a distance.

Yet neither the hunger nor the chill in the air could be staved off by an assortment of dry sticks that we had no idea how to light.

"Oh come on," Ren said after a long silence. "You must have had to do it before. Isn't the north colder than this?"

"Sure," I conceded. "But the palace fires were lit by servants, and as a political hostage I never travelled without supervision. You?"

The prince cocked his head, still gazing at the pathetic stick pile as if he could make it ignite with nothing more than the heavy weight of expectation. "My guards always handled it. Ademar used to kind of…crouch next to the wood and it burst into flames."

"I think there's more to it than that," I said wryly and then frowned, trying to remember. "Rocks, maybe?"

"Rocks don't burn, Mat."

"It was…they smashed them together?" I looked around for some stones we could use, hissing out a breath of irritation when Ren didn't move. "We're still attached, asshole. Could I trouble you to possibly help?"

Ren leaned in and licked my cheek.

I raised an eyebrow, trying not to laugh. "That was not remotely helpful."

"I could lick something else instead?"

"You're still not contributing in any useful way."

He shrugged. "Then I'm out of ideas."

But he gestured vaguely to a spot on the ground with his boot, and sure enough there were a handful of pebbles half-sunk into the soft ground, possibly deposited by the river when it had trailed a different course through these woods long ago. Yet after twenty minutes of fruitlessly scraping them together, which admittedly produced the desired sparks but did not, in any way, result in the sticks catching fire, I finally gave up.

Ren clicked his tongue. "Is it too damp or something?"

"Oh, I don't fucking know," I said, scowling. The sun was now heating up our little glade quite nicely, so maybe we didn't need a fire after all. Still, the waste of time and energy was depressing, and my stomach was growling loudly. "We're terrible at this shit."

"We absolutely are. Next time you have the fantastic idea of leaving a comfortable city to go gallivanting across the country with absolutely no supplies or servants, remind me to tell you to fuck off."

"And the next time you want to stay within a mile of the palace in which everyone wants you dead, remind me to let you."

"I'm sure it's not *everyone*," he protested with visible indignation. "Just Welzes and Navar and Yanev…and probably the rest of my father's Council, and all the nobles and merchants now on their side, and the servants and guards who just follow the authority of whoever's ass is on the throne, and the palace cat whose tail I accidentally trod on when I was six."

"Right," I agreed, trying to stifle a yawn. "So you've got Lord de la Vega and the palace's population of mice in your corner."

Ren winced. "Probably not so much the mice. The cat became twice as mean after she almost lost her tail, and I'm sure they know it's me to blame. Shall we skip the fire thing and get some sleep?"

I faltered, trying to ignore my growling stomach and wondering how to raise my other pressing concern. "I have to…" I waved a hand at the nearest tree, and he frowned, confused.

"Answer a call of nature," I said awkwardly. "How do we…?"

Ren deftly manoeuvred us into position and I flushed, looking away as his own stream of urine hit the bark.

"Really, *mi cielo*, after all the filthy things I've done to you, *this* embarrasses you? I'm sure many people have pissed in front of you before."

"Not while I was tethered to them, they haven't."

Ren laughed, shaking himself off and straightening his clothes. Then he rattled the chain between us. "You have to admit, this is kind of kinky."

"It's kind of *inconvenient*," I retorted.

That earned me a half shrug, like being captured by mercenaries and ending up shackled to another person in the middle of a Quarehian forest happened to him every day. But instead of giving me privacy, the prince rested his chin on my shoulder, peering down attentively and somehow making me feel twice as uncomfortable than when I had my cock out for other reasons.

"Need me to hold anything?" he offered sweetly.

I batted his face away but paid for it dearly, for the moment I was finished, he dragged me backwards and dropped abruptly to the ground a few yards away without warning. I yelped as I was pulled down with him, the shackles biting into the abused skin on my wrist.

"Stop. Fucking. Doing. *That!*"

Ren ignored me and lay down instead, and while I wasn't prepared to admit it, he'd chosen a decent spot for us to rest. The ground was spongy with the layer of oak leaves spread thickly across it, and while it made for a musty smell, the thick greenery above us sheltered us from the direct sunlight.

He inspected his own bound wrist as I tucked myself away.

"We'll find a blacksmith to remove the manacles or…something," I finished lamely, realising as I said it that even if we could afford to pay for such a thing, we looked very much like what we were: a pair of alleged criminals on the run. We could just as easily be turned in for our troubles.

"Hmm," said Ren. "I suppose I should say thanks for not gnawing off my arm to save yourself."

"That was an option? Damn," I said.

He patted my knee. "It's not your fault. You're just not as good at thinking up drastic solutions as I am. Or as good at *anything* else, really, other than being a sullen asshole."

When I shoved half-heartedly at him, careful to avoid his injury, he caught my hand and rolled on top of me. We came to rest with his right forearm pressed lightly against my throat.

"Oh yes," Ren said with a wolfish smile. "You're also excellent at looking deliciously fuckable. How do you possibly make 'cranky' seem so hot?"

"No," I warned. "Don't even think about it."

"You don't want to find out if we can make it work even with these?" Ren asked, shaking his other hand to make the chain rattle.

"You're Renato Aratorre. You'd make it work." He preened at that. "What I *don't want* is acorns in my ass."

"Mat, if you think I'm going to let a bunch of acorns get up in what's mine, you're not as smart as you've been pretending. Trust me, your ass will be far too full for anything else to fit in there."

"We also don't have any oil," I pointed out.

"True."

"And you're injured."

"That's…" He sighed, slumping against me. "Also true. Very well. But so it's fair, I shall ensure your suffering will be just as acute as mine." He rubbed himself against my cock until he coaxed an unwilling groan from my mouth, and then, far too smug at having brought me to aching hardness with no relief, crawled off me and lay at my side.

I forced unpleasant, cock-softening images into my head, although it took a long damn time to undo what he'd done to me so I could get some sleep. Yet each time I began to drift off, I was rudely wrenched back to reality.

"Stop wriggling!" I hissed at Ren after receiving an elbow to the ribs for the fourth time in as many minutes.

"I can't help it," he grouched, shuffling on the ground and driving his hip painfully into my balls. I grunted and reached out an arm to hold him still.

"There's a…Dios-damned rock pressing against my back wherever I lie," Ren complained, and I sighed.

"Careful, *dorogoi*. You're letting your spoilt prince show."

"Oh, and you're finding this *so* comfortable?"

"I've had worse," I shot back, returning the fifth rib-digging elbow as I was convinced that this time it had been deliberate. "Someone threw me in a fucking cell, remember? Twice!"

"Hmm," the prince said, suddenly sounding much more contented. "That sounds absolutely dreadful. Poor baby."

"So maybe I'm not exactly upset that the cause of that unpleasant experience now has a rock in his bed. Would you like me to collect some more?"

"You're being mean," Ren pouted, "and entirely unsympathetic to my horrific situation."

"A barely-inconvenient situation which is the same as mine."

"One might have supposed that a good servant would have fashioned his prince a comfy hammock."

"I'm not your fucking servant," I snarled, "but if you happen to have any rope to make one, I'll gladly string you up in the trees nonetheless."

"That sounds lovely-"

"By your neck, prince."

"Or I could not put you to the trouble," Ren added hastily, and I shook my head as my lover finally fell blessedly silent, sleep taking me once more.

And then I jerked back awake as Ren dug his knee into my thigh.

"Do I have to bite your arm off after all?"

He gave a long, drawn-out sigh. "It's not my fault. It's just too hard."

"Yes, Ren, it's the *ground*. It tends to be hard."

"Well, tell it not to be."

I rolled my eyes. "I'll get right on that."

Ren made a noise of approval and patted the earth at his side. "You won't know what hit you," he warned it. "My Mathias can do icy judgment and impossible stubbornness like you've never seen: you'll be soft and squishy in no time."

He made a noise of complaint as my chest shook with silent laughter. "Now who's wriggling?"

"Your Mathias?"

"Yes," Ren said firmly. "*Mine*."

I reached around and tugged Ren's slim body onto mine so his shoulders and torso were off the ground. He tucked his head under my chin and gave a sleepy, happy hum as he settled against me, his weight a pleasant pressure as we drifted into sleep.

"Good pillow," the prince whispered to my chest, kissing it gently, and those words accompanied my consciousness into darkness.

*

Chapter Eight

Ren

We allowed ourselves only an hour of rest before we forced each other back to our feet and continued the trudge east, having learned our lesson about staying still for too long. I was no stranger to lack of sleep — as a prince, I had many responsibilities and there were only a limited number of hours in the day — but when added to the painful gnawing of hunger in our stomachs, the itch of the dried river mud on our skin, and the army of mosquitoes whose leader had apparently joined Navar in declaring us enemies of the state, it was hard to find my normal upbeat cheer. Those first few days on the road now seemed idyllic compared to our current conditions, and when one found themselves wistfully daydreaming about even that horrendous inn food, one realised quite how far one had fallen.

I might have imagined this to be hell, and that I'd died in the wagon with grimy water pouring into my lungs as I strained at a chain that was never going to give, if it wasn't for the man enduring it all with me. Brilliant, passionate Mathias, and his iron-willed determination thrown at whatever he put his mind to. Hell would never be so kind as to allow him near me, let alone permit me to indulge in the soothing comfort of his presence that was like sunlight and silk sheets and the smell of warm bread all rolled into one.

There was just enough length in the chain for us to walk comfortably side by side, but we'd quickly learned that holding hands as we travelled helped to prevent those awkward, painful moments where we tried to move in different directions to navigate a tree or patch of mud in our path. Awkwardness that I had perhaps manufactured, as I liked having his hand in mine. I liked being able to touch him at all times, to feel his warmth and solidness beneath my fingertips, and maybe I was being a sentimental, soppy fucker right now but when he was the only thing keeping my feet moving, I was bloody well treating myself to as much of him as I could.

Neither of us seemed to want to speak of it out loud, but whenever our conversation veered in the direction of what had happened last night, we squeezed each other's fingers in a silent acknowledgement of how close we'd come to dying. And then we returned to what we did best: unnecessarily bitching at each other.

Really, it was amazing how it made the miles pass beneath our aching feet. Even exhausted as he was, Mathias' wit never faltered, and it invigorated my own heckling long past the point where I might have descended into brooding silence. The teasing banter weaved its way through our discussions about childhood adventures, favourite foods, the importance of theological influence in monarchical power structures, and a rather heated argument when we hit our third round of *fuck, marry, kill*.

"*Ren*," he spluttered, shaking his head, "she's my sister. I'm not going to marry *or* fuck Mila."

"So you'd kill her?" I asked dubiously. "That seems like a terrible choice. Not only would she be the hardest to murder, but it means you end up having to fuck Dr. Sánchez or Viento."

Mat groaned. "Who said you could include a horse in this game, anyway?"

"My rules, darling. Just like the rule where if you don't give me a final answer before we reach that big tree over there, you have to carry me for the next two miles."

He wrinkled his nose. "Fine. Kill Mila half a second before she dies peacefully in her sleep because otherwise it's my ass that would be getting murdered, marry Viento – because the game means you don't have sex with your spouse, right? – and then close my eyes and get it over with…with Dr. Sánchez." He shuddered, and my laughter echoed through the woods.

"Now there's a sight I'll have in my head for a long time," I mused.

"Urgh. I don't envy you that."

"No, I meant you and Viento, *mi amor*. Your face as you walk down the aisle with him. *His* face. I'm not sure which of you would look more pissed off."

"Well, I have to try to kill Mila first. Maybe she'd put me out of my misery before I could endure the unendurable fate of being married to a horse and…nope, I'm not going to say the other thing again. Once was enough." Mat paused, and I glanced in his direction to catch him looking ponderous. "Your turn. Luis, Valeri, and Aksinia."

My guard, my future brother-in-law slash maybe enemy, and the crazy

AN OATH AND A PROMISE

Temarian seer? Easy.

"Fuck, fuck, fuck."

My lover gave a long, drawn-out sigh. "That's not how this works."

"It is now," I told him. "My rules. Nat…"

"I am neither marrying, killing, nor fucking myself," he said flatly.

"The latter I can and will make happen. But I was going to say that I was wrong, before. I'm actually…"

When I trailed off, Mathias cheerfully filled in the silence for me, insolent brat that he was. "An irritating, entitled prick with no sense of boundaries?"

"Oh no," I said. "I've always been all that. But I'm also glad you're with me, even though I know I shouldn't be. I know I should want you safe and far away from all of this, but I don't think my heart could take being alone."

He brushed a kiss against my cheek, his mouth bumping clumsily against my skin as we walked. "It is a rather squishy, cuddly heart once you get to know it."

I scowled. "When I'm king, I shall have you executed for such heinous slander."

He snorted.

"We were also wrong about something else," I said softly, and before he could offer up some nonsense to that too, I added, "and that's about being shit at this. Because we're still alive, Mat. It's been nearly two weeks since we escaped the palace from under Navar and Welzes' damn noses, and we're *still alive*."

Blue-grey eyes met mine and then darted away again, not lit by his usual indomitable fire but steeped in anguish and reservation. Mathias slid his hand free and dropped his head, mumbling something incomprehensible to the ground. Oh, fuck him for not being immediately and irrevocably convinced by my little motivational speech. We'd even been all mature and responsible and shit by not having sex earlier, and *this* was how he repaid such noble sacrifice on my part? By blaming himself for what had happened yesterday?

I gave a hard tug on the chain between us, as I had been doing each time he tried to sink into that morose self-reproach of his. The filthy look I received in return was Totally Worth It, because when he was irritated at me, he wasn't angry at himself. Anger that was entirely fucking ludicrous: why would it be *his* fault that my country was hunting me and had come far too close to catching us? I was capable of making my own bad decisions, thank you very much, and that had included dragging us to an inn each night…when if I'd stopped and thought about it beyond the desire for a bed and warm meal, I'd have known it was just asking for trouble. Yet if I tried telling the idiot northerner that he wasn't at fault, he'd become even more convinced that the opposite was true, stubborn fucker that he was.

I yanked at the shackles again, towing Mat forward where he'd begun to trail behind. He made another of those cute, incensed noises of protest, and I glanced around to find he'd curled his fingers around a length of the chain, ready to pull back against me in turn.

I raised an eyebrow. "Go ahead and try it, Nathanael," I said sweetly. "And see where it gets you."

He took in my overly polite smile, his expression wavering from defiance into suspicious unease, before biting his lip and letting go.

My soft laughter sounded sadistic even to my own ears. "Very good. I'd have you on your hands and knees for even daring to think it, only you'd slow us down terribly."

Mathias grunted out his disapproval of the idea. "I thought we agreed I wouldn't ever crawl for you?"

I'd never heard such nonsense in my life. "We did *not*," I said indignantly. "Are you trying to drain all the fun out of the world? Don't answer that," I hastily added, because his pissed off scowl implied that may indeed have been his goal. "I've decided instead that the punishment for that mutinous attitude of yours is to walk the next hour in only your boots. Give me all of your clothes."

He ignored me so thoroughly that for a moment I wondered if my words had merely been wishful thinking.

Never mind. I knew a sure-fire way to have my northerner strip for me, and it would only take a single sentence.

"You-"

We both froze as a long howl split the air, staring back the way we'd come.

"They have dogs," Mat said hollowly.

"And terrible timing," I agreed, pretending to sulk as that was better than letting the icy fear in my veins freeze me in place.

"We should run?"

"Nah," I said. "I think we should stay here and let them tear us to pieces. Yes, Your Highness, I think *we should fucking run.*"

His answer was to scowl, grab my hand, and take off at a pace I hadn't known either of us were capable of, considering how long it had been since we last ate or rested properly. But I had to admit that the excited barks of the mercenaries' dog as they gained on our heels were *excellent* motivators, and the adrenaline carried us through thick underbrush and up steep inclines that I would not have even attempted half an hour ago.

But it was when the next howl came from ahead of us that I realised running hadn't been the obvious solution my sarcasm had implied. The fuckers were herding us.

"Makes. Sense," Mathias gasped as we pushed our way through spiky, low-hanging branches whose entire purpose in life seemed to be to inconvenience runaway princes. They left shallow yet numerous gashes across our faces and arms. "Catching people is…what these mercenaries…fucking *do*. Did we really…believe…a pair of royals could…outpace them?"

Outpace, likely not. Outsmart? Perhaps.

"This way," I panted, leading us to our right where I knew the river lurked somewhere close. We'd been roughly following its course through the forest – again, that was probably predictable but without food we'd needed *something* to give us sustenance and muddy water was better than none – and if we could get across without being seen, the water would lose the dogs our trail. The men hunting us would hopefully assume we'd continued east, but if we doubled back west for a while, we might be able to evade them long enough to…

"Oh," I said, as we shoved our way through the last of the trees to find the anticipated river.

Only it was a hundred feet below us.

We stood on a cliff, the rocky ground dropping before our feet so steeply it was almost vertical. The river wound its way below, thinner and not as fast-moving as it had been where we'd first met it — and almost drowned in it — but it was going to be difficult to use the water to dampen our scent when getting to it would require either a half hour of careful descent, or a fatal fall that would quickly sweep our corpses away.

"Maybe we can lose them in the trees after all," I suggested, but Mathias shook his head. I stilled when I saw his usual stormy-coloured eyes had been replaced with the blue and gold of my family name.

"If we run now, the dogs catch us alone within minutes," he said, his voice quiet as he reflected on whatever he was Seeing. "But if we stay here, the men will be with them."

"And then what?"

"I don't know. I didn't See beyond them all arriving from over there." He pointed at the tree line a few feet from where we'd emerged ourselves.

"And how is that better?" I demanded, and Mat gave a rueful shrug as the vivid colour receded from his gaze.

"They're people," was all he said, and I was reminded of what I'd told him in the wagon about the involvement of people giving us a chance. But that had been with guards or servants who might be willing to take a bribe to let me escape, not a bunch of mercenaries for whom our entire value rested in our recapture.

Oh.

"Do you trust me?" I asked, buoyed by the lack of any hesitation from my lover when he immediately gave me a warm smile and his unflinching assent. I sneaked a kiss from him because I could, and because there was a very good chance this wouldn't work, and because I wasn't leaving this world without stealing whatever I could from the man who in turn had stolen — and *become* — my everything.

"Are we interrupting, boys?"

I held up a finger in the universal symbol of *wait your fucking turn*, not bothering to look around at the approaching men until I'd finished memorising Mat's mouth with my tongue and the little dimples in his lower back with my fingertips. So perhaps our this-may-be-goodbye kiss had turned a little heated in the minutes we'd been waiting but I noticed my wildcat wasn't complaining, melting into my touch with a soul-warming receptiveness that made my blood sing.

"You are," I said eventually, dragging my lips from Mathias' with reluctance. So much reluctance that I leaned back in and gave him another quick kiss because fuck it, he was mine. "I'd ask for an extra half hour before this all plays out between us so *mi cielo* and I can finish what we were doing, but I don't suppose you'd agree."

"Sure we would," offered José, winking at me. He stood only a few yards away with Filiberto and two of the other men: the rest of the group save for the one who had been killed in the fall. Two dogs with slobbering jowls and heaving chests waited obediently at their feet, their canine faces twisted in near-feral grimaces. "*If* we can watch. Maybe join in when it gets good?"

I glanced at Mat with curiosity, and he snorted.

"*Nyet.*"

"He's very shy," I explained to them. "Maybe you could all turn your backs and take a few steps away while I get him warmed up? A mile or two should do it."

"Or you-"

"*Or,*" hissed Filiberto, clearly not as invested in the idea as the older man, "you two can drop to your fucking knees and start listing reasons why we shouldn't break every bone in your bodies."

"I thought you were going somewhere else with the knees thing." José looked disappointed. "Are you sure we don't have time for a bit of fun first?"

"We sure don't. Because we've spent the better part of a day in this Blessed forest, and we still have to get them back to a town to find new transport. You really want to delay us any further, José?" The man's voice was hitched in a livid snarl, his lips peeled back from his teeth. I guessed we had been more than a little bothersome to their plan of collecting the bounty on me, but I also didn't give a shit, so there was that.

"Breaking bones isn't going to make us move any faster," Mathias pointed out with disdain, and I nodded in wholehearted agreement.

AN OATH AND A PROMISE

"You know what *would* make us haul ass out of these woods? Letting us go."

Filiberto began to angrily march towards us, clearly ready to haul one or both of us over those massive shoulders of his, and as much as I was keen to feel if his muscles were as mouth-wateringly juicy as they looked, I figured he wasn't going to be particularly nice about the manhandling.

So, as he approached, I backed up. One step, two, until my heels were resting on the very edge of the cliff. Rather than protesting, Mathias had moved with me; precise, unquestioning, and with a derisive sneer in the direction of the other men.

"For every step you take forward, we take one back," I called, and that fucking stopped the mercenary in his tracks. "You'll note that we don't have a whole lot to spare."

"This isn't a damn ballad," Filiberto snapped. "There's no heroism or miraculous survival to be had here, boy – you go over that edge, you *die*."

We would. It was the unarguable truth.

"Maybe, maybe not," Mathias said, arguing anyway because he was *him* and even impending death wouldn't change such fundamental principles. "But are you keen to find out?"

"Oh, but it's going to be awfully difficult to collect the reward money when they don't even have our corpses as proof," I mused to him, although my voice was pitched loud enough to include the rest of them in the macabre conversation. "And then that would make this little jaunt of theirs entirely worthless."

"Wait," José said, his brows drawing low in horror as he finally caught onto our threat and the implications for their purse strings. "Don't. I'm sure we can…come to some sort of arrangement?"

"They won't do it," scoffed Filiberto. "Why the fuck would they choose death for each other?"

"He's rather fond of drama," Mat said, jerking his chin at me. "If you take us to Welzes, he's dead anyway, and I don't see a future without him in it…so why shouldn't we inconvenience you assholes on the way out?"

I grinned. The mercenaries bristled.

AN OATH AND A PROMISE

"You're going to toss us the key to these," I ordered, shaking the wrist that bound me to Mathias and letting the links of the chain rattle. "Then you're going to-"

"Call your bluff, little princeling," Filiberto growled, even as his men hissed out pleas for him not to be so hasty in risking their gold. Damn it, if he'd been the one who'd died in the wagon accident, we might have had a chance. "Here's *my* deal. You both get your skinny, privileged asses over here, take the beatings we give you without a word of complaint...and if you apologise nicely enough for the trouble you've caused us, I might consider giving you food and water between here and Máros."

"*Skinny?*" I demanded, indignant, not having heard anything he said after that. "Nat, he's even crueller with his adjectives than you are."

Mathias cocked his head. "So to confirm," he said unnecessarily loudly, "you plan to hurt us, starve us, drag us back to the capital, and then sell us to a man who intends to kill one or both of us?"

"*Sí*," said Filiberto. His lips were twisted with spite.

"And nothing we threaten or offer could possibly change your minds?" Mat was still almost yelling out the words, and I didn't know why.

"No."

The other mercenaries shook their heads in support, Filiberto's confidence seeming to have given them back their own. And then movement in the tree line behind them caught my eye.

My heart gave an excited, relieved flutter.

"And to be *really sure*," my lover continued, "you're saying you wouldn't hesitate to hurt the man at my side? This one, Renato Aratorre, the true king of Quareh?" He gestured at me with his free hand, as if they might have gotten confused with the *other* person standing with him on the edge of a Dios-damned cliff.

Filiberto gave him a filthy look. "Make me repeat it one more time, *bárbaro*, and you'll *wish* it's only a beating you're in for."

I shrugged. "We're just checking."

"For your sake," Mathias added. "We'd hate for you to be killed unfairly."

"I wouldn't *hate* it," I countered, watching the figure in the trees silently close in on the men at the back of the group. "It would probably be quite a pleasant way to end this shitshow of a day."

Mathias reached a hand up to my face and turned it towards his. "I can think of a better way," he murmured, and when he pressed his mouth to mine, I was in vigorous agreement with him for once. Fingers brushed skin, tongues grazed teeth, and I watched his delicate lashes flutter shut before closing my eyes in turn and fully surrendering to the kiss.

I heard a scream, one of those panicked, pained shrieks which are only cut off so abruptly for one reason. There was barking. Swearing. Metal on metal. Noises that meant nothing, close but ever so distant, because all that mattered was the man in my arms who fitted against me so perfectly I knew he'd been made for me. Or I for him.

It felt like I was falling from a great height; dizzy and wild and lost, and with my heart in my mouth as I tumbled towards the exciting and terrifying unknown. I cracked an eye, fearing I'd perhaps accidentally pitched us over the cliff edge such that I'd have a hell of a lot of apologies to make in the seconds before we splattered over the rocks below, only to find us both still standing on solid ground, plastered together so thoroughly we might have been one entity.

It had been one of those metaphorical falls, then, one which felt realer than the sting of my shackled wrist or the ache in my shoulder or the wind in my hair. A realness I only experienced with *him,* the man who set my nerves alight and my senses dancing. Who made me want to laugh and scream and run and fly all at once, although I settled for playfully biting at his bottom lip as we drew apart, just so I could watch his own eyes spark with lust. Or annoyance. Something that was clearly synonymous with him being in unstoppable, incurable love with me.

I reluctantly dragged my gaze from Mat's, landing it on the mercenaries instead. Or what had been mercenaries: they were now nothing more than immobile, bloodied corpses lying face down in the dirt. All except Filiberto, but only because he was on his back, staring unseeingly into the cloudless sky as he suffered the indignity of having his killer use his cloak to wipe his own blood from the sword that had slayed him.

I mean, I assumed that was what had happened. With how distracted I'd been by Mathias and his eager, surprisingly deft tongue, for all I knew the mercenaries had all spontaneously keeled over and died untouched.

Yet that would make the giant crouched beside Filiberto a figment of my imagination, and I was too delighted to see him to entertain that as a possibility.

"I've rather missed you stabbing people for me," I said fondly, and Jiron's lips curled into a soft smile as he raised his head to look our way. "Mathias prefers to *get* stabbed for me, which is substantially more…let's be nice and call it discommodious."

I cocked my head, considering. "Although he did almost have his throat slit last night, so maybe I should give him credit for spicing it up."

"Jiron!" Mat exclaimed excitedly, and the guard cracked a second smile in his direction before fixing me with a look. It said *'you're Blessed lucky I arrived in time to rescue you'*, which clearly meant he'd forgotten how to communicate in our non-verbal language in the two weeks we'd been apart, because he'd mistranslated *'I'm Blessed lucky to have the privilege of rescuing you'* and also left out *'sorry I left it so fucking late'*.

"My prince," he murmured, plucking something from Filiberto's pocket before rising to his full height. Whenever I'd been away from Jiron for a while – which was extremely rarely – I was always struck afresh by his size. Larger than me and only a little smaller than a mountain, my oldest friend exuded a comforting, stabilising presence that others had variously described as 'terrifying' and 'intimidating' and 'argh, please don't-', usually right before their hearts coincidentally gave out.

"Are the others…"

"Luis and El are fine," he assured me, and the emotions I felt at hearing that on top of seeing him alive and *here*, made my knees weak. Mat immediately steadied me with an arm around my waist, wisely moving us away from the edge of the cliff.

"Don't you stop me from swooning in his presence," I objected in a futile attempt to pretend I wasn't dizzy with relief. "Jiron is looking so scrumptiously edible drenched in sweat and the blood of our enemies."

"How did you find us?" Mat asked. I was curious enough myself that I didn't chide him for the boring change of subject, although it was a close thing.

AN OATH AND A PROMISE

"I've been on your heels for the last couple of days, tracing rumours from village to village before I came across the accident on the road. A pair of princes traipsing through a forest is not exactly a subtle trail to follow." My guard hesitated for the briefest of moments and then smoothly added, "but not nearly as conspicuous as your pursuers, of course. I surely wouldn't have found you without them."

"Hmm," I said. Mathias snorted at my sceptical expression.

And then we were all moving closer to each other in wordless urgency, and I found myself pressed between Jiron's solid chest and Mat's slimmer frame as the guard drew us both into a tight embrace.

"*Ren.*" Jiron murmured my name into my hair with a sob, his huge hands gripping me in a way which was almost painful. I expected my own fingers were digging into his flesh just as deeply. "I was so worried. Being apart from you was…"

"I know."

I did. I'd felt it too; an emptiness that had gnawed at me no matter how hurt or terrified or exhausted I'd been. Jiron had been at my side for over thirteen years, and I had very few memories of my life before him.

"And you, little one," said my guard, and as I drew back I saw him gently squeezing my lover's shoulder. "I feared for you both."

"You know Mat's too stubborn to die. It's why I decided the safest place for me was permanently attached to him," I drawled, gesturing at the chain between us. "I offered to be attached in *other* places too, but he was his usual disagreeable self and made me sleep on a pile of rocks for even offering."

The northerner grimaced. "Now imagine *that*," he said to Jiron with a finger rudely jabbed in my direction, "but all day for the past…a thousand years, it must have been." He lifted his shackled wrist with a weary expression. "And unable to escape."

Jiron was far too professional to speak ill of me, even by way of tacit agreement, although he very much looked like he wanted to.

"Mmm," he said neutrally and I cackled, enjoying watching him be so obviously torn between loyalty and what was probably quite well-deserved sympathy.

"Sounds delightful, if I do say so myself," I said. "Jiron, if you can find a spare set of manacles, you're welcome to clip them on and join us."

"Or I could just free you both," he suggested, producing a key between his thumb and forefinger that he must have taken from Filiberto's corpse. It looked tiny in his huge hand.

"Yes!" Mathias exclaimed with an insulting amount of gratitude, just as I gave the opposite response. He scowled at me and held out his hand for the key, so I grabbed hold of the swaying chain between us and yanked sharply at it, sending him down onto his hands and knees. The startled yelp he made as he fell was just delicious.

"Kings *first*," I said in mock reproach, grinning when Mat glared up at me and brushed his palms together to clear them of the damp leaf litter.

Jiron undid my manacle and proceeded to fuss over the resulting wounds left on my skin, while I gazed at Mat thoughtfully.

"What do you say to us shackling his other wrist so we have something pretty and all tied up to play with?" I proposed, and I didn't miss the way Jiron's amber eyes flared with heat as he looked down at Mathias on his knees.

"Funny," my lover deadpanned, snatching the key from the guard's unprotesting grip and working it into the lock.

I pouted. "Don't be like that. Jiron's getting hard watching you too." Mat scoffed, so I nudged my guard with my elbow. "Tell him."

Jiron shot me a wounded look, but obligingly upheld the promise he'd made at Sesveko to obey me despite his better judgment, and his next words, uttered quietly, made Mathias blink. "It is a rather enjoyable sight."

Then he ruined it by reaching out a hand to pull my northerner to his feet.

"*I* decide when he's allowed off his knees," I complained, but when I lunged forward to force Mat back down to them, he neatly avoided me by sidestepping around Jiron's bulk. "Just so you know, it would have been *after* I'd made him properly express his gratitude to you for saving us, so it's entirely your fault that you're not getting a thank you, Jiron."

"Thank you, Jiron," Mathias said from somewhere behind him, and I rose to my tiptoes trying to spot him and the eye roll I knew had accompanied the words.

"You must both be starving." Jiron ran an appraising eye over me before glancing over his shoulder to do the same to Mat. He didn't seem to approve of what he saw. "Have you eaten *anything* since I saw you last?"

I shot him my most brilliant smile. "We've been hunting and cooking ourselves five course meals over campfires we had absolutely no trouble lighting," I said. "But if you *insist* on taking care of us, we will of course graciously and selflessly permit you to do so."

*

Chapter Nine

Mat

"You deal with this," Jiron said, depositing a wriggling bundle of fluff into my arms. "I'll get some wood to get a fire going."

My grip tightened on the struggling rabbit, my fingers curling around its neck and then...stopped.

"Well, fuck me," said Ren as he peeked over my shoulder. The animal twitched its little nose in his direction, its eyes huge and fearful. "That's the cutest thing I've seen all day."

"Only because you don't have a mirror to hand."

The prince laughed and nipped at my ear. "Naww. For that rare compliment, you and the critter can share first place."

"We need to..." I trailed off, feeling the rabbit's pulse beneath my fingers and unable to bring myself to end it.

"Knit it a little pair of trousers!" Ren exclaimed delightedly.

"I'm quite sure that's not what Jiron intended by *dealing with* it."

"You're right, of course. No one in my country should be wearing clothes." He clapped his hands together, startling both me and the rabbit, who kicked against my chest with a surprising amount of strength in its back legs and hopped clear out of my arms. I feared falling from such height would hurt it, but the animal landed deftly in the thick scrub and immediately bounded back into the undergrowth that Jiron had plucked it out of. "But he would have looked *stupendous* in a tiny hat. One with cut outs for the ears and everything!"

I was still picturing that delightful image when Jiron returned to us, a pile of logs in his arms that looked as though they weighed the same as I did. He deposited them at our feet and glanced at me, and then Ren. "Where's our dinner?"

"We...I...couldn't," I said. My fingers absently played with a loose thread in the bandage that Jiron had wrapped around my wrist after tending to Ren's wounds.

The man looked between us both once more, wearing a bland, dispassionate expression which I knew meant he was barely keeping a lid on his emotions.

"You didn't see him, Jiron!" wailed Ren. "He had the most soulful little bunny face. Exactly like *that*," he added, pointing at me.

"Where the fuck…" As Jiron took a steadying breath, I tried to remember if I'd ever heard the man swear before. "Where do you think your meals come from back at the palace, Your Highnesses?"

"The kitchen," Ren said promptly, flashing a glittering, dangerous smile that dared the guard to correct him.

"My prince–"

"*Jiron.*" Ren lifted both hands behind his head, curled his fingers into rabbit ears, and fluttered them. His brown eyes were wide and imploring; a picture of pure *adorableness* that was so incongruous with the prince's true nature that all I could do was blink at him.

Jiron promptly turned on his heel and disappeared back into the thick mass of trees beyond our glade.

"Did we…break him?" I asked.

Ren snorted, dropping his hands and restoring the effervescent arrogance I better recognised in my lover. "He's had a whole two weeks without my company. If that didn't drive him to insanity, I don't think anything will."

"Two weeks? Sounds heavenly," I retorted instinctively, none too surprised when that earned me an indignant huff.

"You no longer rank anywhere near first place, Mathias. Even that dead tree over there is cuter than you."

"Court that tree, then," I said carelessly, and then choked as he grabbed me by the neck and threw me against it.

"I don't need to find you *cute* to bend you in half and fuck you until your voice gives out." Ren's words were a vicious, delighted hiss an inch from my lips. "Take it back before I take your ability to walk tomorrow."

I couldn't even if I'd wanted to: he'd stolen my air with the way his long, sharp fingers were digging into my windpipe, and even when he loosened his grip to replace his hand with his mouth, the way his teeth slid against and then sank into my flesh made me too light-headed to speak.

"Mmfhm," I mumbled eloquently, feeling myself rousing to hardness as a result of Ren's forcefulness as he held me in place and took what he wanted. A satisfied chuckle vibrated against my neck. His fingers roamed possessively down my arms and over my cock where it strained against the seams of my trousers, driving me back against the tree as I tried to thrust into his hand.

Someone cleared their throat politely; not as an interruption, but merely an announcement of their presence. And maybe Jiron wouldn't mind us getting down and dirty in front of him, and Ren *certainly* wouldn't, but I still had some standards of decency despite the prick having worn most of them down during our time together.

Well, I say 'worn', but the better analogy would be that he'd smashed those standards with a battering ram the size of *la Cortina*, stomped on them a dozen times for good measure, and had them exiled to the northern ice wastes where he'd say they belonged. The same north that would undoubtedly faint if they knew even a fraction of the things that the prince and I got up to in private.

Ren, who knew the difference between my don't and *don't* refusals, only licked a comforting line over the bite mark he'd decorated my neck with before obligingly letting go.

Then he stretched, entirely unashamed at the position his guard had just found us in, even as I had to fight against the heat that flooded my cheeks.

"Something faceless and nameless that may be eaten without remorse," Jiron said without looking up from where he was building up the logs, waving a hand at the decapitated, skinned corpses stretched out on the ground next to him. "How either of you expect to lead a country when you can't kill a *rabbit* is…" He cleared his throat again and quietened, evidently assessing he'd gone too far.

I didn't give a fuck, but Ren was never kind when the opportunity to torment someone presented itself, and he gleefully proceeded to spend the next hour making Jiron regret speaking out of turn until he'd wrangled every possible apology and contrite statement from him.

"Yes, my prince," the guard was dutifully saying as he took the cooked meat from the spit and began to divide it into portions. "You are wise, resolute, and benevolent." I snorted in disbelief at that last one. "Irrespective of how many animals you've found it in your gracious heart to spare, you will make a fine ruler-"

"The *finest*," Ren corrected, stretching out on the thick log we'd laid down to sit on. His smile was all teeth.

"...the finest ruler Quareh has ever seen-"

"Just tell him to fuck off, Jiron," I advised, accepting the leg of meat that was handed to me. "Your suffering will be just as painful, but at least it will be over quicker."

"Hush, Nathanael. Some people genuinely wish to express their adoration for me, you know."

"No one here does. Jiron, tell us what happened back in Máros. How did you get away?" The memory of leaving the three men in the palace chapel, irate guards hammering down the door and the windows we'd fled through too small to allow their own escape, had infected my nightmares more than once.

The guard shrugged in his usual, unaffected way. "Not much to tell. They knew you were already gone by the time they finally broke through the door. We didn't see the point in killing more of your men, Your Highness, so we allowed ourselves to be arrested, although it came at the cost of Councillor Navar expressing his...*frustrations* with your escape."

Ren and I shared a glance, knowing exactly what that meant. Yet the guards had either been treated by a healer or the beatings they'd received hadn't been too severe, as Jiron showed no sign of discomfort as he seated himself across from us.

I tore off a piece of the hot, tender meat, stifling a groan at how good it tasted after a day of living on nothing but water. Ren didn't bother to hide his own noises of relief and pleasure, sounding very much like he did when he came, and that brought my blushing back to the surface pretty sharpish.

"Und wen wat?" the prince asked with his mouth full.

"We were held in the cells for a few days while they wondered if we'd be of any use in catching you," Jiron said. "We soon disabused them of that absurd notion."

Ren stilled. It hadn't been that ludicrous an idea: he might act cold and callous at times, but there was nothing he wouldn't do for those he loved.

"Then they made the mistake of only sending seven men to escort the three of us to our execution," the guard continued, pausing with his own food halfway to his mouth. "*Those* men made the mistake of unshackling Elías to have their fun with him first." He shook his head, eyes glinting with a rare malice. "El didn't need our help taking them apart, but Luis and I were only too happy to assist."

"Fucking hell," I said, recoiling in disgust. "Ren, we're culling your entire contingent of palace guards when you make king. Is there even one of them who could be called a decent person?"

"Some," Jiron answered, surprising me by answering on his prince's behalf. "But Comandante Moreno's influence was wide, and bitter. Many men whose ideals were opposed to his didn't last long under his command."

"And under your command?" I asked sweetly, and he struggled to hide his exasperation at the reminder that I wanted him to take up the vacant role.

Ren laughed. "Told you he wasn't going to give up on that. So." He leaned over and captured my wrist, sucking my fingers clean of grease. "Luis. Elías?"

"Keeping the false king from learning your whereabouts, my prince," the guard told him. "Each of those Blessed with the Scent in Quareh's employ will have recently found themselves ill, incapacitated, power-drained, or otherwise inexplicably unable to assist Welzes and Navar in running you down. All except one."

"And that one is…"

"Luis' cousin. And she is *quite* convinced that you're somewhere on the south coast, Your Highness."

Ren hummed, evidently pleased. "And you claim not to have a strategic mind, Jiron?"

"It was Elías' idea. As was me coming after you once we heard the rumours of you travelling east, not that he could have stopped me from doing so." The guard's eyes flashed with steely determination. "May I ask where you're headed?"

"We have no fucking clue-"

AN OATH AND A PROMISE

"You said you were willing to do anything to save Quareh," I said, rounding on the prince at my side. "Is that still true?"

His response was immediate. "Yes."

"Even if it means begging an enemy for aid?"

His gaze caught mine, steady and unflinching. "Yes. What are you thinking, Mathias?"

"Quareh is hunting you. Valeri will turn you in, as would undoubtedly my mother." I paused, hoping he'd put emotion aside in favour of logic. "That leaves Mazekhstam."

"Mazekhstam," Ren repeated, an eyebrow quirking in something like amusement. "Where its regent and I have hated each other since birth, she wants nothing more than to see my country in ashes, and…I swear there's another thing I'm forgetting, *mi sol?* Remind me because I can't quite remember: is it something about…her only brother and us trying to kill him? No, that can't be it. Even you and your contrary ass wouldn't be suggesting that we ask such a person to help us."

"To be fair, Kolya tried to kill us firs-"

"Ah, what the fuck," he said cheerfully, interrupting me for no reason other than he was an annoying prick. "Either we form an alliance that unites the continent, or Panarina kills me on sight. Either way, I get to deny Navar and Welzes the pleasure of ending me themselves."

"Crossing the Quareh-Mazekhstam border won't be easy," warned Jiron, not bothering to protest. He would follow Ren wherever he went, even if it was to hell itself. "And we won't go unnoticed."

I acknowledged his words with a nod. "We know there's a few skirmishes we'll have to avoid."

"No longer just skirmishes, little one," Jiron said gently. "There was a large-scale assault two days ago, and it's devolved into open warfare since then. There's already been hundreds of casualties on both sides."

"War," I said hollowly. "Fuck, after all this time, we're actually at *war?*"

Ren's eyes flashed, an unusually grim expression gracing his face. It made him look older, hardening his features and stealing away a piece of the carefree man I loved.

I let my hand fall to his knee, knowing it offered pitiful comfort in the wake of horrifying news. But it brought a smile back to his lips as he looked at me.

"Mazekhstam," he said slowly, although his next words made me wonder if I'd made a terrible mistake. "I'll bleed for her if I must, but Astrid Panarina *will* help Quareh. Whatever it takes."

*

Chapter Ten

Ren

Mat uncurled from where he'd been draped over me like a blanket, getting to his feet rather unsteadily. He groaned as he did so, stretching out his neck and shoulders.

"Did I say you could move?" I asked.

"You've kept me in that position for the last hour." His tone was dangerously close to an accusation.

"Because I was cold. Really, Mathias, it's like you only think about yourself."

He snorted and nudged my elbow with his knee as he squeezed past, edging through the narrow space between the moth-eaten cot I was lying on and the hut wall, which looked like it was one good sneeze away from collapsing. Or even a moderate, half-stifled sneeze, really. It was a dwelling unworthy of the name, only useful for the rain it mostly kept off our heads, and even then it had been hard work to convince Jiron to let us seek shelter in it for the night. He'd only ceded when he realised how remote and abandoned the place really was, at which point – and for the exact same reasons – I'd been more than willing to find a ditch somewhere for the greater comfort it could surely provide.

"I need to piss."

"*Alone?*" I sniffed, feigning horror.

Mat leaned down and pressed a kiss to my forehead. "I'll just be a minute."

I nodded frantically, hyperventilating. "Our love is strong enough to endure such separation, I'm sure of it. It has to be!" I wailed for extra drama as he slipped through the crooked door that did nothing to keep the heat inside or the weather out, although the heartache wasn't entirely feigned. I missed his presence already, and as humiliating as being chained up had been, it had certainly fulfilled my wish to always keep him within a few feet of me.

I caught Jiron mouthing the word *love* at his feet where he sat hunched in the corner, an expression almost like a grin on his face.

I snuggled down into the cot, trying to ignore the smell of rot and the pain in my shoulder, and eyed him suspiciously. "Something to say?"

"Watching the two of you together..." he began, but it wasn't lust that clouded his gaze. He dropped his chin. "He makes you happy. More human, my prince," he added wryly.

As well as Jiron and I knew each other, despite the many times he'd had to pull me from the depths of my panic attacks, I'd never let my guard see the most hidden parts of me. What I'd faced at the hands of Moreno and the orders of my father, and the fear of failing my people. But Mathias could pull all that to the surface with a single smile or his hand in mine.

"I am happy," I said. It was easy to ignore everything shitty happening in my life, starting with this horrible little hut we were confined in until morning, when my lover's infectiously intoxicating presence drowned the rest of it out.

Jiron laughed at that. "Little Renato, content and committed. I never thought I'd see it."

"Don't be dramatic," I admonished, fully aware of the hypocrisy and knowing he wouldn't call me on it.

The man raised an eyebrow. "You don't remember the day after your fourteenth birthday, when you asked me to beat Lord de Leon's son's face in because he'd made you angry?"

I scrunched up my nose. "Vaguely. What had he done?"

"Told you he loved you."

I blew out a disgusted breath. "Oh, yes." And then I brightened. "But you did it. You smacked around some kid for daring to express such sickening, affectionate sentiment to me."

"Of course I did," Jiron said. "It was *you* asking."

"I also remember you convincing me to send Starling to him only an hour later."

"He was fifteen, Your Highness."

"Hmm."

"And then there was that month you spent avoiding the kitchen girl who'd said the same thing to you. You insisted we take the long way around to the throne room in case you ran into her in the corridors, and you refused to go near the dining halls at all."

I waved a hand. "All of this happened when I was a child."

Jiron's lips twitched. "What about six months ago, barely weeks before Mathias arrived, when Lady Hierro flung herself at you and declared in front of half the court that she'd *positively die* if you didn't return her affections?"

"Well, I'd say Lady Hierro is a fucking liar, because she's still very much alive in...wherever she is."

"The Quarehian peninsula, where you exiled her, my prince."

"'Exiled' is a little strong, Jiron," I said. "I merely suggested that she take a journey as far from *la Cortina* as possible because I never wanted to see her again. I slept with her twice before she started talking about *love*, for fuck's sake."

He raised an eyebrow. "And how many times had you lain with Mathias before you spoke of the same?"

I scowled. "That's different."

"Yes," he said, but he somehow seemed smugly satisfied under that unaffected exterior. "It is."

I shifted on the cot, trying to keep warm, and winced when it brought back the aching soreness in my shoulder.

"We need to find you a healer for that," Jiron fussed, immediately reverting to protective daddy mode upon my flinch.

I rolled my eyes. "You already took care of it."

"I'm not a doctor, my prince. I'm barely a field medic. Dios knows what the damage is like inside, especially with the filth of the river getting into it. That water is full of diseases."

I looked away guiltily before I could meet his eyes, deciding not to confess that before he'd caught up with us, Mathias and I had been drinking the damn stuff.

"The Martinezes have a healer," Jiron reminded me. "We'll stop by their estate and I'll persuade him to help."

"Ooh, can I watch?" I asked delightedly, perking up at the thought.

"Watch him...heal you?"

"Watch you *persuade him*," I corrected. "It's always fun when you go scary, Jiron."

He gave me a small smile, a dark glimmer of satisfaction flickering in his eyes.

The door creaked open, revealing a shivering Mathias stamping his boots on the threshold as if he was worried that treading wet leaves into the hut could possibly make it any less habitable.

"You've been gone for *days,*" I complained, huffing out a breath. "Don't roll your eyes at me, brat. You thought being forced to act as my blanket was bad? I think it's time I introduce you to predicament bondage, so I can get off on keeping you in a stress position all night."

"Except that would require you to move, Your Highness," he shot back unfazed, and damn, he had me there. As disgusting as this mouldy cot was, I'd collected some small measure of warmth curled up like this, and even the pleasure of tormenting my mouthy wildcat couldn't compel me to voluntarily relinquish that.

"Right," I said. "Then make yourself suffer while I watch. Or get Jiron to do it. Oh, and give me your knife."

Mat, far too used to my abrupt changes in subject, didn't even blink. He handed it over, an unfamiliar blade that I couldn't begin to guess where he'd acquired it from. "Planning to slit your own throat so we don't have to endure your cruel comments any longer?"

"Far worse," I told him. "I'm going to cut my hair."

Both men did a double take at that, and I was pleased that I could still catch them off guard.

"My prince?"

"I don't want to," I said in response to Jiron's questioning tone and Mathias' open-mouthed stare as I pushed myself upright, grabbed a fistful of my hair, and raised the knife to it. "But changing my appearance is the smart thing to do. We're on the run, and I can't-"

"*Nyet!*" Mat hissed loudly, and I startled, several strands flicking free as the blade sliced through them.

"A Quarehian with short hair would attract more attention for its rarity," he pointed out, looking fierce as fuck as he folded his arms. "And the first person who recognises you despite it will report to Welzes, and then you've lost any advantage *and* you'll be insufferable for it. It's not smart at all."

"Oh, thank fuck for that," I muttered, letting go with an audible exhale of relief. Mathias knocked the knife from my hand onto the floor, shaking his head and calling me a variety of insulting names in several languages. Then he gave a put-upon sigh that was as dramatic as any of mine. It seemed we had both altered the other, irrevocably entwining until it was impossible to pick the parts of him that had embedded into me and I him.

Jiron rose gracefully to his feet and pushed open the door Mat had just closed. "I'm going to check the traps."

"Can I come?"

I wasn't surprised by the request. Mathias had been watching Jiron closely these past few days; eagerly observing the way he built campfires, set traps for small game, hid our tracks through the woods, and foraged for mushrooms and shit. It seemed he'd taken to heart the guard's half-comment about our lack of ability or willingness to get our hands dirty, and was applying his usual levels of stubbornness to proving him wrong.

I fought a sigh at having to go back out in the rain and swung my legs over the side of the cot. "Let's go."

"Rest," they said in unison, making twin shooing gestures. I quirked an eyebrow.

"Rest up, my prince," Jiron said again. "We'll be back soon."

I didn't bother arguing. Mostly because when it came to my comfort or health, he could prove as obstinate as Mathias, but also because my shoulder was starting to really fucking hurt. Jiron had taken another look at it this morning and proclaimed it fine, yet I'd overheard him anxiously whispering to Mat a few minutes later.

The two fusspots had then proceeded to be annoyingly nice to me for a couple of hours until I called them out on it, fear churning at my gut. For was there any bigger clue that they considered my death both inevitable and imminent than pure, unadulterated *kindness*?

Fuck it. It was just a scratch, that was all. I'd been shot *weeks* ago and I was still standing…or lying down, at least, and with my history I knew I could take my share of pain. There were bigger, more pressing things to worry about, and our plan reverberated in my head as the hut door closed once more and left me in aching, echoing silence.

Cross the border into Temar and follow the mountain range north, before using Cašran Pass to sneak back into Mazekhstam.

Get to Stavroyarsk. Convince Panarina to help us.

Use her army to take back my country from those misogynistic, abusive, uncaring assholes. Do some good.

Fuck Mathias against every wall and pillar in the palace until he can't walk into a room without blushing at the memory.

So maybe that last one hadn't been on the official to-do list we'd drawn up together, but I was taking it as my royal prerogative, as well as one hell of an incentive to get the rest of the shit done.

And maybe there was one more thing to add, an idea that I didn't dare to even think on for too long in case it flitted away nervously, as uncomfortable at receiving its well-deserved attention as my lover himself.

Ask the prick to marry me.

*

Chapter Eleven

Mat

Jiron pointed at the snare, a thin twist of rope waiting just beyond what he'd identified as a rabbit's den.

"Something large has disturbed it since we set it earlier," he said, showing me how the notched trigger had been dislodged. When I took a step forward to move the sticks back into place, he shook his head. "Remember what I said about our scent putting the animals off?"

I crouched and rubbed mud onto my hands, waiting for the approving nod before resetting the trigger. Trapping wasn't a fun activity by any means: my stomach lurched each time we caught something, yet it growled when we didn't. I took relief in the fact that Jiron didn't seem to enjoy it any more than I did – he just got on with it, like the necessary chore it was.

"You're doing well, little one," Jiron murmured as we drifted between the other forest traps we'd set up. "I know it's not something you ever thought you'd need to do as a prince."

"I never thought about anything I'd need to do," I admitted, squinting up into the foliage above our heads to spot the bird who had just let out an indignant chirp at our passing. "Everything was just...on hold in Stavroyarsk. I knew I'd eventually be able to return home when the next round of hostages were swapped, but it felt so far away that I never bothered to wonder about what I'd do when I did."

When I stopped, he paused too, head cocked as he waited for me to continue.

"It hit me, you know, when I was with Val and Mila and they were talking about taking me back to Temar."

"What did?"

"How utterly fucking useless I am," I said bitterly, drawing back my foot to kick at a rock and then remembering the importance of not disturbing the ground any more than we had to – both for the game we were hunting and for anyone hunting *us*. "I have absolutely no skills to speak of. I can't fight, can't navigate politics like Ren can, can't draw or sing for shit, and..." I threw up my hands to emphasise the point.

"And that's all you consider useful?" Jiron asked.

"I just..."

"Mathias. Do you have any idea how many lives you've changed in the last few months alone?"

I scowled. "What, by kissing someone of the *wrong gender* and riling up the continent?"

His mouth twitched fondly. "Somewhat. But I was talking about the people who've met you. Every servant and commoner you were kind to, when they may not have ever received kindness from someone of your rank before. Every noble you challenged into questioning themselves, every woman you inspired into pushing back on what they were told they couldn't have, every Quarehian to whom you proved northerners are not as evil and barbaric as we would have believed." He wrapped a huge arm around my shoulders and pulled me close, tucking me against his side. "Every precocious prince you helped shape into a king."

"He's going to be magnificent," he whispered, and just as I was about to agree, he added, "with you at his side."

I tripped over something unseen on the ground but Jiron held onto me, effortlessly keeping me upright.

"That's not...Ren doesn't need me," I said awkwardly. But fuck, I needed *him*.

The guard hummed. "We both know that's not true. Please do not make me waste my breath recounting all the reasons why."

We walked in contemplative silence for a few moments, yet he couldn't seem to help himself from continuing to speak despite what he'd just claimed. "His Highness helps you see the larger picture; you make him appreciate the smaller. Nerve and compassion, flexibility and tenacity, head and heart. Together, you-"

Jiron's arm tightened around me. As I glanced up to ask what was wrong, his other hand clamped down over my mouth, warm and smelling of earth. I froze, wondering what had spooked him, but not daring to speak as he slowly removed his hand and ushered us behind a large tree.

Yet it was another half minute before I heard them for myself: first, the rustling of leaves and the snap of sticks as they moved recklessly though the forest, and then their words.

"…we're getting close."

"You've been saying that for hours," someone else complained.

"I said we were getting *closer*. Now, he's close," the first voice said. "Within a mile, I expect."

"You hear that, lads? The son of that fucker Iván Aratorre in our hands, at long last." It was announced with cruel relish.

"Would have preferred it to be Horacio, but his youngest will do."

"I expect he'll do nicely. We're gonna fuck that boy up so bad for what his daddy did to us."

There were various cheers at that, enough to suggest the presence of a dozen men at least. I swallowed, tensing up and feeling my hands ball into fists. Jiron remained as cool and collected as ever at my side, but his expression was murderous.

"I'm going to cut out his tongue. Maybe make him swallow it."

"You mad? Then we won't hear him scream."

"…or beg."

"Or *fucking beg*," another man agreed with a laugh. "By the Blessed, I wanna hear an Aratorre begging."

Their noises grew louder, passing us by only a few yards away. Jiron swayed slightly to the left to glance around the tree, and I watched his eyes darting back and forth as he counted their number. The slightest of frowns gracing his brow made my heart sink but I forced myself to remain still. They didn't sound like they were particularly alert to their surroundings, their own voices pitched loud and raucous, but I didn't doubt they'd notice us if we moved.

"…after everything," one of them was saying, to much agreement from his companions. "And when he died without ever having the chance to pay for what he did…I hope Iván is watching from hell as we take his child apart piece by fucking *piece*."

"Can you assholes let me concentrate?" interrupted the first voice, whiny and petulant. There was a loud sniff. "I can't Scent shit with you lot nattering in my ears."

Fuck. They had a tracker. Ren's guards may have ensured that all the Blessed with the Scent in Quareh's service were accounted for, but there were always some who managed to avoid royal conscription. These men, whoever they were, would be able to find the prince no matter where he was on the continent. Covering our physical trail through the forest meant nothing when magic was involved.

Jiron's gaze met mine, steely and ruthless.

"Use your fucking nose instead of your ears, then," retorted another, but he was drowned out by more eager suggestions of the torment they intended to inflict on Ren when they found him, their voices gradually fading as they moved further from us. My blood roared in my ears.

"Jiron," I hissed when I judged they were sufficiently far away not to be heard.

"Get to His Highness," he said, unsheathing his sword. "That way, and *run*. Don't stop for fucking anything, you hear me?" His eyes flashed. "Find somewhere to hide, and meet me back at the hut at dawn."

I shook my head frantically. "There's too many of them for you to take alone."

The guard heaved out a breath, confirming my fears as to their numbers when he didn't deny it. "I only need to remove their tracker. Then the rebels will be blind."

They were rebels? I knew such groups existed: there would always be those who resisted whatever royal rule applied at the time, but I'd never had the misfortune to encounter them in either Mazekhstam or Quareh. Some were self-proclaimed freedom fighters. Others, little more than raiders, murdering and pillaging in the name of liberation.

These particular men apparently held a severe grudge against Ren's father, which I suspected was likely justified considering what I'd known of the man, but to go after his kin in revenge – and it was small comfort to know they believed Ren was of Aratorre blood just as much as we did – was both fucking cowardly and wildly repugnant.

And also dumb, because getting on the wrong side of Jiron was nothing short of suicidal.

Yet as competent as the guard was, even he couldn't work miracles. One man against all of them? If Elías had been here perhaps he could have taken out the Blessed from a distance with his bow, but Jiron would need to get within a sword's length of the tracker. And then he'd be surrounded…

"Go, Mathias!" Jiron growled, shoving at me to get me to move. "Ren comes first!"

"Dawn," I said hollowly, beginning to back away. "Promise me."

He gave me a sad smile. "If I can, I'll be there. If I'm not, get His Highness to Stavroyarsk. You promise *me*, my prince."

I choked up at the address, unable to speak.

And then Jiron was gone, disappearing into the darkness between one tree and the next, and with a prescience that had nothing to do with my Sight, I somehow just *knew* we wouldn't be seeing him at dawn.

*

Chapter Twelve

Ren

"Ren," Mat said gently, shaking my shoulder. I lifted my head and blinked at him with bleary eyes sore from crying and lack of sleep.

"Did you…say something?"

"We're almost at the Martinezes' estate."

"Right," I said dully, not caring one way or another. My head drooped again, and I stared unseeingly at my boots as memories of the past few hours continued to flash on repeat through my head, haunting and mocking me.

The last time I'd seen Jiron as he left the hut with Mathias, not bothering to even say goodbye to him with the assumption they'd be back within the hour.

The door crashing open on its hinges sooner than expected, only it was a stranger who stood on its threshold, bearing a cruel smile and a wicked-looking blade.

The man closing in on me where I lay on the bed, muttering dark threats against my family that sounded like promises, as I desperately tried to scramble away from his reaching fingers.

Get the fuck away from my man! Mathias appearing in the doorway, hissing out angry, possessive words and foolhardily launching himself at my attacker without a weapon or any sense whatsoever.

My fingers closing around the knife Mat had knocked to the floor earlier, reaching up to plunge it through the stranger's throat as he grappled with my lover.

Mathias dragging me from the hut and sequestering us in a thicket a couple of miles away, frantically whispering what had happened in incomplete sentences and choked horror.

Sunbeams drenching the desolate hut hours later, the dead rebel's blood having long dried on the floorboards. Just me and Mat waiting in vain as the sun reached and passed its zenith, the echoing silence of the space meant to be filled by Jiron devastatingly loud.

And the flies buzzing around the corpses in the forest, busy laying their eggs in the mouths and chest cavities of the scattered dead men.

"None of them were Jiron," Mathias murmured to me now, his thoughts evidently sinking into the same place as mine. "We checked all of the bodies twice, darling."

"He would have been there," I argued, following the pattern this conversation had taken each of the dozen times we'd had it. "He would have been at the hut when he said, and he *wasn't*." A dark thought struck me, and I strayed off script for the first time in hours. "Maybe the surviving rebels took his body with them?"

"Why would they do that?" Mat said gently, with more patience than I probably deserved. "They didn't bother to bury or take their own with them. They wouldn't do it for an enemy." He clasped my hand tighter. "Jiron *survived*, Ren."

I knew that. Rationally, *I knew that*. But the fear of his death was overwhelming everything else, as was the knowledge that if he lived and yet hadn't made it back to us, it could only mean one thing.

The fuckers had him.

Dios only knew what they were doing to him right fucking now, and...

"We have to find him."

"We don't know where to look," Mathias reminded me.

That was utterly logical and intolerably frustrating.

"I have to do something!"

We'd remained at the site of the massacre – for that was what it was, a dozen bodies beginning to fester in the heat after being cut down by Jiron's sword – for longer than was safe, hunting for any clue of what might have happened to him. For that many to be dead and the guard still missing…by the Blessed Five, how many men had there been? Why did he have to be so brave and fucking *honourable* all the time to have still tried to take them on, *alone*?

Yes, I'd heard everything Mat had said to me about the rebels seemingly not giving a shit about keeping me alive for the bounty. About how they'd do terrible, indescribable things to me if I was caught. About how, without Jiron taking out their tracker, that would have been my inevitable end.

But I didn't care. Because I'd only just gotten him back a few days ago, and here I was, worrying about him again. The selfish, selfless prick. How dare he do that to me?

Give him back, I'd wanted to scream at the gaping faces and twisted limbs of the dead. But their souls had moved on, preferably down rather than heavenward if there was any justice in the afterlife, and no one was fucking listening to me. My prayers echoed listlessly between the trees.

Mathias had eventually tugged at my arm, wanting us out of there in case any of the survivors returned.

"Good," I'd told him savagely. "Let them come. I'll use that knife of yours to make them tell us where they took him."

"I'm not letting you near anything sharp right now."

"Then I'll tear off their skin with my Blessed fingernails," I'd snarled.

For once, my lover hadn't called me on my bullshit. He'd just kissed me, long and soft and sad, and led me away, my tears blurring everything so badly that I hadn't even been able to walk without his hand in mine, guiding me. But hadn't that always been the way? I'd been so fucking blind before him, not even realising how much I'd missed in front of my own damn eyes, and then the obstinate asshole had appeared and pointed it all out. 'Quareh treats its women despicably,' he'd said. 'Why *can't* there be peace on the continent?' And fuck, I hated myself for not seeing that shit myself but it was so much *easier* with him. Mathias was like a flame in the darkness; a source of light, warmth, and so much damn comfort that I knew I wouldn't have been able to move a step forward without him. Not just now, but…ever.

"We're going to see Astrid," Mat murmured, rubbing circles across my palm with his thumb. His fingers were all calloused as a result of the survival shit he'd been learning from Jiron, and I focused on the sensation of the rough skin to keep me grounded. I'd already had two panic attacks since this morning, and I didn't have the fucking energy to push through another. "We get Quareh back, and then we get Jiron back. You with me?"

What kind of question was that?

AN OATH AND A PROMISE

"Always."

Blowing out a breath to expel the last of the tauntingly brutal images dancing behind my eyelids, I brushed my hair from my face and looked up in front of me for the first time in hours. Mathias was right. Wallowing was Blessed useless, and I didn't do *useless*.

Maybe that hadn't been exactly what he'd said, but I was taking it to heart anyway. I had Things to Do, and while there was now one more item to add to the list, it didn't take away from the rest of them. If I wanted to save Quareh from further generations of gendered abuse and inequity, as well as putting a stop to the absolute waste of life they were calling a war with our northern neighbour *and* send my fucking army to comb the country for Jiron, I had to take my throne back.

"Through there," I said, pointing at a gap in the trees that I was sure Mathias had noticed himself but graciously allowed me at least the illusion of regaining control by letting me lead him towards it. We moved quietly, cautiously, conscious that we were nearing the estate and all that might entail. It was another risk in coming here, but we needed provisions and a healer to tend to my injury in order to make it much further north, and Lord Martinez was supposed to be away at the border where I'd assigned him command of my old militia to keep him away from his poor wife. A smile graced my lips at the memory of Mat standing angrily over the man when we stopped here on our return from the trade talks slash attempted kidnapping in Sesveko, ready to tear into him with his bare hands for the spousal abuse despite it being legal in Quareh. One more thing we would change as soon as I had the power to do so.

We crouched, hidden, in the bushes, something that had unfortunately become an all-too familiar pastime of ours lately. There were too many people roaming the grounds between us and the main house for us to approach it unseen: gardeners, servants, guards. Any one of them could turn us in if they spotted us, and while we were betting on the hope that the Lady Martinez would favour us over the false king, the same couldn't necessarily be said of the household staff.

I idly watched their movements as the shadows across the neatly cut lawn grew longer, devoting half of my attention to listening to Mathias detail his plan for sneaking us into the house, and offering various additions to make it more dramatically awe-inspiring that he immediately shot down with a scowl and a hissed whisper about *unnecessary complexity and utter ridiculousness, Ren* – which, in respect of my suggestion about befriending a pack of local squirrels in order to create a distraction, was incredibly short-sighted of him.

The other half of my mind was, *naturally*, admiring the scrumptious curve of his jaw and the adorning stubble that had devolved into the makings of a beard, and wondering what kind of noises he'd make if I buried my face in it and nibbled until I'd restored the teeth marks I liked to leave on his pretty skin, and-

"Someone's coming," I said reluctantly, dragging my gaze past him to the girl determinedly making her way towards us with a furrowed brow and a basket of unfolded linens tucked under one arm.

Mat glanced up from where he'd been drawing lines in the dirt with a stick, his expression alarmed.

"It's only Abril," I assured him, but that only seemed to make him even more worried.

"The servant with the crush on you?" he asked in a low, anxious tone.

I fluttered a hand. "They all have a crush on-"

"The one I threw out of your room twice last time we were here? The one you rejected at breakfast the following day because you'd…you'd…" He coloured, a delightful pink crossing his cheeks that perfectly reflected the colours of the sunset behind him.

"Because I finally got you into my bed?" I asked, grinning, and then thought about his words and realised that yeah, maybe Abril wasn't our biggest fan after all, and we should probably move.

But it was too late for that. The serving girl loomed over us, dropping her basket in shock as she saw what was in the bushes and sending sheets fluttering to the dirt.

"Your Highness!"

"Shush," I murmured, putting my finger to my lips just in case she didn't understand the meaning of the word *shush*. Abril nodded frantically, eyes wide, and began to lower herself into a curtsy.

AN OATH AND A PROMISE

Mat groaned and put his face in his hands while I waved at her to stop. She faltered, flustered.

"Abril," I said sternly. "Pick up the linens, slowly, and do your Dios-damned best to *not* look like you're talking to your king in a bush. Can you do that?"

She made to nod, caught herself, and dropped to one knee to begin collecting the discarded contents of the basket.

"What are you doing here, my prince?" she asked from the corner of her mouth, not looking at us as she pretended to fuss over the leaves caught on one of the sheets.

"We need someone with the Touch. Is the Martinezes' healer here?"

"No, Your Highness." Abril's eyes flickered from me to Mathias, and the undisguised droop of her lips suggested she was disappointed not to find him gravely injured. Clearly picking up on the same, he threw her a rude gesture. "He's still at *la Cortina,* but my lady could have him called back by sun-up on the pretence of concerns with her own health?"

"Do you think she would help us?" The question I *hadn't* asked lingered in the air, thickening the tension between us as I questioned her loyalty with that of her mistress, but Abril met my gaze steadily as she answered them both.

"We will."

She gathered the last of the linens and stuffed them haphazardly in her basket. "Please stay here, my prince. I will come for you after dark." The servant rose to her feet, wandered to a nearby bush, and in a spectacular display of improvisation to justify her presence in this area, unhurriedly gathered a handful of flowers before returning in the direction of the house.

Mat hummed out a thoughtful noise. "Do you think we can trust her?" he asked, although it was rather telling that he hadn't tried to immediately drag us away in fear of the guards that could converge on our position at any moment.

"I think we can," I declared. Yet I kept a cautious eye out and didn't even *suggest* that we jerk each other off to pass the time, which probably told him everything he needed to know in turn.

*

Chapter Thirteen

Mat

"*Boys*," Lady Martinez said, folding us both into her arms after delivering all the cooing and fretting I'd come to associate with mothers of toddlers. Yet the hug was welcome, and I allowed myself to sink against her as she held us tight, petting our hair and murmuring soft platitudes without a single wince at the state of us.

We smelled fucking terrible, I was sure, and our clothes were layered with so much dirt and blood that we probably looked like we'd crawled from our own graves...but here she was, greeting us in a small chamber off the main hall as if we were her own children. It was nice. It was something I'd never had from my birth mother: sending me off to a foreign country to play political hostage at age two didn't exactly feature among my best memories of Queen Zora Velichkova.

"I have sent for the healer," Lady Martinez declared, finally releasing us with a sad sniff as she looked us over once more with sympathetic eyes. "One of you is unwell?"

"*Sí*," Ren said, but when he didn't elaborate, neither did I. "Thank you, señora."

She waved the gratitude away. "Of course. You are not the first fugitives this house has sheltered this month."

"My lady?"

"That little girl you had with you last time...Consuela?"

I remembered Consuela Sanz all too well. Her father had attempted to sell her off as a child bride, only to drag her before the prince when the deal soured. Not knowing Ren as I did now, I'd tried to help, fearing he'd leave her in the hands of such monsters. But while my loud protests and attempts to rearrange the prince's face hadn't done shit, he'd been acting in the shadows much more effectively, and Jiron had been sent to quietly buy her from her asshole father and provide her with independence and a job in *la Cortina's* kitchens.

"She turned up on the doorstep with a bread knife, a scowl that could melt steel, and a string of palace servants she'd convinced to flee before the false king could have them flogged or executed for their loyalties," Lady Martinez told us, and Ren let out a surprised laugh.

"She's *you*, Nat," he accused fondly, flicking my ear. I batted him away only for him to do it again, harder.

"What happened to her? To them?" I asked, feeling the lead weight of worry in my chest that ached more than my stinging ear.

But the woman's answering smile was reassuring. "They're safe. We managed to get them settled in a village a few miles away, although one of them – the tall, helpful one who's infatuated with the loud dark-haired girl – refuses to stay hidden and returns here every couple of days for any word on you, Prince Ren."

He exhaled with relief. "Camila. I feared for her."

"I don't think you need to. It appears she orchestrated some sabotage before they all fled, and now *la Cortina* has found itself short on servants, unbroken windows, and *tablecloths* of all things."

"She always did hate having to iron them," Ren said, cackling at some memory or another that evidently involved his personal servant. "When you next see Camila, tell her we're well. Do *not* tell her how terribly matted and oily my hair has become, unless you enjoy watching people spontaneously drop dead of horror."

Lady Martinez eyed his locks with a similar level of dismay. "You shall eat, bathe, and rest while you wait for our healer, and I shall have saddlebags packed with everything you need for your travels. Two of my husband's fastest horses will be ready for you in the morning. Oh, you poor things."

"We can't stay."

"Nonsense, my prince," she chided, looking uncharacteristically fierce. "You boys, out in the dark and the cold all night? No. I will not hear another word of it."

I shared an amused glance with Ren. We'd suffered far worse, but I wasn't brave enough to argue further with her and fuck, all of that sounded wonderful. Being able to travel north with more provisions than the scraps of food, bandages, and waterskins left in Jiron's bag that we'd buried in the bushes outside was a relief I couldn't begin to describe.

I bowed my thanks. "Please wake us as soon as the healer arrives, my lady. We must leave before the sun rises."

"Very well." The woman, whose first name I still didn't know, hesitated. There was a tear running down her cheek that she quickly brushed away, and I felt guilty when I noticed the smudge of filth on her perfect skin that had clearly come from touching one of us. "Is there…anything else I can do? I have little usefulness here and most of the staff answer to my husband, but if there's anything you need, just say the word, Your Highnesses."

A sincere offer, if a hollow one. For she was right: a woman in Quareh was more powerless than even two bedraggled princes on the run, and yet it made it all the more dangerous for her to be helping us.

Her and Abril, for the servant stood at her side with a pile of clean clothes in her arms. We hadn't been set upon by guards nor delivered to the local constabulary, so I guessed they'd decided their loyalties lay other than with the Lukian man declaring himself Quareh's king and the treacherous, sly councillor at his side. Although it sounded as though that had already been proved when they'd offered shelter to Ren's servants.

"You've done more than enough," I assured them, taking the clothes from Abril and trying not to wince as she carved her sharp fingernails across my wrist, unseen by the others under the thick fabrics. It seemed that even if she wasn't turning us in, she didn't appreciate me stealing her erstwhile lover from her. "We will repay you for this kindness when we can, I swear it."

"The royal suite has been made up for you, my prince," Abril said, flashing Ren a dazzling smile that held a great deal of eyelash fluttering. "I'd be happy to escort you to it."

"There's no need for that, nor is it wise," I protested. "Space in the servants' quarters will be fine."

"The servants' quarters are full of servants," she rebuked sharply, and then dropped her gaze when Ren lightly growled his disapproval. "With respect, Prince Nathanael," she added, clearly intending none of it.

"Abril's right," Lady Martinez said apologetically, in a much softer tone. "The royal suite is on the second floor and away from prying eyes. Go. Rest up.

AN OATH AND A PROMISE

We can talk more later."

The servant gestured for Ren to follow her, deliberately treading on my foot when she shifted to face him. The heel of her boot ground down onto my toes, and I glowered at the back of her head.

"Are you going to let her bully you all night?" Ren murmured to me as we crept carefully up the main stairway, moving into the shadows of the upstairs corridor. "That's not like you."

"I don't want to cause a scene."

"Also highly unusual. You know you're mine, right? No one else's?"

"I don't think it's me she's after," I said wryly.

"Which means I'm yours," the prince continued without missing a beat, bumping his shoulder against mine. "And when in doubt, ask yourself this: what would Ren do?"

I slowed, staring at his back as he followed Abril through the door into the royal suite.

What would Ren do? Something entirely petty, possessive, and inappropriate, for sure. Not a difficult guess considering that described him most of the time, but did I have that in me?

Yet when Abril *accidentally* knocked off the pile of clothes I deposited onto the dresser so that she could pick them up off the floor, brushing against the prince and wiggling her ass so he couldn't possibly miss how tightly it was stuffed into a dress made for someone half her size, I realised that *yes, I really did*.

I reached for Ren and shoved him back against the nearest wall. The breath left his lungs in a sharp, surprised exhale that I captured with my own mouth, running my hands through his hair, down his narrow waist, and resting them on his hips before thinking *what the hell* and sliding them around to his ass. The prince ground himself against me, curling a leg around mine and drawing a moan from my lips. His reaction spurred me on, and I fought through the discomfort of having an audience to deepen the kiss.

"Your Highnesses," Abril said loudly and pointedly.

I ignored her, tilting my head so I could explore his mouth from a different angle, revelling in the buried citrus taste of him despite him not having eaten oranges for days. He was soft and sharp all at once, his contrary tender assertiveness showing in every brush of his lips and tongue.

Ren bit down and his teeth sank harshly into my bottom lip. I felt the sting of the skin splitting, the tang of blood in my mouth and the thrill that brought with it. When I drew back, letting go of him with reluctance, he moaned his protest.

"We-"

"We're alone, *mi amor*," he murmured, and I glanced around to see he was right. Abril must have left without my noticing, and if that brought a tiny twinge of guilt at instigating the public display of wantonness, it was extinguished by the pleased look I found on Ren's face, eyes bright and gaze adoring. His lower lip was smeared with my blood, and why was that so hot?

"In that case," I said, and eagerly pushed him back to the wall, pressing myself close until he was flattened against it. I wrapped one hand around his nape of his neck and let the other drop down between us to cup the solid bulge in his trousers. Ren's teeth flashed in a broad grin, his head falling back against the wall as I nosed at his neck and delivered kisses down his throat, relishing the way he responded to each one, so hard and warm in my hand.

"I can't decide what my favourite thing is, Mathias," the prince said against my mouth when I moved to capture his lips once more, and he playfully nipped at my bitten lip to reignite the prick of pain. "You throwing me against the wall and kissing the fuck out of me…or the fact that you did it *twice*."

I gave a soft laugh, backing up as I heard footsteps in the corridor. Abril appeared at the doorway with a huffy scowl and a tray in her hands that bore two plates of food, a bottle of wine, and two glasses. When I thanked her – there was no need to be rude even if she needed to learn to keep her fucking hands and eyes off my man – and made to take one of the identical plates, she deftly spun the tray to put it out of reach of my fingers.

"That one's yours, *my prince*," she said, sickeningly sweet, and I stared at her with suspicion as she set the tray's contents on the table, curtsied to Ren, and departed the suite, drawing the door closed behind her.

Ren made a delighted noise and pounced on the food with something akin to reverence.

"I expect she spat in mine," I mused, still eying it dubiously. He wordlessly swapped our plates and began to shovel forkfuls into his mouth.

When I raised an eyebrow, the prince shrugged. "I don't mind. Her and I have exchanged saliva more than once."

I let out an annoyed hiss that was entirely involuntary. "I don't...you didn't need to..."

"Jealous, *mi sol*?"

I felt like I was swallowing something unpleasant despite not having even touched the food.

"Yes," I finally bit out.

Ren shot me a wicked grin that was surprisingly soothing. Perhaps it was how, when he looked at me like that, he devoted to me the whole of his attention as if nothing else on the continent mattered. As if nothing else even *existed*.

"We're going to finish eating, take a gloriously long and hot bath together, and then you'll allow me to fucking worship you for the next few hours, *sí*? I want to prove to you that you have nothing to worry about, because there's only you, Nat."

He paused with a goblet of wine halfway to his lips, which twisted half-heartedly into an expression of feigned disgust. "*Monogamy*? What the fuck did I do?"

I scowled at him and he cocked his head, considering me.

"Oh yes," he purred. "*You*."

—

A hot, wet tongue stroked up the back of my neck. "You awake?"

"No," I said. Even without opening my eyes, I could tell it was still dark, and this bed was fucking *soft*. The smell of dirt and leaf mould was absent from my nostrils for the first time in weeks, and being warm and clean and cozy was a luxury I'd almost forgotten.

Our bath earlier, to Ren's disappointment, had proven less sexy and more utilitarian, as we scrubbed off the layers of grime we'd accumulated until the water was nearly black. Even he found it hard to initiate something when it looked like we were wallowing in pure mud by the end, and the second bath he'd made me run us was a similarly unappealing grey. It had been hard to enjoy the hot water like that, but this? I'd never take sleeping in a bed for granted again.

"I'm bored," Ren whined, kicking the back of my thigh under the covers. "Play with *meeeee*."

Without opening my eyes, I lifted my leg slightly where I lay on my side facing away from him, inviting access.

Yet he didn't move. My leg wavered with the strain of keeping it raised, and then eventually dropped.

"Mathias," he said patiently. "We're not at the 'get on with it while I just lie here' stage of our relationship yet, and I sincerely hope we never reach it."

"When I fuck you," he added in a murmur, nuzzling gently at my shoulder, "I want you present. I want you moaning out your desire and screaming my name, you hear me?"

The words, uttered with heat and promise, spurred my cock to life and my eyes open. We'd kissed and fooled around earlier, once our stomachs were full, our skin washed, and his hair clean and freshly braided – resulting in Ren murmuring many prayers of gratitude to Dios, although the god hadn't shown the patience I'd had to exercise with a hairbrush, did He? We hadn't had the chance to do such things in over a week other than for some casual flirtation and fleeting touches, and it seemed fitting to remedy that in the same room where I'd first given into him all those months ago. And then I remembered why we hadn't gone any further than that, and groaned miserably into the pillow.

"I want to. But you're still injured, Ren."

From the pained looks he'd been making when he thought I wasn't looking, I knew his shoulder had been twinging with increased regularity since our fall in the mercenaries' wagon. The wound was also starting to leak pus through the bandages that I tied around the swollen skin with none of Jiron's skill but twice the fretting, and the only thing keeping me from freaking out about what that meant was the knowledge that the Martinezes' healer would be here at any moment to magic it all away.

"That was just a dream," Ren whispered unconvincingly, drawing out the syllables and waggling his fingers over my temple. I stared suspiciously at them in the gloom. "I'm fine, and you're going to let me have my way with you."

"Nice try. When you're healed."

"When I'm *healed*, I want inside you every hour, on the hour." He huffed and rolled onto his back with a wince, the lack of any further attempts to convince me suggesting that my *pesky stuffiness*, as he described my refusal to let us fuck when the circumstances rendered it sheer stupidity to do so, was starting to take root in him. "If you're going to resist my irresistible advances, you can do something else for me?"

I pressed my face into his bare shoulder, breathing in the scent of him. "Mmm?"

"Tell me what snow tastes like, Nat."

"Snow?" I asked, surprised by the request. "Uh, nothing. It's just water."

"Oh," Ren said, deflating with audible disappointment. "I'd thought it might be sweet. Or maybe fluffy bitterness, like flour."

"Flour," I repeated, snorting against his skin. As Ren shifted to look at me expectantly, his fingers trailing up my arm in lazy patterns, I explained my amusement.

"There's many types of snow. Sleety, hard as rocks, clumpy, fine…but best of all is the crispy snow. The type that crunches underfoot and is thick enough to mould." I snuggled closer, and he shifted his arm to play with my hair. "There was this day, years ago, where that kind of snow had just fallen and all the others were playing outside. Making shapes where they rubbed the snow away from the grass, like angels." My hands and feet twitched involuntarily, remembering the wild movements of the childish game.

"Astrid was recovering from an illness…or something that meant she wasn't allowed outside the castle that day. I don't exactly remember, just that we were forced to watch the other children from the window. We were both so jealous. But instead of complaining or throwing a tantrum, she just looks me in the eye, chews on one of her blonde pigtails, and says, 'Nathanael, I do believe princesses and princes should get to have their *own* snow.' And we go down to the kitchen and haul these massive bags of flour back to her room, and to this day I have no idea how we weren't caught on the way up because those things were spilling powder fucking *everywhere*."

Ren's quiet laughter joined mine, carefree and delighted.

"An hour later, Astrid's tutor walks in to find the princess' room absolutely *caked* in flour. And it would probably have been okay if the stuff was still dry, but one or the other of us had had the brilliant idea of adding water to the mess to make our 'snow' more slushy." I snorted. "Fucking hell. I was apologising to the servants for months after our punishments ended."

Ren stiffened, his amusement instantly stifled, and it hit me what I'd said. What to him, punishment as a child had entailed.

"Nothing like that," I said softly, silently cursing his father and the abuse he'd inflicted on the brilliant, beautiful man at my side. "I was just confined to my room for a week, only permitted to leave for meals and lessons. Not that it stopped Kolya, who snuck in everyday to bring me snacks he'd traded for secrets from the other childre…"

It was my turn to fall still. The northern prince's name echoed around the bedchamber as if the man himself was here, not as the mischievous and demanding boy he'd been, but the bitter, resentful adversary who'd slaughtered innocents and hadn't given a fuck, too intent on claiming both my affections and the Mazekhstani throne to care about their cost.

Ren trailed gentle caresses down my arm until the sick, guilty feeling invoked by that horrible night sank back into the recesses of my mind, soothed by his touch and presence. And then the prince paused, glancing over at the door. "I can hear voices."

I sighed and flung the bed covers off us, which made Ren yelp and toss out a myriad of threats in my direction. "It must be the healer. We better get ready to leave."

We dressed quickly, grateful for the increased cleanliness and warmth our new clothes offered over what we'd been wearing when we arrived – which were now nothing more than embers in the suite's fireplace – but the still, cloudless night held a vicious chill to it that had been kept away while we lay in the bed with his warm skin against mine. Ren shivered, his face pale and expression drawn as he hugged his uninjured arm around himself, and I moved towards the bedchamber door, ready to drag the damn healer in here if he didn't move any quicker.

AN OATH AND A PROMISE

"...it's my own Blessed house, bitch."

I froze, my hands shooting up into frantic gestures to warn Ren to stay still and quiet. Pablo Martinez's obnoxious voice continued to float through the door, too close for him to be in the corridor. He had to be standing in the suite's antechamber, with only an inch of wood between us.

"That slimy fucker who calls himself a driver deliberately ran over every pothole between here and the border. I've been bounced around in that damn carriage for hours, and I need a hot meal and a bath, something a good wife should have had ready. Why is that so hard for you to understand, woman?"

"We didn't know you were..."

The doorknob rattled. Ren and I darted for the window, him muttering a prayer for Dios to ward off squeaky hinges as he eased it open.

"Why the fuck is this door locked?"

"It's...been sticking in the cold weather lately," I heard Lady Martinez say hastily. "How about taking a bath in our rooms, dear?"

"You know I don't fit in that tiny tub. This is...get this open!"

After a silent battle of glares between us, Ren relented with a roll of his eyes, and climbed through the window first.

"My lord." Abril's voice, polite yet cold. "Welcome home."

"I said open the door, not stand there like a gaping dormouse, you imbecile," Martinez snapped. "You there, deal with this. It seems my household has gone to shit in my absence."

I clambered out after my lover, swinging my legs out over the twenty-foot drop and trying to manoeuvre the window closed with my elbow. My fingertips scraped across gritty, cold stone, and I glanced down to find Ren clutching the wall tightly. His face was screwed up in pain.

I heard the sound of a door being broken down amid Lady Martinez's gasps, and hastily lowered myself below the level of the windowsill, my boots scrabbling for purchase.

"What the *fuck*?"

We'd been seen.

Could we climb down two floors quicker than the obnoxious bastard could send his men around, or would we find them waiting for us on the ground, swords already levelled at our throats?

"I'm a tolerant man," Lord Martinez boomed from above us, "but there are *expectations,* girl, and one of those is to keep the standards expected of this house. What if His Majesty were to visit and be subjected to this Blessed mess?"

I glanced at Ren, but he had his eyes squeezed shut. His knuckles were white where they gripped the stone.

"My apologies. I'll make the bed immediately, my lord," said Abril soothingly, and then I winced as a hard slap echoed through the window.

"Pablo!"

"Don't you raise your voice to me, woman! See to it that the girl receives a flogging for her incompetence when she's done."

There was a long silence from the room, and it felt like an eternity. Would the servant attempt to barter her way out of punishment by giving us and her mistress up?

But when the next words were Lady Martinez's quiet assent, I felt relieved, and then shame at that relief. I shut my eyes too, seeking solace in the aching burn of my fingers and arms that would be nothing, *nothing,* compared to what the servant now faced, unless the two remarkably resourceful women could plot their way around that too.

"I tell you," Lord Martinez said, casually conversational as though he hadn't just sentenced someone to a painful and disproportionate punishment over a fucking unmade bed. At least if Abril was the one remaking it, no one else would know how the sheets were still warm to the touch. "King Welzes has a remarkably progressive mind, for a foreigner. If he does half of what he's promised, Quareh will be *revolutionised.*"

I bit down on all the scathing retorts I wanted to offer to that, unused to having to stay silent. Even as a prisoner in *la Cortina,* I'd rarely held my tongue, as Ren would readily attest to.

"Oh, dear?"

"You wouldn't understand it if I told you," Martinez responded haughtily.

"Economics go over women's heads, which now that I think about it, is probably why he wants to introduce such policies." He laughed, long, loud, and ugly, and I used the cover of the noise to begin to climb down the wall, wincing at each rustle of fabric and scuff of my boots against stone.

Ren cracked an eye and followed me, moving at a fraction of my pace. When he adjusted his left arm to take his weight, he flinched and buried his face into his other shoulder, clearly muffling a scream.

Blyat.

I briefly wondered if climbing *up* and silencing the priggish lord would be the better way to go, but when I heard a chatter of male voices from inside the house, I knew our instinct to hide had been the better idea. Of course Martinez hadn't returned home alone, and who knew where his men's loyalties would fall, even with their master dead or incapacitated?

Neither Ren nor I were fighters. Perhaps this whole thing would have been easier if we had been. If we'd had Jiron's skills for survival, or my brother's imposing presence. But we were who we were: two lean, not particularly athletic men, whose talents primarily lay in bickering with each other.

And being seen here meant sentencing Lady Martinez and Abril to worse than a flogging, along with any other members of the household deemed to have been implicated regardless of actual guilt.

My heart twisted. I was sick of leaving people in the dirt everywhere we went.

As the nobleman above us continued to espouse Welzes' plans for Quareh, being vague enough that I couldn't work out exactly what they entailed but gleeful enough that there was no possibility it was anything good, I slid further down the wall until I could safely drop to the grass, holding up my arms to help my prince. Ren fell the final couple of feet onto me with a muted cry, driving the wind from my lungs and any remaining colour from his face.

"We have to get to that healer," I whispered urgently in his ear, but he clutched my arm to keep himself upright and began to stagger away from the house.

"No, *mi cielo*. We can't risk staying here any longer. We'll find another."

Torn by an impossible choice and rendered in uncertainty, I let him drag me into the shadows of the gardens and to the wilderness beyond.

*

Chapter Fourteen

Ren

The air grew even colder as we veered northwards, and we spent the last of our money on furs and food for the days Mat couldn't catch any. It was late on the fourth day from the Martinezes' estate when I paused, squinting at the stream we'd just forded and then the trees around us, which at some point had transformed from oaks and beeches into pine trees without our noticing.

"Welcome home," I said softly.

It took Mathias a moment to catch my meaning. "We've...crossed the border? We're in Temar?"

"I believe so."

"I thought it would be more obvious."

I gave a rueful smile. "The Mazekhstani border is marked by conflict and blood-drenched land. But we've had no real quarrel with Temar for decades, and while there are checkpoints on the roads, we're deep enough in the woods to have passed by them unnoticed. You can't bring an army or trade caravans through here, and that's all either country cares about."

"Home," Mathias repeated, and then screwed up his face. "If we have indeed passed the border, then I think I just left mine."

That made me falter, my breath catching. "Do you mean...?"

He leaned in and kissed me as we stood on the precipice between our countries, or as close as my memory of cartography allowed for.

Was this it? This measly stretch of leaf-strewn dirt, indistinguishable from any other, was what had tried so hard to wrench us apart? Being born on opposite sides of a border...*this* is what demanded we be enemies instead of friends? Instead of lovers?

I made to pull Mat closer but my shoulder gave another pulse of pain and I gasped against his mouth. My northerner's face folded into that concerned unease he'd been wearing so often lately, and while I was used to him looking sullen – and delighted in being the one to coax out a smile – this particular anguished look was not one I favoured.

As a result of his insistent demands, we'd passed through a few settlements in search of a healer since fleeing the estate. While we'd found a couple of helpful locals possessing basic herbal knowledge willing to assist, all they could offer were sympathetic looks, foul-smelling poultices, and leaves to take the edge off my pain. Those payoffs hadn't been worth the risk of capture, but the stubborn brat refused to give up on finding someone with the Touch. Thankfully, this far from Máros either word of the bounty hadn't yet reached my people, or we otherwise hadn't been recognised.

"I misspoke, before," Mathias said fiercely, cupping my face with his gloved hands. "Quareh is not my home. You are."

I closed my eyes, breathing in the scent of him as he pressed his forehead to mine. "*Mi luz. Mi vida. Mi fuente de frustracion infinita.*"

My light. My life. My source of endless frustration.

Mat huffed out an amused breath, a fond smile replacing his worry for a fleeting moment. And then he dipped his chin into the furs at his neck, hiding his joy as if ashamed of it.

I slid my fingers under his jaw and pried it back out. He'd been doing this lately, looking guilty whenever he felt happy, as though he wasn't permitted to experience it while I was in pain. While Quareh suffered under Welzes' rule, and the war at the Mazekhstani border raged on.

"I want your laughter," I told him, as our breaths puffed into the air and a cold breeze tugged at our clothes. "Your happiness is mine, as is the rest of you, so don't even think of keeping it from me."

Another smile, briefly disguised by habit but then allowed to shine, and fuck, he was beautiful. The wintry sunlight dancing in his hair, his cheeks flushed pink from cold, and the way he looked at me as if he'd never let me go.

"So don't," I said.

"*Dorogoi?*"

I stared. Mathias no longer stood before me, but was hunched up, knees to his chest and huffing warmth onto his hands with his breath. And he was…sideways?

AN OATH AND A PROMISE

Blinking rapidly as if that would help orientate myself, it took until he'd shuffled closer to me to realise that I was the one in the horizontal relationship with the ground. I was stretched out on my back on a pile of furs, the air crisp in my throat but flecked with warmth and the enticing smell of cooking meat from the direction of the nearby campfire.

I rubbed my eyes, quickly swapping to my right arm when my left refused to cooperate. "Weren't we just talking?"

"You were talking to *someone*," Mat said. "I'm not entirely sure it was me."

"Then it wasn't a conversation worth having," I retorted, but the concern visibly wrinkling his eyes and mouth was making me nervous. "What happened? We were at the border, and…"

Mathias let out a long, defeated exhale. "That was two days ago," he told me softly. "You've been…in and out of it for a while."

Images swarmed my brain, hazy and distant as if from a dream or an old memory. A bird in a tree, bathing in sunlight. My boots plodding across wet dirt. Snatches of conversation, half-formed words, my confusion when he said things that didn't make sense.

"It's not looking good, is it?"

My northerner glanced at my shoulder before his gaze darted away, refusing to look me in the eye. "It's fine."

I snorted, or tried to, but the effort pulled painfully at the wound. "You can lie better than that, *mi sol*."

His lips formed into a broad beam of a grin, and he laughed as if this had all been a hilarious joke. "Ren," he said. "Seriously. You're going to be fine."

Shit. I almost believed him.

The meat spat and crackled where it nestled above the fire, and I stared into the flames, searing the flickering light onto my eyes so I didn't have to think about...

Had fire always been white? I didn't *think* so, but there it was, a perfect, almost pearlescent white brightness inches from my face. But it was cold, and fire wasn't cold, and I tried to fight it off as it wrapped around my arms and wouldn't let go and-

AN OATH AND A PROMISE

"Let me help you," growled a voice in my ear, and I fell still as the warmth that voice brought with it sank into my bones.

"Mat," I croaked. "I don't...I can't..."

"You fell," he said patiently, easing me up onto my ass from the face-planted position I'd found myself in. The way he avoided my shoulder so adeptly told me that this wasn't the first time he'd had to manhandle me like this, and there was no sign of the clearing with the fire that formed my last memory. "Perhaps we should rest here for the night."

"It's *snow*." The realisation hit me as the white mass before my face resolved into a picture I could make sense of, my cheek seeming to burn as it was wrenched out of its chilled embrace. But the mild pain was nothing compared to how my shoulder screamed at me. "Mat, I've seen snow!"

"You've also tasted it." Wry amusement tinged his tone. "You insisted on catching snowflakes on your tongue for two miles straight."

One landed on the back of his hand, and as he was unable to brush it off while he was holding onto me, I thoughtfully licked it from his skin.

"See?" he asked. "It has no taste."

"Wrong," I told him. "Snow tastes like you."

I thought about that some more. "No. You taste like snow?"

—

It was nearly dark now, which meant I'd suffered another lapse in time. I could feel the warmth of Mat's body where he lay against my right side, but everything ached and I didn't even have the strength to turn my head.

"Mi copo de nieve?" I whispered.

Mathias stirred, appearing above me a moment later. "That is *not* a new nickname," he admonished with mock sternness, peering down at me with sleepy yet undeniably worried eyes. "I am not your fucking *snowflake*."

I coughed, but that hurt too. "Are those really...the last words...you want to have said to me?"

"Ren. You're not dying."

"I'd say I hate to argue...but seeing...as that's our entire dynamic...yes, I am."

"You're *not,*" he insisted stubbornly, his jaw determinedly jutting out as if looking fierce and growly was sufficient to stave off death. "I won't let you."

Oh fuck, if only that was enough. I'd hold him so tightly it hurt, dig my teeth and nails into his fucking soul and never let go if it meant neither of us could be torn away from the other.

"It's time…to stop with the pretty lies now," I murmured, staring at his face and trying to memorise every enchanting line of it. "We both know I don't have long."

His expression washed clean of all deception and attempt at comfort, turning stricken. "No. No, Ren, we haven't had long *enough.*" He wrapped his arms around me, sinking his face into my neck as he sobbed out each word. "You're not going anywhere, you hear me?"

I could feel myself drifting again and gritted my teeth as I tried to fight against it. For whether it was another bout of delirium or the actual end, either meant I would lose *this*, these final precious moments with my lover, my heart, my *everything.*

"Don't you dare, you prick," Mathias snarled, smacking at my chest. *Fucking ow.* "You're staying here!"

"Please try not to…insult Dios like you do me when you eventually stand before…His gates," I hissed, blinking back tears as another wave of pain cascaded through my body. "I'd hate to…have to forsake my comfortable life in heaven to come and…join you in being tortured in the…fires below."

He scowled. "I've not given up on this life yet, Renato, and if you think there's *anything* I won't do to keep you here, then the Blessed cold's already gotten to you."

I couldn't feel the cold, although a quick blink at what I could see past his head told me that the snow had stopped falling. It now lay crisp and glittering, a scene of wonder and magic draped in moonlight.

I also couldn't move my hands. That felt like a terrible shame, for if this was truly my death then it would have been nice to depart the mortal plane with one last sweep of my fingers across his jaw, trace the smooth dimples in his back, feel the weight of his warm and silky cock in my hand. The uptight bastard would probably frown upon getting intimate with someone inches away from becoming a corpse, but hey, he could whine about it all he liked when I was gone.

"Kiss me," I breathed, and he did, teasing my lips with his before sinking his tongue inside to explore my mouth as if he knew as well as I did that we'd never get to do this again. He was crying as hard as he was kissing, hot tears running down from his cheeks onto mine, but I didn't have the energy to call him on it.

I needed my breath to tell him the only thing that mattered.

"I love you, *mi sol*," I whispered as the darkness swooped in and claimed me for its own. "Death…will not dare change that."

*

Chapter Fifteen

Mat

Tears blurred my vision, mellowing the snow-laden landscape into a meld of pastel colours with no detail. It rendered our sack of provisions into a brown lump, my hands into frozen, instinct shapes, and allowed me the illusion that the man I was crouched over was absolutely fucking *fine*. That his skin wasn't blue, his shoulder wasn't gushing pus and surrendering to necrosis, that his eyes weren't sunken in that distant glaze that signalled the infection stealing his mind from me once more.

But my poor vision couldn't imagine away the sound of his harsh, stilted breaths, or the pained whimpers Ren made with each rise of his chest. And no amount of Blessed daydreams could conjure up a healer in any of the Temarian towns I'd staggered into over the last week, begging and pleading and not caring if I was recognised by my people. Yet there had been none gifted with the Touch in these remote communities, none who could save my prince now he'd passed beyond the reach of mere medicine, and as my desperation grew, so did my anger.

Fuck *Dios*. Fuck every single damn god that ever existed or didn't, because not one of them would help him. Ren had been suffering his entire life and no one fucking *cared*.

Drying my face with my sleeve, I pushed myself to my feet. I'd been terrified to leave him out here, knowing the injury or the cold or even a pack of stray wolves might take him from me in my absence, but if the alternative to leaving him alone was watching him fucking *die*, the choice was no longer any such thing.

"I love you too," I whispered and then I was running, my boots crunching down on the fresh layer of snow as I shoved my way blindly through the trees. North was the only destination I had in mind; I knew we were miles away from any cities but none of the settlements we'd passed so far had held any hope, so all that was left was what we hadn't yet been able to reach as Ren's condition had worsened.

AN OATH AND A PROMISE

My breath exhaled in shallow pants, a steady rhythm that matched the single word in my head.

Please, please, please, please, please.

Maybe it was a prayer after all, and maybe it was nothing more than a plea cast out into a void in which no one was listening. But I wasn't waiting on divine intervention to save my prince.

I was fucking well doing it myself.

The trees began to steadily thin and after half an hour I stumbled out onto tilled farmland draped in a thin layer of snow. The soil cracked underfoot, tough and unsuitable for growing anything but the hardiest of foods, but tended to recently enough to give me hope that a settlement was close by. Scanning the darkening sky, I spotted a haze of light erupting from a handful of buildings nestled near a watermill that was crouched over a creek.

It took several impatient thumps on the door and a threat to break it down to bring the occupant of the closest dwelling out into the cold to greet me, which he did with a suspicious scowl and a sickle clutched tightly in his hands.

"Healer," I demanded in Temarian, not bothering with niceties. He was hardly going to invite me into his house for tea, and I wouldn't accept if he did. "I need a healer, *now.*"

The old man squinted at me. "Where you from, boy? You been on the road long?"

"A healer, please," I begged. "My lov...*friend* is injured, and only someone with the Touch can...can..."

The stranger's face expression softened, and he lowered the farm tool. "You're in luck, boy. A month ago, I'd have to have said there's no such person in these parts."

My breath caught. "But now?"

"Now..." The man glanced behind me into the snow, the suspicious look returning. "You don't go causing him trouble, you hear me? You keep your mouth shut when you get to wherever city or town you're going. The last thing we need is the crown's soldiers coming to take him away because some fool ran his tongue."

AN OATH AND A PROMISE

I understood. All Blessed were required to surrender themselves to their ruler so they could be put to work in the palace or army or wherever else their magic was needed. No matter where on the continent, none of them – technically *us*, but I had no intention of ever working as a seer and my gift was too haphazard in any event – were free. Sharing rumours of this healer's presence would see him taken to the capital, forcibly if required, to benefit those whom my mother deemed most worthy.

Which wouldn't be the residents of this tiny, remote settlement in southern Temar.

"I won't," I said. "Please, tell me where I can find him. My friend doesn't have long left."

A sympathetic grimace washed over the man. "He's taking shelter in the watermill until we can get some proper lodgings built," he said, jerking his head to the right in case I'd missed the only distinguishing feature of the entire hamlet. "Poor lad carries his demons, but he's a fair healer. He'll do you right if you can pay, I'm sure."

"*Blagodarya*," I blurted by way of gratitude, and rushed the half mile to the watermill. Further graceless knocking yielded no response, so I shoved open the door…only to find the building beyond empty.

Furs were scattered in the corner of the draughty room, scraps of wood and parchment littering the surfaces of the small table and chair, but my eye was drawn to the incongruity of the weapon leaning against the far wall. Unlike the worn-down, decrepit nature of the building and the rest of its contents – an aesthetic which mirrored the old man and his sickle – the sword gleamed with ill-matched luxury. I stepped inside, peering closer at it. It was an expensive item, polished and gilded, although it was missing the emerald I knew had once been in its hilt.

"Zlatkov said you needed a healer?" asked a familiar voice in accented Temarian, and I sensed someone entering the room behind me, stamping their boots on the hard dirt floor. "As long as he told you I don't do shit for free."

"Well?" the man demanded impatiently when I didn't turn around. "Either you do, or you're wasting my time."

I eyed the sword, wondering whether I could run him through before he

AN OATH AND A PROMISE

realised who I was. But that wouldn't save Ren.

So I turned around and looked him directly in the eye, refusing to let the prick see any of my fear.

"I do."

Kolya's expression went slack with disbelief as he stared at me. "*Natty?*"

*

Chapter Sixteen

Ren

Snow fell onto my face, dainty flecks which quickly melted into wet drops that ran down my cheeks or hung from my eyelashes. Every few seconds, I allowed myself to blink them away.

If I rolled onto my side, maybe I could protect my face from the swirling snow. But I couldn't move. Every part of my body felt heavy and foreign and hot and *wrong*.

"Poor, pathetic Ren," Comandante Moreno drawled, idly stretching out a leg next to mine. I could just make out his mocking smirk in my periphery. "Did you really think you were worthy to rule Quareh? Did you expect you would be *welcomed* to the throne?"

I flinched.

"Kings don't die all alone and unloved in someone else's country," the Comandante continued, inspecting the scars across his palm that he'd been forced by my father to put there himself. "Kings don't fail their people before they're even crowned."

"You're not really here," I told him dismissively, regaining my composure. "Fuck off."

"His Highness was more of a king than you could have ever been, *sir*," snapped Ademar. He was leaning against a tree, glaring at Moreno, with his arms folded and legs crossed at the ankles.

"You can stay, Ad," I said, "as long as you ease up on the insulting past tense when talking about my rule."

"Oh, *mi querido*," murmured Altagracia sadly, and I could have sworn I could feel her fingers carding through my hair, stroking it gently like she used to whenever I lay my head in her lap. "It's almost over. You won't have to suffer for much longer."

"What? No," I protested, trying to bat her hands away but unable to lift either of my arms to do so. "I *like* suffering. Suffering means I can still feel.

Suffering means I get to wail at Mathias until he's suitably annoyed and tries to hit me. Suffering means I *live*."

She made some sympathetic cooing noises. "Shush. Not long now."

"Alta-"

"Speaking of. Where is that little pain-in-the-ass of a northerner?" Ademar interrupted, glancing around between the darkened trees.

I didn't bother to look. Mathias was gone: I knew that more surely than I knew that by conversing with the apparitions gathered around me, I was losing my last vestiges of sanity and reason. The woods felt lifeless without him; a dull stillness like the very air was holding its breath until his return.

"He's not coming back, you know," said Moreno. His teeth glinted as white as the snow that never landed on him, no matter how thickly it fell. "He ran away as soon as you lost consciousness. Even a Temarian isn't stupid enough to risk his life to exposure or starvation for the sake of giving you comfort in your last moments." He shrugged. "Never mind. I'm sure someone will kill the vicious brat sooner rather than later."

"It's okay, Ren," Alta murmured soothingly. "I'll stay with you."

"My prince," Ad said. He straightened up and offered me a sharp, professional bow. "It's been an honour."

"Fuck honour," I spat. "Mat will return any moment."

The looks I received from the three of them ranged from amused to pitying, and I scowled at them all.

"I'm sure Nathanael would be here if he could," Al ventured hesitantly, and Ademar nodded his agreement even as the Comandante gave a derisive snort. "But if something happened to him…"

I swallowed. That hadn't occurred to me. I'd been ready to give him shit for abandoning a dying man when all I wanted was him at my side when I went, but what if he'd fallen in the dark or encountered a wolf or…*mierda*, what had I been thinking, tangling him up in my problems?

"Just die already, little Aratorre," Moreno said with clear exasperation, throwing his head back to stare at the sky. "For once in your life, do what's expected of you."

Hoofbeats drummed through the ground towards me, a noise I felt rather than heard. Hope sparked through me and I laughed.

"That would be Mathias," I told them triumphantly. "And it seems he's brought me a ride."

Alta and Ademar glanced at each other.

"My prince…"

As the horse approached, it slowed, whinnied, and then shoved its wet nose into my face. When it drew back, neighing happily, the other phantoms had disappeared.

"Miel," I said softly, recognising the mannerisms and markings of my dead horse. She tossed her head so that her bridle jangled, and it drew my attention to the person sitting astride her. A woman who was the spitting image of my sister Alondra, only with longer hair that held a tinge of red. Someone I'd only ever seen in portraits. "Mother?"

"Sweetheart," Consuela Aratorre murmured. "You can rest now."

"Mother," I said again, struggling to sit up even though I knew no movement remained to me. "Is it true? What Yanev said about you-"

"I promise to tell you everything when we meet in the next life," she answered. Her smile was broad, but sad. "It's now time for you to sleep, Renato."

*

Chapter Seventeen

Mat

Kolya recovered from his shock quickly, lunging forward with his right hand outstretched. His ungloved fingers came to rest a half inch from my cheek, not quite touching but clear in their threat, and blue eyes simmered in fierce savagery. Then he faltered, as if he'd expected me to flee or cower and was unsure of what to think when I did neither.

"What, by the Blessed fucking Five, are you doing here?"

"I told you," I said, relieved not to hear any waver or tremble in my words. "I need a healer."

The Mazekhstani prince's lips lifted into a pleased, terrifying smirk. "I hope it's painful."

His fingertips closed the distance and pressed lightly against the skin of my cheek, cold at first but then heated with his magic as silver and burgundy sparks flickered in the gloom. He cocked his head, frowning at me. "It's not you who…?"

Then he let out a delighted laugh. "Ah. You're here for your southern bitch? In that case, Nathanael, I hope it's fucking *excruciating*."

"Please," I begged, and that time my voice cracked. "I need your help."

The incredulous scoff I received at that was entirely expected. "You *are* joking? After everything you all did?" Kolya snarled in my face, wrenching his hand away as if I'd burned him. "You stabbed me. Your brother disembowelled me and left me for dead, and then you spread your lies so that I could never return home. You took *everything* from me, Natty."

He closed in on me again, seeming gratified when I backed up a step. His gaze softened at the sight, a tinge of satisfaction tempering the fury.

He wanted my submission? Fine.

If that was his price, I'd willingly pay it.

I forced myself to drop my head, speaking to the dirt floor instead of him and adding a sniffle for good measure. "I didn't mean to. It was all such a mess. And then the delay with the tournament gave Ren's Council time to work against him and he was…was…"

"I heard," Kolya spat, vindictive and pleased. "Made my fucking day."

"I'm sorry for what we did," I said softly, injecting a note of false plaintiveness into my tone instead of the sarcasm I'd have preferred. "I was scared, Kolya. Please, don't…"

He moved closer and cradled the back of my head in his hand as if in tenderness, but the firm grip kept my head bowed to him so I couldn't look up beyond his knees. It took everything in me not to shove him away, knowing my lies were all I had left.

"Say that again."

"I'm sorry?" I offered meekly.

"Not that," he murmured. "I *know* you're sorry. It's me and you, Natty, always has been."

Then what…?

I scowled at the ground but forced my voice to sound even more miserable. "I'm scared."

"Of course you are," whispered Kolya, petting my hair. I tried not to shudder. "But I'm not going to hurt you. And you'll make it all up to me, won't you?"

When I nodded, the pleased exhale of breath against my forehead told me that I had the asshole where I wanted him.

"But Ren," I pleaded. "He's dying and you're the only one who can save him."

The snarl that lit Kolya's voice at that was practically feral. *"Otlichnyy."* Then he said it again, as if I hadn't grasped just how Blessed happy he was to hear such news. "Excellent."

"Is it?" I asked, struggling to keep my tone within a few hundred feet of civil. "Because the reward for delivering him to Quareh alive would be enough to buy you a ship off the continent and set you up with a new life."

"Or," he said slowly, finally letting go of the back of my head and tipping up my chin so he could inspect my face. His eyes flickered intently between mine, and I deflated my expression into one of fearful acquiescence. "I could take half the bounty for delivering a corpse *and* get the satisfaction of watching your little distraction die."

"You'll never find him without me," I said, feeling uneasy at what I was proposing. But Ren didn't have long: if Kolya healed him and sold him back to Navar and Welzes, at least he'd have more of a chance to survive than he had now. "Please, Kolya?"

The prince cocked his head. "Give me more. Sweeten the deal for me, Natty."

"I don't know what you want," I said, my frustration the first genuine emotion I'd showed him, and he clicked his tongue in admonishment.

"You know *exactly* what I want."

Ice ran through me as his sharp fingers tightened around my chin, holding my jaw forcefully enough to bruise. He leaned in so his cold lips brushed against mine, his voice a hoarse rasp. "Say it."

I swallowed, not having to fake my fear any longer. Yet it was an easy decision: *moy dorogoi's* life could have cost the world, and I'd have gladly paid it.

"Save Ren," I whispered. "And you can have me."

Kolya crushed his lips against mine, his tongue spearing into my mouth with demanding, explorative strokes.

I stiffened at the unwelcome intrusion. He hummed his displeasure when I failed to respond to his efforts, drawing away from me after several uncomfortable seconds. I fought the urge to wipe my mouth on my sleeve.

"You're going to need to work on that," he said coldly.

"Sorry," I mumbled. "You just...caught me by surprise."

His gaze darkened, and terror coiled low in my gut at the bitter reminder that he held my lover's survival in his hands. Without letting myself think about it I leaned forward, and it was Kolya's turn to be surprised as I reignited the kiss and gave as good as I fucking got.

I'd thought I could get through the whole thing by imagining it to be Ren's mouth, but the differences between them were too stark. Soft lips, hot breath, keen tongue – everything should have felt the same, but it wasn't *him*. Smoked herring instead of saffron and citrus. Head tilted the wrong way. Hesitation when there should have been resolve, fierceness in place of warmth; he didn't take when he should have taken or yield when he should have yielded. But *fuck*, I didn't...*couldn't* let myself pull away, fuelling the kiss with a desperation I could only hope he'd misinterpret as passion.

In short, I kissed Kolya like Ren's life depended on it.

He groaned into my mouth, a noise of want and desire. One of his hands twisted in my hair, keeping me locked against him, while the other slid down between us. Realising what was coming, I held myself still as he palmed my cock through my trousers and began to rub against it.

Shame burned through me as the friction ignited a response, and I closed my eyes as if that was all it would take to remove his tongue from my mouth and his hand from between my legs.

And yet it did.

"*Blyat*, Natty," Kolya panted against my lips, his voice hoarse with lust. "You feel so fucking good." He took a deep breath as though to steady himself. "Fine. Take me to your southern dalliance so we can get this over with."

—

"Hurry," I hissed as Kolya started to lag behind once more. He shot me a look and I cast my eyes down, already sick of this fake deference shit. *"Please* hurry."

He sighed, yet obligingly hastened his pace. "It's dark. I don't want you to hurt yourself."

I really didn't give a shit, either about hurting myself or what the prick did or didn't want, but I nodded anyway. "I won't."

And of course, it was in that moment that an unseen tree branch scratched across my forehead, thin enough to have escaped any snow that may have otherwise clung to it and given it visibility in the dark. I brushed it away impatiently, only for Kolya to snag my wrist and tug me back towards him.

"You always were reckless," he murmured, stroking a finger across the cut above my eye. Colour sparked in the darkness, briefly lighting up the closest trees. "Even Quarehian captivity couldn't take that from you, huh?"

AN OATH AND A PROMISE

I didn't answer.

"Do you remember that time you fell through a hole in the ice while trying to prove you could cross the lake in spring?" Kolya asked. He'd been doing that for the last half hour, bringing up shared memories in a shameless attempt to remind me of how much of our lives we'd spent in each other's company. As if that meant a Blessed thing when he'd murdered dozens of people, tried to kill his sister, and come close to destroying our efforts at reuniting the continent in peace.

"Mmm," I said noncommittedly. I *remembered* being chased across the lake by Pavel Sluchevsky and his friends while Kolya stood there and laughed as if he hadn't just heard them threatening to bury me under three feet of snow. Letting them do it might have been preferable to nearly drowning in frigid water when the ice gave way beneath me, but the benefit of hindsight and all. Besides, giving them such an easy win wasn't my style.

I decided to change the subject before he somehow managed to transform that memory into *look how good I've always been to you* propaganda too. Sure, Kolya and the others had dragged me out of the lake and gotten my shivering ass back to the castle, but only because they'd have been in deep shit with the king if I'd died. Somehow that wasn't quite cutting it as proof of love, or whatever fucked up thing he thought he felt for me.

"You're using your Touch more these days?" I asked.

"I didn't have a choice." Kolya's tone turned bitter. "When my horse went lame before I reached the border, I knew I wouldn't be able to get to Mazekhstam before you and your whore told everyone what had happened. I wasn't about to hang around in the south any longer than I had to. So I fled to Temar, found the most remote shithole I could," – he flung his arms out, gesturing around us – "and offered my magic in exchange for food and shelter, having to sell myself just to eat."

Sell himself? Like what he was demanding from me?

"But that's over now," he cooed as he stroked my hair from my face, his fickle mood settling once more. "Once we deliver Aratorre to his king, we'll have the money to start over. I'll even let you choose where."

Retorts burned so vehemently on my tongue that I had to physically bite it, everything from denying Welzes' claim to declaring that the only place I would be settling down with him would be as two corpses in the fucking ground.

"I'd really like that, Kolya." My accompanying smile was sickeningly sweet.

The prince chuckled and didn't protest when I began to move on once more, frustration at how long this was taking burning me up from the inside. We walked in silence for a few more minutes, and when I spotted the clearing I'd left Ren in, my breath caught.

"He's just over there!"

"I know you're only pretending," Kolya said casually before I could drag him closer, and my heart dropped to my stomach.

"What? No, I'm not-"

"What you're *not*, and never have been," he drawled, "is meek and docile, Natty. And I'm not an idiot." Then he offered a broad smile which confused the hell out of me. "But that's okay. You're trying, and that's all that matters. You'll soon realise how good we are for each other."

I didn't answer, although he didn't seem to need me to. He may not have expected me to be meek, but he certainly liked it.

"Aratorre?" Kolya called, striding over to where Ren lay, a dusting of snow on his furs. I darted forward and dropped to my knees beside my lover, heaving out a relieved breath when I saw his chest rise and fall. But his breathing was even more laboured than before, his eyelashes fluttering erratically, and I thought I heard him murmur Altagracia's name amid his pained whimpers.

I glared up at the Mazekhstani prince where he stood over us watching Ren's suffering with undisguised satisfaction. "Help him, now!"

Kolya sighed like it was a huge inconvenience, dropped to one knee on Ren's other side, and prodded at him experimentally. "It's going to be annoying having to haul him all the way to Máros," he said with distaste.

Hoping it was just his usual bitching rather than him changing his mind, I dragged Ren's furs to the side and tried to unlace his shirt, only it was caked to his skin. The blood and pus had entirely soaked through the bandage. I muttered an apology as I wrenched it all away, Ren crying out in his unconsciousness and Kolya displaying visible disgust as he pressed the tip of his index finger to the festering wound beneath.

Purple and silver sparks hissed where their skin met, and I watched without daring to breathe as the damage began to retreat and the wound neatly knitted over. The rainbow of colours – black, yellow, red – disappeared from Ren's skin, his bloodied shoulder was now whole, and yet…his breathing remained stilted and his eyes were still closed.

Kolya drew back, wiping his hand on Ren's furs and frowning at him.

"What's wrong?" I asked. "Why isn't he waking up?"

"I don't know," he answered, sounding bewildered. "It should have worked!"

"Fucking do something, Kolya!"

"I don't know what to…oh," he said then, a slyness entering his expression. "I forgot who I was dealing with."

Ren's eyes shot open and he abruptly lunged upright, the knife I'd discreetly pressed into his hand a moment ago flashing towards Kolya's throat. But the northern prince jerked backwards before it could make contact, catching my wrist just above my glove and dragging me with him. I gave a pained shout as my shoulder was wrenched in the wrong direction, but it was the feel of his hand on my bare skin that shocked me the most; an agonising, blistering sensation of heat and pressure.

"Cute," Kolya mocked us as I cried out, his mouth twisted in disdain. "Did you get it out of your systems, or do you need *another* reminder of what I can do to you both?"

Ren stilled, his eyes flickering between us and settling on where I was held. Then he tossed the knife into the snow at Kolya's feet, casually stretching his arms above his head as if shaking off a nap rather than a fatal wound.

My heart leapt at the sight, too overwhelmed by relief at his recovery to do more than stare. He offered me a smile, one of those twitches of his mouth that said he was pleased and pissed off all at once.

"You couldn't have picked a feral beast in these woods to adopt instead, Mathias? A leper or two? Anything other than this prick?"

"It seems God will always return Nathanael to my side," snarled Kolya. When I tried to wrench my arm from his grasp, his fingers only tightened around the seared skin.

"Divine intervention, of course," Ren agreed, his eyebrows raising. "Nothing to do with us all being fugitives and happening to flee north by the only route left to us."

"Ren," I snapped, finally recovering my voice. "*Run.*"

My lover, frustratingly but admittedly predictably, didn't move.

"Are you fucking deaf? Run, Ren, before he-"

My words devolved into a yelp as Kolya reapplied that same magical pain to my wrist as before.

"*Don't,*" warned Ren with a growl, hatred in his eyes as he glared at the other prince. "You can have me and the bounty I'll bring, just don't-"

"I already have you," Kolya interrupted, glancing at me. "For if I hold one of you, I hold both."

And wasn't that the fucking truth?

"And yet all that Natty's affection bought you was another few pitiful days of life, Aratorre," he added, "and me the delightful sight of your body being hung from your own city's gates."

Ren bristled but said nothing.

Kolya knelt to rummage in our bag of supplies, tossing me the last of the bandages before sliding his hand to the back of my neck to free my hands. My wrist was a mess of burned skin in the shape of a handprint, red and raw.

Fingers tightened around my nape. "Ensure our dear *king* stays put until I'm ready to deal with him."

Ren didn't resist as I obeyed, capturing his hands behind him and wrapping the strip of linen around them to bind him to the indicated tree. Knowing how much he detested being restrained, I squeezed his fingers in wordless comfort, only to be instantly shoved aside by Kolya. The northern prince yanked at the knot, seeming satisfied – and surprised – that I'd tied it tight enough, and then circled the tree to get in Ren's face.

"Always knew you were a bastard, Quarehian," he murmured. "Didn't know it was *literally.*"

"If you indeed want to bear witness to my dramatic and tear-jerking execution, it's going to require us to start walking south," my lover said with typical Ren-levels of scornfulness, even as he yanked helplessly at his bindings. "Unless you're hoping a convenient carriage might stop by, Your Highness?"

"We'll leave for Máros soon enough," retorted Kolya. "There's *another* delightful sight I wish to enjoy first, and that's Natty on his knees while he pays me what was promised."

He reached for his belt, tossing his sheathed sword to the ground out of reach and beginning to undo his trousers.

I let out a long breath, and Ren went pale.

"*No*," my prince said in a low growl, fury sparking his gaze. His struggles turned desperate as he threw himself forward, only to be held in place by the knot I'd tied myself. "Take me. If this is about revenge or just getting your cock wet...whatever fucked up reason you have, take me! I'm right *here*."

Before I could protest that never-going-to-happen idea, Kolya scoffed, his lip curling. I'd never been so relieved to see disgust on another person's face as I was in that moment.

"I would not contaminate myself with your filth if you were the last man in Riehse Eshan," he spat at Ren, before turning to me.

"I've contaminated myself plenty," I told him. "Do you really want seconds?"

Kolya's lips thinned. "I may be your second, but I will be your last. Your *forever*."

I snorted out a laugh filled with bravado I didn't feel. "Are you that unused to people turning you down?"

"I am the first prince of Mazekhstam," Kolya snapped, "and my subjects know to please me. But you? Nathanael, I gave you the courtesy of saying no, did I not? I respected your choice all those years ago, because I thought I'd misjudged and you weren't...like me."

"Just because I'm gay doesn't mean I'm-"

I swallowed the rest of my words, grimacing as I tried to rein in my usual tactless self.

AN OATH AND A PROMISE

Ren, whose political upbringing meant he knew a dozen ways to phrase it politely, instead spat out, "just because he likes cock doesn't mean he wants *yours*, you murderous, delusional fucker."

"So then I arrive in Quareh, the cesspit of the continent, and what do I find?" asked Kolya, as if neither of us had spoken. "That you're giving *their* prince something you would deny *me*? I could live with it when I thought you weren't that way inclined. But to lie to me, only to allow a southerner to put you on your back at the first damn opportunity?"

"That's not fair," Ren said, his voice cold. "I really had to work for that. Do you know how much Blessed bathwater he goes through? Mat, please tell me you're going to start running away any moment now."

Kolya scoffed. "He's not going anywhere."

Then his face softened as he gazed at me. "I've loved you since we were children, Natty. We can start over and get it right this time."

"Last chance, Panarin! Leave him alone!"

"I want you to watch this, Aratorre," Kolya drawled, beckoning me over. "Watch how much he enjoys himself."

"*If you dare touch him*, I will bring down the wrath of my entire country on your fucking head," Ren snarled. His face contorted into pure hate. "There will be nowhere you can hide from me! Beg, while you still have a tongue. Run, while you still have *legs*."

Kolya's eyes didn't leave mine. He clicked his fingers and gestured down at his feet; a lazy, princely movement that didn't contemplate defiance.

I shook my head. "Not here."

Not…not in front of Ren. I couldn't do that to him.

"Nathanael."

"Not fucking *here*," I snapped, and then deflated as Kolya trailed a finger down Ren's cheek in clear, wordless threat. I offered a smile that felt thinner than parchment. "Shouldn't it be somewhere not…" I gestured around us, letting him deduce the rest of the sentence.

Not in the middle of a forest. Not in the snow. Not in front of the *other half of my fucking heart.*

"Mat," pleaded Ren, his voice raw and vulnerable. "Get out of here. I'm *begging* you."

I ignored his pleas as he had mine, because there was no way in a thousand hells I was leaving him to Kolya's less than tender mercies. Even if looking at the northern prince's pleased, expectant expression made my insides roil.

I drifted towards Kolya and caught his hands, knotting my fingers with his. "Let's go back to the watermill," I murmured, tugging at him, but he didn't move.

"Here's fine," he said.

"No, I'm not-"

He freed a hand and pressed a sparking fingertip to my lips. "*Shush,*" he coaxed. "You're always so uptight, Natty. I want to see you loosen up."

The strength sapped from my limbs in an instant, my knees buckling and my head lolling forward as if suddenly unable to bear its own weight. I slumped against Kolya with a gasp, my cheek nudging at his shoulder, and he wrapped his arms tightly around me.

"I've got you," he murmured.

I tried to fight but my own arms wouldn't respond, as heavy and useless as if they'd been weighed down with boulders. I could do nothing to stop him as he lowered me down onto my knees and moved my head so my face was resting against his thigh. Fingers stroked gently through my hair while his other hand pressed to my cheek.

And then more colour flickered in the darkness and I glared at the sparks that burst from his fingertips, inhaling sharply as life surged to my cock with blistering speed.

"*Nyet,*" I slurred at him, beyond pissed off. I was fucking livid.

Because it felt *good*. So Blessed good, distractingly intense, and I needed relief *now*. My hands weren't cooperating when I tried to lift them to stroke myself to completion, and I gave a frustrated whine, rubbing myself against Kolya's boot with the acute need to bring myself release.

"What the fuck did you do to him?" Ren's voice was laced in fear and anger, cutting through the pleasure I was drowning in and giving me something real to anchor myself to.

"Just something to get him in the mood," Kolya answered as he tugged open the top of his trousers to free himself, and his tone was comforting, soothing, *nice*. I cast it away, rejecting his false gentleness for the raw, violent edge of my own prince as he snarled out threats and pleas.

"Open your mouth, Nathanael," said Kolya.

I tried to shake my head.

And then my jaw was pried apart and something hot and heavy slid along my tongue and to the back of my throat, forcing my lips wide. I choked, trying to pull away, but the hand that had been stroking my hair turned to steel and his magic continued to hold my body as weak as a kitten and fucking aroused to boot.

If only the dullness in my limbs had taken my consciousness as well. Waves of nausea surged with the unfamiliar weight and taste, screaming in wrongness.

This was actually fucking happening?

"Stop gagging," he said irritably. "From the way Aratorre brags, you've clearly done this before."

"Panarin!" Ren roared. "*I'll fucking kill you!*"

Kolya pushed himself deeper and hummed, settled once more. "That's it, Natty, like that."

Clarity hit my mind then; a fierce, ruthless burst of determination that clawed its way through the blissful state he'd put me in. Did the prick think because he had me on my knees, he had *me*? That I would give in without fighting to my last damn breath?

It seemed despite the years we'd spent together, he didn't know me at all.

And while the rest of my body had been rendered useless by Kolya's Touch, my mouth was still my own. Was it a lack of control over his magic? Or was he really delusional enough to believe that I was going to enjoy what he was doing enough to actively participate?

I brought my teeth down savagely into the flesh that invaded my mouth, Kolya's high-pitched scream slicing through my ears as the hot, iron tang of his blood filled my throat and his hands scratched frantically at my face. I was shoved away from him, winded as I fell hard onto my back without the ability to catch myself, and watched with an odd kind of detachment as he loomed over me with his hands pressed to his groin and his teeth bared in feral, animalistic rage.

And then there was more blood. A spray of it cascading through the air to land on the churned-up ground beside us, accompanied by the sound of metal hitting bone; an arc of crimson amid the slushy grey of the snow and dirt. A beautiful, burning hot line of life…of *death,* signifying Kolya's final mark on this continent.

The northerner slumped gracelessly to his knees, his head tipping from his shoulders where his neck was severed, but not quite fully detached. It fell to an unnatural angle, a sight absurd in its terrifying impossibility.

Blue eyes bore into mine, but there was no longer any life behind them.

Ren, unbound and wild and *pissed,* tugged at the blade that he'd hacked into Kolya's neck. When it didn't budge, he settled for kicking the corpse aside, the man's own sword permanently lodged in his spine. A death so quick Kolya hadn't seen it coming, and one he would never be able to heal from.

And then my prince was on his knees before me. Hands fell onto my shoulders and I flinched, yet it wasn't smoke I smelled, but saffron. And oranges and warmth and comfort and *Ren*.

"*Mi corazón,*" Ren whispered, pulling me into his arms, and I let him, not caring that Ren was wet with hot blood and tasted like metal because that meant we were safe and Kolya was fucking *dead.*

He held me without uttering another word, rocking us both gently.

As control over my own body steadily returned to me, I clutched back at him with a grip hard enough to bruise, and Ren didn't say anything about that, either.

*

Chapter Eighteen

Ren

The cold, once so bitterly hateful, was now a balm to the red-hot rage blistering through my veins. I wanted to tear the whole Blessed continent to the ground for what it had allowed to happen, the heavens and my god along with it.

Because for that monster to have…

As much as I liked to claim otherwise, Mathias was never dull when he was scowling or sulking. He always had a hidden spark which danced in his gaze, one which flared even more fiercely when provoked or teased, and I delighted in drawing it to the surface.

But Kolya Panarin had dared to steal that spark.

The expression Mat wore now was not his usual grumpy countenance. For that would have required emotion, and the man slumped on the ground beside me had none. Just an empty, cold stare as the night passed in silence around us, his eyes not leaving the cooling corpse as if committing the sight to memory.

Every now and then Mathias twitched, his lips peeling back from his bloodied, bared teeth in reluctant confession of his discomfort, and I could see the way his hands balled into fists as he tried to resist the lingering stimulation of Panarin's Touch on his body. When I'd gently suggested that bringing himself some relief might help it pass quicker and wouldn't mean anything, Mat had shot me a scathing glare and returned to his vigil over the body. I'd silently cursed myself. Because of course it meant something to *him*: it was one last fight against the bastard dead at his feet, and if anyone could wager their willpower against the physical impulses of arousal and have a chance of winning, it was my stubborn little wildcat.

I wanted to apologise. For bringing him with me on this ill-fated quest to recover my country, for ever putting him in a position where this could happen. For our love, which bound us so tightly that he'd faced a horrendous fate and still hadn't saved himself by leaving me to mine.

AN OATH AND A PROMISE

But me saying sorry obligated him to tell me not to worry about it, or that it wasn't my fault or that he forgave me, and why should that shit be on *him* to say?

"You memorised the slip knot," I said instead, after his breathing began to ease and his shoulders slumped from the effort of denying himself for so long. "You're so fucking good sometimes, you know that?"

Mathias raised his head, tears having forged gruesome tracks through the blood splattered across his face, and brushed his thumb underneath each of my eyes to wipe away the wetness on my own cheeks.

Fuck me, I should have been able to escape sooner. While I'd tied slip knots myself often enough, no occasions more delicious than those around Mat's wrists or ankles during our playtime, it was always on others rather than myself. And with my fingers numb from cold, my body having only just recovered from imminent death, and the bonds being linen instead of rope, I'd taken far too long.

My lover gave a long, resigned sigh and abruptly stood, walking away into the darkness without a second look at me or Panarin's corpse. Realising he wasn't just stretching his legs when he didn't reappear after a long minute, I hurriedly snatched up our discarded supplies and raced after him, thankful the sun had now risen enough to see our way.

I could only hope that was an omen.

-

It was twenty-seven hours before Mathias ate or drank anything other than the water he obsessively gargled and spat as if to purge Panarin's taste from his mouth. Two days before he looked up from the ground before his feet. Four before I saw him smile.

During that time we continued to pick our way north, living on the gold I'd found in Panarin's pockets, and when that ran out, what I made from pawning my rings. Perhaps I should have had a fit of misplaced pride at using either source – the gold for it being blood money owned by a man for whom death was too kind, or the jewellery for the symbolism that selling it signified. But fuck that. Pride didn't put food in our starving stomachs. Didn't buy extra furs from a street market to wrap my wildcat up in for the night Mathias started trembling and didn't stop until dawn. Didn't purchase a tent from the small town we passed through for us to take shelter from the thickening snow each night as we held each other for warmth, lying together in painful silence.

Spending the money didn't mean we owed that fucking rapist anything, or that I'd given up on the hope of retaking my throne.

Far from it.

All it meant was that I was holding to my dual vows of doing everything and anything it took to protect my man and my country. I might have failed to stop Panarin from hurting him, but I'd be damned if I was going to let Mat waste himself away out here in this Dios-forsaken wilderness like he seemed inclined to do without me pushing him to eat, sleep, and walk each day.

And it was five and a half days before he spoke again.

"You must think it stupid," Mathias said in a voice hoarse from underuse. "He didn't even...it was just my mouth. It didn't count."

I was silent. I knew he didn't believe that, but I also knew it wasn't on me to tell him what he did or didn't think.

"And I agreed," he hissed, kicking at a root underfoot that had clearly pissed him off in a previous life from the way he was viciously toeing it with his boot. "What Blessed right do I have to complain when I *agreed* that he could have me?"

"You said no."

He scowled. "I said *not here*."

"Not here. Not now. Not ever. Whatever form your 'no' took, it was your right to say it."

He bit his lip, chewing on it so fiercely it started to bleed. "I still got hard."

"Because the prick *drugged* you! But even if that wasn't the case, so what? Consent can't be inferred from a body's physiological reaction. You may get off on being dominated, Nat, forced and roughed up," – I glanced away, unable to meet his eyes – "but that doesn't mean anyone can just *do* that to you. It doesn't mean you don't have the right to decide when and with whom, or if at all. You told him fucking *no*. He disregarded that, Mathias, and if I was willing to give the fucker even a *second* more of our time, I'd have taken him apart slowly," I promised, fighting to keep my tone level. "Starting with his hands so he couldn't magic himself fucking better."

Mat hummed, not in dismissal like I'd expected but amused consideration. Had the asshole actually listened to me for once?

Then he lifted his head to the wintry sky and squinted at the ravine ahead that seemed to cut the ground in two. "We need to move quicker. I don't even want to imagine what Welzes is getting up to in your absence."

"Nothing good for Quareh," I agreed, noting the unsubtle change of subject but choosing not to comment on it. Our travels had been slower recently, attributable to the tougher terrain, less light, and our growing exhaustion. It was taking too long to reach Stavroyarsk, and like Mathias, I feared what Welzes and Navar might be doing to my country and how many of my people would be suffering for it.

I frowned as two figures on the opposite side of the ravine appeared from the tree line and moved onto the bridge we were heading for. It looked sturdy enough, if a little weathered, but the snow that coated everything this far north – the ground, the trees, the concealed dips and ditches I'd fallen prey to more than once – gave the structure a serene, almost magical quality, as if the wood had been dipped in ice and preserved. "Speaking of nothing good," I murmured as the pair inexplicably stopped in the middle of the bridge rather than completing their crossing. "You have your knife?"

Mathias flashed me a wild grin. "Always."

Yet it had been too much to hope for that the people waiting for us wouldn't be armed themselves, and a bow on the shoulder of the one on the left and a staff in the hand of the other gave my confidence a good kick as we drew close enough to make out such details. Mat, not hesitating even for a moment, strode right onto the bridge and pushed the hood back from his face even as I sank further into mine and tugged it lower. I hadn't needed the hostile reminders of the townsfolk we encountered when buying supplies to know that southerners weren't welcomed this deep in Temar, regardless of my identity.

"Dobar den," Mathias greeted the pair, feigning a casual cheer he surely didn't feel.

The strangers deliberately stepped into our path, blocking the narrow bridge, and we both drew to a reluctant halt.

"A good day indeed," said the one on the left, and as I didn't dare look up, it was their voice rather than their features that gave away their gender. She laughed, and it wasn't a pleasant sound. "We always enjoy welcoming strangers to Palŭk, dunna we, Milord?"

"I consider it our civic duty, Milady," the other responded. "There are many dangers around here. Wolves."

"Wolves," she agreed, and under the lip of my hood I saw her unhook the bow from her shoulder. "Snowdrifts."

"Snowdrifts. Oh, and terrible, *terrible* falls. Big, deep, falls that would surely render a person naught but fragments of bone by the time they were to hit the ground."

"Like that one there, perhaps?" Mathias asked, his voice low and unassuming, and I glanced sideways to find him gesturing down into the ravine.

"We have a clever one here, Milady," the man remarked. "He gets it, he does."

"I don't suppose you fine people know the best way to avoid such a fate?" I asked, copying Mat's accent as best I could.

"Two clever ones, Milord. I think we should help 'em."

"Just what I was thinking, Milady. Wouldn't want anything nasty to happen to either of these fine, upstanding gentlemen."

"D'ya think they'd be generous enough to donate a gold piece for our troubles?" the woman asked. "To compensate us for the years we've spent gathering such worldly knowledge?"

The man's staff clunked onto the wooden boards beneath our feet. "I think they would, Milady."

I tensed, wondering if Mat was going to object as vehemently to this act of extortion as he had with the captain in Máros, but he obligingly reached into his pocket and pulled out one of our remaining coins. Look at him, thinking all bigger picture and shit. I was proud.

"That seems." Mathias cleared his throat and gritted out the last word, not bothering to keep the irritation from his tone. "Fair."

Our companions chuckled.

"Glad we could come to such an amicable arrangement." Boots shuffled in the snow as payment was made, and then stepped aside from our path. "You and your mysterious companion can head to Mazekhstam safe in the knowledge that all you needa do to avoid a nasty fall down that ravine there, is to *not fall off the fuckin' bridge.*"

"Worth every speck of gold they paid, advice like that, Milord. Good day, friends."

Mathias didn't move. "Mazekhstam? Why do you think that's where we're going?"

"Your accents. We got an ear for these things, dunna we, Milord?"

The next time Mat accused me of failing to grasp the subtlety of his accent while I was mocking the odd way he pronounced his Rs and Us, I was going to remind him of this moment.

"But it seems to me," the man offered, "that these two ain't gonna get very far if that truly is their destination. Assuming they're planning to take Cašran Pass like a coupla idiots."

"What's wrong with the Pass?" I asked. As far as I knew, that was the only way across the mountain range that divided Temar from Mazekhstam, other than travelling the hundreds of miles to the northern reaches of the continent where the Tungsten mountains devolved into glaciers and ice floes.

"What's wrong with the Pass," they both parroted, incredulity infecting their voices as they laughed again like I'd made an excellent joke. I wished I could raise my head to see if their expressions were truly as scornful as they sounded.

"Nothing's *wrong* with it if you're an honest man-"

"-or woman."

"Or woman, thank you Milady, who's making an honest living in an honest world."

"Which none of us are, Milord."

"'Specially not these two, what with them taking such a circuitous route north through Palŭk and that one hiding his face. Anyone mighta think they have something to hide, Milady."

AN OATH AND A PROMISE

"Enough with the bullshit," Mathias snapped. "You're saying the Pass is watched?"

"Oh aye," the man said. "Cašran Pass is locked down tighter than a whore's pussy. If you haven't paid for it, of course," he added, "cos once you have, it's not tight at all-"

"We get it," Mat interrupted hastily.

"I don't," I said, grinning under my hood. "Explain it to me some more. Be as graphic as possible so that I can properly understand."

"Well see, it's like when you getta on her back-"

"There's checkpoints, see?" the woman said. "Two or three on either side, so you ain't getting through with a mere bribe. Everything you 'ave is searched, and if they dunna like the look of ya…"

"*Fuck*," Mat said, stamping his feet to keep warm. I felt the vibrations through my own boots.

Someone clicked their tongue. "Hey now, it ain't all that bad. It just so happens that me and Milady here know another way into Mazekhstam yonder…"

"Of course you do," I muttered. "How convenient."

"It's our job, remember? Lord and Lady of safe transportation through these parts." Milady dipped into a deep, flourishing bow, her eyes flickering up under my hood with sly intent, and I turned my head away before she could catch sight of my face. "Whether that's the horizontal kind of transportation like this bridge-" She straightened and tapped her own boots on the boards.

"Or the vertical kind like the ravine," the man remarked snidely.

"-or the higgly piggly kind like getting over them mountains, we're your people. People who get their goods across to the west in a more efficient manner than going up all the way to the Pass, see?"

We did see.

"Three gold," my lover said unexpectedly. "Get us there safely and don't ask questions, and you can have the same again."

"*Mathias!*" I hissed, shocked. "No. We're just going to take their word for it about the Pass being checkpointed?"

"It makes sense," he said.

It did. Less than fifty years ago the northern countries had still been at war with each other, and a gap in the mountains that would lead an army directly from Temar's capital to Mazekhstam's – or vice versa – was hardly going to go unmonitored. But this...not only would six gold drain the last of what we had, but we'd be fucking stupid to put our lives in the hands of two strangers who had already proven they weren't above robbing innocent travellers.

They didn't need the promise of half payment on arrival to incentivise them when they could just take it from our corpses, did they?

"No."

"Yes," he retorted. Stubborn, *stupid,* fucking brat. "Deal, Milady, Milord?"

"Deal, friend."

The clink of gold had me swearing and lunging forward to knock his hand away, but I was too late. Milady – a pinch-faced woman with raggedy furs and several missing teeth – had the coins already clutched in her gloved fist, and Milord – who had a thick blonde beard reaching down to his chest and was dressed even poorer than her – stepped between us, slapping a hand against his staff threateningly.

They both stared at me.

"Not a chance," Milord spat when he recovered. "We dunna want the trouble that transporting a southerner could bring, do we, Milady?"

"Smuggling is smuggling. And we already paid," Mat reminded them from beside me.

"So you have. And yet we're the ones with the knowledge of how to getta over them peaks."

My lover shrugged. "We have knowledge too. Of what you look like, and which of your activities might be of interest to certain...more law-abiding citizens."

"Or I could just gut you where you stand, you little shit," Milady snarled, swinging her bow forward and resting the viciously sharpened wooden tip of it to his throat.

I flinched. He didn't.

"*Mat*," I muttered, tugging on his arm. By Dios, they could keep the fucking money, as long as they didn't hurt him.

"Bad for business, that," Mathias said lightly to Milady, impossibly calm, and there was a tense moment where neither of them moved.

And then she laughed and rehooked her bow over her shoulder, clapping him on the back. "You've got stones, Mazekhstani," she said and then jerked her head in the direction of the mountains to our left. "Well? We haven't got all day, have we, Milord?"

"We dunna," he agreed, "but we do have just enough time for us to enact our usual precautions." He grinned, handing the staff to his companion before pulling two tatty cloths from the pack on his back.

"Canna have you knowing where the crossing is," Milady explained. "Also *bad for business*."

"Then that's a hell fucking no from us," I spat, fear growing in me when Mathias did nothing but turn around to let the other man tie the blindfold around his head. I couldn't even enjoy the sight of my boy like that, the grey cloth over his eyes drawing greater attention to the shape of his sweet lips and delectable jaw, because his unbounded recklessness froze me colder than the snow resting in our hair.

He didn't care. He'd thrown himself thoughtlessly towards this foolish venture without giving a fuck if he lived or died, and while my northerner had always had an unhealthy relationship with his own safety, it hadn't ever been like *this*. I cursed Kolya some more, fiercely yet silently, and vowed I'd beat some sense back into my wildcat even if I had to do it literally.

"Well?" Milord asked, the second scrap of cloth hanging from his fingers. "You in or out, southerner?"

Mat held out his hand to offer me comfort, but I merely knocked my fingers against his rather than taking it, not wanting to provoke more northern intolerance when I was about to be rendered blind.

"Times a ticking, ain't it, Milord?" Milady sang, although she was beginning to look irritated.

"It is, Milady."

"Ren," Mat said softly.

I huffed out a resigned sigh that fogged my breath in front of my face. I may not have had Mathias' temerity, but if we were ending up with slit throats at the bottom of a mountain somewhere, we were doing it together. That was the least of what I owed him.

"Fine," I said. "But if you dare let us fall off a cliff, we're dragging the both of you down with us."

I tensed as the scratchy fabric stretched taut across my eyes and was fastened behind my head, and again when my hood was thoughtfully pulled back up over it. I appreciated the warmth it offered, although I suspected they only did it to avoid looking at me and my apparently offensive southern complexion.

"Dunna about that," Milord said to me, clearly amused. I could smell the rankness of his breath on my face and tried not to recoil from his closeness. "'Nother gold coin says you won't get the chance."

*

Chapter Nineteen

Mat

I didn't need my eyes to know the exact moment we were herded into a tunnel by Milord and Milady, as the howling, icy wind was abruptly replaced by the strong scent of earth and the telling echoes of a confined space. Neither was my sight necessary for the growing realisation that this tunnel was far from stable: the clods of soft dirt and other unidentifiable detritus I was frequently tripping over told their own tales, as did the eerie creaks of tonnes and tonnes of earth shifting and settling above our heads.

I was glad to not be traversing mountain slopes while blindfolded, but I wasn't sure this was much better. One unfortunately timed rockfall and we'd be buried under the Tungsten Mountains in a tomb so deep that our skeletons would never be found, and wasn't that a cheery fucking thought?

We stumbled along for what felt like hours, gauged by the soreness of my feet and the aching of my stomach rather than any proper time-keeping, as tucked away in this hidden vein of the continent there were no stars or sunlight to indicate whether the day had yet faded into night. The only light that made its way through the cloth wrapped across my eyes was the flickering of a torch held by one of our companions, who were happily chattering away to each other in that inane way of theirs, where they used a whole lot of words to say nothing much at all.

The only source of comfort in this strange, terrifying place was the prince at my side, who occasionally bumped against my arm or hip when Milady or Milord failed to keep us steered straight, or when he considered too many minutes had passed since he'd last pissed me off.

Or maybe Ren was seeking solace too, for the nudges were gentle little grazes that I began to not just relish but crave as the hours dragged on, my sightlessness accentuating every dreadful creak around us until my nerves felt as frayed as my clothes. The smugglers who had originally forged this tunnel must have been fucking crazy. Or desperate.

And then I was yanked to a halt by hands falling on my shoulders, and I saw the torchlight dance through the threads of the cloth as Milady or Milord moved past me. There was a clang of metal, like a bolt on a gate, and then the wind that had been absent this whole time hit me in the face, making me stagger backwards.

By the Blessed, it was cold. And just like how I'd acclimatised to the southern weather during the months I'd spent in Quareh such that I'd felt the chill as we moved north, the shock of the buffeting, frigid wind had me burying my face into the furs around my neck and cursing into their fluffy embrace.

"Through you go," Milady said, and gave me a hard shove between the shoulder blades that almost sent me reeling. My boots slammed down, the transition from soft dirt to snow only evident by the audible crunch it made, and I fumbled at the knot tied at the back of my head.

"Hey now," she rebuked sharply, and my wrist was jerked down. "We may be through the range, but ya ain't getting that off until we're good and distant. Wunna want you to know where to look if you were ever passing back this way, would we, Milord?"

"That we wunna, Milady."

"Trust me," I said through gritted teeth, "I have no desire to *ever* go into that tunnel again."

"Hmm," murmured Ren from a few feet away. It was the first word he'd spoken in hours, yet even that one syllable felt dangerously charged, like a coiled viper or a lit fuse. I wished I could see his face.

"Walk, friends," Milord ordered, and I felt myself being shoved forward again, my feet scuffing into thicker snow as the ground dropped off sharply. I bit my tongue on a retort to the rough treatment, wondering what they'd say if they knew they were pushing around the impending heir to the entire southern half of Riehse Eshan. Then again, it was nice to be unseen for once, treated poorly just because they were uncaring assholes rather than because of who we were or who we fucked.

Ren's darkly muttered threats as we descended the slope told me that he wasn't feeling nearly so appreciative of the anonymity. My prince had always adored the type of public interest I shied from, and I knew keeping his identity hidden since that day we'd fled the Márosian palace hadn't been easy for him, not when the man so effortlessly drew – and sought, flaunted, and basked in – attention.

After the ground levelled out after about half an hour, we were finally permitted to remove the blindfolds. I blinked and glanced around, letting my eyes adjust. It was night. There was a thin layer of snow clinging to the branches of nearby gorse bushes and the blades of grass underfoot which seemed to sparkle in the moonlight drenching the land, the moon itself hanging high in the sky.

"Now. Our fee?"

No one moved, and the tension rippled thick through the air between us. Then Ren sighed, dug his fingers into his pocket, and handed over the last of our money.

"Pleasure," Milady drawled, and they turned back towards the mountain range looming in the distance.

"Wait," I said. "Where are we?"

"They said gettem to Mazekhstam, didn't they, Milady?"

"That they did. And we're in Mazekhstam, are we not, Milord?"

"That we are-"

"Yes," I interrupted. "Care to be a little more specific so we don't freeze to death walking in the wrong direction?"

"Well." Milord looked us up and down. "That'll cost you."

I scowled at them. We had nothing left to give, and I expected they knew it. "No, it won't."

"No it won't," Milady echoed, grinning. "Just 'cos we like you, we're gunna tell you that there-" She pointed over our heads, and I followed the gloved finger to a frozen lake a short distance away. "-marks the boundary on the Grachyov estate, don't it?"

I gave an incredulous laugh. "You run your smuggling operation a handful of miles from the home of Mazekhstam's own fucking Commander?"

"Well," Milord said, scratching his chin through his beard, "he's usually in the capital, ain't he, Milady?"

"That he is, Milord. No one to notice us way out here, there ain't."

AN OATH AND A PROMISE

"Dunna turn around," he ordered. "Not until we're long gone."

My prince was still silent, his expression darkly furious. So I nodded and the two Temarians disappeared behind us, fussing at each other loudly enough that it would have been easy to follow them if we'd wanted to.

"They do realise we could simply retrace our footsteps in the snow?" I remarked to Ren, amused. He didn't respond.

I chanced a glance sideways, the sinking feeling in my stomach doubling when I saw his face was set into a stony glare.

"You're pissed at me," I said.

Ren's lip curled, and then he began to walk away, his boots scuffing up powdered snow with every enraged stomp.

"It worked out, didn't it?"

He abruptly rounded on me, jabbing a finger against my chest. "You couldn't possibly have known that, Nathanael!"

"I…"

"Don't you fucking lie to me, not now," he snapped, spreading his fingers and shoving at me with both hands. Caught by surprise, I staggered backwards. "Don't you dare tell me you Saw how we'd be fine."

"I wasn't going to."

"Well that's something."

"What is this about?" I demanded. "That I took a risk? We're on the fucking run, Ren, do you think any of this is *safe?*"

The prince let out a hollow, unamused laugh. "A risk. That's what he calls it."

I folded my arms. "And what would you call it?"

"How about a Dios-damned suicide attempt?"

I stared at him. "I don't…what?"

"Mat," Ren said, his voice softening. "Those two could have easily killed us. Left us stranded. Screwed us over a hundred different ways, and your self-destructive ass didn't care!"

AN OATH AND A PROMISE

"I care," I said. "Of course I care."

He huffed out a long breath. "Really? Because it didn't look like it. It didn't *feel* like it. And that…"

He crumpled, his head dropping and his shoulders slumping, and I had him wrapped in my arms before I could even blink, holding him tightly. He clutched back at me, fingers kneading into my back and arms through my furs.

"You'd tell me, right?" he whispered, pressing his cold face into my neck and breathing me in. "If you were thinking about hurting yourself?"

Fucking hell. *That's* what he thought?

My first impulse was to laugh it off. And then I imagined how it would feel if I feared what Ren might do to himself, and quickly sobered. "*Sí,*" I assured him, squeezing him tighter until he exhaled against my throat. "I swear to you, *moy dorogoi*. I haven't. I'm *not*."

I felt the tension drain from his body, pressed together as we were. Ren had frequently expressed how little stock he put in the promises of others, knowing words were sometimes just words: easily spoken and easily ignored, but that he trusted me when I made them? My heart beat a little fonder, something I would have thought impossible with how full of love it already was for this man.

"You're right," I said. "It was reckless, and I'm…I'm sorry."

Fuck. It had felt reasonable at the time, but now I thought back on it, it had indeed been stupid to put our lives in the smugglers' hands. I'd just been so intent on reaching Mazekhstam, worried about the delay, filled with a certainty that it was the best thing to do…was that what Ren felt when he called on Dios, or Astrid when she prayed to her own god? A faith that defied logic, was blind to common sense, and made people do stupid shit?

But it hadn't been a deity I'd trusted to see us safe. Just me and him, together.

I pressed a kiss to the side of Ren's head. After a moment he rubbed at his face and straightened out of our embrace, but I didn't let him go far, keeping my arm wrapped around his waist so I could rest my hand on his hip as we walked. His mouth curved into a small, satisfied smile and he did the same to me. It made our steps awkward, and my wrist still ached from the burnt handprint that had begun to blister, but neither of us would let go.

"At the far end of the lake," I told him, steering us towards it, "is the Grachyovs' hunting lodge. It's several miles from the main house. We can rest up there."

"How do you know it isn't occupied?"

"It doesn't have any beds," I said, expecting him to make a joke about that. He didn't. "It's not used for overnight stays, just to take shelter in during the day. I went there once with the real Mathias and-"

And Kolya.

"And uh, Astrid."

Ren seemed to know exactly what I hadn't said.

"It wasn't your fault," he said quietly, angrily. "*None* of it. I don't want you to punish yourself."

"Because that's your job, right?"

I'd meant to tease, to draw out his ceaseless good humour and the interminable filthy comments that I was convinced I'd find carved on his bones, they were layered that deep into the essence of him. Yet Ren didn't offer even a smile in agreement, and his unnerving silence bred a bitter sense of unease and confusion in me as we approached the hunting lodge.

We checked it out together, ready to flee back into the shadows if I'd been wrong, but a thin patina of dust across the floors of the two deserted rooms told us that not only was no one here tonight, but it hadn't been visited in a while. Maybe the Grachyovs had the servants clean it up when it was to be in use, for the air smelt faintly musty, a scent I didn't recall from last time.

I dragged armfuls of furs and coats out of the cupboards and piled them on the floor in front of the fireplace, pleased to find it stocked with neat bundles of kindling and firewood that I could use Jiron's teachings to light. Ren was rummaging around in the next room, a kind of kitchen slash butcher's shed that held a large bench used for skinning and preparing the kills so they could be carried back to the main house. The bench was scrubbed clean and there was clearly no fresh food to be had, but when my lover appeared in the doorway with a bundle of dried herbs and a sack of potatoes that were only just starting to sprout, my stomach rumbled in anticipation.

AN OATH AND A PROMISE

"Fuck yes," I said eagerly.

He seated himself opposite me, mirroring my cross-legged position, and tossed the small sack into my lap. I slid the knife from my boot and began to cut away the sprouts on the potatoes, letting Ren sort the herbs between his long, dextrous fingers, but found my attention frequently wandering from my own task.

It was the first time in many days that we weren't wrapped up in thick furs, with the fire having warmed the room well enough to have allowed us to shed our outer clothing. I admired, not for the first time, the angular shape of Ren's hips, the graceful line of his collarbone dipping beneath his shirt, and the way his long eyelashes fluttered against his tan skin.

"Mathias," he murmured, not looking up. "If you cut yourself because you're not paying attention, I shall have to shout at you again."

I cleared my throat, lowering my gaze back down to what I was doing, only to find myself watching him again a few seconds later. His lips quirked in amusement, and I stared, enraptured, at the way his throat bobbed delicately as he swallowed.

Ren gathered up his hair in the loose approximation of a ponytail and then let it drop. It cascaded around his shoulders like ink, drawing my eye. "You know I love you, right?" he asked, catching me off guard. He raised his head and smiled at me. "I feel like I don't say that enough."

"I suppose you expect me to say it back?"

He snorted. "You're in *that* kind of mood, I see."

I carefully set the knife down on the floor. Ren watched me intently.

"But you do love me, of course," he taunted, drawing a circle in the air around his own face with a sprig of what looked like parsley. "What's not to love?"

"Your narcissism," I told him without hesitation. "Your irreverence. How your hair somehow ends up in my mouth while we sleep, every single fucking night."

"If you're just going to list my finest qualities..."

I dove on him, dried rosemary and thyme and fuck knew what else cascading around us as I knocked him onto his back on the pile of furs and slammed my mouth against his. My fingers found and undid the laces on his trousers by muscle memory alone and I dragged them down to his knees before he could say a word.

Then I rolled my tongue over the head of his cock and Ren went rigid.

"No," he murmured, trying to push my face away. "Nat, you don't need to-"

Shame and fury washed through me, heating my cheeks, and I pulled away before I could meet his gaze.

"I just don't want you to feel like…" He couldn't seem to finish.

"Is that why you haven't touched me since he did?" I asked quietly, irritable resentment seeping into each word.

Ren scrambled up onto his knees so he could crawl closer, trying to tug me back to face him. I ignored his efforts.

"I haven't touched you, *mi cielo*," he whispered, "because I didn't know if you wanted me to."

"Because you think me broken?" I snarled. "Or because you think me ruined?"

Ren's rapid inhale of breath made my insides twist. Because voicing the accusation was a shitty thing to do, but what was I *supposed* to think? Two weeks ago I would have sworn that he didn't care about such things, that I knew him well enough to be certain that he'd never think less of me for it, and yet…in all those days since Kolya had happened, my lover hadn't once tried to instigate intimacy. Hadn't made a single sexually suggestive comment or joke at my expense. Hadn't touched me anywhere other than my hands or arms, as if we really were just two strangers travelling together.

And yet I needed him as close as physically possible. *Closer.*

"*Never.* Mathias," Ren murmured, and as if he'd read my mind his fingers were trailing up under my shirt, across my abdomen and making me shiver. "I want you. Dios knows, I want you. But I was not going to push you before you were ready."

This time I let him turn my face towards his. He grazed his lips across my mouth. "Are you? Ready?"

"*Yes,*" I said, trying not to shout the affirmation at him. I'd needed a moment to get my head back on straight after all the shit that had gone down with Kolya, but not the eternity Ren had apparently been intending to wait. By the Blessed Five, had he been planning to spend the rest of our lives waiting for me to answer a question he hadn't even asked?

Maybe other people who'd had their agency ripped from them, who'd been violated and had their souls left feeling raw, needed longer to process what had happened. Maybe others needed less time.

I didn't fucking know how I was *meant* to feel, only how I did feel, and that was frustrated and worked up and needing Ren to make me forget it all. To get lost in the future I'd chosen for myself; something good and ever so precious and better than anything I ever dreamed I'd get to have. A future with him.

I wanted it rough, like only he could give me. I wanted to be fucked hard and deep, and I told him so, revelling in the way Ren's eyes lit up. And then my mood immediately soured again when his gaze morphed into horrified pity.

"Or maybe we should do it your way from now on?" offered the prince.

I eyed him suspiciously. "What do you mean, 'my way'?"

"Gentle. Sweet."

I frowned. "Is that what *you* want?"

His silence was enough of an answer.

"Then why even suggest it?" The words came out harsher than I'd intended, but this demure, watered-down version of Ren was starting to piss me off. "What's going on with you?"

Ren fidgeted, twisting his fingers in my shirt. "I just...want to give you something nice," he said quietly. "Like you'd enjoy, not how I always insist on."

I had never been more confused in my life. "Like I'd enjoy?" I repeated, dread creeping into my heart at the words even though I didn't fully comprehend their meaning.

Or maybe I did. "Renato. *You're not Kolya.*"

"But that's the problem!" the prince roared, and then winced, as if worried his yell might shatter me like a pane of glass. "Everything I do to you is violent and cruel, and exactly like him!"

"That's not-"

"The first time we fucked, I held you down and made you take me," Ren spat out, his lips curling in distaste. The man could be so full of unexpected self-loathing at times.

"And I consented."

"That doesn't matter!"

"It's all that matters!" I shouted at him, leaning forward to press my hands to Ren's face and hold him still to ensure the prick was listening to every word. My voice dropped to a whisper as I repeated it. "It's all that matters, darling."

His eyes grew wet, and his shoulders heaved. Ren started to sob silently under my touch, and I pulled him close as I rested his head against my chest and wrapped my arms around him.

Kolya may have been my demon, a nightmare that sometimes woke me in cold sweat, but I'd never considered that he could be Ren's too. I had been the one rendered helpless and pliant as Kolya took what he wanted, but my prince had seen it all where he'd been bound to the tree by my own hand. How would I feel watching it happen to Ren?

Absolutely fucking furious, I knew that. Like I wanted to shred the continent down into individual blades of grass and toss them all into the deepest parts of the sea.

But it wasn't just his vulnerability he was lamenting. It was mine as well.

Well, fuck him. I was plenty capable of brooding on my own: he didn't get to do that for me too.

"I don't want to be your monster," Ren sniffled into my shirt.

I dug my fingernails into my palms to prevent myself from hitting him. I figured smacking him across the face while he was crying was something the old Nathanael would have done, and I was trying to show growth and shit.

"For someone so clever," I ground out, "you are incredibly stupid."

That got a reaction.

"Did you just call me stupid?" my prince asked half-heartedly, dragging his face out of my clothes and wrinkling his nose at their smell. "That kind of shit talk from a foreign royal can cause wars, you know."

"Ren. I knew when I first said yes to you-"

"*Yes?* I don't recall you ever saying such a thing. All I remember is trying to get some sleep that night at the Martinezes' estate when you threw yourself on top of me. I haven't been able to escape your annoying ass since."

I swatted at his arm, although the restoration of his playfulness made my heart dance.

"I knew I wasn't just saying yes to being with another man," I said, the words sounding awkward and thick in my throat. "But to being with you. And Ren, do you think I expected you to be *gentle and sweet?*"

I looked him in the eye, needing him to see the truth there.

"Do you think I *want* you to be?"

Drawing in a prolonged breath, Ren straightened up so he could face me properly. "I could deal with what I was and what I liked in bed before you," he said falteringly after a long moment.

"Am I so terrible at it?" I asked, offering an expression of mock affront.

"Fuck no. You're amazing, Mathias. I just...how can I love someone and also want to hurt them?" Brown eyes bore into mine, wide and pleading for answers. "I'm so fucked up."

He ran a hand down his face and then rolled his eyes at me. "Don't do that."

"Do what?"

"Give me that smug grin that says I'm missing something obvious."

"Well," I said. "You are."

Ren threw himself backwards down onto the furs, his arms falling limply at his side.

"Do you really believe I would let you do all those things to me, if I didn't want you to?" I asked, my lips twitching in amusement at how unnecessarily dramatic he insisted on being even in the middle of an existential crisis. "If you're fucked up for liking it, then I am too, and I'm more than happy to walk that road at your side."

I shifted so I was crouched over him, looking down at where he was cradled amongst the pile of furs, looking small and lost. "But I don't think we are. Pain makes me feel alive. All my life, it's just been about surviving. Getting through, existing rather than living. But the pain...you make me *feel it*, Ren."

"That's certainly my intention," he said dryly.

Then he yelped as I smacked him lightly in the stomach for his interruption. "Maybe we don't talk about a scene before we start, but I don't want that. I enjoy the surprise of trying to guess where your mind is going and not once ever getting it right." I gave him a feigned glare that was steeped in fondness. "Fucking sadist."

I received a low chuckle in response.

"I trust you," I continued. "Not to not go too far – neither of us know all of my limits, and I like learning new things about each other – but I trust you to stop when you realise you have. I can stand on the edge of the cliff and jump with you, and know that you'll be there for me no matter how turbulent the fall."

He hummed. "Always."

"I don't want to lose that," I said. "That fear, that newness, that exhilaration. And I don't see how something that makes life brighter can be a bad thing. Maybe some people won't ever understand it. But you do, and now I do, and isn't that enough? Aren't *we* enough?"

The prince rose up onto his elbows and stole a kiss, long and soft and yet with enough of his usual brusque forcefulness to assure me I'd gotten through to him.

"We're enough," he said firmly, and I saw the conviction welling in his eyes, that same faith I'd relied on so many times to see us through. Me and him, against the continent. Against the whole world, if it dared to get between us.

"Hurt me, fuck me, tease me...and don't ever stop," I begged, murmuring the words against his lips. Laughing, Ren pulled me down into his arms, not with the intention of leading to anything more but just so we could hold onto each other. Hold, and never, *ever* let go.

"I'll do all of those things tomorrow, and more," promised Ren, his voice

AN OATH AND A PROMISE

soft. "But tonight, *mi corazón,* can we stay just like this? Please?"

I snuggled in against him. "That sounds absolutely perfect."

"You're absolutely perfect," he said.

*

Chapter Twenty

Ren

We stayed another day in the lodge, making up bullshit justifications to each other about the weather not being right and needing to scavenge more food and fresh clothes from the cupboards, but really it was just so we didn't have to leave. So we could spend hours nestled together on the furs in front of the fire, feasting on vegetables that were probably on the wrong side of aged, and sharing stories. Sitting on the porch wrapped in a blanket and watching the clouds lumbering across the sky above.

The time allowed us to regain everything we'd recently lost. Warmth. Sleep. Feeling in our toes.

And my smile, it seemed, for I hadn't realised how little I'd been doing so until my face began to hurt just from all the fucking *beaming* I was doing.

And every single mote of happiness was because of him.

Mat didn't make regular declarations of affection as I did. His flirting was limited, awkward even, and usually in response to my own overtures rather than self-initiated. But it was shown in the gentle brush of his hand against my fingers, the way he pressed his shoulder to mine whenever we stood close as if he couldn't suffer even air to separate us. The lingering looks that I caught from the corner of my eye, the myriad of excuses he made to touch me – to fix my hair or straighten my collar.

I didn't point them out. I was worried that if his attention was brought to what he was doing, he might stop, and that would be a tragedy of insurmountable loss.

It turned out I'd been so busy worrying about him that I hadn't realised my fear had infected us both. Because while it *had* happened, and there would always be a part of us that felt the impacts of that horrible day in the woods, I'd witnessed time and time again how resilient my wildcat really was. Talking about it hadn't broken him. Touching him didn't trigger him. My attempts to avoid such things had weighed on Mat more than if I'd trusted him to know what he needed.

And fuck me, had he actually said he missed me tormenting him? I was taking that as permission to never, ever, stop.

Mathias yelped as I moved up behind him, my hands slamming against the wall to cage him in.

"*Blyat*," he panted, laughing and throwing his head back so he could rest it on my shoulder. "You startled me."

I nosed behind his ear and he twisted around to kiss me, hot breath against my lips a moment before his mouth found mine.

I closed my eyes and let myself enjoy the press of heat and exhilaration that was uniquely him. Our tongues fought for dominance, Mat giving as good as he got for several seconds before he allowed me his sweet submission.

"Please," he gasped, breaking our kiss to yank his shirt off over his head and toss it aside.

The plea was a reminder of what he'd demanded from me last night, my cock instantly thickening with the anticipation.

"Please?" I murmured, running my fingertips down his bare shoulders. He shivered under my touch, as oversensitive as ever. "Is this what you want?" I yanked down his trousers and slid a finger down the crease of his ass, laughing softly when he whimpered.

I didn't wait for my lover's confirmation. He'd resist giving it to me, as he always did, and if I'd read his mood wrongly then I trusted him to tell me so. Loudly and vehemently.

Instead I ordered him to get on all fours, my desire flaring as he lowered himself into position for me.

Desire...and love. That fucking emotion that overwhelmed all my senses, making me do stupid shit like declare him as mine to my country before I was even crowned, giving Navar both motive and opportunity to undermine my right to rule. I knew that many Quarehians hated the idea of a northerner at their king's side – the disgruntled gossip had reached me even before we'd been forced to run – but there wasn't a single chance I'd do it differently. If it made my eventual reign harder, then fuck it. I didn't do easy, anyway.

Mathias, who was the furthest thing from easy, shifted restlessly on his knees. Slipping one hand into my own pocket to retrieve the oil I'd filched from the

Martinezes' estate, I knelt behind him and brushed the other up the inside of his warm thigh. I was careful not to touch anything but his bare leg, leaving the contact fleeting and taunting.

He made a needy, breathless noise.

"Greedy," I accused.

"Tease," Mat shot back – unwisely, as all it did was make me *really* tease him, fluttering my fingers across his body with too-light pressure that made him squirm and growl out demands to touch him properly. Demands that naturally I ignored, enjoying watching his frustration grow.

And when I judged he'd least expect it, I slid an oiled-up finger into his hole without warning, relishing the surprised squawk and the way he immediately tried to rock back onto my hand. I smirked at the back of his head, moving with him instead of against him to deny him even that, deliberately avoiding his prostate and making my movements shallow and slow enough that they'd build his pleasure without letting it crest.

That drew out soft, unsatisfied whines from the man beneath me, sending my blood pumping southwards.

"Enjoying yourself?" I asked.

Muttering something vaguely insulting, Mat shook his head as if to clear it and tried to pull himself upright. I shoved him back down, not bothering to chide him for the attempt. Neither of us wanted nor expected him to be good this time: it was about how far I could push him before he broke, and…there it was.

Smothering my satisfied grin, I tugged at his hips to yank him back from where he was attempting to subtly rut against the soft friction of the furs beneath him. I was careful to avoid touching his cock, even as the sight of it dripping pre-cum brought me to instant hardness.

"You think I'm going to let you get off?" I said dryly. "With that attitude of yours?"

"Ren!"

It sounded like more of an order than a plea, and so I ignored it.

But harder to ignore was the way his cock twitched when I spoke to him, so

I rewarded myself by reaching around to stroke it. Just once, not enough to deliver him anything close to the satisfaction he was craving, but its heavy warmth in my hand felt divine. I could only imagine how aching and desperate Mat must feel, and I was loving every second of his misery.

Predictably, he tried to thrust into my hand. I chuckled in his ear and loosened my grip, frustrating him once more.

"Ren, I need-"

"I decide what you need, darling. Try again."

His shoulders dropped. "I want to come."

"Permission denied. This isn't about what you want."

Mathias obligingly mewled out his complaint yet neither of us voiced the truth he'd spoken last night that this – me setting the scene in apparent disregard of his wants – was *exactly* what he wanted. It heightened our enjoyment for us both to pretend otherwise, and to be safe in that shared pretence. Fuck, to know that he hadn't just been humouring me…that he truly enjoyed everything I gave him? I'd *known* that really, of course I had: I wouldn't have ever done it otherwise, but hearing him speak it aloud yesterday had eased that ache in my heart that insisted I was taking advantage of a man who, before he met me, really had been so charmingly innocent in such things.

When I'd drawn out my teasing touches long enough to be rewarded with a half-choked sob from my lover at how fucking unfair he undoubtedly considered I was being, I pulled my fingers free and gave his ass a light slap to ground him.

"I'm going to fuck you now," I lied.

"Yes!" Mat growled, raising his face from where he'd planted it firmly in the blankets in visible vexation. "Now!"

And then I paused. "Oh. My braid's come loose," I told him sadly, tugging at my hair with my fingers to make it true. "I need to go and retie it."

Mathias stared at me from over his shoulder, his eyes flashing with warning. "It's *fine*."

"No. I won't be able to concentrate." I drifted towards the door to the lodge's other room, revelling in how his muscles tensed and his glare turned frigid. "Stay there while I sort it?"

"Renato!"

"I'll just be a moment," I said.

I was, naturally, a hell of a lot longer than a moment. Instead, I took my sweet time, loudly clattering around in the kitchen to dissuade him of the idea that I could possibly be waiting as impatiently as he presumably was on the other side of the closed door, even though I really was. But fucking him and fucking *with* him were my two favourite pastimes, and tonight I was getting to do both.

When I allowed myself to open the door again several minutes later, the pile of furs was empty. My pulse ratcheted in gleeful anticipation, before I realised that Mathias…wasn't in the room at all.

His clothes were gone, no longer discarded across the floor. The window hung wide open.

And the third thing that had changed was the scrap of parchment left on top of the furs. It had been scrawled upon in Mat's neat handwriting.

Gone for a walk. Don't wait up.

He'd known as well as I that this had been his chance to set the tone for the rest of our scene. If he'd still been where I'd left him, I'd have been nice – or as nice as I was ever capable of being. If I'd found him no longer bent over but instead lazing insolently against the wall or the fireplace, he'd have earned himself my crueller side.

But leaving the Dios-damned room altogether?

I huffed out a low laugh, glancing back at the open window. I was going to bring the brat to fucking *tears*.

—

I followed Mat's footprints in the snow to find him leaning against a tree overlooking the frozen lake. With his arms folded and the moon at his back, he cut a dashing silhouette of insolence and pure sex.

"*Zdravstvuyte*," he said casually, cocking his head at my approach.

"Don't fucking *hello* me," I retorted, amused and turned on. The best combination, in my opinion, and the heated look Mathias shot me suggested he felt the same. "If you have any last words, I suggest you speak them now."

He only turned his gaze heavenward. "It's a nice night," he commented to the stars.

"Really? That's what you're going with?"

He shrugged with arrogant nonchalance. "Cold, though."

No shit. The temperatures were so fucking low up here that even my *teeth* were cold. That was not a sensation I'd ever wished to experience and I could have gone my whole life quite happily without it, but some stupid fucking Mazekhstani royals had chosen to settle their capital so far north they might as well have planted their flag in an ice floe. It was hard to imagine that my beautifully warm lands lay only a few days' ride south, but it wasn't just distance separating us. It was altitude as well, and as Quareh clearly had the best of Riehse Eshan's climate, the northern countries were left with this freezing – yet admittedly pretty – mess of a weather system.

Mathias grinned at me.

I knew what he was doing. He hadn't appreciated me toying with him earlier, and was now doing his best to sufficiently rile me so that I wouldn't have the self-control to do anything but take him hard and fast.

I knew, but I didn't care. If Mat wanted to unleash that part of me, it was on his own fucking head.

"You won't be cold in a minute," I told him with a smile that was not intended to comfort. "Are you going to run?"

"I am."

"I'll catch you."

"You always do," said Mat, dropping his gaze to mine and holding it with glittering intensity. The words hung between us, bearing more weight than their surface-level meaning.

"And then I'm going to fuck you where you fall, Mathias," I promised, unlatching my belt and hooking it into a loop. His eyes followed the movement hungrily. "Are you sure you wouldn't like to move to somewhere more…comfortable?"

He gave a long, low laugh that sounded like a promise of what was to come. A frisson of excitement ran through me. "Do *you* have any last words, Ren?"

There were so many things I wanted to say to him.

That I would indeed always catch him, no matter how fast he ran or far he fell.

That nothing held any meaning without him.

That he wasn't going to make it six feet before he realised fleeing from me had been a *very* bad idea.

As a dozen other answers ran through my mind, from the romantic to the thoughtful to the manifestly vulgar – because I was me, and that was never changing – Mat shot me a brash grin and darted from the tree. I blinked, caught by surprise.

And yet there was no way in hell I was going to let him have such a head start. Neither would I allow Mathias to win by guile when I had far more tricks and far fewer scruples about using them.

So I forced myself not to give chase despite every ounce of my being rebelling at the restraint, instead staggering on the spot and letting out a pained, gasping noise. Mathias stopped mid-stride, his head swivelling around with a look of utter concern etched across his face and his hand already coming up to reach for me.

I delivered his earlier cocky smirk back to him…and pounced.

"Shit," he hissed, dancing sideways and evading my grasping fingers by a hair's breadth. He twisted away and began to run, yet I was close on his heels now and he knew it.

My heartbeat pounded in my ears as my boots slammed into the snow after his, the cold night air and the primal thrill of all this making me feel fucking *alive*. He made it a dozen feet, maybe two, but I knew I had him.

I forced myself to move faster, eating up the final inches between us.

Mathias swore as I tackled him to the ground, that gorgeous accent of his made thick with fear and exhilaration. Taking advantage of my position on top of him, I quickly yanked his arms behind his back before he could push me off. He struggled to free himself from my weight without them, his face pressed into the snow and his shoulders straining desperately.

Planting a knee in the small of his back to keep him down, I tightened the loop of my belt around his wrists. Yet unlike the other times we'd played with restraints, Mat didn't simply let me tie him up. He fought me with his every breath, resisting my efforts with a fierceness that made me hard just feeling him moving beneath me, knowing he wouldn't yield until I was inside him.

It seemed he was liking this game of ours as much as I was, for when he finally peeled his face from the snow and glared over his shoulder to spit more curses at me, I found his eyes bright with excitement and his lips curved upwards into a broad smile that the normally uptight bastard was either failing or not bothering to hide.

I reached around him to undo his own belt and haul his trousers down to his knees before doing the same to myself, enjoying Mathias fighting back with everything he had. My wildcat was fully unleashed at last, clawing and struggling and yet helpless beneath me.

"That's fucking cold, asshole!" he gasped as the bare skin of his hips and thighs met the snow. I could have told him that I didn't expect either of us to last long enough for it to become a problem, but I enjoyed watching his suffering far too much to ease it.

"Keep mewling," I murmured, sitting on his legs and pressing two fingers to where I intended to invade his gorgeous body. "I love your little whimpers."

"I don't whimper," Mathias said scornfully. I slid my fingers inside him to prove he was once again a Dios-damned liar, rapidly inhaling as I found him still slick and ready from my torment earlier. He bucked and kicked, but I had him pinned and my beautiful northerner wasn't going any-fucking-where.

I knew that, he knew that, and still he writhed, giving me everything I wanted in the form of his resistance. I absolutely adored that he was letting me go all out like this, granting me the thrilling pleasure of holding power over another as I fought to make him mine. His cursing devolved into his native tongue as it always did when he lost control.

"That's it, Nat," I whispered into his ear as I braced myself against him, using my weight to keep him trapped. "Spread those pretty legs for me."

I didn't give him time to either answer or prepare as I forced my way through the ring of muscles that protested every inch of my cock, making him gasp and cry out beneath me. I wanted him to feel it, to suffer the ache of discomfort and wear the pain I delivered to him.

Mathias howled something hoarsely in Mazekhstani as I drew out and slammed back into him hard, instinctively trying to pull away from me. I yanked him back down onto my cock, the breath leaving his body in a gasp as the top of my thighs smacked against his ass.

His hands slid free from the unsecured loop of the belt, but as I'd only used it to get him into place, I didn't bother to stop him. Pale fingers tore up clumps of snow and the grass beneath it as he began to claw desperately at the ground.

I loved taking him apart like this, watching his eyes lose focus and his breathing stutter as I forced his body to submit.

"Fuck, Ren!" Mat panted, squirming beneath me.

"I'm sorry," I said, not feeling sorry at all. Because within mere seconds, I felt him tense and buckle beneath me. His ass clenched tight and he made those delicious moans I knew so well.

"You look beautiful coming around my cock, *mi sol*." I grinned into his hair, delighted at how quickly I'd brought him to climax. By the Blessed, that was an ego boost and a half. "But I hope you know I'm not going to stop fucking you just because you've come."

"Keep going, please," he begged, lost to his high, and I continued to drive into him, listening to him trying to breathe through the brutal thrusts and savouring the inarticulate, garbled noises of pleasure as he sobbed and shivered through his oversensitivity.

"You belong to me," I growled, twisting my fingers through his hair and remembering too late Mat's distaste for expressed possessiveness. But with everything I was doing to him, with everything we'd shared, it felt right to claim him like this; to show him how fucking much he meant to me in a way that no one else had ever come close to. "You're *all mine*, Nathanael."

His noises of half-agreement, half-protest carried me over into my own release. I emptied into him, the stars above our heads seeming to fucking explode into light and colour as I did, and feeling like the luckiest man on the continent.

I'd played with all sorts of people in my years, and yet those experiences all seemed dull and tasteless now compared to the exquisite vintage that was my irritable yet passionate northerner. My precious, exquisite, fucking *unique* mess of a man.

Mathias went limp beneath me, spent and exhausted. His ash brown hair was damp and plastered to his forehead, his eyes were closed, and he had the relaxed limbs and smug, floaty look of someone who had just been thoroughly used.

I ran my fingers through the slickness leaking out of him, drinking in the soft, helpless noises he was still making.

I may have frequently complained about Mat's attitude, I mused, but it was *much* more fun to fuck it out of him.

*

Chapter Twenty-One

Mat

My insides felt suitably rearranged after our fun last night, my body sore and satiated, and I hid my smile as I heard Ren come through the door of the lodge and stamp his boots on the doormat to clear them of snow.

"Brat. Didn't I tell you to stay in bed?"

"You did," I agreed without turning around from where I was combing the cupboards for any supplies we could take with us. "Was I supposed to listen?"

A harsh slap across my abused ass had me hissing out a complaint and spinning around to find my lover's expression wavering between the unimpressed look he wanted to grace me with, and the gleeful smugness he couldn't quite disguise.

"Did that hurt?" he asked slyly. "I couldn't – and wouldn't – have done that if you were still in bed, Mathias."

I raised an eyebrow, refusing to respond to such a loaded and misleading statement, and Ren huffed out a disappointed sigh when I failed to rise to the bait.

"You know, your life would be so much easier if you did what you were told."

"You mean, yours would be," I retorted, and he offered me a wink.

I glanced at what the prince had tucked under his arm, inhaling deeply as the delicious smell wafted around the room. "You brought food?"

"I told you I was going to brave the wilds and hunt us down some breakfast using nothing but my hands and my wits," Ren drawled, "and that you and that pretty cock of yours were staying tucked up in bed so I could play with them when I returned. Unlike *you*, I held up my end of the deal."

I eyed the dead bird he was carrying with a great deal of scepticism. "Hunted down?"

"Indeed." He gestured for a plate and I scrounged one from the cupboard, planting it down on the bench so he could lay his trophy atop it. "Pretty impressive show, if I say so myself, and a *good* submissive would show his appreciation by going down on his master."

In lieu of that idea, I threw him a rude gesture.

Ren made an indignant noise, but it was all bluster. I'd blown him plenty of times since he'd helped me back to the lodge last night and spent hours cleaning us both up, holding me close, and whispering sweet praise in my ear that he would pretend to deny in the cold light of morning. Sometimes my mouth had found its way down there of its own accord, and other times hadn't been given much of a choice when the prince decided that my sarcasm needed to be silenced for a while. I'd told him that it was okay to admit he was losing his edge in our banter, and he'd proceeded to test the limits of both our self-restraint – and the muscles in my jaw – by fucking my mouth slowly for nearly an hour.

I'd gotten my own back just before dawn.

Pulling out two more plates for us to eat off, a luxury we hadn't had in some time, I waved a hand at the bird. "What is this?"

"Um," Ren said, and I knew he'd chosen to deliberately misunderstand my question from the wicked glint in his eye. "Wildfowl? Emphasis on *wild*."

"Really? Smells like chicken."

"Could be," he ventured, cocking his head to examine it from another angle as if that might change its scent. "A *wild* one."

"And wild chickens cook themselves too, do they?" I asked, amused.

"You know what, *mi amor*?" he said, poking a long finger into the crispy skin that had a dozen herbs and peppercorns decorating its surface, "I wouldn't have believed it myself if I hadn't strolled on by and saw her shaking her little feathery ass over a campfire."

I voiced the concern I'd actually been asking about. "At least tell me you weren't seen."

"If I was seen, Nat, do you think I would have come waltzing back here?"

"You are *you*," I pointed out. "I wouldn't be surprised if you'd knocked on the front door of the estate, demanded they serve you food, and then berated the servants for not moving quickly enough."

"That was the backup plan," Ren declared. "Luckily, this little one was left unattended near a window, and I decided to banish her loneliness by introducing her to all those foul potatoes in our stomachs."

I sighed. "You could have been caught."

"You're accusing *me* of recklessness? Fuck off." Ren fidgeted, playing with the hem of his coat and suddenly unable to meet my eye. "I just wanted to get you something…I thought you might be hungry after last night."

Oh, the affectionate little snugglemuffin.

I wrapped my arms around his neck and gently knocked my forehead against his. "It's amazing. Thank you for breakfast, *moy knyaz*."

The small, soft exhale he let out went straight to my heart.

We ate the chicken on the doorstep of the lodge, our fingers soon slick with grease and our stomachs pleasantly full. Ren's leg pressed against mine, warm and comforting, and we watched a family of white-furred foxes venture across the frozen lake, the mother diligently herding her young to make sure none of them fell behind.

And then as the sun rose higher in the sky and we ran out of excuses to linger, we packed up everything of use, tossed the remnants of our meal into the snow for the local wildlife, and left behind the little bubble of contentedness we'd managed to carve out for ourselves these last two days. We'd saved some time by cutting across the mountains early without needing to travel all the way up to Cašran Pass, but it would mean nothing if we squandered it by staying any longer.

It had been nice to recuperate, to build up our strength again and spend time in each other's company in a way I knew we wouldn't be able to do once we reached Stavroyarsk, but it was time to leave. Every day that Quareh was in Navar and Welzes' hands was another day that Ren's people – our people? – were subjected to intolerance and inequity, and what of our attempts at building peace with the north? I could feel those hopes slipping further away as everything fragmented around us: my vision of Val turning Ren over to the false king who had stolen his throne, Kolya's death and how we were to explain it to Astrid, the battles on the border…

AN OATH AND A PROMISE

I paused as an idea hit me. It was over a week's walk from the Grachyovs' estate to Stavroyarsk, but if we had horses, we could reach it in less than three days. We didn't have enough money to purchase any, but…

"Ren," I began. "Remember how Commander Grachyov tried to have me killed while I was in Quareh so that Mazekhstam could hide their fuck up from my family?"

My prince growled at my side. "I haven't forgotten what I'd like to *do* to the bastard for that, I promise you."

"Well, I was just thinking he owes me a lot more than a chicken."

Ren's expression perked up at that. "Are you suggesting we engage in some petty thievery?"

I grinned back at him. "I'm suggesting we engage in *very* petty thievery."

*

Chapter Twenty-Two

Ren

"You know when you do that thing I don't like?" I asked as our stolen horses plodded their way down the street, the salt which was used by the locals to melt snow crunching under their hooves.

Mathias snorted. "You mean talking?"

"Hmm. Close," I said. "I don't mind you talking *sometimes*, Mat. Like when you're sprawled over my bed and begging for it."

"So, never?"

I eyed him with amusement. *Mi gato montés* lived in permanent denial, and no matter how many exquisite noises and pleas I pulled from his lips while in the moment, he disavowed each one when he sobered up.

"I meant the thing where you're occasionally right," I told him, and waved a gloved hand at the city around us. Grey stone buildings cast long shadows at our feet, each one dauntingly imposing in both size and grandeur, with tall peaks and spires straining at the sky. Icicles glittered from windowsills, parapets, the edges of roofs; equal parts stunning and dangerous. "Stavroyarsk is beautiful."

Mat looked surprised. "I didn't think it would be to your tastes."

I hummed as he drew his horse to a halt and I followed suit. "To live? No. But it is indeed a thing of wonder to visit…or to flee to in a desperate attempt to save one's own country."

My boots hit cobblestones and salt as I dismounted, perhaps the first Aratorre in nearly a century to set foot on the streets of Mazekhstam's capital. Mat muttered something in his native language to a boy in furs who was crouched nearby, tossing him a silver piece from the money we'd stolen from the Grachyovs along with the horses – courtesy of a stablehand enjoying a liquid lunch and an impressive distraction on my part that had proven largely unnecessary – and the child eagerly leapt to his feet to take the reins from our hands.

I turned my face away as I passed over my horse, but he didn't even bother to peer up into the shadows of my hood, clearly too excited at what the money might bring him to be curious about its payers.

It was certainly a lot easier to hide me in the north than it had been Mathias in the south: up here, everyone wore thick furs that covered every inch of their skin, including hoods pulled low and scarves wrapped over the bottom half of their faces to keep out the biting chill. It was difficult to determine even a person's gender or size when everyone was bulked up with several layers, and no one had gotten close enough to recognise my southern complexion beneath it all.

I'd also noticed that many of the travellers we had encountered on the road these last three days wore the uniquely Mazekhstani ushankas, eared fluffy hats which had me snickering at how absurd they looked until Mathias had donned one himself. And then the only descriptor my head was capable of supplying was *fucking hot*.

Yet my newly conceived fantasy of having him ride me while wearing it had to be frustratingly put on hold, as the walls of the inns we stayed at were as thin as they were on the rest of the continent and my lover was far too loud – although *that* gave me an idea for later – for such activity to have gone unnoticed. A charge of sodomy bore a sentence of a brutal flogging that usually resulted in death, and would have compromised our plans somewhat.

Because despite our pledge not to go near anymore inns, we'd no longer had a choice: the weather was just too cold this far north to sleep out under the stars without the benefit of a shitload of equipment we didn't have. As Mathias rationalised, if we were recognised we were more likely to be dragged before the Mazekhstani regent than single-handedly hauled back to Máros, considering the embattled border and the south's hatred of northerners. We preferred to present before Panarina of our own accord and not shackled like a pair of criminals, but with the eventual destination the same, the risks of travelling on main roads were lower than they had been to date.

It had brought a great sense of relief to have drawn so close to Stavroyarsk that the road signs to the capital had started to appear, the mile indicators steadily ticking down. Weathering the cold and the antsy temperament of my horse had been enough of a distraction to keep my mind from dwelling on the impossible task that lay ahead, although I'd been busy formulating plans for how we could try to convince the regent to help us.

"That's the Panarins' castle," Mat said now, nudging my shoulder with his own as we moved into a cross street as if he was worried I wouldn't notice the towering structure blocking out the sky ahead of us. As with the rest of the buildings lining the main streets of the city, the architecture of the castle *glowered*, looming and bristling, and the glimmering ice along its edges lent it the impression of further sharpness. Maybe beautiful was the wrong word after all – and in that case, I should really take back what I'd said about the brat being right – because there was a threatening menace around it all that infected its beauty and instead made it...hauntingly impressive. Majestic, yet ominous. Grand, but also forbidding.

"You grew up in *there*?" I said, blowing out a breath that fogged the air before my face. "No wonder you were so sullen and boring when I met you."

He shot me an adoring look. "And the impact on *you* from living among all the sex statues which adorn *la Cortina* is too obvious to point out."

I laughed. "Blame not the statues but a vivacious young courtier who ruined my innocence in a single whirlwind night," I said, remembering little more than bright green eyes, a laughing mouth, and an introduction to sexual pleasure that had left me ravenous for more.

"I don't think I've ever asked you about your first," Mathias mused, leading me through a maze of streets and alleyways. Northerners bustled past us, arms ladened with furs and sacks and crates. "How old were you?"

Then he paused, pulling a face. "Do I want to know?"

"I don't know," I said. "Do you?"

"No," he decided after a moment. "But was there ever anyone more…permanent? Like me?"

"There's no one like you, *mi amor*," I said, leaning in to kiss him and then remembering the danger just in time. I pretended to be craning my neck to admire the castle above us instead.

Mat shot me a sympathetic smile, but it was strained.

I lowered my voice. We were speaking Mazekhstani so as to not draw attention, and while I didn't think anyone was close enough to overhear us, the streets were busy and anyone could be watching without our noticing.

"You're the only one who has ever been about more than the physical, Mathias."

"What about Jiron?"

I shrugged off the pang that the name invoked in me, using the memory of his disappearance to fuel my determination in seeing this shit with Panarina through. "We're friends. He works for me. Occasionally we slept together. Each thing did not affect the others."

"But he was assigned to you when you were five," Mat said, and I was impressed — and perhaps a little touched — that he'd remembered such a detail. "He practically raised you. Didn't that make it weird when you..." He trailed off awkwardly, clearly embarrassed and rolling his hands as if expecting them to finish his words for him.

"Fucked him?" I asked, amused. "Not really. I was of age when we began, and it's not like we're related."

"But he was still a father figure for you," Mathias pointed out, clearly determined to torture either himself or me by reminding me of all I'd lost.

I met his eyes, feeling a chill run through me that had nothing to do with the Blessed weather. "I already had a father, Mat. And I knew from early on that if that was what a father did, I didn't want another."

He swallowed, looking at his boots.

"Why are we talking about my past partners?" I asked, worry starting to gnaw at me. "Do you think there's been anyone since you?"

"No," Mat said. Clear and unequivocal, stated like fact: *no*. He could be insecure at times, mostly about his own value, but he never insulted me by doubting what I told him I felt for him. "I trust you."

That made me warm and giddy and disproportionately happy, messing with my insides like only he could.

My northerner's hands fidgeted again, fingers locking and unlocking with each other as if to hold himself back from reaching out to touch me. "I'm taking you to meet Zovisasha and Lilia," he reminded me.

We'd talked about this during our ride here, after getting over the thrill of stealing the Commander's horses. Directly approaching the castle risked

Grachyov and his soldiers intercepting us before we could reach Panarina, and as we'd attempted to expose the man's treacheries against the regent after Kolya Panarin had confessed his role, there was a good chance that we'd end up diverted into somewhere dank and forgotten rather than escorted to the throne room. Mathias had told me that his friends knew a way into the castle, and I was curious to meet the women who had once...

Oh.

"Are you that worried about me meeting *your* past partners, *mi cielo*?" I asked, teasing. "All two of them, you promiscuous wench?"

Mathias huffed out a ragged breath. "I suppose there's no point telling you to behave?"

"None," I replied cheerfully. "Is this it?"

We'd come to a halt before a row of squat little houses, each joined to another by a shared wall. Through the tiny gaps between every second house I could see Stavroyarsk's river, the water's surface kept clear of ice by the frequent traffic passing up and down it; boats and rafts of all shapes and sizes. Glancing between a pair of houses that looked identical other than for their mirrored nature, down to the colourful green paint adorning the doors and the sea glass windchimes in the windows, he eventually jerked his head at the one on the right.

Had it been so long since he was last here that he'd forgotten where his friends lived? A flush of guilt passed through me at the thought: it had been *me* who had taken him from his life here, and while all I wanted was for him to be happy, I couldn't deny how we'd met. If Mathias had been an inch less obstinate, or clever...or simply less *lucky*, he might have faced his end in Quareh with those he cared for never knowing what had happened to him.

"Chimney," he said now, watching me with a faintly amused expression as if he could read my thoughts like one of the Hearken, the fifth branch of Blessed that complemented the Voice, Touch, Scent and Sight. Five sense-based branches of magic, their origins lost to history but their deeds recorded through the eons. Miraculous cures, villainous compulsions, eerie prophecies: the Blessed did not number many but seemed to feature in a disproportionate amount of tales. Everyone loved hearing about magic used to save the day or threaten the hero, even if in reality, the Blessed were lumped with skills that were difficult to wield and merely put targets on their backs. Mat was lucky:

as a prince, he wouldn't be drafted into working as a seer, although I'd bet against anyone who tried to make him do what he didn't want to do, royalty or no.

"Hmm?"

"Smoke coming out of the chimney," he repeated patiently, gesturing at where it curled from the roof of the house on the right. "They're in Lilia's house today. You'll always find them together; it's just a matter of working out where."

I followed him to the correct door, bemused, and he hammered his fist on the bright green wood in a distinctive pattern. High-pitched shrieks immediately sounded from inside the house, followed by excited chattering.

"It's him!"

"I know it's *him,* you-"

"Of course you know because I said it-"

"Just get the door-"

"I'm getting the door!"

The door opened to reveal a black-haired Mazekhstani woman with ivory skin, striking eyebrows, and full lips. She pursed those same lips as she looked at Mathias, her face completely expressionless as if it was a stranger who stood on her doorstep.

"No thank you," she said politely, and shut the door again in his face.

I glanced at my lover, alarmed, only to find him grinning broadly. He shook his head and twisted the door handle, stepping through into the gloom beyond without waiting for an invitation. I followed with rather more hesitation, flinching as something fast and squealing and *red* pounced on my boy.

"Lilia!" Mat laughed, his voice muffled by the curls of copper hair that obscured his face as the woman hugged him tightly. He wrapped his arms around her slender waist and turned on the spot, diverting the momentum of her excitable leap into a spin so they didn't both end up on the floor.

"Nathanael!" she exclaimed happily, clapping her hands to his cheeks and pushing them together to distort his face as one might do a child. He dropped her back to the floor and pulled out of her hold, glaring, before turning to the one who'd first opened the door.

"Zovisasha."

The dark-haired woman narrowed her eyes. "You expect me to greet you with the same exuberance?" she asked him icily, jerking her chin at Lilia. "You disappeared for months without a word."

"I was fucking *captured*," Mat said with clear indignation, only earning himself a dismissive snort and folded arms. He didn't seem upset by her aloofness, turning to me and eagerly dragging me forward by the arm.

"This is-"

"We know who he is," Lilia cut in.

"You two are the talk of the city," Zovisasha added.

"Of Mazekhstam."

"The continent."

"The world."

"The-"

"We get it," Mathias said.

"He is *very* pretty," Lilia cooed, fluttering her eyelashes at me. "Now we see why you would risk the lash, Nathanael. Look at those legs! His lips!"

Mat groaned. "Please stop objectifying him."

"Why?" one of them asked.

"We've never stopped objectifying *you*," the other said.

"Or did you think it was you we missed?"

"Because it was your…"

Mat flushed and they both giggled, clearly not serious.

"Please continue," I said graciously. Mathias flashed me a warning look that I chose to ignore. "Tell me about *all* of your favourite parts of him."

"My tolerance and sense of humour," he growled out, displaying neither as he smacked me on the arm.

"And your distaste for violence," I said pointedly, trying not to cackle too loudly when he scowled. The women displayed no such restraint, their laughter echoing around the small room that was filled with simple wooden furniture, thick furs, and brightly coloured woven cloth used as everything from blankets on the bed, to curtains, to rugs on the floor. A fire licked hungrily behind a grate, dangerously close to a haphazard collection of plants spilling from their pots.

"Oh, I'm just *so* happy you're back!" one of the women exclaimed joyfully, and with how excited and pleased she sounded, I expected it to be Lilia. So I was confused when Zovisasha flung herself at Mat and pulled him into a long hug that he eagerly returned. Maybe she'd just needed time to come around?

But then I noticed the sulky glare Lilia was now gracing my lover with, and how her shoulders had stiffened.

"Fuck you, Nathanael," the redhead snapped. "You turn up out of the blue and expect us to be happy about it?"

I opened my mouth and then closed it again, utterly confounded.

"Cease your games for an hour, I beg you," Mathias pleaded, finally unwrapping himself from Zovisasha's embrace. "You're going to give Ren a headache." He offered me a rueful smile. "They're never…"

Both women stared at him with raised eyebrows and he seemed to carefully reselect his words.

"*Still*," he said, his shoulders visibly relaxing when they both just shrugged, as if he'd narrowly escaped a death sentence.

Zovisasha flapped a hand. "Unless you boys are here for some fun," – she glanced at me hopefully and I grinned, both of us deflating when Mat shook his head firmly – "then I expect you want something. What is it?"

"Ren and I need to speak to Astrid," he said, "without telling the entire continent we're here, which means the front gates are out."

Lilia clicked her tongue. "So what do you want us to do about it?"

"I know you know of another way in," Mat cajoled, dropping his voice into soft imploration.

"We've told you a hundred times. We can't–"

AN OATH AND A PROMISE

"Can't sneak Mazekhstam's hostage out of the castle because two dozen guards would be on us in moments, yes," Mathias said, rapidly firing off the words as though they'd indeed been relayed that many times. "But how about sneaking an ex-hostage *into* the castle?"

The women glanced at each other.

"I suppose we could-"

"As long as no one found out it was us-"

"Not really fancying being hung anytime soon-"

"My plants would die without me-"

"I *wish* your plants would-"

"We'll do it."

Mat smiled at them, his expression fond. "Thank you."

"And what do we get in return?" Lilia asked, flicking her hair back from her face. She gave us both a sly look that I greatly approved of. "Two extremely hot men willing to let us ride their faces all night?"

"There are a pair of horses tethered half a mile down the road that you can sell," I told them as Mat began to splutter indignantly, and I waved a hand in a random direction because I had no idea which way we were now facing. "Two piebalds, one with an attitude as bad as this one."

I slapped him around the back of the head and he bared his teeth at me, instantly sobering from his embarrassment. "As you can see. Apologies, señoritas, but I will be keeping Nat's mouth entirely occupied tonight."

"*Ren*," he hissed, humiliation returning to pinken his cheeks once more, but his eyes were wide as he glanced at the others. When they snorted out their own amusement at his expense, he frowned. "You're not...it doesn't bother you that Ren and I are...?"

Zovisasha scoffed when he trailed off. "You think we" – she gestured between herself and Lilia – "never got bored waiting for you to decide you were in the mood and had to take matters into our own hands? Once a month might have been enough for you, Nathanael, but we have needs."

Once a month. Dios. My boy was certainly making up for it now.

Mathias stared at them both as if he'd never seen them before. I nudged his arm and he cleared his throat, blinking rapidly.

"Of course," Lilia added with delight, her gaze flicking between us. "It does make sense now why your heart was never really in it."

Zovisasha grinned and glanced back at me, shamelessly looking me over from head to toe.

"He's not nearly as ugly as she said he was-"

"She said *crazy-*"

"And arrogant-"

"And rude-"

"And demanding-"

"And also ugly-"

"You couldn't possibly be talking about me," I protested. "Only half of those are true."

And who was *she* who was allegedly saying such things? The insults could have come from Panarina, but I didn't expect the regent generally hung around with commoners and shit-talked foreign royals.

Yet both women ignored me, continuing to interrupt each other's chattering as they moved around the small house, one filling an iron kettle with water and hooking it over the fire while the other rummaged in a rack of jars.

"He'd look sexy in a crown-"

"*Anyone* would look sexy in a crown-"

"You delightful *whore!*"

"You can talk. Didn't you-"

"I did. But that was one time. Or maybe six-"

"Or seven-"

"Or eighteen times-"

"But the point is-"

"What is the point?"

"I've rather forgotten," one of them said, and then the other turned and fixed us with a smile.

"Your brother didn't wear a crown when he visited us," she accused Mathias.

"I heard you tried to poison him, Zovisasha," he responded easily, and the black-haired woman gave a guilty shrug. I eyed the jar of herbs clutched in her hand with alarm.

"Just *one* cup of tea before we go, Your Ruthlessness," she said coaxingly, mischief flaring behind her eyes. As I prepared to call on every scrap of diplomacy I'd ever learned in an attempt to get out of drinking anything she prepared for me, I felt Mat stiffen at my side.

"I *know* that name," he said.

So did I. It sounded like the nonsense Starling used to call me.

The door at our backs opened to let in a fresh gust of cold air.

"I hope you're not expecting me to curtsy, prince," came a voice behind us, speaking Quarehian. Mathias sucked in a surprised breath.

"Would be nice," I retorted on instinct, staring at the girl I'd thought I'd never see again as she strode into the room and tossed her fur coat over the back of a chair as if she belonged here. Her frizzy brown curls sprang free as soon as she removed her hood. "So this is where you ran off to, Estrella."

*

Chapter Twenty-Three

Mat

"*Star?*" I croaked, half-convinced she was an apparition I'd dreamed up from the stress of our journey. Maybe *all* of this impossibleness was a hallucination, including the revelation that my two oldest friends had apparently lain together in direct violation of Mazekhstani laws – multiple times – and didn't give a shit that I'd declared my love for another man. But the tight hug Starling pulled me into disabused me of that notion, if only for the fact that it *hurt*.

"You're pinching me," I complained, yet she just *shhh*ed me, clutching me tighter and continuing to painfully squeeze my arm.

"I'm just making sure this is real," the healer murmured, her thoughts seemingly drifting in the same direction as mine. "Isn't that what they say to do when working out if something is a dream?"

"*Yourself,*" I protested. "Not someone else."

"Oh." She finally let me draw back, a wicked smile on her face. "Maybe that's why it never worked."

And then there was lots of *can't believe you're here*s and *I'm sorry I left you*s and *look at the state of you* – that last one being directed entirely one way from her to me.

"Well, *really,*" Starling said, planting her hands on her hips and giving me a disapproving glare in that no-nonsense way of hers that made her utterly terrifying. "I made it here without looking like a leprous rat dragged through a ditch, and you're a fucking prince."

I raised my hand to give her the finger. She slapped it away.

I expected Ren to protest the insult or the violence – he liked to imagine he had the monopoly on both of those when they were aimed at me – but when I glanced around I found he'd been backed into a corner by Zovisasha and Lilia, looking suitably distracted and half-horrified as they look turns in fawning over him and yelling at him in that personality-swapping peculiarity they adored so much. Lilia had her arms draped adoringly around his neck, pretending to nibble on his ear, while Zovisasha jabbed a finger into his chest and screeched at him in rapid Mazekhstani for the *nerve of it all* in daring to kidnap me. Yet even as I watched, Lilia's fingernails began to dig into Ren's collarbone and she hissed out angry words about *stealing friends and fucktoys*, with Zovisasha instantly softening and starting to stroke his hand. His head swivelled between them, eyes wide, mouth open, and yet not saying a word.

It seemed Ren had finally met his match in flirtatious capriciousness, although the fact that it had taken two of them to rival him made me smile.

"How did you find them?" I asked Starling, who hummed out her amusement as she watched my friends, who were apparently now *our* friends, ruthlessly torment the prince.

"We found each other," she told me. "I'd spent the journey north healing those I found in need, and by the time I reached Stavroyarsk I'd depleted my magic. Stupid."

"Selfless," I corrected, and her mouth twitched.

"Well, I was barely able to keep my eyes open or my feet beneath me. Ended up damn near fainting in the main square. While it was Blessed amazing not to be looked down on just because of my gender, my skin colour was another matter. Anyone who got close enough to realise I was Quarehian under my furs backed away again pretty sharpish. Except those two."

She nodded at the others. "They brought me out of the snow, gave me a place to recover, and I...never left. I've been able to pay them for board and food by doing some magic for the rich families who don't have their own healers, but when we realised who the other was, I don't think any of us would have let me leave."

Star punched me lightly on the shoulder. "I didn't need their names to know they were the ones you told me about back in *la Cortina*. You have good taste in friends."

When I raised an eyebrow, she laughed.

"No, I'm not counting His Crabbiness. On that one, you're entirely fucked in the head. Although..."

"Although?" I prompted.

AN OATH AND A PROMISE

The healer scowled. "I heard what you two did, with trying to bring peace and all. And that he stood by your side when...don't look at me like that, Mathias. I am capable of admitting I was very slightly, *minusculely* wrong."

"Mat?" asked Ren, his voice wavering into something like fear, and I looked back at him to find Zovisasha holding a chipped clay cup to his lips while Lilia had her hands clamped over his eyes from behind. She gave me a grin filled to the brim with mischief and slid her hands down and around his shoulders, hopping up onto his back and wrapping her legs around his waist. Ren staggered before adjusting to her weight, tucking his hands under her thighs so she didn't fall.

"What's the matter, prince?" Zovisasha purred, trying to pry his mouth open with a sharp fingernail so she could feed him the contents of the cup. "Don't you want to play with us?"

His eyes bore into mine in a silent plea for help, unable to free his hands without dropping Lilia and clearly nervous of what he was about to be made to drink.

But before I could put him out of his misery by assuring him that the herbalist had prepared the tea from the safe jars – it was the tins on the top shelf one had to really watch out for – an unlikely source came to his rescue.

"Let him go," Starling said, barely able to contain her smirk. I blinked, surprised to hear her speaking Mazekhstani. It was heavily accented and faltering, but impressively clear for someone who had been in the country for less than two months. "These two...*como se dice?*" She waved her hands as she searched for the word. "*Drain*. Drain my magic. Always. I do not heal poisoning too, Zov."

Zov? I'd once heard Zovisasha threaten to slice someone's tongue off for daring to shorten her name, and that someone had been *me*. But my oldest friends didn't even blink, reluctantly releasing Ren from their devious clutches.

He cleared his throat and grinned, cockiness immediately restored...although I didn't miss the way he sidled closer to my side. Star hadn't done anything to ease his suspicions about what was in the tea.

The healer held her hand out to him and the prince eyed it with renewed suspicion.

She rolled her eyes and reverted to their native tongue. "Would His Highness do me the absolute honour of placing his royal fingers in mine, or does he fear that his privileged self may catch infectious peasant diseases like *callouses?*"

"You're as bad as him," Ren told her, jerking his head in my direction. I snatched his hand and brought it up to meet hers, and Star wrapped her fingers around ours.

"Hmm," she said after a moment. "You're both suffering from malnutrition and dehydration, there's the beginnings of a mild viral infection in you, prince, and a burn on..."

The healer blinked, dragging her eyes to my left wrist despite it being concealed by the sleeve of my coat. Hot fury ran through me at the reminder.

"Campfire," Ren offered hastily. "Mat got too close when cooking."

Star visibly swallowed. She knew that was bullshit. She'd told me once that her Touch laid human bodies bare to her, and wood generally didn't leave marks in the shape of handprints.

But she flattened her expression into one of nonchalant exasperation and didn't press the matter.

"Careless," she said instead, her tone casual, and when she let go of us I knew she'd erased that final physical trace of Kolya from my skin. "It's all healed. Including the unhealthy amount of alcohol in your bloodstream," she added accusingly when I opened my mouth to thank her.

"Well, there was little else to spend our evenings doing," drawled Ren, deliberately switching back to Mazekhstani to maximise the number of people capable of understanding him, "when the laws of your bothersome country wouldn't let me put this one on his back and-"

I clapped a hand over my prince's mouth, my gratitude at the subject change immediately dispelled. His eyes twinkled with amusement, and I felt his tongue peek out from between his lips to lap at my palm.

"Oh, please," Lilia said. "Like we don't already know what you two get up to."

Zovisasha made overexaggerated kissing noises, which I could endure, but when she offered a teasing wink in my direction and began to demonstrate activities with her hands which went far beyond *kissing*, I felt my face colour. Ren cackled loudly from behind my cupped fingers.

"Indeed," said Starling. She raised a judgmental eyebrow as she spat out the Mazekhstani words. "Not smart place to hide out, Stavroyarsk. You both risk much."

Ren removed my hand from his mouth.

"Is that what you think we're doing here?" he asked, staring unblinkingly at the healer. The tendons in his neck stood out, tension strumming through his posture.

When Star shrugged, the prince let out a low hum that was almost a growl. "We're not hiding. I'm taking it *back*, Estrella," he told her, and the resolve in his voice surprised me. Not at the plan; we'd talked about that many times, but at how seemingly desperate he was to convince Starling to believe his intent. "I will not let Quareh fester in that prick Welzes' hands, and I'm here to ask Astrid Panarina to help me."

Zovisasha snorted. "She'll have your head."

"She *won't*," I snapped, glaring at her.

Ren exhaled slowly, still not taking his eyes off Starling. "She'll have whatever she wants."

"You on your knees, I expect," Lilia mused. She and Zovisasha gazed at Ren, evidently imagining what that would look like, for their faces cracked into identical expressions of delight. I wasn't sure if it was the sexual or political implications that pleased them more, but I didn't dare interrupt the Quarehians' conversation, which was probably the most civil I'd ever seen them be with each other.

"When I do," Ren murmured to the healer, "will you return with us? To Quareh?"

"Is that an order or a request, Your Highness?" Starling asked in their language, glancing down at her feet before meeting the prince's gaze once more.

"A request." He shook his head. "No. A favour. *Por favor.*"

Fuck me. Ren saying please...to *Starling*, no less? The woman he and his family had all but owned, whose magic he had once considered belonged to him?

"I will not be caged again," she spat. "No more forced servitude."

Another head shake. "A job opportunity. I'll pay you a fair salary to work as the palace's healer in Máros."

Starling narrowed her eyes. She didn't answer for nearly a minute, and in that time I swore neither of them even blinked. "Double whatever you consider fair…"

"Done."

She inclined her head slightly in acknowledgement. "…and I will reside in Máros for *half* of each year."

"And the other half?" asked Ren.

"Here," she said simply. "I've been doing some good in Stavroyarsk, and there are many more people who need my help. I will not abandon them."

"Yeah," said Ren, but he was looking at me. A fond smile graced his lips, and he brushed the back of his fingers over my jaw. "I understand."

"Ah," Starling muttered. "Maybe I was more than minusculely wrong after all, Mathias."

—

"This is where we leave you."

With those words, Lilia abruptly stilled in the middle of the corridor, the flames of the wall torches highlighting the glossy bronze strands in her red hair. She cast a glance back at me and Ren, her eyebrows furrowed.

"Coward. We can go further," Zovisasha declared, trying to shoo her friend out of the way.

Lilia folded her arms. "This is practically treason," she hissed back, and they began to bicker in hushed tones.

"We mean your regent no harm," Ren assured them but neither woman seemed to hear him, too intent on winning an argument that didn't need to be had.

"You've done more than enough," I interjected, tugging at Zovisasha's arm as she tried to drag Lilia further along the corridor. "You got us in. Please return home before someone sees you."

Zovisasha deflated beneath my hold. "We have to leave," she insisted, even as Lilia began to draw away...*deeper* into the castle.

"Just a little longer," Lilia taunted, "unless you're scared?"

I blew out an exasperated breath. Now was not the fucking time for this.

"*Go. Home,*" I ordered, attempting to lace my voice with that indisputable dominance Ren did so well. The prince's shoulders shook with silent laughter at my side, but it was the unimpressed expressions of the two women that hit my ego the hardest.

"Are you trying to boss us around, *Nathanael?*"

"I think he's trying to pull rank-"

"Poor, delusional Temarian-"

"Someone should really tell him-"

"He's like a growly little kitten-"

"One with no teeth or claws-"

"Just a ball of cute fluff, really-"

"*Mis queridas,*" Ren said smoothly as he took advantage of their rare united position, "as much as I would love to join you in your appreciation of my boy's adorableness, he's right."

"Oooh, speak sexy Quarehian at us again," Zovisasha cooed, batting her eyelashes at him.

He winked and offered a stream of compliments in his own tongue before gently ushering them both back the way we'd come.

"Thank you for everything," I said, and Lilia beamed at me. She then repeated everything the prince had just said to them, word for word, and as much as I might have found it odd being called a pair of stunning women whose bravery and compassion were outmatched and whose wit kept one gladly on one's terrified toes, I was too busy being impressed at the perfect memory recall to complain.

And then they were gone, sneaking back through the maintenance tunnel and rusted gate they'd brought us in by, and leaving me and Ren alone in the

AN OATH AND A PROMISE

Mazekhstani castle.

It was eerily silent, the heavy stone dampening all noise and light that may otherwise have seeped in if we were back in the airy halls of *la Cortina*, and making it feel like we were in the bowels of the earth. I saw Ren shiver, and knew it wasn't just from the cold.

"This is terrible," he said, but before I could attempt to reassure him, he cracked a grin. "If we *were* here to assassinate the regent, she's making it remarkably easy for us."

I snorted. "We're nowhere near Astrid. Do you have any idea as to the size of this place?" I scuffed my boot against the flagstones, kicking up dust. "Those torches are only lit out of tradition. There's probably a near mile of corridor and stairs before we reach anywhere habitable, let alone the royal chambers. We'll be stopped by guards long before then."

"That's my Mathias," he said. "Always so fucking cheery."

Well, there was the opening to the thing I needed to ask him and yet had been putting off for weeks, too terrified as to his response to have broached it before now. But in mere minutes, it would be too late.

"Ren," I whispered, and it felt like the dust was thickening, clogging up my throat until I could barely speak. I forced the beginning of my question out, but at the last moment changed it to a statement, too afraid of him saying no. "Are you...you need to be prepared to walk away if Astrid asks for something we can't give."

"I told you," he said, somehow managing to answer with a Blessed *no* anyway. "Whatever it takes to help Quareh."

"Not you!" I hissed. "If she demands your life or freedom in return, you don't accept. You hear me?"

"Mathias-"

"No, you'll fucking listen, Ren!" I was shouting at him now, but I didn't care. I grabbed his arm, tightening my fingers and digging in my heels so he couldn't pull away. "You don't get to sacrifice yourself! We're not taking another step unless you promise me that."

"I promise."

AN OATH AND A PROMISE

"Mean it, asshole," I snarled, and he gave an amused huff.

"*Dorogoi?*" I begged, and apparently the musty air was devolving from inconvenience to a major health hazard, because the tears forming in my eyes were clearly due to dust motes and nothing else.

Ren hummed out a low note of distress and raised his thumb to wipe them away.

"I promise," he said softly, and this time I could hear the sincerity in his voice. We pulled each other into a tight embrace, the gravity of what we were about to do seeming to hit both of us at once, far too late and far too close to the end to not see it through. Although, maybe it had never been a choice. Because from the moment I voiced the realisation that Mazekhstam was our last hope for recovering Quareh from Welzes and Navar's slimy clutches, we'd set ourselves on a path we couldn't divert from. Ren cared for his people too much, and I...well. Ren accused me of caring for people *generally* too much, and it was one protest I never won.

"Hands in the air, Quarehian."

Ren tensed and detached himself from me slowly, his eyes darting to something over my shoulder.

"How the fuck did you get in here?" someone barked, their tone incredulous. I heard the sound of steel being unsheathed. "Hands in the *fucking air!*"

Ren complied. I raised my hands too, but there was immediate recognition in the two guards' eyes when I turned around and their gazes flickered to my face, although their swords remained levelled at us.

"Prince Nathanael?" the one with a scar across his chin asked, his brows scrunching so much that they seemed to disappear into the creases on his forehead. I recognised him from my time in the castle, although I'd never learned his name. "I...don't..."

"We need to see the regent," I said. "Now."

His confusion deepened. "You..."

"Yes, me. And him." I began to gesture at Ren and remembered the two deadly pieces of steel clutched in the guards' hands, nodding at him instead. "Please take us to Astrid. It's rather important."

AN OATH AND A PROMISE

Their eyes moved to Ren. "And he is?" the other guard demanded. He was starting to bald, but unevenly, as if someone had plucked huge tufts of hair from the top of his head.

"Prince Renato Aratorre of Quareh."

Their mouths dropped open. It would have been quite comical if the air had not felt charged with danger: one wrong move from either of us, and news of our corpses may never even reach the regent upstairs.

"Please," I said again, and when the pair's expressions didn't change, I tried a different approach. "That's an *order*, soldiers. I may not be a Panarin but I'm still a Blessed prince, so get a move on and escort us to the fucking throne room!"

When they didn't snicker at me like my friends had done but instead snapped to attention, I allowed myself to breathe.

That was hot, Ren mouthed at me.

The two men muttered something to each other and then began to usher us up the corridor, keeping their blades drawn and pointed at our backs. I couldn't object, considering we were two foreign royals who had seemingly magically appeared behind their own walls, but the amount of fussing it caused among the castle guards as our request was passed up through the ranks was exhausting.

Two hours later, Ren had gotten over the 'fun' of the frisk search we'd been subjected to and was starting to torment the guards, testing their patience with overexaggerated sighs and increasingly inappropriate comments.

He managed to systematically drive off all but our original companions that way, sending each of the three higher ranked guards scurrying away with hurriedly tossed excuses about checking on the progress of our request to meet with Astrid. We'd been escorted to the upper levels of the castle so the air was warmer and the surroundings more homely, but a draughty corridor was still a draughty corridor, and even I was beginning to lose my patience.

"I know what you both are," the balding guard spat out unexpectedly, his lips twisting with distaste as he glared between me and Ren. Clearly, he'd been building up the courage to say it. "Disgusting, is what it is. They should put the lot of you down and be done with it."

AN OATH AND A PROMISE

"We don't recall asking your worthless opinion," Ren drawled. Both guards tensed, adjusting their grips on their swords, and he gave them a lazy, unaffected smile. "Imagine, Nat," he added to me, "being so concerned about what others get up to that they feel the need to work themselves up about it."

"It's unnatural," the scarred guard agreed, but there was a hesitation behind the words, a sideways glance at the other man that suggested he was only saying that because it was expected of him. I didn't call him out on it – here in the north, sympathising with sodomites could attract punishment of itself – and was glad Ren didn't either, although he gave them both a contemptuous snort that conveyed how little the prince thought of it all.

"I don't know how you dare show your face here, *Your Highness*," the balding guard said to me disdainfully. "After you outed yourself as one of *them*, do you really think we'd have your kind-"

"Soldier." The word, spoken sharply with dismissal, had the man stepping back into place with a crisp salute. The woman who approached us had been one of those flitting around earlier in the chaos our arrival had caused, and the symbol on her stiff collar marked her as significantly higher in rank than anyone else we'd yet seen.

She gave us an assessing once over and then lay her hand on the hilt of her sword, still sheathed at her hip, in wordless warning for us to stay in line.

"Come. Her Majesty will see you now."

*

Chapter Twenty-Four

Ren

Astrid Panarina of Mazekhstam was nothing like her brother. Despite all his faults, Kolya had been an emotional creature: eager to be liked, easily riled, and throwing his whole self into whatever held his interest at the time. That had led to regrettable results, but as both a reluctant ally and an enemy, the late prince had at least been *attentive*.

The woman seated on the austere Mazekhstani throne could not have shown less interest in our entrance. She gave us one passing, aloof glance before turning back to the grey-haired man hovering at her side, his arms wrapped around a pile of thick ledgers. He murmured something too low for us to hear and she nodded thoughtfully, not even resting her gaze on us but on the grey flagstoned floor as if she found it the more fascinating of the two.

Our guard escort held out an arm to bar us from moving closer. Resisting the urge to push past her and claim the regent's undivided attention, as I might have done if Mat was not at my side and capable of being punished for my disrespect, I reluctantly drew to a halt.

Panarina's blonde hair was tucked neatly under the silver crown that rested on her head, several locks cascading down to her shoulders in such precise, orderly design that it gave the appearance of a portrait rather than a real person. Her hands were folded elegantly across her lap, her legs crossed, and the train of her white dress flowed silkily down the base of the throne and across the dais. Not a strand of hair or fold of cloth had dared to sag or fall out of place, and combined with her disinterested, regal expression, it was though the ethereal royal had been cast from stone.

Offering a faint but lengthy sigh as if this were all a major inconvenience, the regent waved her assistant and his books away and dragged her eyes back to us. When she gestured us forward, Mathias dipped into a formal bow at the foot of the dais and I mirrored his enthusiasm with the slightest forward motion of my head.

"Prince Nathanael," Panarina said, and I thought I saw a crack in her armour for the briefest of moments, a smile that dared to shine through all that steely impassiveness. Yet it was gone before I could even blink. "Prince Renato. My apologies for how long you were kept waiting," she added, her tone insincere.

Knowing how the game was played, I smiled and shook my head. "It was no trouble at all," I responded, making sure I sounded suitably gracious and unconcerned. "We appreciated the chance to catch our breath after our travels."

Mat, somehow having no Blessed clue how to play the game even after all this time, let out a low huff of objection. Thankfully it wasn't loud enough to reach Panarina, and he kept his face carefully neutral so she couldn't read our shared irritation from his face. All three of us were acutely aware that she would have been informed of our presence in the castle within minutes, despite the late hour. Making us wait had been a flex of power and a reminder of how little we held in turn.

The regent said nothing more, watching me from her throne with steady blue eyes that held no emotion. She didn't even look human; a queen of ice both figuratively and literally.

Flour snow, I reminded myself, barely able to believe that this was the same person who featured so regularly in Mathias' tales. Panarina had given a piece of herself to Mat through their friendship, and when he'd entwined his heart with mine, I'd been granted a glimpse of that fragment. Beneath her cold, impassive exterior was a woman who loved confectionery and cakes, who absently chewed on the ends of her hair when she was worried or deep in thought, who had once decorated her rooms in sticky, wet flour. Her haughty, regal exterior was as much an act as my own courtly pretence of don't-give-a-fuck flirtation.

"Regent Panarina," I began cautiously, "we-"

"Queen," hissed our guard sharply, her shoulders rising as if I'd offered great insult.

Mat's breath hitched. "What?"

Panarina let out a soft exhale. "My father passed nearly two weeks ago."

"I'm so sorry, Astrid," Mathias said sombrely, his face crinkling in empathy and looking rather more distraught than the news called for, considering he had barely known the man. My boy was too fucking sweet.

I struggled to keep my emotions from my own expression. King Oleg Panarin had been a bastard and a half, and the cause of many of Quareh's woes over the last few decades, so I certainly wouldn't be shedding a tear over his death. "Whether I offer you condolences or congratulations depends, I suppose."

One of Panarina's pale eyebrows rose fractionally. "On what? Whether he was a good king?"

"Whether he was a good father," I said, and Panarina looked faintly surprised at that before quickly recovering her indifference.

"You missed my coronation, I'm afraid."

I shrugged. "You're invited to mine."

Her smile showed teeth this time. "Forgive me if I hesitate to accept, Aratorre. I heard your first one didn't go so well, and it's remarkably audacious of you to assume there'll be a second."

Mat bristled at my side. "Can we fucking not?" he snapped, glaring at her and then belatedly me as if he was trying not to show favouritism between the two asshole – and exceptionally gorgeous – royals he found himself in the company of. Although he could certainly count himself among us. "You don't like Ren, he doesn't like you. We get it. Let's cut the shit."

Oh, the political suaveness of Nathanael Velichkov. It was an incredible sight to behold, and my heart swelled at his passion; at that no-nonsense way of his that struck at the heart of an issue.

To my surprise, Panarina inclined her head in his direction and stood up from her throne, her white dress seeming to shimmer around her legs as she descended the dais towards us. The heavy stone seat looked even more foreboding without an occupant, looming and bleak, but it was the queen now only feet away from us that held the threat. With a single word or gesture to the many guards lining the walls of the throne room, she could have us both executed.

As a prince in exile, if my country even bothered to give me a royal title anymore considering the lies that had been spread about my heritage, my death would not spur any political ramifications. And Mat's people, many of whom had been eager to see him flayed for his public admission of sodomy, similarly might not care, although I imagined Val and Mila at least would raise hell over it. But if Panarina hid word of our arrival? If she had us quietly killed?

It was a possibility we'd contemplated many times on our journey here. Contemplated and then discarded, for there was nothing that could be done to avert it. Without the resources of Quareh to keep us protected, I had to trust in my wildcat's assurances of Panarina's beneficence.

"We need your help, Astrid," he said. "Help us to free Quareh from the monsters who have taken it."

She gazed at Mathias, tilting her head slightly as if to take him in after all these months of separation. *You owe him*, I wanted to scream. After what Kolya Panarin did, she should be on her fucking knees before my lover.

But it wasn't my story to tell, and Astrid wasn't responsible for the sins of her brother.

"It's the start of a new era," Mat continued, ardent and animated. "You're a new queen. Ren will soon be a new king. Forge peace between you, the same as we began between my family and his, and make a legacy to be celebrated and remembered for centuries to come. Or, you can all continue the pointless bloodshed of your ancestors like puppets pulled around on strings."

His voice dropped to a whispered plea. "Astrid, you have a choice here. Do the right thing?"

"Aratorre has a lot to answer for," Panarina said slowly after a long moment of silence. "He was responsible for taking you from my side at St Izolda's Monastery and making me mourn a great friend for many weeks until Valeri delivered the tremendous news of your survival. But you stand by him, Nathanael?"

"I do." There was no hesitation from Mat, the words thrown out with undaunted surety that made me shoot him an adoring glance. "If you could know him as I do, Your High…Majesty, you would see it. He may have begun as my captor, but beneath Ren's flirting and jokes and fucking eyeliner, he's got a good heart. He has *my* heart."

I blew out a breath. "Please don't undermine *all* of my mystique to the prickly northern queen, Nat."

They both ignored me.

"Then I will hear him out for your sake," Panarina conceded, and then turned her shoulders to re-include me in the conversation. "But not tonight. You both need rest, and I need to consider my…position. The situation here is fragile and this will be a delicate issue to manage, as I'm sure you appreciate."

"Thank you," said Mathias, beaming at us both as though the ink was already drying on a treaty instead of her merely having promised not to take my head in the next few hours.

The queen blew out a breath, suddenly looking tired. She reached up to wrap a strand of hair around her finger and brought it to her mouth, and I tried not to smile as I watched her chew on it fretfully. "I make no guarantees, Nathanael. With my father dead and Kolya still missing-"

"Kolya's not missing," he said quietly, his mood souring. "He's also dead. Really *fucking* dead."

She inhaled sharply at that, her blue eyes flashing with more emotion than I'd seen so far. And not in satisfaction as I might have expected from someone whose sibling had tried to have them killed to steal their royal inheritance, but in *pain*.

"What? How?"

When Mat merely ducked his head, Panarina whirled on me. "Tell me what happened!"

"I thought Nat covered it quite succinctly," I said helpfully. "He's dead."

"By your hand?" Her voice was ice.

"Absolutely."

"Guards!" Astrid screeched. I heard the high-ranked guard at my back draw her sword.

"I don't think you want them to hear this," I said in Quarehian.

"You dare," the queen hissed, having transformed from a serene statue into a rabid, frothing animal, "seek my aid when you murdered my *brother*?"

"Your brother sold you out in the hope you'd die," I reminded her coldly. "He kept your father in a coma and was probably responsible for his eventual death. He got Nathanael captured, he conspired with Commander Grachyov to take your throne, and most unforgivably of all-"

Mathias' shoulders tensed as if expecting a physical blow. But what Kolya had done in Temar wasn't something I was going to yell out in the middle of the castle.

"-he tried to kill Nat at the tournament, Panarina. So no, I don't give a fuck that your brother is dead, and I only wish it had happened before he'd had the chance to hurt and murder as many people as he did."

She faltered, her hand shooting up to cover her mouth.

"Astrid," my lover said gently, putting aside his own feelings to protect her from hers in that selfless streak of his that I both loved and despaired over. "I know Kolya could be sweet, at times, but he lost his way. We're sorry it came to that, but Ren really had no choice."

Panarina swallowed, her eyes shooting to his and seeming to take comfort in whatever she saw in their depths. And then she made a careless gesture and the guards retreated back to their original positions, weapons once again sheathed at their sides.

"Yes, I...I know my brother was not always...on my side," she said delicately, and in the twist of her mouth I saw hints of their turbulent relationship, that of both hate and love. "Or that of anyone but himself. But I..." She drew herself up to her full height and seemed to snap out of her grief in the way that royals were forced to do, her voice returning to the brusqueness it had been steeped in when we arrived.

"*Da*. I am willing to consider your plea, Prince Aratorre, before I make any decision on whether to assist you and your country. And normally I would invite you both to dine with me," the queen continued dispassionately, "but considering the circumstances and Quareh's demands for your heads, I think it best you stay in your rooms until I call for you."

"*Rooms*?" I asked, a low growl creeping into my tone as I noted the use of the plural. I stepped closer to Mat, threading his fingers through mine. "You're not separating us."

She looked down at where our hands were joined and narrowed her eyes.

"I will remind you that you are in the north, gentlemen," she said, averting her gaze back to our faces with a cool stare. "I expect I will already have to navigate demands from my court for Nathanael's arrest on the sodomy charge he invoked on himself: do *not* make it worse for yourselves."

AN OATH AND A PROMISE

"If you leave Mat on his own and Commander Grachyov finds-"

"Nikolai Grachyov is no longer my Commander," Panarina told us sharply. "Nikolai Grachyov no longer *is*."

Mathias and I glanced at each other.

"Did you think I would not heed your warnings in your letter to me?" Astrid asked, looking almost exasperated. "I had him investigated and then executed when I secured proof of his treason, along with those helping him. Grachyov is no longer a threat to you, Nathanael, and I regret that is another thing I did not see sooner."

A wave of her hand, and our guard began to politely, but very firmly, guide me back to the door we'd entered through.

"But despite your preferences or objections, I do not need the strife you two would otherwise cause me," Panarina said, and her tone held a note of despairing finality. "You will be given adjoining guest rooms to rest in for the duration of your stay, but the door between will be securely locked. Do *not* attempt to use it."

Mathias let out a low hum, but to my surprise, didn't even try to argue with her. And when I realised that I was being escorted out without him, my hissed demands to stay at his side resulting in nothing more than fingers folding around my arm so the guard could unceremoniously *drag* me out, he surprisingly didn't protest that either.

"Mat!"

"It's okay, Ren," he said, and his warm, reassuring smile even made me believe the deceitful little wretch, despite everything else in this place screaming out danger. He turned to watch me go, seemingly unbothered by the dangerous ice queen at his back, and mouthed out a little *I love you* as the heavy doors of the throne room slammed closed between us.

—

The servant finished with my hair and removed the towel that had been draped over my shoulders. She adjusted the cushions behind my back for the fourth time since she'd seated me here after my bath, but I still didn't lean back into the armchair's embrace, too on edge to relax.

"Would you like me to ready you for bed, Prince Renato?"

"No, that will be all," I said absently, staring at the door of the bedchamber I'd been ushered into over two hours ago.

Mat would come, I knew he would. Even if he was meant to be confined to his room as I was, his stubborn ass would manage to beg or trick his way in here.

It was then I realised the servant had given me an obvious opening for flirtation with her offer, and I hadn't even *thought* about taking it. The Mazekhstani was pretty, perhaps unconventionally so, but beauty had always been a secondary consideration to enthusiasm when inviting someone to my bed.

Yet when I opened my mouth it was to thank her for her assistance instead of making myself feel better with a lewd comment, as gratitude was what *he* always gave those who helped him, regardless of their status. The servant blinked, the frosty, professional demeanour she'd shown me up until now melting into a genuine smile.

"You're welcome, Your Highness," she said warmly. "Please have me called for if you require anything else."

I craned my neck hopefully as she left, but saw nothing through the doorway but the grey, monotonous stone of the corridor and the guard who approached wordlessly to relock the door as though I was a prisoner here.

I blew out a shaky breath. I *was* a prisoner here. Panarina held all of the power, and whether she justified it as for our safety or hers, I wasn't going anywhere without her permission. If she decided that it was better for her newly crowned ass to hand me over to Welzes and Navar, there was nothing I could do to stop it.

All that stood between me and that fate was the worth she assigned to hers and Mathias' friendship, and the distaste I could only assume she held for the misogynistic beasts currently in control of my country. But hey, she might consider me the same as them: as I'd seen with Alta, my own fucking best friend, my politically cautious approach towards the rights of women in my country had made me no better than those who actively enforced such laws. I could swear all I liked that it was going to change, but words were just words, and what reason did the queen of Mazekhstam have to believe me?

I continued to stare at the door, hearing something rustle behind me but assuming it to be nothing more than the crackle of the fire in the grate. Mathias would open that door any moment and I couldn't look away, didn't want to miss even a second of his wry grin and those blue-grey eyes that-

And then a hand slid around my throat from behind, fingers resting below my jaw and gently squeezing.

Pleasure shot through me, but for once, the arousal was less potent than the feeling of sheer *relief*.

He was here.

Mat let go of my neck and climbed over the back of the chair into my lap, clearly too impatient to spare the extra second to walk around. Sharing the sentiment, I gathered him close, relishing his warmth and making little exclamations of happiness in his ear.

"How did you get in here?" I asked after I got him settled in my arms.

"The connecting door between our rooms," he said, snuggling in against my chest.

I twisted around in the chair to look at the door in question – made more difficult by the Temarian prince curled up on my lap, not that I was complaining – and frowned as I found it thrown wide open.

"But...Panarina said it would be locked," I protested, rather upset with myself that I hadn't even thought to try it.

"Ah," Mat murmured, tracing my shaven jaw with a finger and evidently pleased that I'd lost the beard I'd earned in our travels, for he began to kiss and nibble at the freshly exposed skin with contented noises of approval. "She had her *listen to my eyes not my words* voice on when she said that."

I stroked his own beard, enjoying the scratch of it against my fingertips. While I also preferred him clean-shaven, what I loved even more was knowing that he'd eschewed his own bath in favour of coming to see me first. Coming from Mathias, that was one hell of a compliment.

"So she wants us to fuck?" I asked dubiously.

Mat snorted. "I doubt she *wants* that. More...that she doesn't care if we do. Tolerance rather than approval is the sense I got, although it's now making me wonder what Astrid knew about Kolya's preferences."

He hummed against my skin, sending delicious tremors through me. "You were waiting for my return?"

"You know I was, asshole," I said, feeling grumpy and sulky and overwhelmingly jealous that the queen had had his attentions all night. "Mathias, you were gone for hours!"

He pressed an apology to my lips in the form of a soft kiss. "We needed to talk. About everything that happened since I..."

"Gave your life for hers and ended up imprisoned in my cells?"

Mathias pulled a face and wriggled on my lap. My hands fell to his waist to keep him still.

"Not...Kolya. I couldn't leave her with that memory of him." The dead Mazekhstani prince didn't deserve Mat's protection, but I understood. He'd done it for the sister, not the brother. "But everything else, *sí.*"

"You told the queen of Mazekhstam all the sordid details of our sex life?" I asked smugly, unable to maintain such a draining, negative emotion as *grumpiness* for long.

He rolled his eyes. "There were no sordid details shared. No details at *all*, Ren."

"Well, then I can't imagine why it took you so many hours to relay everything," I said.

Mat shot me a knowing smile. "Were you *lonely*, darling?"

Fearing a trap if I answered honestly, I shared another truth instead. "I was worried about you."

"I was fine. Astrid's a sweetheart."

"She's terrifying," I said flatly.

"Val said that too," he told me, and my boy frowned as if he couldn't possibly imagine why we might both think that. "But she's just...she's nice."

Not the word I'd choose to describe a woman I'd be afraid of cutting myself on in the unlikely event she deigned to touch me, but one he'd frequently used in the past.

"She also needed to grieve Kolya," Mat added quietly. "I couldn't just leave her alone."

My heart lurched at his words. Because fuck, *of course* the self-sacrificing *idiota* wouldn't think twice about offering his friend comfort in the wake of her brother's death, despite the cost on his own soul of doing so. I couldn't even begin to imagine listening to someone reminisce fondly about your fucking *rapist*.

I didn't care that Astrid wasn't aware of the full extent of what Kolya had done to Mat. She knew enough of it, of his actions at the tournament if nothing else, and yet had still sent me away. He'd had to endure hours alone with his secret, his sweet nature compelling him to help her even as it forced him to relive his own trauma.

I gripped him tighter, burying my face in his hair until I could compose myself. I couldn't afford to fall apart in front of him, as he'd take the responsibility for fixing that, too.

Mathias settled in, seeming content to be snuggled without needing to speak.

"You should bathe while the water's still hot. Where's your servant?" I asked when I could be sure my voice wouldn't crack.

My lover made a noise that was mostly a grunt of complaint. "Gone to bed, I imagine. I told them I didn't need anyone waiting on me."

"Nathanael," I said disapprovingly, although I couldn't be mad. Not with him, and especially not with that endearing quality of his that made him awkwardly embarrassed to be served, as if that wasn't at least half the fun of being royalty.

"I don't need a servant to attend me," Mathias said slowly, deliberately pausing to draw the rest of the sentence out, "...when I have a prince to do it?"

He cracked an eye, peering up hopefully from where he was cradled against my chest to check my reaction to that statement, and it meant I couldn't even attempt to hide the surprised, delighted laugh that bubbled up my throat.

"Oh, *mi corazón*. It would be my absolute pleasure to take care of you."

I extracted us from the armchair – with difficulty, as his limbs had spilled into each crevasse and angle like wine poured into a goblet – and directed him into the adjoining bedchamber. It was decorated identically to mine but in a reverse layout, and a tin bath full of water waited on the rug in front of the flickering fire. Filled by hand, the poor fools.

Mathias began to shrug off his coat, but I steered his hands away and guided it from his shoulders myself. Untucking his shirt from his trousers, I slid my hand up his chest, slowly undoing it as I went and relishing the warmth of his skin beneath my fingers.

I moved without urgency, savouring each inch of skin I exposed as I continued to remove his clothes as carefully and languidly as unwrapping a gift. Not that I'd *ever* unwrapped gifts slowly, being an impatient bastard at heart, but perhaps I should do it more often, because this was a treat all in itself. It didn't matter how many times I'd seen him naked before: each brush of my fingertips or knuckles against his skin felt like something new and precious, and as I leisurely stripped Mat bare, I realised we were both trembling.

When I led him to the bath he sank down into it pliantly, letting out a soft sigh as the heat enveloped his legs and chest. The water sloshed gently against the edges of the tub. I lifted his chin so I could apply the thick lathering soap around his jaw, enjoying running my fingers through his beard in its final moments before I began to scrape it off.

The blade flashed, sharp and deadly as it carved across his throat again and again, yet Mathias never once flinched. To be utterly trusted like this; to hold his life in my hands and not glimpse even a fraction of doubt or fear on his face?

Mathias' eyes had fluttered closed amidst all the sensation, and I paused for a moment to watch him without being observed in turn. His expression was serene, his shoulders heaved with each of his deepening breaths, and his arms rested loosely at his sides.

There were times, like now, that I still couldn't believe that he was mine.

Mine to protect. Mine to care for.

And I was his.

Carefully setting aside the straight razor, I wrapped a hand around the clean, slightly irritated skin of his neck – not tightly, as I knew he panicked when he lost his air – but possessively. Keeping him where I wanted him, and I felt his body surrender to that control, his throat bobbing against my palm as he swallowed.

When I dragged my gaze to his face, I found Mat watching me. Quietly, patiently, his storm-coloured eyes full of keen acceptance.

I dropped my head and ghosted my lips along the dip of his collarbone in silent reply, fingers dropping down beneath the water to trace his spine and those dimples in his back I loved so much.

Wet skin shimmered in the firelight, his and mine.

My lover sighed in contentment, letting me manoeuvre him into place as I lathered more soap and began to drag a washcloth over each part of his body. First his chest and shoulders, and then his arms, carefully drawing the cloth across his alabaster skin and dipping it back into the warm water. When I parted his knees to clean between his legs, Mathias gave a delighted, breathy moan, which made me linger there longer than I'd intended before instructing him to lean forward.

Wrapping his arms around his legs, my boy rested his chin on his knees and I realised he looked exhausted. His eyes were drooping closed, and he gave a small start at the splash of the cloth dropping into the water after I'd washed his back slowly and reverently. We'd been on the road since dawn, and it was now well past midnight.

Not to mention the pressure of his past colliding with his present, including reuniting with the only people in Mazekhstam who, to my knowledge, had ever given a damn about him.

Mat needed to sleep, and I wanted nothing more than to spend the next few hours just holding onto him as he did so, letting his soothing presence wash away my own exhaustion and fears. So I helped him stand and then as he swayed on his feet, looking like he might pass out any moment, patted his skin dry with a towel. This time my movements were brisk rather than idle, and I quickly ushered us both into his bed, stripping from my own clothes and pulling the blankets up over us both.

I gathered him into my arms, humming out my intent and pressing a kiss to that spot behind his ear that made him whine.

"Try not to worry about anything for a while," I murmured to him, and on the precipice of unconsciousness Mathias used the last of his energy to smile sleepily at me.

AN OATH AND A PROMISE

"I don't need to worry, Ren. You're here."

Chapter Twenty-Five

Mat

The whipping posts stood menacingly in the city square, easy to spot even from the window of my room in the castle high above. Thankfully they remained unoccupied, Stavroyarsk's citizens rushing past with their heads bowed to the sleety wind and sacks of food tucked in their arms, and seemingly unconcerned about the instruments of torture – and death – that loomed so close. Yet my mind all too easily dredged up memories of the leather restraints cutting into straining flesh, hot blood dripping down into the snow, the agonised screams of the men and women sentenced to the ruthless bite of the whip.

The posts were used for more than sodomy and the other alleged sexual deviancies, but those were the crimes that most frequently saw the death of the person sentenced. I'd never been someone who made a point of watching the floggings being carried out, but fuck, you couldn't live in this city and avoid such spectacles entirely. I'd been lucky that my old rooms had been situated on the opposite side of the castle, because every time I looked out of the window now, it forced me to confront the grim reminder of how the north judged me and Ren. Of the future the Temarian seer Aksinia had once predicted for me, describing how I'd be outed and dragged to the whipping posts, just as it had played out only a couple of days later. If it hadn't been for Jiron and Valeri refusing to let the men go through with it, I might not even be standing here.

The north had to change. For everyone. For every child who believed there was something wrong with them, for every unhappy adult chastising themselves for a fantasy. For every person flogged or imprisoned or killed for daring to act on who they were.

There was little else to do but dwell on such things when I was alone like this, the door between our rooms firmly closed while the castle seamstress waited on the prince, because we'd been sequestered in these rooms for days. If it wasn't for Ren's company, I would have gone Blessed crazy, and I knew he was only barely keeping it together.

My lover was an extrovert who gained his energy from being surrounded by people. He was also enough of a narcissist to need those people to love him.

And I did love him, so fiercely it hurt, but I wasn't capable of the same group worship offered by an entire palace. A *country*. Being locked away was a particular kind of torture to a man as gregarious as Renato Aratorre, and I wondered how much of that was by Astrid's design.

The guards outside our doors had obviously been ordered to give us anything we wanted, for any request we'd made had been fulfilled — Ren had been enthusiastically testing the limits of that generosity by making increasingly absurd demands, but he hadn't been denied yet — except to allow us to leave our gilded prison cells. Or to see the queen apparently, for while generic holding messages were delivered from her each day requesting our patience, she neither visited nor invited us to do so.

I heard the adjoining door click open and glanced over my shoulder to find Ren slipping through it, his face broadening into a wide smile as he spotted me by the window.

"What do you think, *mi cielo?*"

My prince performed a flamboyant little twirl in front of me, spinning around on an elegant heel. Complete with an entirely needless and yet fucking sexy flick of his long dark hair.

"Where did all this come from?" I asked. I ran my fingers reverently across the embroidery that hadn't been on his clothes when I last saw him, the plain Mazekhstani shirt and coat transformed into a whirlwind of colour and intricate shapes that drew the eye. It wasn't exactly Quarehian dress, but it was far from the usual blandness of northern clothing.

"I persuaded the seamstress to add some necessary style," he retorted, his eyes glimmering with mirth at the overt mockery.

I raised an eyebrow. "And how much flirting did that take?"

"A good ten minutes. But she didn't agree until I'd made her come twice, once on my fingers and once on my cock...joking, Nat, joking!" Ren's voice rose in pitch and he hastily raised his hands in surrender as I swatted at him. "There was only a *tiny* bit of flirting. Mostly flattery about her skills...with a *needle*," he added, clearly worried I would try to hit him again, or worse, take a pair of scissors to his pretty clothes. "Did you want to see my latest acquisitions?"

Hiding my grin, I followed him back through the door and dutifully surveyed the new items Ren had piled on top of the table. He'd already collected a hefty stack of books about Onnish cattle farming, a sheath of papers covered in backwards writing, a pot of mustard yellow ink that smelled like it was actually mustard, and a handful of quills from birds whose names began with 'S', but since I'd last been in here the prince had apparently received a delivery of new, bizarre...*things*. There was now a goblet that looked to be entirely carved from ice, a platter of unripe chestnuts, and a framed charcoal drawing of a wolf dressed up in courtly attire.

Dragging my eyes from the realistically drawn slobber drenching a starched collar, I fixed them on the ebullient prince practically bouncing on his toes at my side.

"And why did you need more?" I asked, only for him to dart forward and sweep the whole fucking lot of it off the table. I jumped as it all crashed, thumped, and shattered onto the floor, the mess spilling haphazardly at our feet.

"So I could do that," Ren declared cheerfully, and then wrapped his arms around my waist and lifted me just high enough to seat me on the edge of the now entirely empty table. "And this." He leaned in and pressed a demanding kiss to my lips.

The door rattled with three heavy thumps. "Your Highness?"

Ren sighed against my mouth. "Everything's fine!" he called back, and then groaned, more quietly. "Damn it. If they heard that, they'll hear *you,* Mathias."

"Hey," I protested. "I'm not that loud."

He snorted. "Like fuck you're not. Luckily for you and that needy little hole of yours, I planned for contingencies. The seamstress was only too willing to give me the extra cloth when I asked."

I frowned at the long strips of fabric he produced with a flourish from behind his back: black, gold, reds, and oranges.

"What do you need those for?"

Shit. I had less than a second's warning from the mischievous glint in my prince's eye before he was on me, pinning me down onto the table and scrunching up the gold cloth to shove it between my teeth.

"You're delightfully vocal when I get inside you," Ren said happily, clapping a hand over my mouth to stop me spitting it back out, "and you know how much I adore it. But I doubt your screams and moans are going to go down so well in this stuffy, bigoted castle, Mathias, and as I can't bear to leave you empty or wanting, I really have no choice but to keep you quiet."

We struggled some more as he wrenched a second strip of cloth over my mouth and tried to tie it in place, although I snatched it away before he could secure the gag.

He tugged at my trousers next, which was his mistake because with my hands free I could still fight back and managed to shove him off me. He rolled his eyes and shoved back, only there was rather less tabletop than either of us had realised, and I fell heavily to the floor just as I heard the door opening.

And that was how I found myself lying at the feet of the queen of Mazekhstam; gagged, red-faced, covered in mustard-scented ink and with my trousers wrapped around my knees.

Astrid raised a perfectly sculpted blonde eyebrow.

"Nathanael."

I choked on the cloth, my fingers frantically scrabbling to tug it free of my mouth and straighten my clothes. Brushing off feathers and shards of what were either ice or glass, I hurriedly got to my feet and bowed to her.

"Your Majesty."

Ren, I'm going to fucking kill you.

"Your Majesty," he repeated, his face bland and expressionless as though he wasn't responsible for the complete and utter mess he'd just made of both me and the floor.

Astrid sighed. "You two are *exceptionally* lucky that the only person the guards would let through that door without your authorisation is me."

My cheeks were still burning. "Yes, my queen. And…sorry."

"Make yourselves presentable and join me in the throne room," she instructed, her eyes raking over us both with stern disapproval. "*Promptly*, Nathanael."

I bowed again, choosing to keep my head lowered until I heard the door close, because words were insufficient to describe the levels of humiliation I was currently drowning in.

"Well, *that* was poor timing," Ren said with unapologetic cheer. "And you're standing on my wolf portrait, had you realised?"

I ground it into the rug with the heel of my boot, and he let out a pained whine. "Mat, you're being-"

"As long as we both live," I growled, "you will owe me one. No matter how many times you think you have repaid me for this, it will *never be enough*. Do you hear me?"

Ignoring his splutters of complaint and flagrant batting of eyelashes, I stomped past him to return to my room and retrieve clean clothes, peeling my ruined ones off and scrubbing at my skin in an attempt to rub the ink away.

"How come Panarina gets all your bows and I've never received a single one from you that wasn't either forced or steeped in sarcasm?" my prince asked, trailing after me.

I glanced at him in exasperation. "Ren, I bent the knee to you in front of your entire court."

"Oh," he said, happy and satisfied once more. "So you did."

Taking a cursory glance in the mirror to check for any lingering mess, I shooed him back into his own room. There were a handful more innuendo-laden comments flung back at me but I had the pleasure of cutting one of them off mid-implication when I slammed the door in his face, only to be greeted by him mumbling vicious threats under his breath in Quarehian when we met again a few moments later out in the corridors, having departed through our respective bedchambers.

We gave the barest attention to pretending we hadn't seen each other in days, and our guards must have been given the same orders for haste as us, for we were quickly ushered through the castle and into the throne room with little fanfare. I'd expected Ren to whine about the lack of fuss made over his entrance, or the hypocrisy in being hurried up when we'd been left to stew for nearly a week, or anything else that he judged would be sufficiently annoying to our escorts, but my lover was uncharacteristically silent, his fingers worrying at the fresh embroidery on the hem of his coat despite his expression being of carefully crafted unconcern.

He was nervous, I realised. A rare miracle, to be sure, but these were hardly normal circumstances. Ren thrived on politics, on conversing with, manipulating, and performing for his opponents, but the weight of what now rested on his gifts of persuasion had never been greater. If we couldn't convince Astrid to help him retake Quareh, what was left to us? What other hope did we have?

I was so busy watching him that it took me a moment to notice that there was again someone standing by Astrid's side, a travel cloak draped over his arm and his feet planted two steps lower than her throne in a gesture of respect. But unlike last time, this man wasn't some nameless assistant.

I felt Ren flinch as he recognised the betrayal at the same time I did.

I stumbled to a halt, glancing around in panic to find our guards had already closed rank behind us, barring us from any attempt we might make to flee. Grabbing Ren's arm and dragging him behind me – we may have been trapped but I'd be damned if I was making it easy for any of them to take him – I shot a hurt look in Astrid's direction.

"You sold Ren out?"

She shook her head.

"Nat," Valeri said, descending the remainder of the dais' steps and moving towards us, one arm outstretched like he intended to haul my prince away right in front of me.

"You're not taking him!" I snarled, stubbornly keeping myself between them as my brother tried to move closer.

He faltered, his eyes darting back to Astrid as if seeking an explanation. She didn't offer one.

"I'm not taking anyone," Val said slowly. "Why would you think…"

"I Saw you do it."

Astrid's mouth opened slightly at that, a crack in her proud royal façade. I'd told her about my Sight when I relayed to her everything that had happened since my capture when we spoke upon our arrival, although I hadn't been brave enough to recount my vision of Valeri and the horrifying realisation that he'd cut out my prince's tongue. I'd never expected she would be the one responsible for making such a future happen.

"You're going to hand Ren over to Welzes!" I accused. I felt Ren's sharp exhale on the back of my neck.

My brother frowned, his face creasing into a pained expression. "No. I wouldn't do that."

I scoffed.

"Nathanael, Aratorre and I may have had our differences, but that was before..." He shifted his weight between his feet, clearly uncomfortable, and cautious hope flickered through me at the confession. "Before I realised what he meant to you. Before I watched you two together and saw how happy he makes you. Before..."

I stared back at him, unable to speak.

"Fuck, you're really going to make me say it?" he pleaded.

"Yes," Ren said from behind me, clearly enjoying his discomfort. "Say it."

Valeri sighed. "Before I realised that he wouldn't make the *worst* king."

Ren snickered and rested his chin on my shoulder. "Told you he's in *loooove* with me."

I folded my arms. There were still some things that weren't adding up, regardless of how sincere my brother sounded. "Then why did you double the bounty for his capture?"

"Because the original amount was for his head," Val said. His eyes shifted to Ren. "I made the very *public* offer of a greater sum in exchange for you being brought in alive, Aratorre. Welzes couldn't refuse without admitting they wanted you dead without trial."

He sighed. "It was all I could do at the time to help. I was being closely watched in Máros; I couldn't get a message to either of you. Other than through that laundress."

Oh.

"You said we had no hope of escaping the city," I said, realising, "knowing that upon hearing that, it would make me doubly determined to do so."

AN OATH AND A PROMISE

My brother grinned. "Was I wrong?"

"No," I grouched. I hated that he knew me so well.

"I could only pray the message reached your ears before the false king and that fucking councillor implemented their city-wide raids. They were...*brutal*." Valeri's expression sobered. "It was an excuse for violence that had clearly been festering for a while: arrests without cause, punishment without reason, executions without crime – all under the pretext of finding their so-called treasonous prince."

"Bastards," Ren hissed, ducking out from behind me. His face was carved from angry lines, pain etched in his eyes. "How fucking dare they?"

"I'm sorry I couldn't stop it, Aratorre. Your sister quietly alerted me to Welzes' intentions in coming after me next, and I was forced to flee like a thief in the damn night." Val swallowed. "I didn't want to leave Alondra with that monster, but she refused to leave and I was powerless there alone. I just..."

His shoulders sagged, and I didn't think I'd ever seen my brother look so beaten as he did in that moment.

"There was nothing you could do," I said softly, and the words were for both princes. "Not then. But now?" I glanced up at Astrid, still seated perfectly motionless on her throne. "*Now*, we can. We might not have been able to help those people, but we can stop it happening to anyone else. Please?"

The queen rose gracefully and inclined her head. "Then let us speak. I will *consider* granting aid to our southern neighbour despite our long and bloodstained history, but as it is a decision that concerns the whole of Riehse Eshan, I wanted Temar present at our discussion. That," she added, her expression turning wry, "and I rather hoped your brother's presence here would explain why you had not gone to him first, Nathanael. It was certainly...illuminating."

My stomach knotted at the glimpse of the coldness Ren and Val had tried to warn me about. Astrid had always just been *Astrid* to me, clever and independent and often apprehensive, but when she was playing the political part of Mazekhstam's monarch and not my friend, the callousness was evident. "You could have just asked, Your Majesty."

"I recall a certain nine-year-old Temarian prince swearing up and down that he had no idea where the curtains in the second dining hall had gone," she mused, and her eyes danced with a mischief I recognised from years past, "when he'd watched me cut them into cloaks for our games not half an hour before. I learnt a long time ago not to trust your word, Your Highness." Yet the words were spoken with fondness, and Astrid gifted me a smile – something she'd done often when we'd been alone a few days ago but hadn't yet allowed herself to show in front of Ren – before gliding through into one of the antechambers along the throne room's left wall.

"Nat," Val said on an exhale, raising his arm again. This time, not struck by fear, I recognised it for the hug it was and let him pull me into a tight embrace, amazed when his other arm reached out and wrapped around Ren's shoulders. My lover stiffened in similar surprise before quickly recovering, winking at me and pressing his lips to Valeri's cheek in an exaggerated, noisy kiss.

My brother immediately shoved him away with one huge hand, the movement abrupt yet playful. "Fuck off, Aratorre."

I laughed into his shoulder, relief cascading down my spine at the realisation that I didn't have to choose between my family and my heart. I'd been so terrified of what I'd Seen Val do to Ren that I hadn't let myself believe what I knew: that he *wouldn't*.

Valeri glanced at the door Astrid had left through, and then lowered his voice. "Our mother won't allow Mila to mobilise Temar's army unless Mazekhstam is willing to send its own," he murmured. "You're going to be negotiating for both armies."

Ren caught and held my eye. Maybe if I didn't know him as well as I did, I'd have been fooled, but his tense posture betrayed the anxiety he was hiding behind a cocky smirk. "If I can entice your brother into my bed, Velichkov, I doubt winning a few thousand more people to my side will pose a challenge at all."

Rolling his eyes, Val shooed Ren ahead of him, waiting for the prince to leave through the door before turning to me and ruffling up my hair with a fond smile. Then he frowned, rubbing his fingers together and bringing them to his nose to sniff.

"Is that…mustard?"

"Serves you right," I snapped, but without much bite, attempting to flatten my hair down from where he'd mussed it up. "How did you get here so quickly?"

It had felt like eons while we were isolated in our rooms upstairs, but by my count it had been less than a week. A rider couldn't have reached Delzerce and returned with Val in that time.

"I was in Kiripul," he said, naming a town in eastern Mazekhstam. "Aksinia said she'd Seen you might come through the Pass. I was looking for you."

"Oh." I fidgeted under his gaze. "I'm sorry I didn't trust you."

Valeri sighed. "The Sight is a difficult gift to manage, Nathanael. I don't blame you for fearing what it showed you, but you shouldn't have had to be alone all that time. To reach Stavroyarsk whole and uncaptured..." He shook his head and chuckled. "I really shouldn't be surprised by your resourcefulness by now. You and Aratorre are the only ones who can keep up with each other."

And with that, he followed the others into the antechamber, leaving me blinking after him before hurrying to catch up.

The room was smaller than I'd expected, still grand in the way that the whole castle was with its tapestries and looming pillars and huge slabs of grey stone forming the floor and walls, but only just large enough to fit a table of four. A shaft of sunlight allowed in through the single slitted window highlighted the dust motes dancing in the air before landing upon a large map stretched across the surface of the table and held down in the corners by carved paperweights. Astrid was seated demurely in one of the high-backed chairs, her eyes settled on Ren across from her, who was lazily lounging in his own chair like he'd been sitting in it for hours.

He looked up as I entered, winked, and patted his lap in invitation.

I rolled my eyes and took the seat at the far end of the table instead, placing myself opposite Val but instantly half-regretting my decision not to grace my ass with the warm squishiness of Ren's legs instead. Because fuck me, these chairs were uncomfortable.

My brother made a similar wince to me, but Astrid looked entirely unconcerned at the unpleasant hardness. I expected she could be made to sit on a row of spikes and she'd somehow manage to pull off the same serene expression she was wearing now, a gracefulness that couldn't be further from how Ren had put his feet up onto the edge of the table and was using that leverage to rock onto the back legs of his chair, clearly already bored.

The queen waved a hand. "You may begin."

Ren's brown eyes glittered dangerously. "Oh, how *kind* of you."

"If you're not-"

"I'm nothing like my father," he interrupted. "Let's start with that, shall we? All the bloodshed and the aggravation and the cruelty of the last twenty-five years…that's not what I want for my people. Or yours."

Astrid regarded him coolly. "Nothing like your father," she repeated. "And I'm supposed to just believe that?"

Ren's laugh was short and sharp. "Everyone else in Quareh seems to. A single lie spread about my illegitimacy, and a day later there's a new king on the throne. I suppose I should be grateful you're not so easily fooled."

"Yet you still believe you're entitled to that throne?"

"He *is*," I said firmly, making three pairs of eyes turn to me. "Ren will be a good ruler, Astrid, and whether you agree with me about that or not, you can't deny he'll be better than the pricks in charge now. Didn't they declare war on Mazekhstam within a fortnight of taking power?"

She sighed, letting the tiredness show in her expression again. "I cannot deny that I would like to see that Lukian lose his ill-gotten crown," she admitted, fingers fluttering through the air as if she could so easily waft Welzes away, "but interfering in another country's politics is not an action I take lightly. If I provide soldiers to you to invade Quareh, Aratorre, if I support what would essentially be a rebellion considering the claims against your heritage, then what's to stop someone doing that to me?"

She looked at Ren, and then at Val, who swallowed in unease.

"My word?" Ren asked, moving his hand in mimicry of hers. "If I promise *really hard* that I don't want this fucked-up ice block of yours, assuming the Mazekhstani throne is as uncomfortable as these chairs and will only serve to make my ass flat, will that be enough?"

She fixed him with an unimpressed stare.

"For fuck's sake, Panarina," he snapped, his voice losing its playfulness. "We're talking about *tens of thousands* of Quarehian lives here, not to mention those of your people dying on the border. That's more important than your insecurities."

"Security and stability is vital, Aratorre. A *good ruler* would know that."

I glared at the map laid out before us, not liking my words to be used that way. "A promise could work."

"Nathanael, he was being sarcastic-"

"I'm aware," I said. "But that doesn't mean it's not a good idea. You wanted all of Riehse Eshan in on this, right?" I nodded over at my brother. "So make it a whole-of-continent treaty. The north helps the south, and each of the three countries pledges to support the current monarchies against any threats moving forward, whether from foreigners or local rebellions. Any one of you breaches that, and the others have the right to sanction them."

"*Sanction,*" Ren echoed suggestively, suddenly sporting a vicious grin. "Let's make it a good hard spanking and hope Temar is the first to fuck up, hmm?" He turned his sadistically gleeful expression onto Valeri and brought his palm down hard on his own thigh, the sound of the echoing smack sending an involuntary shiver running up my spine.

"Keep him in line, Nat," my brother said sourly, his hands clenching into fists. Ah, five minutes after reuniting with Ren and the man was already at risk of committing murder.

"I doubt I could if I wanted to," I retorted. "You know Ren does what he likes."

As if in confirmation, my prince jokingly slapped his leg again, making Val's scowl deepen. I felt my face flush with heat.

Ren happened to glance over at me then, instantly noticing my discomfort and dragging his eyes down to where I was squirming on my chair. His face lit up.

No, I mouthed at him as he raised his hand again with wicked anticipation. He shook his head at me pityingly, clearly having no intention of listening and *every* intention of embarrassing me in front of my brother and friend by getting me all worked up with nothing more than the movement of his

AN OATH AND A PROMISE

Blessed hand.

"But I will remind His Highness of Quareh," I gritted out, "that the future of his country may rest on this discussion. In such circumstances, one would consider it a wise idea not to antagonise the other participants."

There was a moment of expectant silence.

And then Ren sighed, uncrossing his ankles and pulling them off the table so he could sit straight in his chair.

"It's lucky you're such a phenomenal lay," he said casually, evidently not quite done taunting us, and Astrid huffed out an irritated breath that was matched – and outdone – by Valeri's.

"And it's extremely *unlucky* that you don't understand the meaning of the word 'antagonise'," I told him, finding it easier to breathe when I wasn't looking his way.

"Perhaps we should start by agreeing on the language in which to have these discussions," Val offered smoothly, and I shot him a grateful look. "Considering we've changed tongues a dozen times since we sat down."

"Aren't we all just going to suggest our own?" Astrid asked. The men shrugged.

"So let Nat act as tiebreaker," Ren suggested brightly, followed by consenting murmurs from the other two, and fuck me, *that's* what they chose to agree on?

I froze, glancing between each of them. My lover, my brother, my friend. Whatever I decided would probably lead to insult with the other two, but I didn't speak any non-continental languages such as Onnish or Lukian well enough to suggest a fourth, more neutral option.

"Mazekhstani," I said, refusing to sound apologetic when they'd all put me in this damn situation to begin with. "Seeing as that is where we find ourselves."

Astrid looked pleased. Valeri nodded briskly.

And Ren gave me an easy smile, not an ounce of condemnation or disappointment in his gaze as he looked over at me adoringly. "Perfect."

And he gave every indication that it was. If Valeri or Astrid had hoped that forcing him to speak a foreign tongue would reduce his innuendoes, they'd thought wrong. Ren knew all the double meanings of Mazekhstani words – many of which I'd taught him – and even Val struggled to keep up with some of his backhanded compliments and implications, though the language had a similar sentence structure to Temarian. But it wasn't all jokes: the three of them veered dangerously close to causing serious political offence several times as they navigated the potential terms of the tri-country treaty I'd proposed, fiercely campaigning for the rights of their own peoples. An argument about the haste at which sanctions would be applied occupied the discussion for over two hours, and I found myself frequently acting as mediator when they reached what would otherwise have been an impasse.

Ren showed no signs of exhaustion even when the other two began to flag in the early evening, despite not only having had to keep up with the negotiations in a language other than his own, but also applying his usual manipulations throughout the whole thing. It was nothing particularly nefarious. Just whining and grouching, interspersed with expectant grins that broadcasted what he was thinking...or allegedly thinking. I may have fooled the Quarehian court for months into believing me Mathias Grachyov, but that had been largely due to a misunderstanding on their part and a tendency not to correct them on mine. *This* was pure political guile, as Ren played at being easy to read while seamlessly hiding his true thoughts behind the exaggerated actions. Whether they realised what he was doing or not, Val and Astrid showed their own hands, relaxing their hold on their emotions as they responded to his wails of complaint or eager bouncing in his seat with unguarded reactions in turn. I could practically feel the smugness radiating off Ren as he soaked in both the information they were inadvertently gifting him and the satisfaction of a worthy performance.

"So," Ren said finally, rapping his knuckles on the map where Máros was drawn. "Now that we've agreed you *can* help me, what's your answer to whether you will?"

Astrid tilted her head, flyaway strands of hair finally starting to betray her otherwise composed appearance.

"You want me to force my army through the border lines and march on your capital," she said bluntly, "so that you can bully your way back to your crown?"

Ren raised an eyebrow. "I could try asking them real nicely for it instead," he offered in a dry voice, "if you think that might work better?"

"Panarina." That was Val. "It's this in the short-term, or enduring another reign of a monster in the long. Welzes is..." He swallowed, and I wondered if he was thinking of Alondra and the fearful expression she'd worn in the presence of her husband. "Nothing good for anything of us."

Glancing at the parchment in front of me where I'd been scribbling down the concessions Ren had agreed to make to his northern neighbours if he returned to power, Astrid let out a low hum of consideration.

My prince raised his chin. "You help me arrest Navar and Welzes so I can plant my ass back on my throne, and Your Majesty, Your Highness, you need never worry about a threat from the south again. One last act of war to achieve peace."

Val let out a long breath, looking as pleadingly at Astrid as Ren and I were.

"Fine. I will *consider* it," the queen said, a note of warning finality in her voice. "Happy?"

Ren smiled broadly, leaned back in his chair, and sipped from his wine glass before answering. "No. I also want Algejón."

We all stared at him.

Then Astrid laughed, and it wasn't a nice sound. "You come here to beg me for favours and then meet me with demands? You have guts, Aratorre, I'll give you that. I wonder what they'll look like spread over my floors."

Ren didn't flinch. He merely continued to smile as if it was all of great amusement to him.

"This all started with you taking Algejón," he said. "It will end with me taking it back."

"Perhaps *don't* remind everyone here how you tried to kidnap Astrid and ended up with me instead," I hissed at him. "Besides, it was Commander Grachyov and King Oleg who took your city."

"Then Her Majesty should have no objection to handing it back," Ren said smoothly, continuing to recklessly court danger in a way that made him a fucking hypocrite for ever admonishing me for the same.

From the deepening glare she was sending his way, Astrid clearly *did* have objections. "Arguably, the city belongs to Mazekhstam. Quareh invaded it and renamed it Algejón several hundred years ago."

"*Arguably,* that's just a rumour. The records from that era are far from clear on what happened."

"We've held it for over a year now," she said. "A further change in control would be disruptive to the local populace."

Ren narrowed his eyes. "Continuing to evict Quarehian citizens so that your own people can take up residence there is *disruptive to the local populace.*"

"You just want to control the border, Aratorre."

"Ah. So *that's* why you won't give it up."

"We get it. The city has strategic importance," Valeri said with a sigh.

"It also has a human cost," Ren snapped. "Those are *my* people suffering under Mazekhstani rule, forced to comply with *your* ridiculous laws and customs, Panarina, that prevent a woman from lying with her wife or a man from kissing his husband."

"Your people are welcome to leave," Astrid said. "That has always been made clear to them."

"One of you gets the city," I interrupted. "The other is allowed to maintain a garrison in it and elect a representative to its local council to ensure that the city can never be used against you."

Astrid glanced at me and then pursed her lips. "But who decides who gets which?"

"Chance," I said, pulling a coin from my pocket and slamming it down onto the table. "Reach agreement on the terms now, while neither of you know which position you'll end up with. That will ensure you give yourselves – and each other – a fair deal."

Val looked surprised. Ren did not.

"Yes," my prince said, shooting me an affectionate smile. "Your brother is the second cleverest person on the continent, Velichkov, if you weren't already aware."

Valeri frowned and opened his mouth as if to ask something foolish like who

AN OATH AND A PROMISE

Ren believed the *cleverest* was, and then seemed to think better of it.

Astrid and Ren descended into rapid-fire discussions, negotiating the terms for Algejón quicker than I could write them down. When they fell silent a few minutes later, holding identically tense poses as they watched each other carefully and tried to work out if they'd distributed the rights evenly enough to be acceptable no matter the outcome, I slid the coin across the table to Val.

"Tails for Mazekhstam keeping the city," I said, and my brother deftly flipped the coin, catching it in mid-air and slamming it down on his wrist.

He pried his fingers up to reveal the profile of the late Oleg Panarin stamped in the copper disc.

"Very well. Algejón is yours, Quarehian. As for the rest of what you're asking of me...I have much to think on," the queen said abruptly, standing. We all rose from our own chairs as she swept from the room in evident dismissal. "I will provide you with an answer tomorrow."

Then she paused in the doorway, glancing back over her shoulder. She was chewing on a lock of hair, an anxious tell that she'd begun to succumb to about half an hour ago as the discussions started to draw to a close. "I can't promise it will be an answer you like."

My brother stared after her long after she'd disappeared.

"Fucking hell," he said in Temarian, drawing a weary hand over his brow. "Dealing with her never gets easier."

For the first time, I didn't disagree. I'd seen more of that other side to Astrid today, the merciless politician who didn't cede an inch of ground without securing a greater benefit in turn, and while I expected it would make her an excellent queen to her people, it also turned her into a formidable...*adversary* wasn't quite the right word, considering Ren was hoping to win her as an ally.

"It's been a fun day," my prince agreed, cracking a smile in Valeri's direction that surprisingly held hints of his own tiredness. To allow such a thing to show through was either a lapse in attention – which Ren didn't have, not when he was working like this – or an offer of camaraderie.

To my *brother*.

I shut my mouth before either of them could catch me staring.

AN OATH AND A PROMISE

Ren drummed his fingers on the table, drawing our attention. "One of you Velichkovs cheated," he announced delightedly, "and I couldn't be prouder. I just can't work out if you Saw how it would land," he said, glancing at me before turning his head to Valeri, "or you've learned to flip coins with precision."

"We have no idea what you're talking about," I said, yawning widely, and my prince smirked.

"I'm going to get some sleep," Val declared in lieu of his own denial. His palms fell heavily to the tabletop as he shoved his chair back and stood. "Night, Nat. Aratorre."

Ren shot his departing form a lazy salute with a hand that was missing its usual rings, although the leather cuff still adorned his wrist. "That went…"

"Terribly?" I suggested.

"Well," he said. "Terribly well?"

I grunted out an irritable snort that summed up my feelings. "We still don't know if Astrid's going to help us."

"Of course not. It was the first day, and everyone knows nothing is agreed on the first day. It would be far too suspicious."

"But every day that passes–"

"I know, *mi sol*. But trying to hurry her up appears desperate," he said, "and there is nothing so dangerous in a negotiation as desperation."

I groaned. "I hate this politics shit."

Ren stood from his chair and moved over to me, pressing a kiss to the top of my head. "You're doing exceptionally."

I frowned, not understanding. "What? I didn't do anything."

"Think of it this way, Mat. Astrid is a vegetable."

I peered up at him. "Excuse me?"

"Your brother is the appropriately shaped chorizo," my prince explained, making a lewd gesture in case I'd somehow missed his meaning. "And I am the chicken. And the prawns and the sauce and everything else tasty, but you, Mathias! You are the rice."

"Is this supposed to do anything other than make me hungr-"

"You cannot have paella without rice, darling," Ren informed me very seriously, his brown eyes wide and surprisingly sincere. "You are the key ingredient. And if the rice stuck only to the chicken, it would be a terrible dish indeed."

I narrowed my eyes. "I'm...relevant?" I guessed, and Ren chuckled.

"Yes, Mat. You're relevant. You're *vital*. Every one of us around that table cares for you. You're what pulled us together, and you're ultimately who they've been listening to today, not me."

I shifted on the chair again, somehow far more uncomfortable in its unforgiving embrace now than I had been for the last several hours. "I just..."

"Hate being the centre of attention and are far too absurdly modest to ever admit your importance," Ren finished for me, holding out his hand to help me to my feet. His fingers curled through mine and he gave a fond shake of his head. "Blessed help me, I *know*."

*

Chapter Twenty-Six

Ren

The following day, while alone in our rooms and waiting for Panarina's answer, Mathias handed me a roll of parchment filled with his neat, tight lettering.

"What's this?" I asked, unfolding it with curiosity. "A list of all the things you love about me?"

"Wouldn't need nearly as much parchment for that," Mat shot back. "It's...well..."

"It's law," I said in wonder, my fingers tracing the indented paragraphs and the meticulously worded decrees. "A draft law for gender equality."

He fidgeted awkwardly, playing with his sleeve. "Obviously it would have to be cross-referenced with Quareh's existing legislation to see what needs to be added, and my translation might need some work, but..."

"I love it," I said, rising to my feet and kissing him. Dios, he had such a huge heart. Even with everything going on around us he'd found the time to draft this up, to campaign for people suffering hundreds of miles away. And that he'd put this much work into it meant he really did believe I'd find my way back onto the throne.

Mat coloured and shifted his weight between his feet, clearly embarrassed.

"Although I'm a little insulted that this was first on your list," I told him, tapping the parchment against my thigh, "and not the Statute of Mandatory Desserts to be Served at All Palace Functions, or the Prohibition Against Temarian Royals Wearing Any Clothes in the Presence of their King."

"Well," Mathias said, as I drew his shirt over his head in a respectful effort to comply with my own imaginary laws, "to help with financing the legislative changes, I did draft up the rules for a Fund to Which Renato Aratorre Must Donate One Gold Piece Each Time He Says Something Inappropriate."

I wrinkled my nose and tugged at his trousers. "The treasury would be empty within a week," I said, and he snorted.

"A week is exceedingly generous."

"You know what else is generous?" I asked sweetly. "Me taking the time to lay my belt across your ass."

"Wouldn't want to disrupt your busy schedule, Your Highness," he drawled, and I offered him the full force of my sadism-drenched smile.

"It's really no trouble," I said, shoving him backwards so he fell onto my bed with his trousers twisted around his shins. He looked up at me from under those long eyelashes of his, and fuck, if anything should be deemed illegal, it was those.

Mat lifted a leg and elegantly extracted himself from the remainder of his clothes. As I'd made the decree, I wasn't protesting, especially when he then laid back down and very deliberately spread his legs for me.

"I stand corrected," I said, trying to remember how to breathe. "You're lots of trouble. Roll over."

"Make me," he said. His expression was coy, and the filthy heat in his voice made my cock thicken in my trousers to the point of discomfort. Damn him. All I wanted to do when he was stripped and splayed out like that was sink inside him, and my lover knew it. And if I fucked him instead of spanking or belting him, he won.

He knew that too, which is why he was dragging a hand down his chest, his stomach, stroking his pretty cock and biting his bottom lip, because fuck him, and *fuck* him, and I was halfway out of my own clothes with my hands braced on his thighs before I caught myself.

"When did you get so brazen?" I asked between heavy breaths, and Mat just grinned up at me. "What happened to my shy little brat who blushes at the slightest of innuendoes?"

"You were liking it too much. We couldn't have that."

I raised an eyebrow, delighted at the challenge he was presenting me.

"I can either warm you up first with my tongue, or bury my fingers in you dry," I said, watching him squirm shamelessly at my words and loving the hell out of it. "Want to guess which one you'll get if you continue to mouth off?"

Oh, but to watch his gorgeous face as he struggled to decide which he wanted more. And then defiance flashed in his gaze, and I knew my wildcat needed it rough.

I worked a finger into him and he hissed out a delectable whine when he realised I'd indeed gone in without oil, trying to pull away.

"Uh huh," I said, my other hand falling to his hip to keep him in place. I knew I should be trying to keep him quiet, but it was hard to give a shit when he was looking at me like *that*. "I don't feel like letting you misbehave today. If I can't make you feel it *across* your ass, I'll make you feel it inside."

Mathias let out another pained noise as I pushed deeper and encountered resistance, but the way he wrapped his own hand around his cock to give it a swift tug told me everything I needed to know about how good it was making him feel.

"What do you want?" I murmured, continuing to watch his face as he screwed his eyes shut. "Do you want my cock in this hot, tight hole of yours?"

Pink blossomed across Mat's cheeks and I preened, pleased that I could still bring him to embarrassment even after everything he'd done and had done to him.

"Beautiful," I said, leaning down to kiss his flushed cheeks and forehead.

"*Ren*," he moaned, opening his eyes, and it was a sight I never tired of. My Mathias, looking up at me, blissed out and turned on...there was nothing like it in the whole fucking world.

I turned him onto his stomach before he could protest, pulled his cheeks apart, and licked a hot stripe between them, making him moan and shiver as my tongue lapped against his hole. But as much as I'd loved eating him out that time in the inn, today I was far too impatient to get inside him.

My boy glanced over his shoulder, his hazy expression sharpening in an instant when he saw what I held. "Where did you get the oil?"

"I asked for it."

His gaze shot to mine and then flickered to the door, alarmed.

"Oh, don't worry, *mi sol*," I reassured him. "I also asked for three and a half drops of goat's milk, a chair missing a leg, and a blanket woven from the wool of a blind sheep. No one will think twice about the seventeen vials of oil."

Mat blinked. "Seventeen?"

I pursed my lips. "Not enough?"

"How many times-"

"If you're going to ask me how often I plan to bury my cock in you, Nat, then the answer is that we're definitely going to need more oil. I'll order it immediately in case we run out before nightfall."

He rolled over and wrapped his legs around my waist before I could move.

"You're not..." Blue-grey eyes peered up at me, tentative and unsure. "You won't get bored with me?"

I frowned. What the fuck? Where had *that* come from?

"Are you bored with *me*?" I asked.

"No!" my northerner exclaimed. "*Blyat,* no. I just...you're used to...more," he finished, flapping a hand pathetically. "What if I'm not enough?"

What if I'm not enough. This man.

I closed my eyes. "Take that back, Mathias," I ordered. "You are more than enough. You are *everything.*"

I felt his legs tighten around me.

"You once said you could never give up flan or crema catalana, Ren," he whispered, and damn, maybe he'd been right about the food analogies inciting wistful hunger for Quarehian dishes. "With me, you'd not only be giving that up, but every other dessert too, because I don't think I could stand to see you with...with others."

I opened my eyes. "Don't think?"

"Couldn't," Mat corrected, and then added with a growl, "*won't.*"

"Better," I said, pleased. "*Mi cielo,* I knew when I said yes to you-"

"Yes? I don't recall you ever saying such a thing," he teased, parroting my words from a few days ago. "I do remember you shamelessly feeling me up under the pretence of frisking me, and all but hauling me to your bed."

I pinched his side, hard, ignoring both his yelps and attempts to wriggle free.

AN OATH AND A PROMISE

"When I *said yes*, I knew it was just me and you," I said. "You and me."

"Da," Mathias breathed, gazing up at me with a soft, happy smile on his face.

"And yes, maybe before I met you, Nathanael, such a thing would have seemed dreadful. Impossible. Dreadfully impossible. But you have a way of changing one's worldview." I pinched him again because I wasn't receiving nearly enough whimpers and curses from the man beneath me, and then bent down and followed the trail my fingers had taken with my tongue, giving kitten-like licks to the abused, reddened skin until he settled once more.

Mat hummed, his arms reaching up to wrap around my neck and pull me down onto the bed with him. I fell heavily, not expecting it, yet hardly protesting the opportunity to feel his warm skin against mine. But then he rolled us over and straddled my hips before scoring his nails down my bare chest – not hard, like I would have done to him, but enough to make me shiver.

"Close your eyes," he murmured, before prying the bottle of oil from my unresisting fingers. And just as I was about to give him shit for trying to take charge, he added, *"por favor?"*

By the Blessed Five, I found it hard to resist my man when he said please. If I'd been Panarina yesterday when he'd turned those big, soulful eyes on her and pleaded for her assistance, I'd have been a wreck on the floor and Mathias would have had my army wherever and however he wanted it.

He stripped my clothes from me, gentle yet insistent.

"Mat?" I asked as I felt him move away from me and heard the rustle of fabric from the other side of the room.

"Stay there," he said hurriedly. "And keep your eyes shut."

"If you're getting dressed so you can leave me here all worked up, please know that I will chase you down, clothes or no clothes, and take you in the middle of the fucking corridor," I promised, delighted to hear the sudden exhale of breath that escaped his lips.

"A tempting thought," he responded after a long moment, evidently trying to sound unaffected.

Too late, little wildcat.

AN OATH AND A PROMISE

"Claiming you in front of half the Mazekhstani court? I agree."

"Leaving you here."

I laughed, reaching my arms above my head to give a lazy stretch. "You had your chance to be rid of me. Now you're mine, permanently."

"Now, that," Mathias said from above me, "I can agree with." His fingers ghosted along my hip and then disappeared, making me let out a frustrated mewl.

It was his turn to laugh, excited and with a touch of wicked daring in his voice. Yet when I felt wispy fabric brush along one of my outstretched arms, I tensed.

"Easy, Ren," my lover murmured, calming me with a hand resting on my throat, and pressed the cloth into my palm. My fingers curled around it instinctively. "It's for me."

My rapid heart rate immediately stuttered from *oh fuck, I can't be tied up*, to *oh fuck, this just got hotter.*

"You were right," Mat told me, and I turned my head to the side to follow the sound of his voice. "No one can be allowed to hear us here, and I...I don't want to have to be quiet."

I smirked. I honestly didn't think he was even capable of it, and one day I wanted to watch him try.

But every single one of my plans for today involved Mathias screaming into the gag I held as I tormented him for hours. Suddenly and entirely coincidentally, I hoped Panarina took her sweet time in coming back to us with her answer.

"I'm opening my eyes now," I said, and when he didn't object, did just that, a harsh breath escaping my lips as I found him seated on the rug before the fireplace, with his knees bent and his hand dipping between his parted legs. Firelight flickered across his bare skin, aptly reflecting the heat that pooled in my lower half at the sight of his oiled fingers disappearing into his body as he prepared himself for me.

"Fucking hell," I whispered, my mouth going dry.

Mat ducked his head shyly. His movements slowed.

"Don't stop," I begged. "*Please*, don't stop."

He bit his lip and forced his eyes up to meet mine before beginning to move again, his face conveying everything he was doing to himself. And when his eyes widened and his mouth parted as he caught the spot inside him that brought such pleasure, I had to squeeze the base of my cock to warn away my own.

"Deeper," I ordered, and what do you know, the brat actually obeyed, his eyelashes fluttering as he adjusted his position on the floor to be able to push his fingers in further.

They slid in and out, synced with his breathing and shiny with oil, and I couldn't have looked away if my life depended on it.

"Add another finger, Mathias," I said, getting off on the sight and *loving* this ability to control what he was feeling without even touching him.

"I'm already-"

"Then make it two," I corrected, and that shut him up, his dismissive expression quickly turning to apprehension as he did the maths.

I cocked my head. "I know you heard me."

Mat swallowed, his chest heaving, and then slowly, ever so *slowly*, eased four fingers into himself. His back arched, and a beautiful whimper escaped his lips.

I was across the room before I knew it, shoving a chair under the door handle and swooping down to kiss my man from his quivering ankles to the tip of his nose. I brought the cloth across his mouth just in time, muffling the cry he made as my attentions jostled his hand inside him, and then pulled his wrist away and impatiently replaced his eager fingers with my equally eager cock.

"*Fuck*," I hissed, feeling his smooth, slick channel clench around me. "Nathanael, you have no idea how damn irresistible you are, do you?"

He couldn't respond, gagged and held down as he was, but that was fine by me. The way he mumbled out incoherent words and attempted to shake me off to *try* to respond was fine too, and I grinned as I pretended to misunderstand.

"Shush," I soothed, letting the rest of my weight press down onto him as I settled between his legs and began to fuck him ruthlessly. "You don't need to waste your energy returning the compliment. We both know how fabulous you think I am."

Mathias bucked against me indignantly and I chuckled, sinking my teeth into his neck to mark him. But it was only a few minutes later when he finally gifted me his hard-won submission and I felt him fall still, that I spilled deep inside the man I loved, affection and euphoria flooding my soul.

-

Panarina's expression was of carefully sculpted impassiveness, not a single laughter line or eye twitch giving away what her position would be. We stared at each other across the heavy table without blinking.

"...and I want you to uphold safe refuge for anyone who asks for it," Mat was excitedly saying to his brother, who smiled warmly at him.

Astrid frowned, her attention temporarily diverted from me. "Refuge?"

"You'll allow any northerner who would otherwise fall afoul of the sodomy laws to cross the border into Quareh," Mathias said, looking at her and then Velichkov to make it clear that it applied to both of their countries. "Call it a penalty of exile if you must, but you'll permit them to leave without punishment."

The queen considered his words. "And in return, we give shelter to Quarehian women who wish to flee abuse inflicted on them because of their gender?"

"That will be the offer made," responded Mat, glancing at me. I shot him an encouraging nod. "But we're hopeful that, in time, it will no longer be necessary." He pulled out the draft law reform from his coat and rolled it across the table. Panarina's eyebrows rose when she read it, and she passed it over to Velichkov as she began to speak again.

"That will be agreed, regardless of any other...terms."

Mathias hid his flinch well, but I saw the way he clenched his jaw. "You have decided, then."

Her eyes flickered back to mine where I sat across from her. "This endeavour to liberate your throne would come at great cost to my people."

Valeri made an irritated noise. "None of what we do is ever easy or safe, Your Majesty, and Aratorre has agreed to compensate you for-"

She held up a delicate hand to cut him off, her fingers perfectly still as they hovered in the air. I hid my own shaking fingers in my lap.

"I don't find your company easy to endure," Panarina said to me, the words spoken with precise care. "But I expect it may become so in time."

Mat snorted. "Don't count on it."

But I couldn't join him in his teasing, for I'd finally noticed a slip in the queen's otherwise flawless poise; a slight tightening of her lips that told me no one at the table was going to like what she had to say next.

"No," I whispered, my head turning between her and my lover as it fell into place. The perfect solution from a political perspective...and yet also the most horrifying. "Don't do this."

"Your hand in marriage, Aratorre," said Panarina, not heeding my plea. "That is my price for aiding you and Quareh."

Mathias knocked over his empty water glass. It hit the floor and shattered, punctuating the end of her terrible pronouncement.

"Stop," I growled. She didn't.

"Our firstborn child will be named heir of Mazekhstam," continued the queen, holding my gaze as I stared at her in dismay. "Our second will rule Quareh. Both will carry my name."

Mat pushed his chair back, his face like stone, and shoved open the door without a word, before disappearing into the throne room and the corridors beyond.

Fuck.

I stood up.

"We have not finished our discussion," Astrid rebuked me, her voice cold. "Leave this room before we are done, Aratorre, and I will offer you nothing. Algejón will remain with me. You might as well have never come here."

I looked at the door, and then at Mazekhstam's queen. I thought about everything she could give me; how she could help in recovering my country and my crown, all the people I could save with her as my ally.

AN OATH AND A PROMISE

And then I followed Mathias outside.

*

Chapter Twenty-Seven

Mat

I dug my fingers into the snow that had piled up on the low stone wall where I was sitting, hoping the tingling cold would distract me from all the emotions that swirled around inside, hot and turbulent. But although the discomfort began to turn painful, it still wasn't enough to stop my mind returning to *him*. Because even the hurt reminded me of Ren.

He always took care of my pain, delivering the right type in the right amount and then soothing it away afterwards, never letting it damage me but instead building me back up stronger than before.

But I wasn't strong. I was fucking dependent on Ren, on his laughter and little gentle touches and the way he spun and danced through life, buoyed with confidence and excitement and *rightness*. He'd shown me far more of the world than I'd ever realised existed.

I couldn't go on without him.

I *couldn't*...but I had to. Our relationship was no longer just a daring *fuck you* to societal norms: it would cost us continental peace.

I sighed, pulling my hand from the snow and sticking it in my pocket to warm the chilled skin. This had always been my favourite place to escape court life for a while, the raised garden bed I was seated on home to a dazzling array of snowdrops which stubbornly clung to life despite the freezing temperatures. Their drooping, upside-down petals emanated a beautiful, quiet sadness that resonated with me, now more than ever.

"You're in my spot."

I raised my head to find my lover with his hands on his hips and snowflakes nestled in his black hair, one perfectly groomed eyebrow raised expectantly. He shooed me to the side and I obligingly shuffled over, snow dampening the seat of my trousers while he sat down on the drier section of the wall I'd already cleared.

"How did you find me?" I asked. I was in a part of the gardens that couldn't be seen from the castle, and I'd dodged the guard sent to follow me.

"Mathias Grachyov," said Ren. "The annoying one who insists on using your name even though he should just accept it suits you better and get another one. Ran into him and he said if you were anywhere, you'd be here."

I heaved out a breath. "I'm surprised he answered so forthrightly."

But my joke about the lord's infamous circumlocution fell flat, my voice dull, even though I knew I should be treasuring these last moments of banter while I could still pretend my world hadn't just imploded around me.

"Well," Ren said, screwing up his face and clearly not ready to stop pretending himself, "maybe the man's vocabulary disappeared with his parents."

"*Ren,*" I chided. "That's not funny. His father was executed."

"And his mother."

"What?"

"Mmm," said my prince sagely. "Heard it from one of the guards. Both were found guilty of treason and Panarina had them..." He drew a finger across his throat and made an odd choking noise that could have as easily meant decapitation as a hanging. Not that it mattered.

"Poor Mathias." My heart went out to him and what he must be going through: not just losing his family but having everyone in the court know what they'd done. Did they think him a traitor too? Had he had his lands stripped from him?

"I should repay him for the horses we stole," I muttered, aware I was freaking out but unable to stop it. "And the chicken, and the potatoes. And I should see if he wants to-"

Ren put his hands over mine and pulled them onto his lap. "Nat. You're not doing any of that. Didn't he bully you as a child?"

I scowled. "So that means I should treat him like shit?"

My prince muttered a hasty prayer to Dios, rolling his eyes at me. "You can't save everyone, *mi amor.*"

I swallowed, knowing we couldn't avoid Astrid's marriage proposal forever.

"Speaking of…"

"Speaking of," he repeated, blithely cutting off the words as if they formed a whole sentence. "Aren't you cold? May I take you inside and *thoroughly* warm you up?"

I pulled my hands free of his, and he sulked.

"Ren," I said. "We shouldn't…we shouldn't make this more difficult for ourselves."

"Darling, you *always* make things more difficult. I've grown quite fond of it, actually, and would be terribly disappointed if you stopped now." My prince leant his head on my shoulder. "Want me to stab her?"

"Astrid? You're going to stab the queen of Mazekhstam, are you? Incur the wrath of an entire country and end up in some gruesome torture chamber for regicide?"

"For you? Yes," he murmured. "She should have known better."

Heaving out a breath, I carefully pried his weight off me, but that just made him pout harder, his bottom lip jutting out and his eyes welling with exaggerated fake tears until I gave in and let him settle his head against me once more.

"Ren. I didn't leave because of what Astrid said. I left because of what you would have to say."

"And what would that be, Mathias?"

The prick knew perfectly well *what*.

"*Moy knyaz*," I said in exasperation. "If you agree to marry her, you would unite the two most powerful countries on the continent. You wouldn't have to worry about Mazekhstam invading Quareh ever again, and my mother wouldn't dare to so much as say a bad word about you for fear of being wiped off the map. You and your people would finally be safe."

"Sounds kind of boring," he griped, twisting around to look up at me. "What else you got?"

I swallowed against the lump in my throat. "What we have…*us*, we stand in the way of peace. I know you can see it, Ren. Look at the riot I caused by kissing you in front of my people that day: I risked everything the tournament

AN OATH AND A PROMISE

was trying to achieve. And now again. We're fighting an unwinnable battle."

"Aren't those your favourite kind?" Ren asked with amusement, and then snorted. "Why am I even listening to you? You seriously imagine I'm going to accept Panarina's offer?"

"You have to," I whispered.

My lover just gave me a crooked smirk, grabbing my face and tugging it his way so all I could see was him. Unnecessary, for that was all I *ever* saw.

"Do you still think, after all this time, that I'm going to do what you tell me to?" Ren shook his head vigorously, strands of hair coming loose and falling down around his ears. "Nuh-uh. You're not getting away that easily, for I plan to torment you for the rest of our lives, *mi cielo*. Earthly *and* heavenly."

"You said you'd do whatever it took to retake your throne and help your people," I reminded him, my insides feeling tender and raw.

"So I lied," Ren murmured back, his thumb stroking across my bottom lip and dragging it down. His eyes followed the movement. "Mat. I don't want *anything* if I can't have you. My life has no meaning without you in it. My freedom means nothing without you to enjoy it with. And a crown is worthless without you to rule by my side...and to tell me how stupendous I look in it."

"It's certainly an adjective that begins with S," I said, hearing my voice crack as the weight of what he was doing for me started to sink in, but needing to say something so I wasn't just sitting there with my jaw open and drooling over this impossibly perfect man. "I'm just not sure it's *stupendous*."

"Sexy, then. Splendid. Superb. Sterling. Super...eminent."

He kissed me between each word, his tongue darting in to claim mine and then pulling away all too soon. It was sweetness and tenderness, and the exquisite kind of frustration that only Ren could cause with his teasing and fondness for denying me.

I gave doing the right thing one last pathetic attempt before I let the temptation of getting to keep him sweep me away. "This is our only hope for saving Quareh from what Welzes and Navar will do to it."

"Then we'll find another," he said simply.

"Where? How?"

"I don't know and I don't care." Ren's grin was bright, sly, joyful. *Beautiful.* "You think our relationship is in the way of peace? I say peace is in *our* way, Nathanael, and I'll let the whole fucking continent burn before I give you up."

"You'd really do it?" I asked, getting lost in the depth of those warm brown eyes and his gentle kisses. "You'll turn Astrid down...for me?"

"*Mi corazón*," he murmured, his hands threading through my hair so he could pull me closer. "I already have."

*

Chapter Twenty-Eight

Ren

Mathias spluttered out a half-apology when he knocked the rest of the game board to the floor, his hands waving wildly as he tried to stop it falling. He moved with all the grace of a blind and deaf cow. One which was four days dead.

As the pieces scattered across the length and breadth of the room, I wondered how much of it had truly been a drunken accident, and how much was a deliberate attempt to prevent me from beating him in any more rounds of checkers. When my northerner had initially explained the rules of the game to me – unnecessarily, as I'd played it before, but I liked listening to him talk – he'd failed to mention that I *couldn't* prevent his counters from eliminating mine by biting his fingers every time he tried.

He probably *had* advised that I could only move one piece at a time and that the squares of the opposite colour were out of bounds, but hey, no one got to a score of forty-nil without a little bit of innovative thinking and adamant insistence that he'd said no such thing.

"You," he said to me now, adopting a fierce scowl that made him look utterly adorable. The last of the vodka sploshed around the bottom of the bottle he was holding. "You're…you're…"

Mat staggered on the spot, laughing when he fell against the wall and thanking it for its assistance.

I shook my head, amused.

"Give me that." I held out my hand but he clutched the vodka to his chest in horror, keeping it out of my reach from where I was comfortably seated in one of the armchairs in his room.

"*Nyet.* You're going to do something mean to it. Or me. Or both of us." He held the bottle up to the light and peered at it dubiously. "You already have. You've stolen it!"

"*I've* stolen it?"

"Ren!" Mathias wailed. "Why do I feel so…?"

"Inebriated?" I suggested wryly. "I fear your new companion might have something to do with it. How about you hand it over and let me put you to bed?"

My lover narrowed his eyes and glanced between me and the vodka as if deciding which of us to trust. Then he bared his teeth at the bottle, tossed it to the floor – I winced, but it landed at the edge of the rug and stubbornly refused to shatter – and proceeded to settle himself in my lap. It seemed it was one of his favourite places to be, even while drunk.

I buried my face in his hair and breathed him in, wrapping myself in that crisp, delightful scent that felt like home. Mat was mine to hurt, to fuck, to hold. To care for, to fucking *love*.

Mine. End of story.

Panarina could keep her beautiful, prickly self and her marriage proposal far, far away from us. Nothing was ever getting between me and my wildcat, and I hoped that spending an afternoon repeating that to him in various ways until he'd begun to awkwardly fidget and shush me had finally gotten it through his thick head.

But this was Mathias we were talking about, so next I'd showed him without words, bending him over the table while I spanked his ass red and he acquainted another gag with his cries, and again when I'd taken my sweet time eating him out.

And then, when we finally allowed ourselves to discuss how screwed we were – and not the fun kind I'd just delivered to him – Mat had had the bright idea of drowning our sorrows in liquor. I suspected it was half intended to numb the stinging of his sore ass, but when I'd dared to voice that accusation he'd fixed me with a scathing look and told me a gentle breeze hit harder than what I'd just delivered. By the time I'd gotten over my spluttering indignance, he was too deep in the bottle for me to prove him a fucking liar.

Clever, insistent fingers now tugged at the fastening of my trousers.

"Mat," I murmured, "you're drunk." I caught his wandering hands. "We can pick this up in the morning."

"Don't worry about any of them," he said nonsensically, yanking his wrists free and putting the index fingers of both hands to my lips. He misjudged the force required and ended up smacking me on the mouth. "They don't matter like you do."

And then the door to his room opened and Velichkov and his wolf strode in as if they owned the damn place.

"I wanted to see how you were…"

His jaw set at the sight of Mathias sprawled on top of me, his knees resting on the outside of my thighs as he straddled my lap.

"Nat, for the love of God, find your own seat. There's plenty of them." Velichkov gestured helplessly at the rest of the room.

"We're busy," Mat responded instantly, not bothering to look around at his brother. He ran his hands down my neck and under my shirt. "Fuck me, Ren," he murmured, his words slurred but content.

Valeri abruptly choked. "Nathanael, that's-"

My lover yanked roughly on the collar of my shirt, giving up on undoing all of its fastenings. "Take me hard and fast how I like it," he begged.

I had no intention of doing any such thing while he was this intoxicated, but Velichkov didn't have to know that. I smirked around Mat's needy, desperate form to where his brother stood frozen and horrified.

"I know *just* how you like it," I purred, pressing a kiss to his cheek without breaking eye contact with the elder prince, who'd turned exceptionally pale. "Did you want something, Velichkov, or are you just here to watch?"

Oh, Mathias was going to *murder* me when he remembered this sober, but right now he was nosing into my neck and rubbing his hips against mine in a shameless attempt to get me to cede to his demands. And by Dios was it difficult to keep my hands to myself, but I'd be damned if I was taking a half-delirious, drunken mess to bed when I doubted he even remembered his own name right now, let alone how to say no.

"Aratorre," Velichkov growled out, echoed by Wolf, but I shushed them both, wrapping my hands under Mat's ass and lifting him as I rose from the chair. His long legs wrapped around my waist instinctively and I carried him to the bed – not without difficulty, as he was a similar weight to me, but it was only a few steps and he'd never forgive me for dropping him – and lay him down on it.

"If you think," the Temarian heir behind me spat out, "that I'm going to let you bed my brother in that condition, then you're going to earn yourself four missing limbs. I…"

He fell silent when I pulled a blanket over my boy's curled up form, brushing his hair from his face.

As Mat murmured into his pillow and closed his eyes, I straightened and gave Velichkov a caustic look.

"If you expect I would even consider doing so, you're still as much of a dumb brute as I've always believed," I said evenly, and then in the same tone, gestured at the chairs near the fire. "Shall we talk?"

He faltered and then nodded brusquely, swallowing away his complaints and seating himself opposite me. Wolf nestled at his feet and lay his head on his huge paws. "How is he?"

"Giggly," I said with amusement. "It's not something he lets me see often, but when he does it's utterly hilarious."

Velichkov didn't bother to hide his smile, his eyes flickering back over to where Mathias had already fallen asleep and was beginning to drool onto the pillow.

"He's fine," I added softly. "He doesn't hold grudges well, and I doubt he'll remember to be angry at Panarina tomorrow, vodka or no."

The man frowned, his gaze returning to me with suspicion. "Yet you're still sober?"

"Your brother challenged me to a drinking contest, only he foolishly failed to specify what I'd be matching him mouthful for mouthful with." I nodded at my own glass of Quarehian wine that the door guards had miraculously procured for me. "Needless to say, the straight spirits he chose did not help him to win."

The heir's mouth drew into a thin line. "So you acted dishonourably and tricked him into inebriation?"

"Velichkov," I said exasperatedly. "He obviously knew I was cheating from the very first sip. It was his decision to get drunk, and neither of us will thank you for assuming that Mat...*Nat*, is incapable of making his own choices."

He cleared his throat awkwardly.

"Right." He played with Wolf's ears. "I just wanted to say...thank you for putting Nathanael first, earlier," Velichkov murmured. "For showing him that he has worth, as I fear he all too often misses it. You did well today, Aratorre."

"Gosh, I didn't realise I was being *rated*," I said sarcastically, letting my back slide down the chair until I looked appropriately uninterested in my companion in case he got any ideas of us being friends or something equally stupid. "If I'd known that, I'd have tossed out a grandiose speech or two before running off."

Velichkov winced. "That was...I didn't mean it like that. I'm sorry. I...fuck me," he cursed.

Ah, but there was that promise of monogamy I'd made. "Regrettably, I can't."

The northern prince exploded into an unexpected and deep laugh, Wolf eyeing him with surprised disgruntlement before shifting closer to the fire and closing his eyes.

"Did you just *reject* me, Aratorre?" he asked, still chortling and holding his side. It hadn't been *that* funny. "I didn't think it possible."

"And now you're calling me a whore," I pointed out , trying to maintain a straight face although his mirth was beginning to affect me too. "I see your reputation for adept diplomacy is well earned, Temarian."

"No worse than you slighting the queen of Mazekhstam and her marriage proposal by walking out on her without a word," said Velichkov, but he was grinning now. "I've never seen Panarina so shocked. She couldn't speak for at least ten minutes. Just sat there gaping like a fish."

"I'd liked to have seen that," I admitted, allowing him to see a hint of a smile.

Wolf got to his feet, stretched, and sniffed my feet before settling himself between them. Valeri and I both stared, and I tentatively reached down to run my hand across the coarse fur of his back. When I still had all of my fingers attached half a minute later, I let out the breath I'd been holding.

"It seems I owe you both one for what you did for us in Máros," I said, talking to both the prince and his pet. "Although without Panarina's help, I doubt I'll be able to repay you anytime soon, unless you happen to have a use for a penniless, usurped southerner? A use that *doesn't* involve sucking your cock, brother dearest," I added, just to see him flush like Mathias, "because I'd gladly do that for free."

"What happened to not propositioning me?" The trademark Velichkov scowl was back on his face, although I'd gotten my blush, with the pale skin of the prince's cheeks and neck turning delightfully pink.

"That moment of foolishness has passed."

"It did seem rather unlike you."

I stretched in the chair and winked at him.

The man shook his head ruefully, glancing back at Mat. "I wanted to come by and see him earlier," he murmured, his voice low, "only I thought I'd take the chance to speak to Panarina on your behalf."

"Oh?"

"I told her that after spending only one afternoon in your company, I'd wanted to take a ship from Riehse Eshan and flee the continent entirely," Valeri drawled. "I think she's starting to get it."

"Well, we couldn't have her thinking I'm nice," I agreed.

"I'd say no one would be daft enough to believe that, Aratorre, except the proof to the contrary just started to snore."

I flashed a fond look over at the bed. "I know. Isn't it adorable?"

Velichkov rolled his eyes. "I also convinced Her Majesty that she didn't really want your children. That they would be vicious little beasts; sly, sharp-tongued, and utterly uncontrollable."

"Fuck, prince, we're trying to persuade her *not* to want to bed me," I said.

He ignored that, pushing up from his chair and gesturing for Wolf to follow him. "So she's agreed to not toss you in the river for your insult earlier, and will meet with you in the morning to continue our talks. You're welcome."

I watched him prowl towards the door, blinking at him in surprise.

"What do you hold over Astrid Panarina?" I asked, curious. "You convinced her to dissolve the northern hostage exchange, too. There's no way you're actually that good of a negotiator, because let's face it, I've *met* you."

Where once he would have responded with growls and threats, now Velichkov just laughed. "Leverage disclosed is leverage weakened, Aratorre. *Leka nosht.*"

"Goodnight," I repeated absently, my attention caught and held by a noise from the other side of the room. Mathias seemed distressed, clawing at the blanket in his sleep and muttering something incomprehensible yet clearly panicked. I ran my fingers over his cheek but it didn't seem to soothe him, so as the door clicked shut, I slid into bed beside my lover.

"Nyet, Kolya!" he snarled, and I heaved out a shuddering breath, not knowing whether to pull him closer in reassurance or give him space. Just as I resolved to wake him so he could make that choice himself, Mat let out a long, sleepy sigh and yanked me over onto his side of the bed before wrapping his arms and legs tightly around mine. Attached to me like a limpet and pressing his face into my neck, he soon settled and didn't stir again for a very long time.

*

Chapter Twenty-Nine

Mat

"You know, you slumped helpless over a table seems to have become a habit," Ren said cheerily, his breath hot on my face, and I cracked a reluctant eye to find him only an inch away. He had his cheek resting on the surface of the table, mirroring my own pose, only his was mocking and mine was the inevitable result of consuming far too much alcohol the night before.

"I don't know what you're talking about," I said firmly, although my tongue was declining to cooperate and the sounds that actually erupted were closer to *erdunna wat yur tawkinbart*.

Luckily, my prince seemed to understand me, or else he knew me well enough to know I'd protest the claim, for he just grinned.

"I know you remember," he coaxed, and even with my fuzzy eyesight I could see the wicked glint in his brown eyes as he whispered the words. "I liked the look of you bent over similar to this yesterday, legs spread wide where I put them and my palm coming down on your bare skin, over and over."

"Never 'appened," I denied, feeling heat spark through me at the memory. Fuck, that had been hot, and the ten promised smacks had turned into a punishment five times as severe when I refused to count as instructed and he'd just kept going until I did. It had been difficult to maintain my obstinacy when my ass was on fire, even if counting strikes while fucking *gagged* was sadism only my lover could deliver.

"Did it not?" Ren asked, pulling a disappointed face. "It was such a fun fantasy though – for *me*, at least. Tell you what, we'll re-enact it when we get back upstairs so you don't miss out."

I scowled, wincing at the pain that shot through my head as a result of doing so, and he chuckled before leaning in to boop my nose with his.

I closed my eyes. The surface of the table was comfortably cold against my cheek, and was being much kinder to me than my lover. And especially my brother, whose loud voice was inconsiderately echoing around both the room and my tender skull.

"Shhh," I grumbled, and then felt a gentle touch in my hair.

"I've sent for my healer, Nathanael," Astrid murmured from above me, continuing to lightly stroke my head. "We'll have you back on your feet in no time."

"Blorgiriarchi," I slurred incomprehensibly instead of a thank you in Mazekhstani, giving up the painful talking until I felt a different pair on hands on my head a few minutes later, with briskly efficient fingers that pressed against my temple and the base of my skull.

The magic took longer than Starling's, but soon I could think again without the sensation of being battered by a thousand heavy rocks, and muttered out my gratitude to the healer.

Opening my eyes and lifting my head, I found three concerned faces peering back at me. It seemed my hangover had achieved something positive, at least: Val, Ren, and Astrid were standing shoulder to shoulder without swapping so much as a dark look or a sharp elbow to the ribs.

"Your Highness," the Blessed said from behind me, a man I'd known my whole life and that insisted everyone only ever call him Doc. "Would you also like me to heal the bruises on your knees and your, uh...backside?"

"Certainly *not*," Ren shot back sharply, the uncompromising tone making me obediently shake my head before I could stop myself, but at my subsequent expression of utter mortification, he descended into loud and uncontrolled laughter.

"It seems that will be all, Doc," Astrid said delicately, the only one in the room able to maintain their composure. Val was steadfastly looking over my head, refusing to meet my eyes, and Ren was so lost to his amusement that he would have fallen over had Astrid not clutched his arm to keep him upright.

Doc cleared his throat. "Very good, Your Majesty." He scratched his stubbled chin and gave me an awkward half-smile. "You always were a clumsy child, Prince Nathanael, covering yourself in cuts and bruises from the countless times you fell down staircases. I only pray God will bestow fewer black eyes on my son when he becomes old enough to walk these halls."

Ren's humour abruptly disappeared and his lips curled away from his teeth, clearly ready to unload on the inattentive man.

Val, who as far as I knew had never learned of my...*encounters* with certain other inhabitants of the castle, just shot me an exasperated glance.

"I've delayed you all long enough," I said quickly. "Shall we resume our talks?"

Astrid eyed me cautiously before nodding. Ren was harder to convince, but a few well-placed glares in his direction persuaded him to drop the matter until we were at least alone, and he surprised us all by graciously pulling out the queen's chair for her.

"Nathanael, Renato," she began, stroking out the folds of her dress with slow, deliberate movements evidently designed to keep her hands busy. "I regret any...difficulty I caused yesterday. Your brother helped me appreciate that I had underestimated what you mean to each other."

I looked at Valeri, who gave a faint, dismissive shrug as if to say it was nothing. *Nothing*, to have convinced the fucking queen of Mazekhstam to recognise my illegal relationship with a foreign royal as above that of her own political needs.

"I will assent to everything else we have settled these last two days," Astrid continued, "including Algejón and the complete cessation of hostilities between us once you retake your throne, Aratorre. But..."

She faltered.

"I can't offer marriage," Ren said firmly, and she bobbed her head in acknowledgement, clearly not expecting his answer to have changed. I shifted uncomfortably on my chair, the ache I felt across my ass making it ten times worse.

"Then I can't give you my army." Astrid brought a lock of blonde hair to her mouth and chewed on it before speaking again, her brows furrowed. "Please understand. I will not risk the lives of thousands of my people to conquer Quareh, only to hand it back to a foreigner. I won't ask that of them."

I did understand, and I loved that she cared about such things. But it also left us with nothing.

Yet Ren cocked his head, looking shrewdly across at her as he picked up on something I hadn't. "And what would the offer of *friendship* between us buy me?"

Astrid considered him for a long moment, her blue eyes eventually settling on me. "A secret."

"What type of secret?"

"The type that may be able to unravel others," was all she said.

"Cryptic. I like it." Ren grinned and held his hand out to her. "I believe we have a deal."

-

"I don't know why we have to be out here freezing our asses off," Ren grumbled the following day, "when Panarina could have just had him brought to us."

"The word 'secret' doesn't mean much to you, does it?" I said conversationally, pretending to enjoy the brisk air when really I was just as eager as him to be out of the cold.

"Not unless I can lick it," he replied, and proceeded to lick *me* instead, swiping a hot trail of saliva up my cheek that quickly cooled against my skin.

"Just knock on the damn door, Ren."

The prince raised his hand to the door of the cabin we'd trekked four hours from Stavroyarsk to reach...and then yanked it open without knocking. A heavy cloud of smoke surged out as he did, making my eyes water.

"Inhabitants of this creepy, lonely little hut," he called loudly, pushing his way inside, "you're graced with our royal presence. Bows and curtsies are acceptable, hot beverages preferred, and a carriage ride back down that Dios-damned mountain would be the greatest gift of all. Why did you have to go live somewhere so inconveniently remote?"

That last was squarely directed at the older man who had clambered to his feet upon Ren's entrance. He had a pinched face, grey eyes squinting in disgust at the snow melting from the prince's boots onto his floor, and a shock of pale hair that was more than just aged: it was a bright, brilliant white that outshone anything else in the dingy hut.

"Royal?" he said slowly, peering at my lover. The white hair seemed to shine where it curled around his ears. "A bold claim for one hunted as an imposter and traitor."

Ren faltered and I stepped neatly in front of him, sheltering him from the stranger. It seemed we'd certainly found who we were looking for.

"Nathanael Velichkov," I said by way of introduction.

He harrumphed in response. "I know."

"I know you know," I said. "But considering you're meant to be extinct, shouldn't you be better served pretending you don't?"

The man sighed, dropping back down to the dirt floor and folding his legs beneath him. He stared into the flickering flames of the small fire he was warming himself by, a kettle and teacup set untouched to one side. While there was a dedicated firepit and chimney space above to funnel the smoke outside, I still found myself coughing as the air rethickened around us.

"I do not care to hide what I am," the man said morosely. "It is Mazekhstam's kings and queens who would keep my existence a secret."

"And one hell of a secret it is." Ren gave a low whistle, beginning to prowl around the hut in what was perhaps supposed to be intimidation, but I knew was just him being a nosy prick. Not that there was much to look at other than a bed and a few shelves: it was clear the man lived a sparse life. "A living Hearken. Capable of reading our fucking thoughts from our heads."

Even standing before the man as proof, I was still reeling from the impossibility of the information Astrid had divulged, her voice lowered to a whisper and the words uttered in Quarehian to minimise the chance of us being overheard. For Riehse Eshan believed the Hearken, the fifth type of Blessed in addition to those with the Touch, Sight, Scent and Voice, to be long dead. None had been born in over a century, and while the sense-based abilities of the Blessed could manifest almost randomly and later in life, with my own gift as evidence of such, it was always one of the other four magics that emerged.

I hadn't thought anything Astrid could have said would have made up for the absence of her army at our backs – and that of Temar – but if this was the value she was placing on friendship with Ren and the south, then she was truly serious about achieving peace. It was one hell of a gift.

Except people couldn't be owned, so if we wanted any chance of unseating

Welzes we had to be ready to beg for this stranger's help.

"Close proximity," the man said to me just as I opened my mouth to ask him what he needed to work his magic. "Not exactly voices, but close enough not to bother explaining it any other way," he added, seemingly anticipating my next question about how he read a person's thoughts. "Name's Dima. White sparks – they blend with my hair so you can barely tell in the daylight. Yes, I'm doing it now. No, I can't stop it. Yes, I expect that constant drain on our magic is why we died out. Your sympathy for that is not needed; I never knew any others of my kind."

I sucked in a startled breath.

"Hmm," Ren mused, although I noticed he kept himself as far away from the man as was possible in the tiny room. "It would have been a lot easier to get you into my bed if I'd had that little handy trick, Mathias. You wouldn't have been able to feign disinterest nearly as well."

"Feign, right," I said, because with how accommodating and agreeable I'd been to him last night, he deserved me playing hard to get today.

Dima shuddered, reaching into his pocket and stuffing something dark green and leafy into his mouth. He chewed quickly, his lips turning down as if the flavour was unpleasant, only when he spoke again I realised it wasn't the leaves that he was finding distasteful.

"I have already seen far too much of your naked bodies than I am comfortable with," he said sourly, glaring at each of us. "If more of this is what I am to expect on our journey, then I shall have to change my mind about helping you."

"I…"

I glanced helplessly at Ren, who for once, didn't seem overjoyed about being able to torment someone with sexual implication.

"Then avert your fucking eyes," my prince hissed. "Mathias doesn't like to be looked at, and he's *mine*."

Dima crammed more leaves into his mouth, chewing and swallowing like he couldn't get it down fast enough. "You think if I had a choice in the matter, I'd want to see what you two…what *anyone*…"

"Do your best, Hearken, before I turn my thoughts decidedly nastier and drown both them and you in blood," my lover spat at him.

Ah, a line. I never thought I'd find one, not when it came to Ren and oversharing, but apparently there was a difference between encouraging someone to use their imagination about what he and I got up to behind closed doors, and actually *seeing* it.

I shivered, feeling uncomfortable and violated. All those moments were private, precious, and *ours*.

But when Dima swallowed and dropped his head as if attempting to comply with Ren's order despite the futility of physical movement against such magic, I realised that the violation wasn't one-sided. To have other people's thoughts thrust into your head without your consent, unable to stop whatever was in their own minds from polluting yours…fuck, no wonder the man lived so remotely.

I tried my best not to think about Ren without clothes, but of course, that's all my mind would latch onto. The older man shot me a hateful glare from underneath his thick, bushy eyebrows.

"See us?" I asked hurriedly, hoping to distract both my thoughts and his. "You said it was like voices, before, is it-"

"I said *close enough*," he snapped, and then sighed. "Think of it like a book, with words that conjure mental images. You two are particularly graphic in your descriptions of each other."

Sorry.

Dima sighed again. "I know you do not intend it, Mathias. Your apologies do not need to be quite so loud and insistent."

Then he glanced at my lover. "And Ren, I see you make none at all even though you *are* doing it intentionally."

It was odd hearing this stranger refer to us so familiarly, as though he'd been with us the whole time. I supposed, in a way, he had.

I swallowed down that thought and hoped the Hearken wouldn't comment on it either.

Ren shrugged, sticking his hands into his pockets. "I'm not thinking of you, Mat," he assured me, and then winced, closed one eye, and peered at me

AN OATH AND A PROMISE

gingerly through the other. "Except for now. And...now. Shit, sorry."

Dima swayed on the spot, his hands crossed and clutching at his ankles where he was still seated in front of the fire. "I assure you that I am not as bigoted as many of my people. With all minds laid out to me, it would be difficult to judge something that everyone has imagined or fantasised on at least once, but that doesn't mean I *want to see it, Ren!*"

I wasn't sure if he was talking about us both being men, or the kink, but I really *really* didn't want to hear the answer. My mind lurched, desperately trying to pin down something to change the subject to, but it flailed helplessly in a sudden void of desolate befuddlement.

"You said you'd help us," the prince blurted out, looking rather *un*-Ren-like as he lost himself in his own panic. "We need you to-"

"Get close enough to the healer Yanev to read his thoughts so you can use the Hearkens' gift and inability to lie to publicly denounce *his* lies regarding your heritage," Dima interrupted, his words starting to slur together. "Yes, I got that when you walked in."

Fuck, that was unnerving.

"There's-"

"Horses at the base of the mountain to take us all back to Stavroyarsk."

"Do you-"

"Want to know what I'll be offered in turn? I know," he mumbled quietly, and I was barely able to hear him now. His eyes were hazy and unfocused. "I'll take it."

"What's wrong with you?" I asked, my concern only heightening when the man let me finish my question.

He gave a lopsided smile, green mush staining his teeth, and I swore. I'd never seen it in person before – although Mila had once used it on me in its concentrated form – but the leaves he'd been chomping down on could only be one thing. *Molchaniye*.

Ren met my gaze and rolled his eyes.

"Let's get going," I growled. I did *not* need the Hearken losing consciousness from the narcotic before we reached the base of the mountain.

Dima uncurled himself from the floor, swaying dizzily as he stood, and when I snatched his arm to keep him balanced he waved an imperious hand at Ren. "Bring the box," he ordered, the *molchaniye* clearly already addling his mind as well as his ability to speak coherently if he believed, having the benefit of reading the prince's own thoughts, that he would obey.

Ren opened the lid of the small wooden box on the shelf being gestured to, peering in with curious eyes and then recoiling in disgust.

"We are not," he hissed, "fuelling your fucking drug habit!"

"Bring it," I said wearily.

"I would have thought you would have had some disapproving, judgmental words to say on the matter, Nat."

"Would you like to carry him and *I'll* handle the box?" I asked snidely, and my prince immediately shook his head, snapping the lid closed and swiping the box of *molchaniye* off the shelf. He clutched it in his arms, pretending to stagger under an enormous weight, and I glared at him as I heaved and dragged an almost limp Dima to the door.

But even Ren's self-centred nature apparently couldn't stand to watch us both struggle through the narrow doorway, me almost bent double under the older man's weight, and he tucked the box under one arm so he could help.

Bitingly cold air abused my face as soon as we left the protection of the cabin, the wind howling past my ears in sharp protest. The visibility had dropped to almost nothing, and any view that may have existed was firmly blanketed in white.

"I can't condemn...him for it when...it's us...who drove him to it," I panted, as we each wrapped one of Dima's wiry arms over our shoulders and began to pick our way down the ice-ladened mountain. I supposed I should be thankful that the man hadn't chosen to live at the very top, but the journey upwards had been horrible enough; few proper paths and treacherously loose snow had made it an arduous trek.

"What...do you mean?"

"He lives alone for a reason, Ren. He wanted to...get away from our thoughts."

My Sight wasn't as convenient as the gifts of the Voice, Scent, and Touch, which could be used at will, but at least seers weren't plagued by their magic all the time.

To never be able to turn it off like Dima had suggested...it wasn't that much of a surprise that one would turn to mind-numbing and dangerous drugs to ease its effects. Perhaps the desperate, reckless need to avoid the unrelenting bombardment of other people's thoughts was another reason why none of the Hearken remained.

The man between us grunted, and I instantly regretted the direction of my thoughts.

This was...both odd and terrifying. Having someone know exactly what you were thinking, as soon as you thought it?

No filters, no delay, no deception?

Being exposed to everyone's genuine, raw selves with all their flaws: the shameful instincts that would normally be smothered, the spiteful thoughts that weren't otherwise spoken, the dark desires that should remain unacted upon? How could someone *live* like that?

Another grunt, and I bit my lip, sending a silent apology to Dima that was probably unnecessary. He would have felt my guilt and remorse in my initial mental flinch, and perhaps now I understood what he'd meant about not shouting at him. Were targeted, focused thoughts more painful than general musings?

"You think too much," the Hearken complained, and even though his words had been quiet and barely enunciated, Ren gave a hearty agreement that was quickly snatched away by the wind. I could barely see beyond him now, the world around us having turned completely white. All we could do was put one foot in front of the other and follow any path that looked like it would take us downwards.

"How far do you think we're-"

The overwhelming bleak whiteness of our surroundings suddenly burst into vivid colour, the bellowing of the wind quenched in an instant.

I blinked to orient myself – or tried to, but I couldn't move. Or more accurately, there wasn't any of me *to* move. I didn't feel solid at all, like my mind was present without my body, and it took me a moment to recognise the formless sensation as similar to what I'd felt when I'd Seen Ren lying on the floor of *la Cortina's* throne room being tortured by Comandante Moreno.

So this was a vision, and one I apparently wouldn't be present for when...*if* it ever happened. Only the more skilled seers could See events outside of their own future, but the excitement of that realisation quickly faded when the colours focused into distinct shapes and I recognised the shrewd, bald face of Councillor Navar. He was wearing a dressing gown I recognised as one of Ren's; gold silk with red roses stitched along its edging, and the familiarity of both that and his surroundings made my non-existent insides swirl with foreboding.

Navar bared his teeth in my direction.

"You can't get anything out of a dead man," he crowed and turned to the northerner who stood by his side, an old man with salt and pepper hair and a heavily wrinkled face.

By the time I realised what he held in his hand, the councillor had sunk the knife into the stranger's chest, roughly jerking it back out and making the embroidered roses on his sleeve swell with colour as the blood soaked through the fabric. The other man gave a wet, desperate gasp, staggering backwards and instinctively clutching at the wound. I knew the impulse well: each time I'd been hit with the recurring vision of Ren similarly stabbing me I'd tried to hold myself together as if my fingers could stem the flow of blood, but it had never saved me and certainly wasn't doing any better for whoever Navar's victim was.

Although...sparks sputtered beneath his fingers, the pale orange of a rising moon. I waited expectantly for the healing magic to take effect, but the sparks were weak and irregular. They fizzled and then abruptly died, as if they'd had water poured on them.

There was a commotion behind me, a flurry of noise and movement, but it was muted like I was hearing it from underwater and I couldn't turn my head to look. My Sight evidently only wanted to show me the northerner's death because it narrowed in on him, amplifying the man's heaving, uneven breaths, the way he collapsed heavily to the floor, how he stilled a moment later with dull, staring eyes.

Cold and monotonous white rushed in once more, bringing me back to my body, although it wasn't where I'd left it. I was lying down, aching and wincing, with my left arm twisted beneath me. I also wasn't entirely sure which way was up until I felt Ren wrench me to my feet, fussing and cursing and brushing loose snow from my shoulders.

"Are you alright?"

I saw his lips move and heard traces of the yell reach my ears, but it was as if he'd shouted it from the top of the adjacent mountain. The wind was somehow even *louder* now, dreary bleakness staring back at me from all directions and leaving my prince the only spot of colour – and warmth – in what felt like the entire world.

I nodded, checking him over. There was snow everywhere, including tucked under his chin and in the buttonholes of his fur coat, but otherwise he seemed uninjured. "What happened?"

"Fucking Blessed!" Ren shouted back. "You went into a vision and apparently your mind dragged Dima along with you, for you both collapsed and fell down the damn slope. It was an expeditious way of descending the mountain, I'll give you that, but I'm also prepared to quite literally *murder* you for scaring me so badly, Mathias!"

Instead of making good on his threat, he yanked me into a tight hug. I wrapped an arm around him, blinking snow from my eyelashes, and stared over his shoulder into the piercing white. I couldn't see a thing.

"Where's Dima?"

"How the fuck should I know? If my fucking heart throws himself off a mountain, I'm going after him, not hanging around to take a head count!"

"Ren," I yelled into his ear. "He's high on *molchaniye!*" The plant-based drug was known for its depressant effects, the leaves often chewed to relax or sedate their user, and the Hearken had already been deep in its embrace when I sank into my vision. If he'd fallen, he might not have the energy or inclination to get back up, and with the weather making it impossible to see more than a few feet in any direction…

The prince nodded briskly, knowing that it wasn't just the man's life at risk but our chance of unseating Welzes. He threaded his gloved hand into mine so we couldn't lose each other, and we staggered deeper into the snowstorm.

Foot by foot we searched in vain, calling Dima's name until our voices were hoarse and our legs ached from fighting the wind. The snow was falling quickly enough to hide our own passing, let alone any footprints he might have made.

Panic surged through me, knowing time was precious in these temperatures, and that if the man wasn't moving whether because of an injury or the narcotics in his body, the cold would quickly find him.

A pained wail split the air for a brief moment, snatched away by the wind, but it was enough. Ren and I darted in the direction it had come from, soon rewarded by a splash of colour against the bitter white, and hauled a kneeling Dima upright. His face was screwed up and gloved hands were pressed to his ears where white light sparked through the wool.

"*Lo siento,*" Ren shouted at him, looking vaguely guilty, and I realised he'd been using his thoughts to provoke the man into making noise. But it didn't seem like it was our bedroom activities this time: the look of anguish on the Hearken's face was far beyond embarrassment or disgust, and his expression seemed haunted before it slackened once more. I wondered what Ren had showed him, swallowing when my mind jumped to what he'd suffered at Moreno and Iván Aratorre's hands as a child.

Dima slumped against us, his body limp even as he blinked in confusion, and we hitched his arms back over our shoulders before continuing the descent down the mountain, our boots sinking into loose and slippery snow. I only hoped my Sight would stay firmly dormant until our feet were on stable ground once more.

*

Chapter Thirty

Ren

"It sounds like Yanev," I said when Mathias had finished describing what he'd Seen up on the mountain. The description of the elderly northerner with burnished orange magic fit everything I knew about the healer, including my father's complaints that his Touch had been weakening in his old age. The late king had been the only person Yanev had ever treated, allowing him to maintain his strength long past the lifespan of most Blessed healers, one of the many favours he'd received in exchange for defecting to Quareh all those decades ago.

"That's what I was thinking," Mat confessed, his teeth worrying at his bottom lip. "And feared. So Navar's going to kill him?"

"It would make sense. Dead, his story about my parents can't be contradicted. Alive, someone might do what we're planning and force the truth from him. Although they're probably more concerned about torture than an extinct kind of magic."

We both glanced behind us to where Dima was slumped unconscious over the third horse in our little party, its reins tied to a lead rope attached to my saddle. The base of the mountain had thankfully been sheltered from the storm, the improved visibility giving us no trouble in finding the horses – alive and only a little grumpy – yet that stroke of improved fortune had been countered by Dima's deterioration into the *molchaniye,* and we'd been dragging his passed-out form the final couple of hundred feet. If the man didn't give enough of a fuck to have held off taking incapacitating drugs until we'd gotten him down the mountain, I didn't give enough of one to be careful when manhandling him into position. Fortunately for the Hearken, my lover was a much more compassionate soul. Mathias had not only done his best to keep the man comfortable, but had frequently called us to a halt to check he was still breathing.

"The question is when," Mat said quietly as we turned our horses onto the bridge that ran directly from the northern hills up to the gates of Panarina's castle. It was elevated on huge stone pillars above the city, grand and imposing and about as subtle an entrance as announcing ourselves with a fanfare of trumpets, but Dima might rouse any moment. With how overwhelmed he'd been with only two additional minds in his own, I didn't dare think about how quickly he'd be driven to insanity if we carted him through the populated streets of Stavroyarsk. All we could hope was that the late hour, the swirling snow, and the height of the bridge would keep our return from too many prying eyes.

"And where," I agreed, but he had an answer for that one.

"*La Cortina.* Your rooms…your old ones. I recognised the tapestry behind Yanev as the one in the antechamber."

Oh, so Navar fancied himself a prince, did he?

Dima groaned. We wordlessly urged our horses into a trot, their hooves clicking against the cobblestones of the bridge. Because wood would have been too *common,* apparently, with some ancestral Panarin having spent a fortune and much of their sense in constructing the massive bridge that soared up to the castle in a showy gesture of wealth and pretentiousness that I was finding it hard not to admire. Less impressive was the hulking shadow it cast over the city below during the daytime, but seeing as Stavroyarsk was fucking freezing and gloomy regardless, maybe no one had noticed yet.

And while our companion's identity remained a secret to all but us, Panarina, and Velichkov, it seemed our return was anything but secret, because we were quickly ushered through the several checkpoints of guards who manned the bridge and past the gates.

Where we discovered that we weren't the only royal visitors this night.

Astrid Panarina stood on the steps to the castle, framed by the open doorway at her back. Her thin white dress billowed airily around her, snow cascading down onto her bare shoulders, and the ethereal appearance she cast was only heightened by her abject refusal to do anything so human as *shiver.*

Velichkov was a few feet away, bundled up in furs like any sensible person, but both his and Panarina's eyes were locked on the third royal in the courtyard. The woman had her back to us, her grey hair pinned up in a severe bun, but as Mat and I dismounted from our horses and handed over our reins to a pair of stablehands, her shoulders turned fractionally in our direction. Familiar blue-grey eyes took us in with a terrifyingly intense scrutiny, and I felt my wildcat stiffen at my side.

"Mother?" Mathias croaked out, his voice breaking on the word. A word that was a *question,* as if he was unsure of the answer.

Queen Zora Velichkova's gaze swept coolly from him to me and then back to her son, her mouth thinning. Whatever she saw, she wasn't impressed.

Valeri cleared his throat, miming a bow with the crisp tilt of his upper half, his right arm clenched in a fist across his chest. But Mat, who I'd seen bow in the Temarian way before, instead sank into the traditional gesture of the Mazekhstani, settling his arm across his waist.

Reminding her of what she'd done to him.

"Your Majesty," I muttered, half-assing my own bow and not bothering to give it the usual flourish favoured by Quareh. Yet it seemed I'd used up my allotment of her scant attention, for the Temarian queen didn't bother to even acknowledge me.

As the silence grew, I waited for the condemnation I was sure Zora was about to deliver on her third-born son. The fury, or the disappointment, or the bigotry – however she chose to communicate the clear disapproval on her face, I was ready to fucking *unload* on her about how Mathias was a thousand times the royal…the *person,* she could ever be.

But it didn't come, and that was almost worse.

"Nathanael," Queen Velichkova said evenly, dispassionately, as though she was addressing a stranger instead of her own Dios-damned child she hadn't seen in nearly two decades. Then she turned away without another word, gliding up the stairs and past Panarina, who mutely stepped aside to allow her entrance.

"Mother," Mathias begged. His voice echoed around the torch-lit courtyard. "Please let Val and Mila have your army. Let them help Ren."

Zora didn't even pause.

As she disappeared inside the castle, I glanced at Mat. His jaw set, his eyes filled with a steely hardness I recognised as his *getting shit done* expression, and he jutted his chin at Dima.

"He needs to be kept sedated by Doc until we leave tomorrow," he told

Panarina, and she nodded, ordering her servants to take the man inside to the healer before descending the stairs towards us.

"Nat?" she asked gently, tentatively, the ice queen thawing before my very eyes. The worry on her face as she raised a pale hand to his cheek had me reassessing what I knew about her, because Astrid Panarina was apparently a complex fucking creature, oscillating between cold-hearted bitch and sweet, vulnerable tenderness. While I appreciated more than most the importance of maintaining appearances, hers seemed more than surface deep. Like she really was both personalities, and saw no difficulty in maintaining such a juxtaposition of character.

Mat's hand was already entwined with mine: I'd reached for it as soon as I realised who the surprise guest was and that there would be no warm reconciliation between them, and now he squeezed it gratefully.

"I'm fine, Astrid. I just…didn't expect her to be here."

"None of us did," Panarina said softly.

"Apparently Aksinia Saw the treaty we'd reached," Velichkov added, giving the doorway his mother had disappeared through a dark look. "While it was within my delegated authority to agree on Temar's behalf, Her Majesty wants to look it over before it is signed."

I felt my northerner tense. "She's not…it won't…"

"*Nyet*," said Panarina. Her bare arms were smooth from bumps, showing no sign she was even feeling the cold. "I consider the matters between Aratorre and myself settled, and will not accept any amendments Queen Velichkova may propose if they are detrimental to *either* of our countries."

I murmured my thanks, she gave an apology, and then everyone else in the courtyard retreated into the castle or the stables, leaving just me, Mat, and his brother.

Mathias' shoulders slumped, emotion finally overwhelming him, and I held him tight. His cold cheek pressed against mine.

"Fuck her," I said firmly. "You don't need her."

"She's my family," he mumbled.

"She sold you as a child to finish a war you had nothing to do with," I snarled, barely able to keep my rage in check. Oh, if it wouldn't undo everything we were trying to achieve with bringing peace to the continent, I'd march in there and rip the woman's fucking head off for how she'd dared to treat her son: all those years ago, and just now. "She's not family."

I pulled back to look him in the eye, hating how it took him a few seconds to work up the nerve to meet it. "I am. Your friends are. Valeri, Mila, even Viento, the little shit."

Mat cracked a reluctant smile. "I hope he's not letting any of the pricks back in Máros ride him."

"You and I both know he isn't. And you can't let a horse beat you in wilfulness, can you? So. *Fuck. Her.*"

Velichkov drew close to us and wrapped a broad arm across his little brother's shoulders.

"Hands to yourself, Aratorre," he said wearily, rolling his eyes, and I blinked innocently up at him. How he'd felt my arm creep around his back with the thick layers of furs he was wearing, I didn't know, but I hadn't done it to cop a feel. I'd done it to more securely squish Mathias between us, making sure he was kept warm and loved, and the small, happy smile on my boy's face said maybe it was working. Mat kissed our cheeks, one after the other, rising up on his toes to reach his brother.

"You're right. I have you both."

We stood there in silence for a long moment, our backs blocking out the wind and forming a quiet, private space between our bowed heads.

And then I made a comment about how, if that was Mathias proposing to have a threesome with the surly northern heir in our huddle, I would have to regrettably, unfortunately, *immediately* accept.

Velichkov snarled curses at me and we descended into mindless bickering, but all I could see was Mat closing his eyes, that content little smile only growing wider.

*

Chapter Thirty-One

Mat

The next morning, after checking Dima was being cared for, I found myself pulling up short at the sight of a familiar Temarian waiting for me outside Doc's surgery and accompanied by his own Mazekhstani escort.

"Parvan," I said, surprised. The last I'd seen of the royal guard was him bleeding out on the tournament grounds after taking a blade to the gut for me. While I'd ordered him healed and Mila had later confirmed his survival when I'd asked, Valeri had made it clear that the man was no longer welcome in his retinue and hadn't brought him with us to Máros. "I thought my mother had already returned home?"

"Her Majesty left just before dawn," Parvan confirmed and sank into a deep bow. "Although I have resigned from her service."

"Oh. That's...good for you," I said awkwardly, trying to inch past him to get to the stairs.

"My prince."

He lowered himself further until one of his knees rested on the hard floor, and I faltered. The man may have saved my life, but he'd also made no secret of how he considered my sexual preferences to be contrary to God's wishes. In fact, I was fairly sure one of the last things he'd said to me was that he still believed I deserved to be flogged for it, and there certainly hadn't been any damn *bowing*.

"I should not have judged you, Your Highness," Parvan muttered into his beard, his eyes cast down in respect.

I cleared my throat. "Whatever this is, I can't do it with you on the floor. Please get up."

He rose smoothly, his hand sliding automatically to his hip where a sword would have been, had he still been on active service and not alone in a foreign castle. His fingers flexed, searching for a hilt that wasn't there, before he forced his hand down to his side.

AN OATH AND A PROMISE

"My niece," Parvan began, an adoring smile stretched across his lined face. I wasn't sure I'd ever seen him wear an expression that wasn't professional neutrality, other than the disgust he'd sent my way after I'd outed myself. "Fifteen years old, never shuts up, and certainly knows her own mind, much to her parents' displeasure. She asked me rather excitedly when the army returned to Delzerce whether I'd had the privilege of guarding Prince Nathanael."

I shifted my weight between my feet.

"I...I'm afraid I said something about you that she did not like," he continued, glancing down as if ashamed, "and then she told me...she told me I should have been proud to stand at your side when you did what you did. That you were brave. That she'd never dared speak of it before, but she feels things for men *and* women, and those who identify as both or neither."

Parvan dropped back down to the floor, and I growled in exasperation because that was easier than processing what he'd just said.

"I cannot apologise enough for my behaviour," he said frantically to my boots. "I've always trusted God to see me through, but if He would ask me to condemn my niece... That girl is an angel, not a single evil bone in her Blessed body, and if that is her truth, then...maybe yours is also something I should have listened to."

I let him speak, sensing he needed this confession. And maybe I needed a moment too, because to hear that what I'd done had inspired someone else's courage was...hard to comprehend, but also so fucking amazing.

"It's taken me a while, but it made me realise the world is bigger than I'd thought," murmured Parvan, "and that I have been terribly short-sighted. I won't ask for your forgiveness, Your Highness, but I will try to earn it."

"You stopped Andonov from killing me," I pointed out. "I think that's enough to-"

"Will you have me at your side?"

I blinked. "What?"

"The next time I see my niece," he said gruffly, "I want to be able to say that *yes,* I do have the honour of protecting you from those who would do you harm, my prince. Will you accept me as your guard?"

AN OATH AND A PROMISE

"Parvan, I..."

I blew out a breath and ran a hand over my face before hauling him to his feet. He uncurled from his deferent position with surprising elegance considering his age, muscles straining under his shirt and his eyes flickering around intently to assess for threats even in the midst of making his plea. If his apology was genuine, he'd make a good ally, but...

"If this all goes as planned, I'll be living in Máros," I told him. "Are you sure you'd want to be so far away from your family? It's not easy being a northerner in Quareh."

"I will endeavour to learn the language, Prince Nathanael," the man said stiffly.

I raised an eyebrow. "And if you're at my side, you're going to see me and Ren kiss. You know that, right? Maybe worse. *Probably* worse, knowing him."

Parvan bowed again. "So is that a yes, Your Highness?"

I gave a low hum of assent. "Only if you find yourself a sense of humour."

"I'll start looking immediately, my prince," he said, and although the words were uttered in the driest tone of voice I'd ever heard, his lips twitched.

I snorted.

He trailed me through the corridors until I reached my own room, only to be nearly bowled over by Ren bursting out of his. I watched Parvan closely, looking for any indication of disgust, but found none.

The prince cheerfully looped his arm through mine and gave our Mazekhstani guards a look that dared them to comment on it. "Panarina has asked for us," he told me, steering us in the direction of the throne room. "That was about half an hour ago, but you were busy and I was...not inclined to make the effort. Now seems as good a time as any to wander down."

When we arrived, my attention was immediately drawn to the Quarehian with the frizzy hair and wide grin, who was wedged between two of Astrid's guards.

"Starling!"

"She is one of yours?" asked Astrid, rising gracefully from her throne.

Ren squinted at the healer. "Never seen her before in my life."

Star threw him a rude gesture without looking his way.

"That answers that," Astrid said resignedly, and motioned for the guards to step back. Starling brushed off the shoulders of her coat as if their presence at her side had all been a terrible inconvenience.

Ren, who I was sure secretly approved of the dramatics, gave a disapproving tut, but when I glanced at him his gaze was soft.

"What happened?" I asked her, worried. "Why are you here? Did you not get the message I sent?"

"We got it," Starling assured me. "Lilia and Zov are fine," she added, "and appreciated knowing you were too. But I expected you were having far too much fun without me in this big old castle, and wanted to come see what the fuss was about. So I asked the girls to show me the way to..." She faltered, glancing at the queen. "...to the *front gates of the castle*, where I happened to find another entrance in all by myself."

Astrid clicked her tongue, far too dignified to offer the scoff that she clearly wanted to make.

"I know your friends helped you inside," she told me wryly, "and I'm in the process of having that entrance sealed. Thankfully I took the precaution of ordering the area guarded after your own unexpected arrival."

I let out the breath I'd been holding. If she'd known who aided us all this time and still hadn't taken any action against Zovisasha and Lilia for it, I figured that meant nothing worse was heading their way.

"Will you come with us?" I asked Starling. I'd been thinking of reaching out to her, but I should have known she'd make the first move. "I know you and Ren talked about you coming back afterwards, but we could really use your help now with..."

I fell silent, not wanting to speak it out loud in company even if we were already conversing in Quarehian. Astrid silently gestured for her guards to leave the room.

"With a Hearken," I said after the doors creaked shut, and Star's eyes widened.

"What the fuck?"

"I *know!*" I agreed, and we shared a moment of incredulousness before she gave a brisk, elated nod.

"I'm in. That's far too damn crazy for me to ever say no to, and if whatever you have planned gets that lump of shit off the Quarehian throne, I'll do what I can to help." She side-eyed Ren. "Not that the alternative is much better."

The prince clutched at his heart and batted his eyelashes at her. "You say the sweetest things, you pesky irritation."

She blew him a kiss.

"Is the Hearken well enough to travel?" Astrid asked me.

I winced, feeling vaguely guilty about Dima's extended and magically-induced unconsciousness but knowing it was the best way to protect him from the minds of the castle's hundreds of occupants. "Hard to tell at the moment, but if you can lend us a carriage, it won't be a problem. We can revive him once he's out of the city and away from so many people."

The queen's expression thoughtful. "I've received word from my Quarehian contacts-"

"Spies," Ren said with a meaningful cough into his hand. She eyed him with amusement.

"From my *spies*, that Welzes will shortly be travelling to *la Cortina* to solidify his position with the nobles of north and east Quareh. There's been rumours of unrest in those provinces, and I expect he's wanting to clamp down on it before it gets worse. If he leaves the healer behind in the capital, you might be able to-"

"No. He'll be taking Yanev with him," I said in a low voice, recalling what my Sight had shown me. I turned to Ren. "He'll use Yanev's lies to convince them he's the rightful king as he did the nobility in Máros, and then he'll dispose of the man. We're running out of time."

The prince nodded sharply. "Then we'll leave immediately."

"I'm coming with you," Val said as he entered the throne room behind us.

"You are *not*," Ren retorted after giving an abrupt and rather loud laugh, clearly caught off guard. "That's the stupidest idea I've ever heard from you,

AN OATH AND A PROMISE

Velichkov, and that's saying something."

"Why?"

I expected my lover to complain about inconsiderate northerners stomping all over his lands, or the difficulty of sneaking the heir to Temar into a Quarehian palace.

"Because you might die, and that would be terrible," Ren said instead.

Valeri stared at him, his mouth opening and closing awkwardly as if he wasn't quite sure what to make of the prince's unexpected concern.

"Terrible?" I prompted, suspecting there was more. There always was, with him.

"*Sí.* Valeri dies, you get even more dour and crabby than usual, and then *I* don't get laid," Ren explained in a tone that said it was obvious, and my brother sighed.

"Nat?"

"I would love you to come," I said, ignoring Ren's childish snort at the phrasing, "and we would greatly appreciate the help. But I would also prefer you didn't die."

"I'm not going to *die*," Val assured me, his exasperated tone suggesting I was being ridiculous. As if there weren't literally tens of thousands of people on this continent who'd gladly put all three of our heads on spikes for the money or glory it would bring them, and that our so-called *plan* consisted of little more than a vague goal: get Dima close enough to Yanev to read his mind and discover the extent of his lies, and then produce the Hearken to the nobles as evidence that Ren's birthright remained intact. How exactly we would do any of that when we were wanted men, Dima couldn't function around too many other people, and Yanev's remaining life was ticking down to a messy end at the end of Welzes' knife, I didn't know, but I *did* know that having my brother at our side made me feel more optimistic about our success.

Ren offered me a cheerful wink, letting me know that he didn't actually have a problem with Val accompanying us, and then proceeded to ferociously argue with him about it for over half an hour while we made plans to depart. Because *moy dorogoi* could never do anything as simple as saying *"thank you, Valeri."*

*

Chapter Thirty-Two

Ren

I had just gotten Mathias exactly where he belonged – beneath me and openly panting – when Velichkov ripped open the door of the carriage we'd sequestered ourselves in. Even without looking around I could feel the heir's irritated displeasure filling the air, a heavy, tangible thing that needed a good flick on the nose to send it scurrying away.

"I have to *sit* there," he growled.

I gestured with my foot at the opposite bench to where we were making out. "Sit there instead."

"And spend the day watching you molest my brother? No."

A huge hand grabbed me by the nape of my neck and hauled me bodily off Mat, undoing all of my work in climbing on top of him as if that shit had been effortless instead of a violent, intensely hot struggle that had occupied most of the last five minutes.

Seating himself on the empty carriage seat, Velichkov roughly yanked me down beside him. My wildcat hurriedly pushed himself upright and tried to flatten his hair from where it had gotten all mussed, but before I could move into the spare space left next to him, the Temarian guard that had been following Mat around all morning climbed in and snagged the spot. Wolf darted inside just as the door was closed from the other side, settling himself across all of our feet.

"Ren," Mathias said with a deepening scowl, his lips red and swollen and disappointingly not occupied in the way we both preferred. "I think we're being *chaperoned*."

He was right. We'd been carefully separated by the two men so we were sitting as far away from each other as possible in the tiny space, with another 120 pounds of lupine flesh and teeth nesting casually between us. I pulled a face, wriggling to free myself from where I was pressed against the wall by Valeri's massive bulk.

"That's it. We're taking the other carriage, and you can have Dima and Starling." I leaned forward to open the door just as Velichkov rapped on the roof with his knuckles and the carriage lurched forward, throwing me back into my seat. I opened my mouth to call the driver to a stop instead, and the heir slapped a meaty hand over my mouth.

"You know I'm a king, right?" I asked testily after I'd managed to free myself.

"Not yet, you're not." Velichkov eyed me unfavourably. "But you *are* an irksome, talkative little pest."

"Nathanael," I drawled. "Did I ever tell you about the plan I once had to kill your brother slowly and horribly by dunking him into a shallow pond full of eels? I've suddenly decided to revisit the idea."

"A shallow pond?" Mat asked testily. "Wouldn't a deep one be better? Make it harder for him to escape?" He growled out that last part.

Velichkov had seemingly decided to ignore us both, watching the world slide past through the little window to his left.

"I didn't want the eels to find themselves a nice spot to settle down in and raise little eels and visit their eel neighbours on the weekend," I explained, because *duh*. "A shallow pond meant that all their attention would be on him, and if they wanted an inch of space for themselves, they'd have to take it from his flesh."

"Charming," the man opposite me muttered.

I beamed at him. "Many people say the same, and I can only assume it's due to my infinite kindness to those less fortunate than myself. Which is everyone, of course, but especially this brute here." I patted Velichkov's thigh in what was totally a friendly manner, and then abruptly found myself in a lot of pain as my wrist was twisted in a way wrists were not meant to go.

"Val!" Mat rebuked, and the heir reluctantly let go.

"Couldn't you have found someone *sweet* to fall in love with and upset an entire continent for?" Velichkov complained loudly to his brother, who smirked and pulled his feet up beneath him on the cushioned seat, settling in for the ride.

"Speaking of people who aren't sweet," I said, staring at the other man in the carriage whose name I remembered but wouldn't be using because I couldn't have him think I cared, "aren't you the one who wanted Nat flogged?"

"That's all behind us," Mathias said.

I rolled my eyes. "You're too forgiving, *mi amor*."

Parvan met my accusing gaze without blinking. "I did say that, but believe it no longer. I wish to atone for my past mistakes."

"*Right*," I said, ensuring my tone communicated how I wasn't nearly as merciful as my lover. I'd be having Dima check out the truth of what he claimed as soon as the Hearken woke. If Parvan retained even half an ounce of ill intent towards Mat, I'd make sure he choked on that glorious salt-and-pepper beard of his, the practicalities of such a thing be damned.

But as the day drew on and the carriage bore us steadily south, I noticed Velichkov was keeping a wary eye on the guard too, and relaxed slightly with the knowledge that there was no way he'd be able to try anything with the heir on his back. Regardless of how good Parvan might be with a sword, nothing could stand in the way of Valeri Velichkov and protecting his little brother.

As I knew all too well. I'd been on the receiving end of his ire – and his fists – more than once, and even if the damage had been healed long ago, I remembered the look of sheer fury on the man's face when he'd found Mathias and me in bed together. Of course, that slightly less-than-pleasant memory quickly gave way to one from half an hour earlier when my northerner and I had joined fully for the first time, and as attuned to my thoughts as always, I saw Mat shift in his seat and give me a wickedly teasing smile.

Watching his teeth drag slowly and deliberately across his lower lip occupied my attention for the remainder of the day's journey, until we finally came to whatever private lodgings had been arranged for us and I almost tripped over in my haste to get him alone.

The next day, as we all stood waiting for the carriages to be brought from the stables outside the house that belonged to whatever Mazekhstani noble Panarina had paid or threatened into letting us stay, Mathias nudged his shoulder against mine and passed me something.

"What is it?"

"The gender law reform," he said.

I hefted the roll of parchment in my hand, assessing its weight. "Why is it twice as heavy as before?"

"Because it's twice as thick," retorted Starling from Mathias' other side. "*Obviously.*"

I glared at her. "*You're* twice as thick."

"Not one of your best, darling," Mat said affectionately. He gestured at the scroll. "It's been modified to account for feedback from stakeholders."

"Stakeholders?" I raised a meaningful eyebrow at Starling. "Meaning you?"

"Me," she confirmed happily. "And Astrid." I marvelled at this tiny Quarehian casually referring to the fucking queen of Mazekhstam by her given name. "And Zovisasha and Lilia and Alina and Olga and…" She continued to rattle out names that didn't mean a fucking thing to me, and I had no idea how she'd found the time between arriving at the castle yesterday and us leaving barely two hours later, but her visible excitement was kind of endearing.

"You didn't think we were going to implement a law to help women without speaking to them first, right?" Mathias asked grumpily.

I couldn't answer, for the healer was already chattering to him about who else they'd planned to ask when we returned to Quareh. The feisty little señorita and I might never have seen eye to eye – mostly my fault for hoisting onto her my shame of what my father did to me, but I'd *hated* anyone seeing me so vulnerable – yet the insightful way she was speaking was making me see her in a different light. Mat was incredibly fond of her company, but I'd thought it born from their shared shitty circumstances of living at other people's wills.

Yet from the animated way they were both speaking now, throwing out ideas to have them delightedly built upon and refined by the other, they clearly bettered each other mentally as well as emotionally. I could practically hear the melted *drip* as my heart thawed just a little more.

They both glanced at me during a pause in their discussion and I cleared my throat.

"Well," I said awkwardly, intently watching the carriages draw closer across the gravel drive so I didn't have to look either of them in the eye. "That's all assuming we get Quareh back."

"You will," Starling said softly, and I was so busy waiting for the remainder of the sentence and the insult I was sure was coming but *didn't*, that I barely noticed Velichkov ushering me into the first of the carriages.

"Wait, you're leaving those two alone?" I said in horror as Dima's unconscious form was laid in the other carriage by Parvan, and Mat and Starling climbed in after him. "Do you know what utter fucking catastrophes they could wreak?"

Velichkov patted my head like he would his wolf, and I smacked his hand away before he could crush the wildflowers my boy had found and carefully threaded through my hair this morning. "Relax, Aratorre. It's just a few hours."

―

Just a few hours wasn't a term that applied to Nathanael Velichkov, not really.

He'd consumed my every thought and sentenced me to drown in unceasing, burning obsession within minutes of meeting him. Mere seconds in his presence could light both my soul and body on fire.

If I thought about how much he'd changed me in the weeks we'd known each other, then I really shouldn't have been surprised that *a few hours* produced innovative theories on an entirely new system of educational governance, scrawled down excitedly – and almost incomprehensibly – across scraps of loose parchment that he or Starling had somehow scrounged up while stuck in a moving carriage. But his fervour was infectious, the ideas thrillingly intriguing, and to my great shame when I hauled Mat away that night it was not to a bedroom but a small study, where we found writing supplies and a lantern full of oil. We talked well into the night, expanding on the initial concept of universal childhood education, and when Mathias fell asleep at my feet with his head in my lap, I carried on working until dawn, stroking his hair and crafting those grand and aspirational ideas into something that could be feasibly implemented without emptying the treasury and requiring more hours from the teachers than the day allowed.

And the next couple of nights were much the same, leaving me exhausted but in a pleasant, satisfied sort of way. I'd even let Mat take charge when we'd finally collapsed into bed together, too tired to issue orders about where I wanted him.

Although he'd put himself there anyway.

Now we were approaching the Mazekhstam-Quarehian border after several days of constant travel, and Starling had just roused Dima from the artificially-induced coma she'd been keeping him in. The healer had kept his body healthy but confessed the torment of his mind was beyond her gifts, and the chaotic ramblings the Hearken had already sunk into as he glared at each of us were evidence enough that the brain was not something easily fixed, even for the magic of the Blessed.

If Dima had been driven to *molchaniye* by only mine and Mat's presence, I couldn't imagine what the combined thoughts of our motley group were doing to him. The two Mazekhstani drivers had departed back north with the carriages, but that still left five people able to fuck him up by doing nothing more than *thinking*.

Well, four. Velichkov had disappeared a short while ago into the descending fog to scout out a surreptitious route across the border, leaving Parvan and Wolf to keep an eye on his brother. And the rest of us, I supposed.

"It hurts, it hurts," Dima muttered, clutching at his head, and although Starling anxiously pressed sparking fingers to his temple, it didn't seem to help. "Too many, so loud, just make it *stop*..."

Fuck. Maybe we should have tried harder to find his box of *molchaniye* leaves from wherever I'd dropped it on the mountain when I saw Mathias fall into his vision, or else sourced some from Stavroyarsk before we'd left. Although we needed the man conscious now that we'd be travelling on foot, perhaps it wasn't the worst idea in the world to let him take the edge off…

The Hearken's head swivelled to mine and he gave me a frenzied, expectant look. His pupils were blown and his fingers were seized into claws.

"We don't have any," I said aloud, unnecessarily. He groaned, slumping against Starling, and I was forced to catch his arm to stop the man's weight from sending them both to the ground.

Then Velichkov appeared from the mist, silent and wraithlike despite his size. "This way," he hissed with an urgent note to his voice, waving a broad arm. "I've found a boat."

The border in these parts lay along a body of water that was too narrow to be called a river, but fast and wild enough to form an effective boundary between the two countries. Further to the east and west, particularly where there was contestation around the city of Algejón, the border was defined by guardposts on the road, but those areas were also a lot more heavily watched. We'd hoped that crossing here, where both Quareh and Mazekhstam primarily relied on the rivulet to keep the other's armies out and we could more readily sneak through the patrols, would keep our return to the south secret long enough for us to reach *la Cortina*.

And then we stumbled down to the water's edge and I saw the craft that Velichkov had generously termed a 'boat'. Because to me, the word suggested a sturdy vessel…or at least hardy, something with a prow and stern and the capability to you know, fucking *float*.

This thing was sitting barely an inch above the water line, encrusted with tar and algae and looking as sorry for itself as was possible for a bunch of rotten boards held together by optimism. It was also tiny, capable of fitting maybe four people but certainly not our whole party, and I gave the dozen yards of swirling water between us and Quareh a dubious glance as we strode up to the end of the little dock the boat was roped to.

"In you get," the northern heir said cheerily, peeling Dima off my arm and dumping him unceremoniously on the back bench. The boat bobbed, seemed to consider sinking for a moment, and then remained resolutely aloft. I could practically hear it gritting its little boat teeth.

I peered inside. There were several inches of muddy water washing across the bottom, along with a large frog, which promptly hopped out onto the dock. When even an amphibian wouldn't take its chances, I knew us land-dwellers were fucked.

"That's okay," I said graciously. "I'll…"

"Just move your ass," Starling muttered, shoving me in the back so I had no choice but to clamber in. I narrowed my eyes and she gave a half-curtsy as she settled herself beside me on the middle, widest bench. "*My prince*."

I glanced around only to find my view of my lover blocked by Velichkov as he manoeuvred himself into the remaining scintilla of space at the back of the boat. "Mat-"

"Will be fine without you for ten minutes, Your Pretentiousness," Starling said, and then sighed as she took in my horrified expression. "And you'll be fine without him."

"I don't think you know what you're talking about," I protested, nearly whining. "I *need* him."

"Thats what he always says. You're both so fucking codependent."

I stared blankly at her. Why was she saying it like it was a bad thing?

"I'll drop these three off and come right back for you," Velichkov told Mat and Parvan, and I craned my neck to see them nod at him and take a step back. Wolf, his tongue lolling out of the side of his mouth like swimming across such treacherous, fast-moving water was the highlight of his day, leapt in and began paddling madly.

I didn't like how Mathias' face began to slowly shrink as the river carried us away, because leaving him wasn't a thing I liked doing.

At all.

"He's right there," murmured Starling, and to my surprise, lay a reassuring hand on my thigh. I looked down at it, considering, and then nudged her wrist with my own hand to move it between my legs. Only she snatched her arm away before it got anywhere *close* to interesting.

"You're an asshole."

The words were spoken with the same weary irritation as Velichkov always injected into his words, and the heir himself shook his head exasperatedly from where he was sitting across from us, heaving on the oars. I made sure he noticed me staring at the way his muscles bulged beneath his shirt with each stroke, pleased we'd ditched the heavy fur coats as soon as we'd reached warmer climates.

"If you wish to toss him in the river, Starling," he huffed out as he rowed, "I'll help you do it."

"But it's *dirty*," I said, reluctantly drawing my eyes from the hunk of tasty Temarian to the swirling water that surrounded us. It was too cloudy – or deep – to see the bottom. "And cold, and dangerous, and if you let me drown, you'll have to explain it to Nathanael."

I saw Velichkov visibly wince. "On the other hand..."

"Mathias will get over it," Starling declared. "Or we'll just find him *another* attention whore with a loud mouth and pretty hair, and he won't know the difference."

"He will," I argued petulantly, thankful for the distraction the inane conversation was providing from the way the boat was ominously creaking with each stroke, and how the water in the base seemed even deeper around my boots than before. "You think you can sum me up in one measly sentence, Estrella? You failed to mention my cleverness-"

"I really didn't," she muttered.

"-my gorgeous figure, and my huge, *huge* cock that makes Nat go absolutely fucking wild."

Velichkov blanched, looking gratifyingly nauseous, but unable to let go of the oars to cover his ears or smack me like he clearly wanted to. *Needed* to, from the way his fingers were clenched tightly around the wooden handles.

"You forget," Starling commented casually, "that I've seen-"

"Finish that sentence and the first thing I'll do when I'm king is arrange for every single Quarehian with a venereal disease to present to you for a *thorough* medical examination," I said in the most pleasant voice I could muster. "And when you dare complain, I'll expand the invitation to those suffering from gangrene and tapeworms."

She fell silent.

Only Mat was capable of winning against me when I was sulking like this, his stubbornness sometimes outlasting even my love for causing destruction, although brattishness versus sadism always made for a delicious combination. His reckless, headstrong nature could occasionally get the better of mine when he truly wasn't in the mood to submit, and that was pretty much anytime we *weren't* in the bedroom.

I suppose what that added up to was me being secretly grateful that Mathias wasn't on the boat after all, because he'd have eviscerated me with that ruthless tongue of his and left Velichkov and Starling the ones looking smug.

Was I out of line? Was I not respecting boundaries, being inappropriate, and making myself into an extremely annoying prick?

Yes to all of the above. But while I was teasing them – and they me – we weren't thinking about what awaited us at the end of our journey. How terrifying our odds were and how there was a good chance we'd all find ourselves imprisoned or dead, considering we were returning to the south without the support of an army.

And if I was going to die, it would be how I'd lived: hedonistic, troublesome, and without any filter.

"*Ebasi*," snarled Dima, and I twisted around at the unexpected Temarian swear word to find him staring up at Velichkov. It took me a moment to realise he was reading the man's thoughts, and while the prince's face was impassive, not giving anything away even as he began to row harder and faster, Dima's loose tongue conveyed everything in his head. "We're sinking. We're barely going to make it ourselves, and Nathanael is still-"

"On the other side of the fucking river," I finished hollowly, for despite all the cartographers' snobbery about this not *technically* being classified as a river, it certainly felt like one: wide and deep and wild. Wolf was on the south bank now, but even the strong limbs of an animal hadn't been able to prevent him from being borne a fair way downstream on the crossing, and Velichkov was having difficulty keeping the nose of our doomed boat pointing towards the shore.

"Ren! Star, Val!"

Mathias and his guard had been moving with us, wading along the edge of the Mazekhstani bank to keep pace as the water carried us away. He was so close – enough that his concerned yell easily reached my ears – and yet with the boat sinking beneath us, too damn far. There was no way they could cross without it, and I couldn't see any other craft in either direction, although the fog blocked everything beyond a few dozen yards.

"Time to swim," Velichkov said bluntly as the water reached our laps, tossing the oars aside and reaching for me and Starling. I pushed Dima into his arms instead, knowing the older man would need the assistance more than me, and threw myself into the river towards the Quarehian shore despite my heart being pulled in the opposite direction.

The icy shock of it made me gasp.

Cold water assaulted my nose and mouth, and I desperately thrashed against the force that threatened to tear me away, bracing my boots against the rocks beneath my feet. The water was only neck height here but fiercely strong, and I flailed for a long moment, hearing Mathias' alarmed shouts but unable to look his way.

All I could do was press forward, throwing all of my weight and strength into it, and slowly, ever so *slowly,* beginning to inch towards shallower water.

Velichkov waded closer and heaved at my arm, having already helped the others to make it safely and returned for me because he was apparently recklessly sweet like his brother that way – or he *really* didn't like the idea of having to explain my death – and between the two of us, we made it up the incline and onto dry ground.

I didn't bother taking a breath before I was spinning around, finding Mathias' own arm snagged by Parvan as he paced anxiously on the opposite bank. Considering my northerner looked like he wanted to throw himself into the heaving waters after us, I could only be glad that someone had sensibly taken hold of him, although it made me uncomfortable that it was a man who had once wanted him dead. Yet now would have been a perfect time to get rid of Mat if that was what Parvan really wanted – simply by letting go and allowing the brash fool to drown himself.

"Stay the fuck there!" I yelled back at Mathias, unable to believe I had to voice such an order when he'd had a perfect view of how the four of us had almost been swept away.

"We'll find another place to cross and catch up!" Parvan shouted in Temarian, and Velichkov raised a weary hand in acknowledgement, water dripping from his elbow.

Mathias' face darkened. "Don't go getting yourselves killed, *svolochi!*"

Then Velichkov's arm dipped into a sudden, slicing motion, a gesture I was unfamiliar with but which made Parvan stiffen on the opposite shore. The guard nodded, muttered something to Mat which made him similarly flinch, and then with a final lingering look our way – and an awkward little half-wave from my lover – fled into the fog.

"Soldiers coming, Aratorre," Velichkov hissed in my ear before I could ask, jerking me away. I stumbled, my clothes and boots heavy with water, and he barely bothered to let me right myself before pulling harder. "Stay silent and stay low. As nice as the peace and quiet would be if you were to lose your head, it would make all of this rather pointless."

A chill ran through me which wasn't entirely the result of my wet clothes.

Drenched, exhausted, scared, and most devastatingly without my northerner by my side, it wasn't exactly how I'd envisioned returning to Quareh.

*

Chapter Thirty-Three

Mat

The bridge and its occupants were silent and still, an anticipatory and foreboding air hanging over it all that felt as heavy as the thickening fog. We were only a dozen yards from the closest of the soldiers and couldn't even see those who waited further across the bridge, but no eyes wandered our way. We were behind them, after all, on their home side of the border, and the danger for these Mazekhstani soldiers lay to the south.

A danger they must have felt more keenly than usual, for I was sure that the border guards did not always hold themselves this tense, with their hands clutching drawn swords and their chests heaving out terrified breaths.

Leather creaked. Metal clinked. And then a cry cut through the air, muffled by the fog but still piercing and haunting, and chaos was unleashed.

I stared in dread as figures emerged from the gloom, hacking and slicing indiscriminately. The northern soldiers leapt forward, throwing themselves into the melee with courage or desperation or something indiscernible between the two, and what had been silent a moment ago was now an unbelievable amount of noise. The fog gave the scene a surreal quality, washing out both colour and sound, but nothing could disguise the sheer amount of death that the seconds delivered.

Seconds.

That's all it took to transform the bridge into a slaughter ground, bodies not even having time to fall before more were tumbling down on top of them. Some Quarehians, mostly Mazekhstani, but what did the colour of their skin or the language of their dying screams matter when the corpses of friend and foe lay together in death?

Horror had frozen me in place, but as the Quarehians surged from the bridge onto solid ground on our side of the river, I looked to Parvan. The man was crouched next to me, watching the carnage with a sorrowful sobriety, and only shifted his grip on my shoulder to push me lower behind the hedge we were using for cover.

"We can't just *watch*," I hissed. "They're dying out there!"

"And what do you propose to do about it, Your Highness?" His voice was calm, only a note or two from unaffected, and I envied the way people like him and Jiron could keep themselves removed from such sights even as I pitied them for it at the same time.

I gave the sword at his hip a meaningful look. It may have been Mazekhstani in design as his old Temarian one had been forfeited with his resignation from service, but it still had a sharp edge and a pointy tip, did it not?

"I am a guard, my prince, not a soldier." Parvan's voice was unnecessarily quiet: I doubted anyone would hear us whispering over here past the sounds of dozens of people *screaming*. "My job is to keep you safe, and I cannot do that if you send me into a battle I have no place being. Nor any purpose, for my presence would not achieve anything but my death...and yours. You know this."

Oh, how I'd missed the man's condescending remarks and indirect reminders of how shit I was at acting like a royal. I knew he was right, damn it, but that didn't make keeping ourselves hidden any easier. Not when the last of the northerners fell, and the Quarehians took a moment to plunge their blades into the hearts and heads of the dead to ensure they really were. Not when the wounded were treated the same, no mercy offered to those who weren't their kin despite their anguished pleas. Not when the southern force pushed forward, swelling past where we hid, and disappearing into the fog.

"*Cera*. Now," Parvan said, and we darted onto the bridge. There was a terrible stench of piss and blood and something else that maybe wasn't even tangible but just the scent of pointless fucking death, and I held my breath as we picked our way through – and twice, where the fighting had been thickest, *over* – the piles of corpses. My boots skidded in a puddle of slick blood and Parvan caught my arm to keep me upright, but my fingers still touched warm, sticky flesh before I snatched them away.

Bile rose in my stomach and up my throat. I swallowed it back down, diverting my eyes from the nauseating mess around us.

We tracked bloody footprints as we left the bridge that were soon lost in the long grasses beyond, and managed to obscure ourselves in the fog just as shapes loomed behind us and we heard more screams.

It was mostly Quarehian pleas and prayers this time. That held its own kind of terror because it was a stark reminder of the senseless waste of it all: an eternal push and pull between the north and south that never granted either one true victory. The border had been fought over for centuries, with thousands of people dying on both sides, and for what? The chance to do it all again the next day?

We passed through the border lands without speaking, the sounds and smells of the horrific battle still echoing around my head even a day later when I woke to a brisk, cloudless morning. As a result of needing to find somewhere else to cross the river, we were nearly a day behind Ren and the others, and it was only when I'd tripped over my own feet from exhaustion that I'd finally agreed to take a short nap. And of course, because Parvan was far too good at his job to let me sleep unguarded, he'd pushed through and stayed awake the whole time, which meant I had to subsequently give him some rest in turn. I don't know how he slept with me anxiously pacing around him the whole two hours, but I was nearly ready to explode with frustration by the time he roused.

"Regretting pledging yourself to me yet?" I asked, only half-teasing as we set off south once more, trying to ignore the ache in my belly that told of how pitiful our supplies were compared to the huge, over-luxurious meals I'd been enjoying as a guest in Stavroyarsk.

"Never, Your Highness," Parvan said blandly, and I snuck a glance at him to see if I could tell whether he was just humouring me. But other than for the man's rare bouts of emotion – like when I'd outed myself to Temar, or when he'd apologised in the castle – he was a difficult one to read. He didn't entirely have Jiron's stoic professionalism or his quiet confidence; it was more that Parvan seemed to empty himself while working, as if he were no more of a person than a suit of armour or the sword he wielded.

Yet he couldn't hide the pained lines around his eyes and mouth when we caught sight of a platoon of Quarehian soldiers later that afternoon. They traced a glorious long line up the road, the shiny metal buckles and weapons of fifty men glittering in the sun, although the uncoordinated movement and nervous expressions told their own story. These weren't soldiers. Recent recruits, perhaps, willing or not, but ultimately just fodder that the false king could throw at his northern neighbour to overwhelm Astrid's lines or bolster his own.

More human lives to be lost so needlessly in a war that had never needed to be waged.

Parvan let himself sigh then, as he reached the same realisation as I had. These men were marching straight for the border, ready to be cast against swords and arrows and other instruments of death and mutilation, and they'd be lucky if half of them – untrained as they were – would survive the week. Each of these awkward, fumbling not-soldiers who passed us where we stood with our faces hooded in the throng of travellers who'd been moved to the side of the road by the platoon's demanding heralds…each one would soon see things, feel things, *do* things they might never recover from.

"My prince," Parvan murmured, but it sounded less like a warning than resigned acceptance. I supposed I was anything but subtle in my urge to help; I was practically bouncing on my toes, my lips peeled back from my teeth as I listened to the officers bark out orders to *straighten up, hold formation, keep the pace*. What the fuck did such things matter?

I hadn't been able to save either the Mazekhstani or the Quarehians at the border. They'd died, just as more probably had today, and might keep dying until Ren wrestled back his crown and instilled the peace we'd fought so hard to secure with the northern countries.

But it didn't mean *these* men had to die.

I'd given myself for Astrid Panarina at St Izolda's Monastery. For Val, at Sesveko. It seemed fitting that there was one last heroic act left in me for the third country of Riehse Eshan, and if it couldn't be for Ren, at least it was for the people he loved. These Quarehian men might never have met my prince, and I might not know their names, but I had their faces engraved on my soul.

A man with tears welling in his eyes as he stumbled along, clutching the spear he'd been assigned so tightly that its tip wobbled above his head. Two elderly gentlemen, stooped from hard labour, their faces creased with the pain of being ushered along at a pace unsuited to their age. Another man – a boy, really, far younger than myself – muttered something that could only be a prayer from the way his hands were wrapped around the cross at his neck. He didn't look up, not once, and despite the noise of the platoon I somehow heard his shuddering, *terrified* sob as he passed.

I exhaled.

"Down with the false king!" I then yelled with my next breath, expecting all eyes to turn my way.

But as if they'd been expecting it, *waiting* for it, the commoners milling around me transformed into movement and anger. They quickly took up the cause, bustling and shoving and jeering out similar cries to mine.

"Dios fuck the false king!"

"Down with Weasel Welzes!"

"One throne, one king!"

Parvan tugged me back into the protective ring of his arms as the crowd surged forward against the line of soldiers, confusion reigning for several seconds as everyone began pushing, fighting to get to nowhere and everywhere at once.

Fuck me, it was as if I'd ignited a barrel of black powder. *Explosive* was the only word for it: these people were riled, and it was more than my words that had done it. I'd merely been the fuse, lighting something that had clearly been simmering for a while, because the shouts soon turned personal. Men and women screamed out about their families, their livelihoods, their hope, their *children*…these people were grieving for things that had been taken from them, whether by Welzes or Iván Aratorre.

It was a sight to behold. Or it might have been if there had been any jubilant triumph to it, like an oppressed people rising up against their tyrants. But this was just a bunch of civilians shoving and hurling abuse at another bunch of civilians, where one side had weapons merely because they'd been told that they were soldiers now, primed to fight and die for a country which had never done anything for them.

It got ugly quickly, as the crowd lost track of who was right and who was wrong, and all that hate had nowhere to go but into each other. Parvan and I stared in disbelief as the crowd descended upon itself, hitting and kicking and scratching and *stabbing*.

I'd wanted to distract the platoon and its leaders, sure, but I didn't want anyone else getting hurt. I'd incited this: the least they could all do was fucking *recognise* that.

"Long live King Ren!" I shouted in an effort to draw their attention, shoving

AN OATH AND A PROMISE

back my hood to expose my fair skin and hair, but my words were lost in the yelling of those around us.

Fuck.

"*Renato Aratorre e istinskiyat kral na Quareh!*" Parvan boomed, and *that* declaration of the true southern king certainly got their attention, the Temarian words cutting harshly through the resonance of Quarehian accents.

The crowd seemed to freeze, and then eyes began to turn to us as they spotted and pointed out the northerners in their midst. An officer barked out orders, stabbing an irate finger in our direction.

Parvan hauled me backwards.

"Run, Your Highness," he growled, and shoved me towards a slim gap between the people closing in on us.

And we ran.

*

Chapter Thirty-Four

Ren

Dima's eyes were screwed up tight, his teeth clamped down on his bottom lip and his hands squeezed tightly shut. The man was clearly in pain but the warning hand Starling had rested on his shoulder proved unnecessary, for he made no sound until the riders had passed out of sight. Then he grabbed a fistful of Velichkov's shirt and pulled the heir close to his face, muttering something that had both of their eyes flickering to me.

Velichkov stood and peered along the road the riders had disappeared down. With time being so short we'd decided to travel fast rather than safe, taking the main road to *la Cortina* and ducking down into the ditches and orchards whenever we spotted someone coming. We weren't exactly inconspicuous, but we'd lost the luxury for overabundant caution and it had been working for us so far.

Yet rather than immediately setting off the way we'd been heading, Valeri strode back towards me with determined steps, shrugging his hooded cloak off and throwing it over my shoulders. I squirmed, trying to escape as he wrapped it tighter around me.

"What are you doing, you idiot? With your hood off, someone might recognise you!"

"Better me than you," he growled.

That made no sense at all. Sure, my people were divided in their loyalties, with some on my side and some supporting Welzes, but the animosity towards the northern royals was a lot less ambiguous.

"Aratorre," he snapped as I continued to protest the humiliating manhandling. And was what with him trying to dress me in his clothes anyway? Some weird territorial marking on behalf of his brother?

Velichkov threw up his hands in surrender. "Fine. Keep your face uncovered and see what happens."

I glared at him. "What are you talking about? Why are you worrying about

AN OATH AND A PROMISE

that *now?*"

"Dima says they're claiming..." He glanced over my shoulder along the road to the north, looking...nervous, for fuck's sake. Valeri Velichlov, first prince and heir to the throne of Temar, built like a horse and with a sword bigger than any I'd seen other than Jiron's, was *nervous*. "There's a rumour going around that you have the Voice."

"Well I don't," I said flatly. Dima nodded sharply, knowing it as the truth, but I had a much more compelling argument at hand. "If I did, you'd all be enjoying yourselves in a huge naked orgy right now instead of being your usual annoying selves."

"If I thought that was remotely in my future, you'd be dead before you could Tell us any such thing," Velichkov snapped. Starling gave a slow nod of agreement, looking at me distastefully. "But it's a smart move on the Lukian bastard's part."

"Then that means it was Councillor Navar's idea," I said sourly. Because fuck, now that I was thinking it through? *Genius.*

What better way to ensure I was never brought in alive than to tell the continent that I had the Voice? An instant death sentence no matter my status or lineage, or any lingering loyalty my people might have felt for me. If he'd had more time to plot, maybe Navar would have used that as his opening move back in Máros: it would have avoided relying on that liar Yanev, and Velichkov wouldn't have been able to manipulate them into agreeing to a higher bounty for my capture.

"You sure?" Starling asked Dima in stilted Mazekhstani. A stupid question, for Hearken couldn't lie – just another burden on the poor creatures – but he didn't look offended. How could he take offence when he knew it wasn't meant?

It was why he called us all by our first names, touched us with familiarity, never asked us questions. He *was* us, living in our minds if not our bodies, no secrets or reflections or fears to divide us from him.

It was utterly fucking creepy, and if I thought that, he thought that.

What was even left of Dima the man? Did he have any sense of self, or was the Hearken merely a melting pot of everyone he'd ever come into contact with, his own personality and hopes and dreams chafed away by ours?

AN OATH AND A PROMISE

I saw him swallow uncomfortably.

Maybe we could...

Dima's head shot up. "I'd like that," he said to me softly, and then I was forced to explain my idea to the others.

Not that I *had* to, of course, and I was sorely tempted to remind them that I owed the two pains in my ass nothing, least of all my valuable breath...but I suppose I wanted to tell them what I'd been thinking. And when they both smiled at me in approval, I felt all weirdly warm inside.

Devotion and praise was nothing new to me. I'd been born a prince, wanted for nothing, and quickly became addicted to the feeling of holding power over others that demanded they indulge me at my whim.

But there was a huge fucking difference between being simpered at because they had to, and genuinely impressing someone. And while I wasn't an idiot and was familiar enough with putting on appearances to well recognise that distinction, I'd never truly experienced the latter until Mathias. He was the first to value honesty over how he was expected to act – ironic, I knew, considering our very first meeting had been shrouded in lies about his identity, but Mat had never given me false compliments. If one of my ideas was shit, he told me so. If the idea was pure unadulterated fabulousness, he still told me it was shit, but the point was that I could trust him not to undeservedly bloat my ego.

And through him, I'd gotten to know Starling and Velichkov, who were much like him in that way. So when the two of them gave me *smiles of approval*, it felt pretty fucking good.

And my idea of having Dima trail far enough behind us to keep out of range of our thoughts while still remaining within view, the tension within our little group seemed to ease somewhat. The man had less of a grimace on his face whenever I glanced back at him, and the rest of us inevitably relaxed now we weren't worrying about our minds being overheard.

Although it meant that I let myself truly stew on the implications of what I was being accused of, and hell, I'd laugh at the irony if it wasn't so fucked up. My father had hidden his magic for decades, only using his Voice to manipulate those who either knew about it or wouldn't live long enough to tell anyone...and yet Navar, a man in Iván Aratorre's trusted Council, had not only been blind to it but had the audacity to blame the king's favourite victim of his crime?

"You're being unusually quiet," Velichkov remarked, nudging me with his elbow. I'd discovered there was a quiet thoughtfulness to him that had surprised me, although it really shouldn't have. Mat could be the same, and as we'd passed through Temar, it had become evident that its people adored their first prince. Valeri's name had always been spoken with reverence.

Not that I'd tell him that.

"I'm trying not to trip over this fucking tent you call a cloak," I said instead, widening my arms to prove how large it was. "Is that your devious plot, heir? Trick me into breaking my neck so you can rescue Mathias from my far-from-innocent attentions?"

"It's weird," he said with an irritated sigh. "You calling him that when you know perfectly well what Nathanael's name is."

"I like weird," I countered.

"It's annoying," clarified Valeri.

"I *especially* like annoying," I said.

"You don't fucking say."

"What I'm not saying," I said, "is thank you. At the river...you've saved my life several times too many now." I glared at my boots and the grasses that flattened beneath them as we walked. "It's becoming embarrassing."

"You've never thanked me, either," Starling pointed out from my left, injecting herself into the conversation in the kind of nosy, attention-attracting way I liked to practice.

"I can't speak for the little healer," murmured Velichkov, "but I consider us more than even, Aratorre." As she began to mutter under her breath that he certainly *didn't* speak for her, he added, "even if I was required to pull your incorrigible and irritating ass out of the fire ten times over."

"Only ten?" I asked. "And second question, much less important...why?"

"For putting a smile on Nat's face," he said quietly, and that eliminated all of my flippancy. "For accepting him and his whole self, even when I wouldn't, and letting him be...*him*. For that, Aratorre, I'll get you your fucking crown

AN OATH AND A PROMISE

back even if it means burning to death under this God-damned sun."

I thought about that for a long moment.

"Damn it, Velichkov," I said. "Now I have to be nice to you."

*

Chapter Thirty-Five

Mat

Parvan's eyes snapped open, his body lurching instinctively into action only to reach the end of the chain attached to his wrists and be yanked back down. He made a strangled kind of noise, his hands shooting to his bruised throat where a handful of hours earlier someone had had their boot pressed down on it.

"Are you alright?" I asked.

Parvan glanced around, taking in me, the identical chains that secured us both to the floor, and the open-air, barred wagon we'd been travelling south in since he'd been knocked out.

"What...happened?" His voice was hoarse, a crackly, raspy quality to it that reminded me of my sister Mila.

I tried for a grin. "We succeeded in diverting the recruits from the border. They're too busy escorting us to their king for them to die horrifically in unnecessary inter-continental conflict, so I call that a win."

Grey, unimpressed eyes stared back at me before flickering around to study more of our surroundings. The sun had dropped below the hills about an hour ago, taking some but not all of the Quarehian heat with it, although the bars of our portable prison cell were still warm against my back. A dozen southern soldiers closely ringed the wagon, with scores more in front and behind, and there were always several pairs of curious or hostile eyes on us at any given time. Martinez wasn't taking any chances.

I'd half-expected my guard to query the likelihood of *us* dying horrifically, but he was far too composed and dull for that.

"A win?" he asked instead, wincing as he dropped his head and felt at the wound on the back of his head. I'd seen the sticky mass of blood knotted in his hair as he lay unconscious, but the chains and shackles that bound our hands and ankles had been purposefully fastened too short to allow us to reach each other.

"You did your job," I said softly, sensing he needed to hear it. "You protected me."

But Parvan swallowed, still staring at the men surrounding us and not looking comforted at all. "Apparently not very well, if you're here."

"It's just that..." I began awkwardly, raising my bound hands in surrender when he turned that exasperated look on me again that made me feel about two inches tall. "What was I supposed to do? Let them *kill you?*"

"If it got you away, Your Highness, yes!"

I snorted. If he thought I'd buy my own freedom at the cost of another's life, he still had a lot to learn about his new charge.

After inciting the mini riot, we'd led the soldiers pursuing us on an exhilarating chase through the crowd still booing and jeering at them, but we'd soon reached the edge of the throng and lost our cover. Parvan had drawn his sword, pushed me behind him and muttered something stupid about me running and *saving myself*, and then had held out admirably well against dozens of soldiers without killing a single one of them. It was inevitable that he'd eventually been overwhelmed by their numbers and we'd been pushed to our knees before the glowering senior officers, but what I *hadn't* expected was to recognise the man assigned to lead the unskilled, quavering group of men to their deaths at the border: the slimy leech Lord Pablo Martinez.

While I'd most recently encountered him being his usual abusive, misogynistic prick self at his estate a few weeks ago, the last he'd seen of me was when I'd been a little physical with my condemnation the night I found him beating his wife...basically, when he was being an abusive, misogynistic prick. His beady little eyes had lit up with the anticipation of getting the chance to repay the favour on me, only for Parvan to break free of his captors' hold and get a perfectly-aimed, *glorious* punch straight to the nobleman's jaw.

Unfortunately that had redirected all the hits Parvan's way instead of mine, and now my guard had a collection of darkening bruises around his face, in addition to the boot-shaped mark where Martinez had ordered one of his men to crush Parvan's throat until he passed out. Well, he'd said *until the northern bastard breathes no more*, but a hastily constructed lie on my part had bought Parvan the chance to at least wake up.

Which he'd just done, and wasn't looking particularly happy about it.

"Did you *want* to die?" I asked, nudging his ankle with the toe of my boot, which was all I could reach him with.

"I want *you* to live, my prince. And I fear…"

He trailed off as a shadow swiped overhead. I recognised its looming shape and didn't need to turn around to know we were passing through the main gates of *la Cortina*. A place we'd hoped to reach when we set off from Stavroyarsk with Ren and the others, but I'd expected it to be in a slightly better position than chained to a wagon like common prisoners. It wasn't like we could pull off our plan of forcing Yanev's – and Navar and Welzes' – truths out into the open when we had neither a Hearken nor the freedom to move more than half a foot in any direction.

Parvan began coughing. Huge, racking coughs that made his whole body contract, and he doubled over as they forced more air from him.

"Water!" I called urgently. "He needs water!"

The wagon lurched to a stop and the back gate was unlocked and heaved open. But the hands that reached inside bore no water, and offered no kindness.

Instead, they unlatched our chains from where they'd been locked into the floor, and then we were both hauled ruthlessly from the wagon. Unable to get my feet beneath me in time, I fell heavily to the cobblestones of the palace's outer courtyard, jarring my knee.

"Prince Nathanael."

The voice was smooth, smug, and held the telltale lilt of a Lukian accent. I lifted my head to find Zidhan Welzes leering down at me, his wife Alondra hovering anxiously at his side.

"For fuck's sake," I snapped, and glanced over at Parvan, who was still trying to recover. "Is no one going to help him?"

Welzes' mouth twisted as he followed my gaze. "Who even *is* he?"

"Your Majesty," said Lord Martinez imperiously, waddling over to us from his carriage. Parvan heaved in shaky breaths as he got his body under control. "Don't you recognise the king consort of Temar?"

I tried to hide my amusement behind a scathing look of disgust. Martinez himself certainly hadn't realised my desperate claim as to Parvan's identity to be the lie it was, but I found it funny that he should be acting so haughty about it now.

The false king faltered and stared at my guard. The man regarded him back, equally as nonplussed about what was going on.

"This...is your father?" Welzes demanded of me.

I kept the disdainful expression in place. "My father's long dead. This is Anton Velichkov, the *second* husband of Queen Zora Velichkova. Do you not keep up with continental happenings at all?"

"Mind your tongue, young prince," Councillor Navar admonished sharply, and my body turned rigid as I glared up at the man joining the impromptu crowd in the courtyard. If he'd met the real Anton, if he knew-

"Show some respect to your king and master," he ordered, and realising that no one knew enough to challenge my lies or the life of my guard that relied on them, I let out an uneasy breath. Parvan remained silent, not understanding our conversation, and I could only thank Ren's god that he was choosing not to interrupt as I undoubtedly would have in his position. If they realised he wasn't royalty and held no value as a prisoner, they'd kill him without hesitation.

"We were travelling peacefully through your lands when we were unlawfully detained. We demand you release us back to our family," I said, pushing myself to my feet. No one stopped me, although the soldiers closed ranks to prevent me from drawing any closer to their king. "And promptly, else my mother discovers your delay."

Navar shrugged, raising and lowering one shoulder lazily and eyeing us both with vicious glee. "What's one more upset northern whore?"

I scoffed. "You wish to go to war with both Mazekhstam *and* Temar? Are you fucking insane?"

"I told you to be quiet," he snapped, not seeming at all bothered at the prospect of so much death and destruction. He stroked a hand across the top of his bald head as if to admire its smoothness. "I doubt your bitch mother even wants you back, *Your Highness*. Word is that you were to be stripped of your familial ties and royal status after it was discovered you were bending over for our bastard false prince."

I gave him a cold look, refusing to let the man know how true his words were. But there was no longer any doubt in my mind who was controlling who here: Welzes hadn't uttered a word since the councillor had shown up.

"But first," Navar continued slyly, "you'll help us catch said bastard. For the safety of all Quarehians everywhere."

Whatever that meant.

"As I told Martinez when he asked me ever so nicely," I said flatly, "I don't know where Ren is. We split up weeks ago."

"I don't believe you."

"I don't give a fuck what you believe."

He stepped forward and grabbed my chin, fingers digging in painfully into my jaw. One of the soldiers caught the chains around my wrists to prevent me from pushing him away.

"Your…Nathanael!" Parvan snarled in outrage, having apparently been keeping up enough to realise the persona expected of him. I heard the rattle of his chains and mine as I struggled against the grip of the two men holding me in place.

"The next time you dare open that little barbarian mouth of yours," Navar promised me darkly, "I'll make sure it's filled. My guards would love to have their way with you."

And then he let go, releasing my jaw with a smug look as if expecting me to immediately speak. I swallowed down the retort I so desperately wanted to make, glancing over to where Parvan was tightly held by two of the palace guards.

"Take them to the cells," Navar ordered, only for Welzes to repeat the command in a rather louder voice.

"Please, my dear," Alonda said, clutching at her husband's arm. "We really shouldn't aggravate Temar. If we were to offer mercy to Prince Nathanael and-"

"This is why women and politics don't mix," he said dismissively, turning away from her – and us – as if none of us were worth his time.

Navar watched the exchange with a knowing look on his face, and then gestured for us to follow him. I refused to take a damn step of my own volition but it really didn't matter, as Parvan and I were shoved and heaved after him anyway, dragged unceremoniously out of the twilit courtyard and down the corridor to the cell block.

It all felt a little surreal.

History was fucking repeating itself, only this time my captors knew who I was and there was no sly southern prince offering inappropriate flirtations and distracting enticements. Perhaps fate had always intended my capture and death at Quareh's hands, and was correcting the mistake it had made the first time around by putting Ren in my path…or me in his.

When they tossed Parvan into the first cell on the right where I'd once watched Ren slit the throat of a prisoner, I could only hope that not *everything* would be repeated. And maybe that memory dug its talons a little too deep into my fear, for I didn't hesitate to snap back when Navar made a snide remark about Parvan disgracing his gender by going to his knees for his slut of a wife.

"If you're jealous that no woman would look at you twice," I said sourly as I was pushed into my own cell without even the courtesy of having the shackles around my wrists and ankles removed, "know that no man would either, Navar. A noxious personality like yours needs more to compensate for it than the delusion of royal power."

The councillor turned, his lips bared in a rictus grin, and it took me a long fucking moment to realise what he was so happy about. I hastily snapped my mouth shut, but it was too late.

"It seems I am able to make good on my promise to you after all, Prince Nathanael," he murmured delightedly, and gestured for my two guards to re-enter my cell. "For a moment, I feared you were actually going to be *quiet*."

Navar smirked as I backed up in horror, and nodded at the guards. "Enjoy yourselves with him, gentlemen."

And then he ascended the stairs and left us in the dark.

*

Chapter Thirty-Six

Ren

"Starling!"

"I'm *trying*, Your Vexatiousness!" she shrieked back at me, red and green sparks radiating from her fingertips as she ran her hands frantically across Dima's chest and throat.

She was the best fucking healer on the continent. If she couldn't help him, no one else stood even a *sliver* of a chance.

"How did he get his hands on *molchaniye* without any of us seeing?" Velichkov spat out from where he stood over us, his dawn shadow radiating a long and extremely pissed off shape across the fallen masonry.

We didn't have time for this. We had to get inside the palace to find Yanev before he was killed, but the man who was supposed to help clear my name was currently spasming in the dirt, green-tinged spittle decorating his slack lips. It wasn't hard to imagine how Dima had found the *molchaniye*: any citizen we'd passed within a dozen yards of would have had their minds scoured by the Hearken, and thoughts or memories about the illicit plant wouldn't have escaped the addict's scrutiny.

But Velichkov was right in that we should have seen him take it, especially an amount that had caused his body this much damage. How had we all been so damn distracted? Dima had the advantage in that he'd have *known* when we weren't paying him attention, but it seemed my willingness to give him space had backfired spectacularly.

Starling heaved out a shallow breath, sweat glistening on her forehead. She sank back onto her haunches and shot a dirty look at the Hearken as he began to groan and roll around on the ground. Velichkov dropped a boot onto his leg to keep him still.

"I've cleared the effects of the drug from his body," the healer said tersely, "but I can't do shit about the way it fucks up your mind."

I swore quietly, clenching my fists until my nails dug painfully into my palms.

Not for the first time, I glanced towards the northern entrance to the ruins, but the dark archway remained mockingly empty.

"We can't wait for him," said Velichkov, apparently taking over Dima's job of reading my Dios-damned mind. "We have no idea how far Nathanael is behind us, and by the time he gets here it could be too late."

"I promised I wouldn't make decisions without him," I muttered, more to myself than the heir at my side. But I knew I was just wallowing in excuses. Mat had gotten angry when I made decisions without him while he was *there*, because he'd accused me of shutting him out and trying to deal with things alone. This was…different. My lover wasn't here, and every minute that passed risked his vision of Yanev's murder coming true.

First we'd left my guards behind in Máros. Then Jiron had disappeared…and now Mathias was gone. I'd started this whole thing with an oath to take my country back, a pledge which had actually felt possible when he was by my side, and yet now seemed like an insurmountable, absurd, *impossible* task.

I didn't want to do it alone.

I *couldn't* do it alone.

"Aratorre," Valeri said softly, and I sucked in air, fighting back the urge to crumble at his feet. Heavy bands pulled across my throat and chest, my anxiety leering in cruel, imminent threat, and it beat down on me with all the doubts I could no longer keep at bay.

You're useless. Shallow. Inconsequential.

I am.

Dios, I really am.

Inept. Rotten. Worthless.

Those too.

Fuck you, Ren. This was a different voice in my head. It sounded suspiciously like Mat, acerbic and incensed. *I'm the only one who gets to insult you.*

Hell yes you are, I snarled silently into the recesses of my brain that normally hid all my ugly, self-loathing thoughts and was clearly shirking its duties today in failing to keep that shit locked down. I thought of Mathias instead; those storm-filled grey-blue eyes crinkled in a fond smirk, his northern accent

AN OATH AND A PROMISE

butchering perfectly normal words, the warmth of his chest pressed against my back as we slept.

He may not be *here,* but he was still with me. I'd told him he had my heart, and it was about time I acknowledged that in turn, the bastard had snuck his own into the space mine had left behind. It was bossy and grumpy and refused to sit still, but it belonged there more than anything had ever belonged anywhere.

Besides, this was *our* place. We'd once spent a glorious night lazing together among these ruins, free to be ourselves for a moment under a starry night sky that held none of the judgment cast on us by our respective peoples.

"Alright," I said as the memories of my lover eased my breathing back to normal. "If the alternative is hanging around with you three all night, then I'd rather take my chances of being disembowelled by my enemies."

Starling grinned and helped Dima to his feet. The man swayed on the spot, looking extremely unsteady, which didn't exactly bode well for what we had planned. I could only hope he'd stay lucid enough until we found Yanev.

"This is your last chance to back out from what is probably an impossibly doomed mission to recover my throne," I continued, wanting to give the others every chance to come to their Blessed senses, "but don't blame me when our daring storming of the palace becomes legend and the bards exclude you from the most epic ballad *ever* sung. Or they pronounce your name wrong."

I gave Velichkov a meaningful look, and he snorted.

"Alright, *Renato,*" he said, as if that was supposed to mean something.

"We came all this way. It would be a pity to turn around," Starling added nonchalantly.

Dima gave a slow nod in support, the pain in his eyes telling me he felt the same driving need and passion to rescue my people as was in my own heart…because of course he did.

"Are you now going to tell me how you expect to get a traitor, two northerners, and a woman inside a palace full of Quarehians who can't decide which of those they hate more?" Velichkov asked, his expression insultingly sceptical.

AN OATH AND A PROMISE

"Pretty sure it's women they hate the most," I responded, and waved my wrist with its leather cuff in front of his face. "Secret passageway, prince. You can go first and clear all the spiders out of the way, *sí?*"

*

Chapter Thirty-Seven

Mat

The door at the top of the stairs clanged open and polished shoes appeared on the steps. I hurriedly pushed myself to my feet, my shoulders and knees aching in protest from lying on the cold stone floor all night, and the shackles having long since rubbed the skin of my wrists raw.

"There," Councillor Navar crooned by way of greeting as he reached my cell and peered through the bars. "Did that quieten you down?"

His satisfied smile sent a shiver down my spine, and I didn't need to adjust my expression to keep the truth from it. The revulsion on my face was all too real, even though the guards hadn't touched me after he'd left last night — it seemed not all of the men participating in Quareh's new regime could be painted with the same brush, and these two had shown no inclination to carry out the rape he'd so casually condoned. Even now, their faces showed their distaste at the reminder, but they still unhesitatingly obeyed Navar as he demanded I be taken upstairs.

"Nathanael!" Parvan hollered from the opposite cell, and while the rest of them seemed content to ignore him, I shot a reassuring smile in his direction as I was hauled past him and up the steps. I wasn't naïve enough to imagine he'd be left in peace, but hopefully while Welzes and Navar's attention was on me, Parvan might avoid the worst of whatever torment was coming our way. Yet my guard seemed to be trying to incur the opposite, shouting and cursing and heaving at the bars between us, and I didn't let myself breathe again until the door between the cells and the guardroom slammed shut and cut off his yells.

Navar led us through the corridors of *la Cortina*, offering sly little comments about what he assumed my silent companions and I had been up to last night, and fearing they'd get into trouble for disobeying or that he'd find men who *were* willing to indulge him in his sick games, I stayed quiet.

With great effort, because the man was a bigger prick than I'd realised. It seemed holding the strings of his puppet king Welzes had given the councillor a confidence boost that let his full perversity shine through, because when I'd previously met him he'd been conniving and repellent but not *this* much of a loathsome bastard.

And when his dark, gleeful mutterings turned to Ren, I couldn't hold my tongue any longer.

"Don't talk about him like that," I hissed as Navar launched into a blisteringly cruel account of *that little good for nothing cockslut* and his apparent role as *a filthy, profligate burden who should have slit his wrists the moment he took his first breath*. "You have no fucking *idea,* do you?"

"And you think you do, Prince Velichkov?" the man spat without the need to even take a breath between his sentences. "You and your people are a fucking scourge on the continent. One I will relish removing."

He flicked his fingers dismissively before I could respond and my guards dragged me ahead of him through the doors to the throne room. Their handling became rougher as more eyes fell on us, as if to prove their loyalties lay far, far away from me. The clink of the chains between my shackled wrists and ankles was the only noise in the hall, and it drew intense, undivided attention from every gathered noble and servant. Parting silently, the court watched me pass with sombre faces and mouths drawn in tight lines, and I glared back at each of them as I was hauled to the centre of the room.

Lord de la Vega and his impressive stomach were here, as were the Lords Lago. Isobella hovered next to Alondra Welzes, both women in equally breathtaking dresses. Lords González and de Leon stood beneath the archers' balcony, not sniping at each other for once but wearing identical grave expressions that made them look far older than I knew them to be. Nearly a hundred other faces I recognised from my time in the southern palaces made up the rest of the crowd, but each one had skin darker than my own and for the first time since being brought here nearly six months ago, I felt lost among the sea of Quarehians.

My chin was shoved down to my chest in a laughable mimicry of a bow to the man seated up on the dais, and I let out a long, slow exhale that I hoped conveyed just how tiresome I found all of this, because that was better than showing them my fear.

"Nathanael Velichkov," Zidhan Welzes said from the throne above me, choosing to inject a note of surprise into his tone as if we hadn't already met in similar circumstances last night. He must have realised that it gave him less of an air of mysteriousness and more befuddled ineptness, for he repeated my name and gave it rather more force this time.

"*Nathanael.* I'm glad you could join us."

I lifted my head and fixed him with an unimpressed scowl. "*Us?* So you admit that your crown is not really worn by you, but by the fucker on my heels?"

I sensed the court shift uneasily around us. Navar might have been clever to set up a figurehead to take the attention – and any potential assassination threats – away from himself while he pulled the strings from the shadows, but not clever enough to have found someone who didn't make it bloody obvious what was happening. Welzes was hardly king material, but his marriage to Alondra Aratorre, who was hovering at her husband's side with her huge brown eyes fixed worriedly on mine, made him eligible for the role in a way that Navar would never be.

Welzes' face split with fury at the comment and he made a gesture with his hand that was evidently to order me smacked hard across the face, for that was immediately what happened. I rotated my jaw, unable to touch it with my hands still bound and chained in place, and tried to look like that hadn't fucking *hurt*.

"Tell me, how long do you think it will be before my brother-in-law…my mistake, *half* brother-in-law," he said loudly, emphasising the correction for the crowd, "comes running to try and save his little whore now we've spread the word you're to be executed? One day? Two? I doubt he's far away."

"Or perhaps I'm just a distraction," I suggested blithely, "and he's actually in Máros right now, taking back his fucking throne."

The false king's gaze shot to mine, looking gratifyingly alarmed, but Navar just chuckled behind me. "Renato always was a jealous, possessive child," he assured him. "He won't like anyone else playing with his toys."

Then he lowered his voice, his mouth moving close to my ear. "Perhaps His Highness will be stupid enough to use the tunnels we know he still has the key to?" the councillor mused, sending my blood cold as he guessed exactly how we'd planned to sneak into the palace. "Oh, the look on his face when he realises he can't talk or fuck his way out of what we're going to do to him. Or you."

"I'm not helping you catch Ren," I gritted out, keeping my head high because I'd be damned if I was giving them anything but defiance until my final breath.

"My dear boy, you don't have to do anything but die." Welzes laughed, loud and deliberate, and glanced earnestly over my head at the gathered court. The words were for their benefit, not mine. "Isn't that the only thing you people are good for?"

*

Chapter Thirty-Eight

Ren

We hurried along the dirt-packed floor of the tunnel, the lantern mostly shielded to only let out the faintest glimmer to light our path. I was silently commending us on how impressively stealthy we were being when Dima let out a sharp, unexpected shriek that made me jump.

"What part of quiet-"

"*Mierda!*" he wailed in terrified Quarehian, and Velichkov glared accusingly between me and Starling before slapping a massive hand over the man's mouth to keep him quiet. But the healer looked as confused as I felt.

"That's not me," she whispered. "Maybe we're close enough to the palace for him to have picked up the thoughts of someone above us?"

And then something flashed further along the tunnel and I threw myself at Starling, crushing her to the wall just as I heard the twang of a bow string and felt the air move by my left ear. Dima cursed again, and this time maybe it *was* because of me, for my heart was pounding and my head spinning as I grabbed the lantern from Starling's trailing hand and flung it away from us. The little light it had provided instantly died with the shattering glass.

"Get down!" I hissed, dragging us both to the ground and pawing in the darkness at where I thought Velichkov had been standing. If my fingers happened to scrape down his groin instead of grabbing at his hand, then it was mere coincidence and Dios' impeccable sense of humour, because it wasn't like I could fucking *see*. Not that the heir seemed to appreciate that from the rapid-fire insults he tossed back, but even he was smart enough to shut up when we heard a second arrow pass by overhead and thud into something solid. I could only hope from the lack of screaming that it had hit a wall and not one of us.

"What the fuck, what the fuck," Dima moaned from somewhere close by. "He's here...what if he makes us...can't...my children...the trap worked...do I fire again?...execution of the other one...His Highness...should have taken...don't want to die-"

The tunnel echoed with his screams as the minds of us and our attackers overwhelmed his own. I felt Starling wriggle away from me and the Hearken fell abruptly silent.

More arrows slammed into the walls. We were pinned down, and it was only a matter of time before they refined their aim to reach us on the floor.

"Stay here," Velichkov breathed. I heard him draw his sword. "Wolf and I will try to get closer."

"They have fucking *bows*, Temarian," I hissed. "You're both going to get shot before you make it even halfway there."

"Do you have a better idea?"

"Of course I do," I said, having no such thing.

"Then do it!"

What if he makes us, Dima had said in an echo of the thoughts he was hearing. What had our opponents been thinking about?

I cleared my throat. "Gentlemen," I said loudly, making sure my voice projected down the tunnel. There was a rapid intake of breath, some shuffling feet and a faint whimper, and I bared my teeth at the darkness. In making me into an enemy of the continent, Navar had inadvertently handed me a weapon. "You've been advised, I assume, of what I can do to you with a mere *word?*"

They only gave me their silence.

That was okay. The anticipation made it more terrifying anyway.

"Have you ever seen anyone under the compulsion of the Voice?" I asked them thoughtfully. "I have. What would it feel like, do you imagine, if I were to Tell you to put your own blades to your veins and bleed you out without even touching you? Or maybe I'll have you blind yourselves. Blunt fingernails clawing at your own eyes, compelled to scratch and scratch and *scratch* until you've carved them from your head, and then I'll Tell you to gouge deeper into your skull until your fingers scrape against-"

"Please!"

I hummed. "Please *what?*"

"Please, Your Highness! Don't...we won't..."

AN OATH AND A PROMISE

"What you'll *do*," I said clearly, "is lay your swords on the ground and walk over here slowly with your hands on your heads. Reckon you can manage that, or do I have to start instructing you on how to best pull out your own fingernails?"

By the time I'd finished talking, I saw nearly a dozen shapes moving steadily towards us in the gloom, a lantern unfurled a moment later as one of the soldiers at the back raised his hands and pulled his cloak from where he'd been keeping the light covered. And thank fuck for the terror on their faces keeping them from realising that if I really had the Voice, I could have just Told them to surrender without the need for threats. Some admittedly looked less convinced than others, yet with more than half their number eagerly surrendering, the rest fell into line for fear of being singled out by my alleged magic.

But there were too many soldiers to tie up with the scraps of rope we had with us. I faltered, not having a plan beyond disarming them, and wondering how the hell we were supposed to keep them still and quiet without killing over a dozen of my people in cold blood.

And then Starling slipped wraithlike between them, fingers gliding across their shoulders and hips, and each one dropped like a stone to the tunnel's floor. It wasn't pretty, and more than one of the men ended up with someone else's elbow or knee to their face as they collapsed, but they were still breathing and it was more than they would have given us.

"You have one hell of a gift," Velichkov remarked to Starling, impressed.

"Back off," I said. "She's mine."

The healer scowled at that and stalked away with Wolf at her heels, leaving me and the northern prince to hurry after them. An unconscious Dima was unceremoniously slung over Velichkov's broad shoulder and I scooped up the soldiers' lantern, catching up to Starling as she began to ascend the steps that led to her surgery. Emerging directly from the tunnels to my old rooms would have been better, considering what Mat had Seen about Yanev's eventual location, but there was no reason to believe that the exit had been unblocked since I'd last been down here, and the fact that so many men had been waiting for us in the darkness had me more unnerved than I wanted to admit.

Navar, as one of my father's trusted councillors, would have been made aware of the tunnels' existence. But to sacrifice the secrecy of his own escape route to send guards to lie in wait…on the mere chance that someone might pass through here? And that someone would also have to know about the tunnels and have in their possession one of only a handful of keys ever made in order to enter them, and…*fuck me*, that was what Dima had meant by *trap*.

"They knew I was coming," I hissed, and the dawning horror of that realisation drowned out even my ability to snigger at my own word choice. Had we been sold out? Were Welzes and Navar's spies just that good, or had Panarina set us up? Had-

"What happened?" I heard Velickov ask from ahead, and finding myself alone, scurried through the tunnel's opening to find Dr. Sánchez passed out cold on the floor of his bedchamber, his nose and cheek squished into the rug. "Did you really knock him out without touching him?" His tone was lilted in wonder.

"No," Starling said, amused. "He fainted. I'd like to say it was at the sight of the apprentice he thought long dead, but I believe it was the wolf sitting in his favourite chair."

Wolf yipped happily and jumped down from the rocking chair before fastening his jaws around the unconscious doctor's ankle, dragging him back towards me. I skipped out of the way as the man began to tumble down the steps into the dark, and then slammed the tunnel door firmly shut on him.

"They knew we'd be here," I said again, but the shutting of the door had been for more than dramatic effect. We weren't turning back now, no matter what stood in our way, although Navar anticipating our arrival had suddenly made this a thousand times more difficult. Perhaps he'd assume the dozen guards would be enough to stop us, and we'd encounter less resistance now we were inside the palace, but if any of my companions hadn't been at my side: Dima, Starling, Valeri…I'd already be dead.

I could only hope that wherever he was – hopefully somewhere far, far away from this whole mess, and preferably still on the northern side of the border – Mathias was faring better than us.

*

Chapter Thirty-Nine

Mat

They hadn't tortured me like I'd expected. Perhaps that would come later.

Perhaps they couldn't be bothered dirtying themselves with my blood and tears.

Perhaps they believed me when I'd said I didn't know where Ren was, or they really were so confident that he would come for me that they didn't need to wade through the inevitable turmoil of truth and lies that torture produced.

And that pissed me off. Because they were right: Ren would be on his way if not already here, not for me but for Yanev, and my capture meant that his enemies could lay their trap for him without him even *knowing* that's what it was. Hell, if Welzes and Navar's plan had been the only thing in motion, then at least my lover would have been aware of what faced him in a rescue attempt, but he was coming in here blind, expecting his arrival to be a surprise.

Once again, I'd fucked everything up with nothing more than good intentions.

If I'd been left alone in a cell, I could have redirected my frustrations into attempting to escape or somehow warning Ren and the others, but I was held securely between two guards – a different pair to last night, who'd apparently finished their shifts and got the pure fucking luxury of being allowed to *rest* – and kept on display for the false king's court as he took oaths of loyalty from his people, one by one.

Even Navar had retired from the hall a short while ago, perhaps sensing that his constant presence was undermining Welzes' perceived authority. An impression I'd done my best to foster with a few sarcastic comments whose cost came in the form of more physical blows, but the pain in my jaw and ribs was well worth the unsettled mutters it drew from the crowd. And when I'd loudly suggested that having me gagged would be the sensible response from a ruler who feared what I had to say, I'd ensured I suffered no such thing, Welzes not having the political savviness to manoeuvre his way around that one like Ren would have easily managed.

Yet my presence here was calculated, I knew, including parading me chained, bloody, and exhausted. Juxtaposed against the fresh appearances of those gathered in the hall, I was marked as *other*, their unworthy enemy. A visible target and reminder of what Welzes professed to protect Quareh from, made more potent by the fact that I wasn't just a nameless northerner but their royalty...and aligned with *that fucking traitor Renato Aratorre*, which of course was twisted to portray Ren as in league with the south's enemies on top of the already long list of his alleged crimes.

"Lord Pablo Martinez, Your Majesty," a man snivelled, his nose nearly touching the floor as he bowed, and I narrowed my eyes at the creep who had obviously replaced Clementina as the palace's herald.

But then Martinez shuffled forward and my distaste resettled on the lord.

"Martinez," said Welze, sharp and brusque. "You've already sworn your loyalty, have you not? I thought Navar...I thought *I* ordered you back to the border?"

"Ah yes, my king, I was hoping to appear before you today to discuss that small matter," Martinez said hastily. "I could only assume there had been a mistake when the message was relayed?"

"There was no mistake?" Welzes said, sounding confused why such a thing would be assumed.

"Ah, but you see it was me who brought you the northern prince-"

"There was no mistake." This time his voice was the cold authority of a ruler.

"But-"

"My lord," I said loudly. "Even I realise that he's telling you to fuck off, and I'm just the dumb barbarian. Isn't that right?"

Both Martinez and Welzes floundered, clearly torn between wanting to concur with my words and disagree on principle. I snorted.

"It's a sorry state of affairs for Quareh when you're the heads of the country and its army," I mused. Someone in the crowd gave a cough that sounded like a laugh, and they both bristled.

"Remind Nathanael of what I have repeatedly told him this morning about speaking in my court," Welzes snapped, and a moment later there was the familiar dull pain of a fist embedding itself in my stomach.

I grunted as the wind was driven out of me, and then raised my head as soon as I was able to redraw breath. "It's not...your...court."

He jeered and tapped the toe of his boot on the dais. "Didn't you once stand here and pledge loyalty to the crown I wear? It seems the trustworthiness of a northerner's word is as poor as-"

"I pledged loyalty to *Quareh*," I confirmed. "Which is why I aided Ren when you and Navar betrayed him, and why I will not bow to you now. You are *not its king.*"

"You will not bow to me?"

Welzes stood from his throne, and the room began to buzz with anticipation, that unsettled kind of murmuring that said the court knew *something* was about to happen, even if they weren't sure what.

He gestured for my guards to let go of me. They stepped back, leaving me standing free but for the chains that still weighed down my aching limbs.

"You will bow," he said, his lips curling back as he spoke each word with precise pronunciation. He was careful not to let any trace of his Lukian accent seep into the words, augmenting the lie that he belonged among these people even as he disdained my own heritage with the derisive comments about *northerners* that had clearly come from Navar.

The space around me rapidly grew, as if the other occupants of the throne room were afraid of catching the dirt from my skin, or the fatal accusations of treason which had been hung around my neck.

Welzes cocked his head, letting his crown glitter in the sunlight streaming through the windows.

"You *will* bow, little prince. Or you will not like what happens next."

*

Chapter Forty

Ren

With Starling leading the way through the familiar courtyards and corridors, no one we came across presented any true challenge. Half a dozen guards and a pair of bitter servants who hissed out slurs in my direction before attempting to raise the alarm succumbed swiftly to her Touch, felled by the merest brush of her fingertips against their clothing or skin. Allowed to draw close to them out of a massive and repeated underestimation for her size and gender, she was a one-woman fucking *army*, and I felt my eyes grow wider and wider as the number of unconscious bodies grew in our wake. *Dios mío*, she was getting anything she wanted when I had the power to give it to her.

Velichkov had tried to help, at first, hefting Dima's unconscious body onto me and diving into each fray with Wolf at his side. But the huge Temarian quickly realised that his sword and muscles didn't hold a candle to Starling's impressive magic, and that I was doing no one any good bent almost double under another man's weight – in the non-sexy, *it's not Mathias so I don't want it* kind of way.

And when the guards standing outside my old rooms crumpled to the floor and I shoved my way into the antechamber to find my father's healer reclining on the worn lounge, I finally let myself smile.

It wasn't a nice smile.

"Yanev," I said, watching him slowly push himself to his feet. There was a faint twitch, like he'd felt an old urge to bow, before he creased his already wrinkled face into a frown.

"Renato," he rasped. "What are you..."

He glanced behind him to the closed doors of the bedchamber.

"We're here for you, Yanev," I said, gesturing for Starling to wake Dima. She rolled her eyes, having already reached for his trailing wrist where it rested at Velichkov's waist. "I hear you've been telling lies about me."

Yanev shook his head frantically, wisps of grey hair fluttering around his scalp like a halo.

"No, my prince, not lies!"

"How could you destroy my mother's memory like that?" I demanded, anger surging through me. "To accuse her of-"

"Of what, Your Highness?" He was almost crying now, hands wringing uselessly at his sides. "Of doing what she had to do to survive your father? We all did!"

I faltered.

"Your mother loved you," whispered Yanev miserably. "She held you as she died, did you know that?"

Dima began to mutter frantically from behind me, but I paid him no heed. All I could hear were the old healer's words, circling softly around my head.

Your mother loved you.

No one who knew her had ever spoken to me about her before.

"I remember her tears," Yanev told me through his own. "She was so happy as she looked down at you. *Renato*, your father said, and she nodded and smiled. *Ren*, she breathed, as she kissed your face and you wrapped one of her fingers in your whole tiny hand, and then the king..."

Swallowing, he dared to glance up at me for the briefest of seconds. "He ordered you be taken from her arms, said Consuela needed her rest, bent down to whisper in her ear..."

He whimpered, and I fear I made a sound that mimicked it. Everything felt impossibly heavy and still.

"I didn't hear what he said, but I didn't need to. I knew his tongue would have shone as black as his magic."

My breath caught. "You knew he had the Voice?"

"Your father was many things to many people, my prince."

I didn't know what that meant, but it seemed Dima did, as he gave a shuddering, pained breath. Had the healer been another of Iván's victims? Would I ever know the true depths of my sire's cruelty? Yanev had apparently said he'd terminated my mother's preceding pregnancies: had that been as unwilling an act as my own forced submissions before the king: kneeling, back bared, and head bowed as I waited for the blows to fall?

Or were these more lies constructed to save his own skin?

"Dima," I whispered, tearing my gaze away from the healer. The man was knelt on the floor, held up only by Velichkov's hands on his shoulders, rocking and sobbing.

There was no point ordering anyone to leave the room. Too many people occupied the palace for his mind to be clear, and I felt a pang of guilt that could have only come from the portion of Mat's heart resting in my chest, because my own was incapable of such feelings.

"Dima," I repeated, urgently. I knew I didn't need to speak the words out loud, but it was a difficult habit to break. "Dima, I need you to focus, just for a moment."

He knew the importance of this. Felt it as I felt it, as we all did, and the weight of our combined expectation turned his tear-stained face towards Yanev. He squeezed his eyes shut, flinching and slapping his hands over his ears as if bracing against a great cacophony, and heaved in a rattling, helpless breath.

"Everything Yanev just spoke was true," Dima hissed in a voice little louder than a whisper, and we all leaned in closer to hear him better.

"And what he-"

"Told Navar and Welzes? What Lord de la Vega relayed to you in Máros? *True*," gasped Dima, and then as if a string had been cut, he shuddered and began to beg and plead, his voice rising to such pitch and cadence that Starling, after a cautious glance my way, leaned over to brush his sweaty forehead and send the man back to unconsciousness once more. He slumped into Velichkov's arms.

I felt numb. After everything...*everything* that we'd given and fought through to get here, and we'd succeeded only to fail?

Was this really where it ended?

*

Chapter Forty-One

Mat

Welzes was angry now, getting even more so each time I forced him to repeat himself. I watched his fingers curl into claws as he steadily lost his patience.

"I will have you bow to me, Nathanael Velichkov. Let Temar recognise my claim to this throne."

The court was grim. Indistinct whispers swept through it as the people watched on with a keen yet wary interest.

"Last chance, you irritating child," the false king snapped. "*Bow.*"

I didn't move.

Welzes let out an extended, resigned breath. For one long, incredible moment, I thought he was going to give up.

And then he spoke, but not to me. To one of my guards, and I didn't even know if it was the man on my right or my left who obeyed, but one of the fuckers pulled out his knife and strode towards me where I stood alone, facing off against a king with all I had left to me.

Pure, bloody-minded obstinacy.

"*Hobble him,*" Welzes had said, but the words didn't register until after the pain did, a slicing hot, *agonising* line across the tendons in my calves. I dropped like a stone, my cry echoing through the hall as my knees slammed down hard onto the tiles and my vision swerved through blackness.

And it was then that the crowd moved, surging forward like a living thing, and although they got themselves in check before it could be viewed as aggression, the buzzing and muttering grew louder. Dark looks were shot in Welzes' direction, anger and fear and disgust, and to me they gave…sympathy? Compassion? Commiseration?

Softer, tenderer expressions.

Lord Hierro had his hand held over his mouth while Alondra's were pressed to her heart, both of their eyes wide in horror. Lord de la Vega's fingers twitched as if he'd thought to stop the knife that was half a room away from him. Quintín Lago looked ready to murder Welzes where he stood.

"Stop it! Hasn't there been enough bloodshed already?" Isobella cried, tearing herself from Alondra's side to stand protectively between me and the dais, arms folded. But the false king barely looked at her.

"Arrest her," he ordered, in a tone as unconcerned as his expression. He was watching me on the floor, lips curling in something close to gratification. I grimaced and snarled at the floor beneath my face, biting back a scream.

Isobella's father choked and threw out his hands as a pair of guards turned her way. "Please, Your Majesty! She was just..."

"Arrest them *both*," Welzes corrected.

"My dear," Alondra interjected hurriedly. "Your people are understandably distressed at the sight of such violence, that is all. We shouldn't act rashly."

"*Rashly*? When they object to me delivering justice in my own palace?"

"Prince Nathanael is well-liked here in *la Cortina*," said his wife in a soothing voice. "Such...justice can be a difficult thing to witness."

I'd thought it just placating bullshit until I saw the nods of those around her. I was *liked*? It was news to me.

But when I looked past the fear and the worry and the panic that infected their faces, I saw the people I'd gotten to know over my months here at the palace. The younger Lord Lago, who I'd held until Starling arrived to take the arrow out of his leg. The servant whom I'd convinced Ren to exonerate from his sentenced flogging for an ill-timed joke about his masters. The kitchen boy I'd gone to my knees for all those weeks ago.

I stopped looking, then, because it was making me feel awkward imagining all these people feeling indebted to me. I hadn't done it for that, although it was admittedly nice that not *everyone* around me wanted me dead or hurt, for once.

The false king scoffed, his gaze sweeping across the room of riled nobles and servants as mine had a moment before. There were some who bristled in unity with him, but the atmosphere of the throne room had turned sour the instant he'd cut me down. Just like how the commoners had risen up against the platoon with the slightest of provocation, this crowd had also been primed for revolt.

But this time it had been Welzes who lit the match.

"What the hell do you all care what happens to him?" he spat, waving a hand at me. I saw Isobella's father quietly pull her back into the crowd while the false king's attention was elsewhere. "He's a son of Temar who was raised Mazekhstani: the same fuckers who are slaughtering your brethren at the border!"

"Because *you* incited war," I hissed out, clawing my hands beneath me so I could lift my head. Pain thrummed through me, incessant and fucking *loud*, but I redirected it into the effort it took to get the words out. Fuelling the rising anger, both mine and theirs. "You took these people's chance at peace, and you don't even fucking *care*."

Murmurs of assent danced through the crowd, not traceable to any one individual and nothing him or his guards could pin down. Shifting moods that held dangerous threat. It felt like we stood on the edge of a precipice; one wrong move from either of us, and it could all come crashing down.

"I will have your oaths," he snarled at the people gathered around us, fighting to reassert his power over them. "Any man who does not do so, on behalf of himself or his woman and children, will be branded a traitor and executed alongside this one." He flicked a dismissive hand in my direction without looking. "Do you stand with Quareh, with your friends and your country, noble in heart and loyal in spirit? Or do you seek damnation of your souls and wish destruction upon us all?"

The court shifted uneasily, growing even louder in its collective protests, yet this time no one dared to stand up against the man who would claim to be their ruler. No one spoke loud enough to be heard. No one stepped out of line. But they were clearly unsettled, dragging their gazes down to mine and then back to their king.

With my tendons slashed, I could do nothing but kneel, bleeding and unwilling, on the floor at his feet.

Welzes may have gotten his bow from me, but it had cost him dearly.

*

Chapter Forty-Two

Ren

"Fuck." I smacked the edge of the lounge, hard, relishing the hot burn that shot across my palm. "Fuck!"

Starling and Valeri were silent, watching me with a quiet wariness that bordered on pity.

"It doesn't mean you *are* a bastard," said Starling eventually, her words slow and reluctant as if fearing my reaction. "Mathias said that Yanev only offered circumstantial evidence that supported a conclusion of illegitimacy, not..."

"It seems no one knows for sure," I said dully. "Perhaps not even my mother did."

I heaved in a breath, the familiar scents of the room tangling in my nose and throat. The cedar and oak furniture. The oil of the lanterns lit each night, which were currently hanging cold on the walls. The underlying scent of stale sweat and baked food that told of its many years as a home for my guards.

"What Yanev saw and knows gives the rumour credence, which will be enough for most of my people," I said. "It's *already* enough for them. I have nothing with which to prove them wrong."

Valeri's blue-grey eyes met mine. He didn't blink, a ferocity burning behind them that was bittersweet in its familiarity.

"We force Yanev to recant," he growled. "Make him publicly admit that he was lying. Without his word to rely on, even the accusation that you're not Iván Aratorre's son would be treason."

He was right. It wasn't much, but it was *something*.

"Velichkov," I accused, feeling a flicker of hope. "That sounds deliciously dishonourable of you, and I'm all fo-"

"You can't get anything out of a dead man," said a voice, unpleasant and nasally, and I spun on the spot to find Councillor Navar with his hand pressed to Yanev's chest.

No, not pressed. It was curled around a knife that Navar was now yanking back out, blood gushing onto his sleeve. Yanev's eyes were wide, uncomprehending. He gasped loudly as he fell backwards and slapped his hand into the bloodied mess, but just as Mathias had described, the old man didn't have enough magic to save him. Feeble sparks flickered and faded.

Starling lurched forward across the floor, her fingers outstretched, but Navar slashed the knife wildly at her and she was forced to roll away before it could make contact. I grabbed her collar and yanked her backwards out of his reach, hearing her curse when Yanev's choking fell abruptly silent.

"Navar," I snarled.

Fuck him for immediately quenching that small pinch of hope I had dared to indulge. Fuck him for making everything we'd done to get Dima here…the miraculous existence of a Hearken, entirely pointless. Fuck him for taking everything I had left.

No, not everything. I still had Mathias. We just had to escape the palace and find him and…

"Renato." Navar drew himself up to his full height and it was then I realised he was wearing one of my Blessed gowns. Never mind the blood on it; the fact that the silk had touched his skin made me want to burn the entire wardrobe of clothes I'd left behind here in *la Cortina*. "That didn't take you long, but I'm surprised you sought out Yanev before going after your feral little pet. Don't tell me you were having trouble finding him with all the screaming I expect he's doing."

I returned the disdainful expression. "What the fuck are you talking about?"

The councillor blinked. "You didn't…you *don't know?*" he asked, seemingly perplexed. Then his face slackened and he glanced between me and the heir at my back, his countenance lighting into one of sheer delight. "Nathanael Velichkov, my dear princes."

"What about him?" Valeri growled, but I knew. I just *knew*.

"We have him," Navar answered, confirming my worst fears.

The rest of his words were drowned out by Velichkov's howl of fury as he flung himself forward, Navar hurriedly scurrying through the bedchamber doors that now hung open.

"You can't kill me," the councillor hissed acidly as he continued to back away, repeatedly slicing the air with the knife to keep Velichkov at arm's length.

"*Watch me*, southerner."

"If you do, your brother dies."

"And if we don't, you let him go?" Starling asked, her voice cold as her and I stalked the two men across the bedchamber floor. "Bullshit."

"Zidhan will-"

"Zidhan Welzes doesn't give a damn about you," Velichkov assured him darkly. He stopped when he had Navar backed up against the wall below the window, his bare heels jutting against the stone and his balding head casting an ugly silhouette against the mid-morning azure sky at his back. Sun shone brightly through the open window, lending the moment an unfairly cheery feel that didn't at all suit the horror flooding through my soul.

I didn't stop. I passed Velichkov and kept closing in on Navar until he had the knife at my throat, my fingers swiftly wrapping around his to stop him from sliding it home. The silk of the gown's sleeve fluttered under my uneven breath.

He swallowed. He knew he was fucked.

"The men had your boy last night," he whispered to me with relish; one final, bloody parting shot. My eyes followed the shape of his mouth as he spoke those awful words that rattled around my head.

No.

"I found him on the floor of his cell this morning. Bruised and sobbing and broken, bent over on all fours and letting them have their fun with him…one after the other. Why didn't you save him from that, Ren?"

I didn't respond. Not with words at least, but I did shove him backwards out of the window, releasing his hand as he toppled over the sill.

Councillor Navar wavered and then fell out of sight, his earth-shattering shriek growing in volume before being abruptly silenced.

I turned to find Velichkov and Starling staring at me, looking horrified.

"He was lying," I told the silence between us, and saw their expressions ease into tentative hope as if I had all the answers. And maybe in this, I did. "Nat

AN OATH AND A PROMISE

wouldn't *let* anyone do shit."

I led the way back to the doors, glancing at where Dima lay passed out at one end of the antechamber, Yanev's cooling body at the other.

They'd both keep. Mat wouldn't.

"Come," I ordered the others, attempting to sound unconcerned. "I must retrieve my man from the palace cells, *again*."

But when we made it through the guard room, the last of the soldiers falling with a heavy thump to Starling's magic, we only found one northerner being held behind bars.

"Your Highnesses!" exclaimed Parvan with uncharacteristic fervour, leaping to his feet with a clatter of chains. His neck was black with bruises.

"Where's Nathanael?"

Parvan's mouth arched into an expression of self-flagellation. "They took him away this morning," he rasped, curling his hands around the filthy iron bars. "I am sorry."

"They're likely in the throne room," Starling murmured from somewhere behind me. "Prince Ren, you know if Welzes is with him then that whole wing will be swarming with guards. I might be able to take out a couple, but the rest would be on us before we even came close."

"I know," I said. I did. Welzes was fucking *king* now, and kings didn't leave their security to chance.

"Then how do we get to him?" snarled out Velichkov.

"There's really only one thing left for me to try," I said, staring at the chains that bound Parvan's wrists.

"What?"

"Act like your brother," I told the heir grimly, "and make a foolish gesture of grandiose self-sacrifice."

Then I turned to Starling, my heart racing. "I expect you're rather going to enjoy this next part, señorita Ortega."

*

Chapter Forty-Three

Mat

The two guards solemnly collected me from the floor of the throne room, hauling me upright between them with their fingers digging painfully into my forearms. I hissed out a sharp exhale when I tried to stand, the agony that flooded my body threatening dark oblivion, so I resentfully let the men bear my weight and that of the chains which still hung from my wrists and ankles in useless restraint. Because injured and hobbled like this, I wasn't going anywhere.

Welzes gestured impatiently as if to shoo me from his sight, and my guards dutifully dragged me away to the side of the hall, leaving a gruesome smear of crimson across the tiles. Tiles that had seen their fair share of blood in their time, but there was something grotesque and faintly ridiculous about it being *mine*, and that only minutes ago it had been inside me and was now drying on the floor.

I blinked back the dual images of Lord de la Vega as he was called forward by the herald, fighting the waves of dizziness that insistently encircled me. The nobleman gingerly picked his way up to the very edge of the pool of blood and with a quick, impassive glance at me, bowed to Welzes. The false king had reseated himself in his throne, his lip curling as he gazed down at his subject.

"Closer," he ordered, and Lord de la Vega visibly swallowed before complying, moving to the standard distance one was expected to stand when presenting before their ruler. It put his shiny shoes directly in the centre of the sticky mass of my blood, and Welzes smiled as he saw he still had his people's obedience no matter how distasteful the command.

"Kneel, my lord," he drawled, smug as all fuck. "Kneel and swear your irrevocable loyalty to-"

The double doors at the far end of the throne room opened with such force and abruptness that we all flinched, each head in the hall swivelling to the source of the commotion. A guard stood there with his hands still outstretched from pushing the doors open, his eyes wide in awe.

"Your Majesty," he breathed. "There's...he's...it's..."

And then Valeri strode impatiently past and I forgot all about the nameless guard, my eyes locked on the man my brother was heaving ahead of him with fingers twisted cruelly in his hair. Ren was just as I'd Seen him in the vision all those weeks ago: hands bound, gaze angry, and glistening blood coating his lips and chin.

"Here's your bastard prince."

Val shoved Ren down to the floor just shy of de la Vega, my lover's knees hitting the tiles as hard as mine had done minutes before. He swayed, unbalanced with his wrists tied behind his back, but my brother didn't give him the chance to fall, keeping hold of his collar and tugging him back upright. He radiated anger as he stood tall over my prince, glaring at Welzes.

"Renato," the false king said, blinking back his surprise. His expression lit up with elated satisfaction and he reached up to adjust his crown. "You've led us on a merry chase, dear boy."

Ren, I mouthed, unable to find my voice. Because *fuck, fuck, fuck,* what the *fuck had happened?*

Welzes' face suddenly fell and he looked uncertainly at the gathered crowd, belatedly remembering the lies he'd been telling them even as recently as ten minutes ago about Ren having the Voice. If they'd been on edge before, it was nothing compared to the tension that strummed through them now as they watched their old prince be delivered to their new king as a bound, bloodied gift.

"And yet, considering what he can *do,* Prince Valeri, I find it disturbing that you've brought him here."

Val glanced down scornfully. "You needn't fear. The little snake cannot weave his manipulations while he's missing his tongue."

And then he forced open Ren's mouth to show everyone he spoke true, and the horrible sight of his mutilated, severed tongue was a thousand times worse now that it was *here* and it was *real* and it was my Ren, no *please-*

My beautiful prince, on his knees and hurting. The pain of it all struck me down to my very soul.

AN OATH AND A PROMISE

"*Ren!*" I cried, and everyone looked my way. Neither my brother nor my lover had seen me until that moment, hidden partly within the crowd as I was, but now their gazes flickered to mine – and the blood still pooling at my feet – and they winced.

In the next moment, Ren and I threw ourselves at each other, both knowing that if we could just *touch*, everything would be alright.

Yet I was held firm by my guards and Valeri's hands landed heavily on Ren's shoulders, keeping us both in place. There were still *yards* between us, and it felt frustratingly endless.

Both princes' expressions were identical in their wide-eyed, irate snarls, but while Ren could only choke out an incomprehensible noise, Valeri spat curses at Welzes.

"What the fuck did you do to my little brother?"

"Your *little brother*," Welzes shot back icily, "has been enabling the traitor at your feet to escape justice."

"I don't give a damn about your justice," said Val. His lips curled back from his teeth and he lifted Ren to his feet by the back of his collar. My prince stumbled, grimacing, his boots slipping in my blood. "Only that you give him back to me and never lay a finger on him again or the Blessed Five help me, my mother and I will lay your country to *waste*."

"So you've come to barter for Nathanael's life?"

Valeri scoffed, full of that dismissive contempt he did so well. He threw Ren at the closest Quarehian guard, a short man with a shaggy beard and frizzy hair who I didn't recognise, and yet seemed oddly familiar. The man wrapped a tanned hand firmly across the prince's mouth as if he didn't trust that losing his tongue had robbed him of his fabled magic.

"No bartering," Val said loudly, striding forward to close the distance between him and the false king. All eyes followed him except mine. "Just one prince for another. And I find it exceptionally odd that upon hearing how you planned to execute a member of my family, I managed to find Aratorre in mere hours when you've had *weeks*, but that's a matter between you and your people." They stirred at that, as he would have known they would, the restlessness that had infected the court earlier continuing to grow. "Give me Nat, *now*."

My brother's bullshit continued to flow over me, but all I could see was Ren. With Temar's heir directing attention to himself and Welzes, no one else seemed to notice how he'd brought his hands out in front of him, seemingly no longer bound, or the way the Quarehian guard's palm over his mouth pulsed with red and green sparks.

Weakness overcame me then, the potent solace of relief making me loll against the ruthless grip of the men who held me.

"You can have your brother or your father-in-law, Prince Valeri," Welzes was saying from up on the dais, his gaze flickering spitefully, "but not both. The other will swing by sunset, so I hope you choose wisely-"

"*Or*," growled Valeri, drawing his sword to buy those final seconds of vital distraction, "you can remove your unworthy ass from that fucking throne, Welzes, before I do it for you."

Every guard in the room but Ren's tensed, unsheathing their own swords and closing in on my brother. The men at the foot of the dais reached him first, cutting across the base of the steps to prevent him from ascending them, but Val merely twirled his sword in a lazy arc to keep them all at bay.

"Stand down," Ren demanded as he rose to his feet, his voice echoing around the room despite the clamour of metal and frantic murmurs. He looked every inch a royal: head high, shoulders back, gaze proud and unflinching. Even the blood on his clothes gave him a heroic war-drenched appearance rather than the feeble victim he'd seemed a moment earlier. "Consider that an order from your king."

*

AN OATH AND A PROMISE

Chapter Forty-Four

Ren

"Needless to say," I said, because I was sure there were some in the room who needed it spelled out for them, "I do not have the Voice. If I did, you would already have obeyed, and yet here you all are, staring at me instead of lowering your swords like I told you to. So I'll point out that you've been lied to, and thank you *not* to kill me."

I didn't move to Mathias like I wanted to: Velichkov had very deliberately pushed me beneath the lip of the archer's balcony when he tossed me to Starling, and I didn't dare move out from beneath its shadow until I was sure that I wouldn't be shot based on a mere rumour of dark magic.

Starling herself edged away from me and into the crowd, her face still disguised by the thick beard she'd grown by agitating hair follicles with her Touch. I'd told her that her height and stature needed fixing as well, for no one would believe that someone as short and skinny – and *ugly*, remembering what she'd said about me to her and Mat's Mazekhstani friends – as her would have been appointed as a palace guard, but that was when she'd smirked and taken my tongue. I could only thank Dios that Starling had bothered to disable my pain receptors first...and that she'd actually followed through with our plan by returning it to me as soon as Velichkov had distracted the room, because with her, one never knew.

Just like I hadn't known if the real guards outside the throne room would let us enter, even with me supposedly muted and bound. If we'd arrive in time, if Velichkov could get me to Starling without anyone else seizing me first, if Welzes would have us all killed on sight.

But with Mathias' life on the line, I hadn't hesitated.

Because it was what we did, throwing ourselves into danger to save each other time and time again without thought or logic. Maybe it was unhealthy and maybe it would get one of us killed one day, but as long as it was me, I was alright with that.

I flashed him a quick grin.

AN OATH AND A PROMISE

Mat didn't return it. In fact, he *scowled* at me from where he was pressed between two hulking guards, but considering the amount of blood that was gathering on the tiles beneath his trailing feet, the lack of appropriate adoration and appreciation on his face was undoubtedly a result of blood loss. I was sure the well-deserved gratitude would appear eventually.

"What the fuck, Ren?" he snapped. "Get out of here!"

Or not.

Welzes stood from my throne, sneering down at us all derisively. "Arrest the traitor prince. If he resists, *kill him*."

At first, no one moved, perhaps from the shock of hearing me speak when a minute ago I'd had no tongue. And then, like a wave building from a ripple, one of the palace guards took an uncertain step towards me and was swiftly copied by a dozen more. Those surrounding Valeri and Mathias watched on cautiously, but didn't move from their own assignments.

"You do not take orders from him," I told the room, meeting the eyes of anyone who would look at me in turn. Guards, nobles, servants. "Zidhan Welzes is not your king. I am."

Welzes scoffed. "No, he's a bastard, which means he doesn't have a drop of royal blood in his veins. You all heard Yanev when he spoke before you yesterday."

Mat's eyes had been fixed on mine this whole time and now they widened in hopeful expectation, assuming I'd produce Dima like we'd planned.

I wished I had an answer better than the one I was forced to give him, which was a small shake of my head. There would be no miraculous proving of my heritage, no persuasive flourish that would send them all down to their knees before me.

My lover strained against the hands holding him, his beautiful face creasing in anguish and fear.

Not for himself: he was far too selfless for that, but for me.

"He's a bastard," Welzes hissed again, when the guards didn't seem inclined to take hold of me.

"And thank fuck for that," I said loudly. "Iván Aratorre was a coward, a bully, and a man both blind and deaf to the suffering of our people."

There were a few shocked murmurs from the crowd, a sharp gasp, and more than one faint nod.

"Whether he was my father or not, I am not him," I continued, similar to what I'd told Astrid Panarina, and I felt the words flow from me with the same conviction as they had then. "And I will not rule like him. I will aim to be fair. Just. I will not tolerate crime nor misbehaviour, but I will ensure the punishments are proportionate to the wrongdoing. I will uphold rights, enforce obligations, and recognise the value in *all* of my subjects."

I saw the mouths of a few women open in surprise, understanding the meaning behind the promise in a way that most of the men evidently did not. They shared hopeful glances – not daring to believe, not yet, but wanting to.

"I have a duty to you," I said. "To you all. And I swear to take that responsibility seriously and with all the accountability it requires."

"Adorable," Welzes mocked, reclaiming the attention of the room. "But pretty words will not save you, sweet boy, nor grant you something that is not yours by right. Now *arrest him,* and know that any man who disobeys my order again shall face the same fate as the rest of these traitors. You *and* your families."

The threat was enough: the civilians hurriedly glanced down at their feet, the guards fell into motion once more, and hands grabbed roughly at me. Across the hall, Mathias snarled out curses and howls of pain as he struggled against his own captors, and Velichkov growled ineffectually as he was cut off from us by a wave of assailants bearing down on him.

*

Chapter Forty-Five

Mat

"Just when I thought you could sink no lower, Renato, you attack my palace with filthy barbarians," the false king said in disgust, finally deigning to descend from the protection of the dais now that Ren, Valeri and I were held tightly by his guards. My brother was bleeding from several cuts on his face and arms, and it had taken a while for him to fall to the sheer number of armed Quarehians who'd surrounded him. He was a formidable warrior but also one who'd deliberately put himself in the middle of enemy territory, *alone*, to serve as a distraction in a plan that had clearly had no Blessed point to it other than *get in there and cause a fuss*. It was on the level of one of *my* plans, for fuck's sake, and I'd thought more of Ren and Val than that.

"You mean Prince Valeri?" Ren asked from where he hung from the hold of two guards nearly twice his size, looking as casually unconcerned as he did when he lounged across his bed. It was all for show, of course: I could see the tension in the lines of his neck, but the prince had always lived to the power of appearances. "He's not so bad. Far more honourable than you, Welzes, much better looking, and there's no question he'll wear his crown with more grace and capability."

Oh fuck me, Ren was complimenting my brother? Within his *earshot?*

We were all going to die.

"I challenge you to a duel," Val said abruptly, surprising us all. His eyes were narrowed on Welzes. "Fight me."

But the false king made a disdainful noise, dismissing his words with no more than a flick of his fingers. A king did not have to accept such a challenge and no one would blame him for refusing when his opponent was the heir to Temar, a man skilled in warcraft and yet less than even the lowliest Quarehian peasant. Even if Valeri won, none here would accept his authority over their own ruler.

"An excellent idea," drawled Ren. "But as enthralling as it would be to watch you get all hot and sweaty again, Velichkov, I fear it's my turn to show off."

AN OATH AND A PROMISE

He locked eyes with Welzes. "You call me a bastard. I call you one in turn, although admittedly for different reasons. You call yourself king. So do I. Let's settle this, shall we?"

"You would fight *me?*" Welzes asked incredulously, and more than one of the gathered courtiers and guards laughed at that. As well they might: Ren was hardly known for his skills on the battlefield. He may have had a reputation for his proficiency at court – and in the bedroom – but as a fighter?

"I would," my lover agreed. "Isn't that the proper way to determine a dispute about who is owed the crown?"

Murmurs of agreement broke out amongst the nobility. He was right. The death or concession of the ruling monarch was the only means of taking a throne on Riehse Eshan, and Welzes evidently wasn't conceding shit.

I stared at him. What the fuck was he doing? There was no way Ren could take Welzes in a fight, no matter how many tricks he had up his sleeves. The Aratorre line was far from well-built, and Iván had only killed King Padilla by using the Voice.

Ren was just a skinny prince with a brilliant mind, and he was *not* going to fucking die at the end of Welzes' sword.

Damn his stubbornness, and his love for a country that would see – had seen – him bleed for it.

Glancing around the throne room, Welzes sized up the mood of the crowd and quickly realised how eager they were for this. A showdown between the two men who would claim to be their ruler? The bastard son of a bastard king, or a foreigner: this was Dios' chance to show who He favoured. A duel like this meant one would be dead on the floor by the end, leaving no question as to who was more worthy to be named the king of Quareh.

"Very well. This is going to be exceedingly embarrassing for you, Renato," Welzes said, accepting a blade from one of his guards. My blood boiled when I recognised it as Valeri's. "Although perhaps the pain of your inevitable death will quell the humiliation somewhat."

He gestured for Ren to be released, and the guards formed a line behind him so he couldn't flee from the fight. One of the men tossed his own sword to the floor at his feet, but my prince didn't move to retrieve it.

"It is tradition," Ren said slowly, "for the victor to grant the vanquished a boon. One last request, as it were."

Welzes sneered. "You would beg for your life?"

"No," answered Ren. His eyes found mine through the rows of men that separated us. "I would beg for his."

"Fuck you," I said.

My blood ran cold as I realised that was the entire point of this. The reason for fighting when he knew he couldn't win, just so he could scrape a favour from the man who killed him.

He wasn't doing this for Quareh. He was doing it for *me*.

The faces of those gathered in the hall, especially those like Lord de la Vega who supported Ren, showed enthusiasm. Excitement. Hope.

Because they all expected one final, glorious trick from him, the clever plans he was known for. They didn't realise that this *was* the plan. Why couldn't he be the self-centred prick I'd thought him to be when I'd met him?

"Pick up the sword, Renato," the false king said. "Pick up the sword, and I will allow you to plead for your northern pet's life before I take yours."

*

Chapter Forty-Six

Ren

I was under no illusions as to which one of us would walk away from this fight. Zidhan Welzes may not have been a warrior but he was broad of chest and shoulder, twice my weight, and had undoubtedly gone through the two years of conscription forced on all Lukian men. The way he held Velichkov's heavy sword casually at his side told me that he knew his way around it easily enough.

Me? Not so much. I'd killed before but never in *battle*. I'd barely even been in a duel: there had been one time a handful of years ago when I'd insisted on facing Jiron in the training ring despite knowing he was duty bound to let me win, and the amount of pretending to trip over his own feet he'd had to do to make that happen had been unspeakably embarrassing for the both of us.

I took a breath.

Let it out.

Took another.

But really, I had always known it would come to this. Since the day I'd finally let myself admit what Nathanael Velichkov meant to me – much, much more than anyone ever had before, in a way that was etched onto my very soul – I'd accepted that my life would be his. A price well worth paying, even literally, and my only regret was that I didn't have more lives to give because the reckless bastard would inevitably get in more trouble sooner rather than later, and then where would he be?

Far away from this mess, at least.

Parvan had been sent through the tunnels with Dima and was waiting a short distance from the palace, should he be needed to escort his charge away from here. Velichkov and I had entered the throne room with the hope of having all three of us princes walk back out of it whole and free, but also knowing that Mat came first, and we'd both do whatever it took to keep him breathing.

Although he was barely even doing that.

My heart shattered as I took in his paler than usual skin, the uneven fluttering of his chest, the way his face was twisted up in a pained grimace as he slumped in the arms of the men holding him. And all the fucking blood.

Welzes had hurt him somehow, and if there was ever a reason to wish someone carved to Blessed ribbons while they were still conscious to feel the agony of it, it was that.

I picked up the sword.

"Wait!" Mathias cried, desperation and pain lancing his voice.

I didn't look back at him. I couldn't. I'd just collapse with the weight of it all, and then I'd die before I'd even *tried* to fight for us.

"This is a kings' duel," Mat added, now full of that haughty dismissal of his that demanded attention. "When neither of you are kings. It means nothing!"

It wasn't just me who paused at that.

He raised his chin defiantly as everyone looked at him in confused expectation, his grim satisfaction catching us off guard.

"Only one of them needs to hold the throne," Lord Hierro tried to explain, "while the other challenges-"

"We've been through this," interrupted Welzes. "With Renato admitting himself illegitimate," – a strained interpretation of what I'd said, but I couldn't fault him for twisting it to his advantage when I'd have done the same – "I am next in the Aratorre line."

"No," Mat argued. I marvelled at the endless *fight* in him: the man could take on the world and still have determination to spare. "You're not."

I realised he wasn't even looking at Welzes, but was staring past us to someone in the crowd. That person blinked, comprehending his meaning a moment before the rest of us.

"I am," Alondra whispered. Then she cleared her throat. "*I* am the eldest living child of the deceased King Iván Aratorre, and in the absence of any full blood brothers, the Quarehian throne belongs to me, to be held by either regency or husbandship."

"Which means I'm king after all," Welzes said dryly. "Glad we could get that cleared up."

He turned back to me, dismissing her.

I saw my sister's eyes flash with anger. Lifting her chin, her next words cut clearly through the low buzz of the crowd.

"And I renounce all claim to it."

There was a shocked silence and then the room erupted into gasps and shouts, eclipsed only by Welzes' snarl as he lifted a finger and pointed it at his wife. "You can't do that!"

He took a menacing step towards her but Lords González and de Leon closed ranks between the two of them, united for the first fucking time in *ever*.

"She just did," Velichkov spat, and even bleeding and restrained – and now gagged, as a cloth was immediately drawn over his mouth by one of the many guards struggling to keep him on his knees – the statement came across as the threat it was.

"What does that mean?" someone whispered, and the question was taken up by several others, echoing around the hall until everyone was staring at the elder Lord Lago, who was somewhat of an expert on these types of laws. He also hated attracting so much attention, and fidgeted uncomfortably until his husband lay a reassuring hand on his elbow.

"Uhm," he said awkwardly, "it means the only remaining claimant through hereditary succession is the youngest Aratorre daughter, whose reign would also be held by regency or husbandship."

"Another damn foreigner," someone in the crowd muttered.

"But...but Mariana Janssen ceded all rights held by herself and her heirs to take a crown when she voluntarily abolished Onn's monarchy," Lord Lago hastily continued, referencing how my other sister and her husband were in the process of dissolving their rule in favour of an elected government. "In the absence of any other...*blood claimants*, the Quarehian throne may be filled by popular vote of the nobility, should they so choose."

"I choose," the younger Lord Lago said eagerly. His voice was pitched high with excitement. "We can crown our new king ourselves!"

AN OATH AND A PROMISE

"Or we can get on with the fucking duel," snarled Welzes, the tip of his sword aimed at my throat.

*

Chapter Forty-Seven

Mat

"Actually, you can't." Quintín Lago stepped forward, his face flushed with triumph. "Prince Nathanael is right. Under Riehse Eshan's laws of displacement of sovereignty, a kings' duel is only for when one of the duellists already holds the throne. Your fight will not determine anything at law." He looked to the man at his side and pawed at his arm. "Did I get that right, love?"

His husband paled further as all eyes in the hall turned back to him.

"Y-you did," the elder Lord Lago stammered, shrinking behind his other half.

But what the two noblemen appeared to be naively missing was that if Welzes killed Ren, the candidacy options for the crown would be helpfully lessened. My prince swiftly tossed the sword back to the closest guard, winking at me as if he'd had the same thought. It wasn't that we believed Welzes honourable enough not to cut down an unarmed man, but at least he'd risk losing any remaining support in the court if he did.

Now Welzes and Ren were equal, neither with a stronger claim than the other. It all came down to the people's choice.

Not all of the people...that would be quite an effort, and it was an interesting idea for the future. But the nobles here ruled over every corner of Quareh, representatives from across its fertile, sun-baked soil.

"Where is Navar?" demanded Welzes. "Get him in here, now!"

"You'll find Councillor Navar in the inner palace courtyard," Ren drawled, inspecting a scratch on the back of his hand as if that was the worst he had to worry about. "You're welcome to go find him if you need to be told what to do, but be sure to use a fifth storey window like he did, won't you?"

Welzes went pale.

"Fine," he said to the court after a long, tense moment. The word was drawn out, reluctantly uttered when he evidently saw no other way forward. "We will travel to the capital and hold your *vote-*"

"We have a quorum of lords here," Lago chipped in, his enthusiasm unintentionally stymieing the man's attempt to seek support from the rest of the Council back in Máros. "We can vote now."

"It is tradition to put forward positions first, my love," his husband said in what was maybe supposed to be a whisper but the anticipatory silence of the hall made echo.

Ren made a courteous gesture towards his opponent. "*Por favor, señor.* The wisdom you must have gleaned through the many passing of seasons surely outweighs the advantage bestowed on me with fewer."

The fucker did not just say age before beauty.

There were a few faint snickers from the crowd but Welzes either missed the implication or chose to ignore it, for he immediately launched into vehement speech.

"This *boy*," he snarled disdainfully, making no secret of how he was leveraging his position with the overt emphasis he put on the word, "is not a fit choice for a king. He lacks the experience, the understanding, the *gravitas* of what it means to lead a people into their golden age. Quareh has the potential for magnificence, my dear lords, and Renato would have you all cower in your homes while you make obsequience to your northern neighbours.

"His single week as your so-called *ruler* speaks for itself. A bloodthirsty Temarian army was allowed to invade your lands," – I glanced at Val, who looked amused even through the cloth the fuckers had gagged him with – "and the little prince mysteriously disappeared in what I can only assume from the reports meant he was either captured or attempting to flee."

"That little bit of fun? Nah." Ren waved a hand. "I was merely spending some valuable time getting to know my northern counterparts. Did you know Prince Valeri's idea of a first date is taking someone to a flogging?"

My brother's smirk dropped into a glare.

"Ever the comedian, Renato," said Welzes contemptuously. "Were the appointments of women to men's positions such as those of this palace's herald meant to be a joke, too?"

"Absolutely not," I spat.

He rounded on me. "Ah, and then of course, my lords, there's *that*."

AN OATH AND A PROMISE

Ren's eyes narrowed.

"A vote for Renato is a vote for a Temarian king consort," Welzes sneered, and despite the disdain in his tone, my heart fluttered at the implication.

But I swallowed that shit down. This wasn't the place for fucking *love*, let alone marriage.

All Ren had to do to negate Welzes' accusation was announce his intentions to take a Quarehian spouse. Hell, he could probably declare a spontaneous engagement to anyone in the room, and I doubted they'd decline.

I was well used to him needing to be something different to his people than he was to me. He'd might have turned Astrid down but one didn't mess foreign queens around: on the other hand, it would be easy enough for Ren to later wiggle his unfairly attractive ass out of a marriage proposal to one of his own court.

And expecting that bit of ruthless subterfuge, I stared in surprise when he cocked his head, smiled fondly in my direction, and said, "*sí*."

Not everyone was struck as happy or charmed by that answer as I was. There were some scoffs, some scowls – I caught Isobella's dark glare from where her father had protectively tucked her behind him – and one long, low whistle from the gaggle of younger lords from my left that was either highly complimentary or highly insulting.

"Lying with the enemy," Welzes murmured, clearly pleased with Ren's admission. "Where does that leave your fickle loyalties, he who would be king? How could your people ever trust you to protect their interests over those of a foreign royal?"

"Interesting choice of words, Lukian." Ren turned to the crowd, projecting his words to the farthest reaches of the hall. "And yet Nathanael is as Quarehian as you and I. He has bled for our country, fought for its peace and safety, pledged himself to it. Only yesterday, he risked his life and freedom to save fifty of our families and friends from being sent to the border to die pointlessly, and it is why he stands before us now, still bleeding for us, despite red not being his colour at fucking all."

Liar. How many times had he revelled in turning my skin that exact shade, either by his words or his hands?

Even now, that thought sent a flush of entirely inappropriate heat through me, and I blamed it on watching my lover in his element. There was something incredibly attractive about Ren being his most competent self, weaving mastery over his audience with his speeches and sense of theatre.

And there were always so many hidden meanings to what he said. Like just now, revealing knowledge of my capture told me that they'd rescued Parvan from the cells, and relief over my guard's fate washed through me.

As did an unexpected and comforting warmth: not as a result of embarrassment or interest this time, but the familiar sensation of healing magic.

I subtly glanced to the side to see Starling, still disguised as a man, brushing her elbow against the guard on my left as she pretended to scratch at her neck. The guard shivered and shook his head as if to clear it, seemingly feeling her Touch flow through him but not realising its source. I pressed my face into my shoulder as the magic knitted together the slit tendons and skin, trying not to make a noise.

"So Zidhan is right," Ren continued. "If you choose me, you indeed choose Nathanael as well, for he has stood by my side this whole time and I will continue to do the same for him. Because that is loyalty. That is love."

"And what I find incredibly curious," he said, furrowing a brow as though he'd only just come to the realisation of whatever it was although I knew his sharp mind would have immediately picked up on it, "is that Welzes has spoken much of what my rule might look like, but not his own. Are we truly so afraid of unity with the north that we would choose anything but which brings that future closer?"

We, I noted. Despite it being unlikely he'd get the opportunity to vote himself, Ren had effortlessly slotted himself into camaraderie with his people, whereas Welzes had fostered his own exclusion with his use of *you* and *yours*.

"Because what I want for us is a place we can call home and not fear we will lose to our enemies the next day," said Ren, his face softening into a smile. "Friends who will grow old with us and not be sent to the afterlife at the edge of a blade. Children who do not have to go through what *we fucking did.*"

There were a few side glances at that from the older men in the room, evidently wondering what someone as young as Ren could possibly have to say about it. But the fierceness in the set of his mouth and the weight of his gaze silenced them, and even not knowing what abuse Iván Aratorre had put his youngest son through, none dared to say a word.

"A place where spouses," my prince added, looking at me now, "are chosen for love not obligation, where borders are just lines on a map, and where your body does not define you. *That* is our Quareh."

*

AN OATH AND A PROMISE

Chapter Forty-Eight

Ren

Perhaps in Máros, a speech like mine wouldn't have meant much.

But here, in the northern province of Quareh, these lords had suffered from the conflict my father had stirred up with Mazekhstam during his rule. They'd lost countless children to the border skirmishes, had their lands ruined and bloodied, risked their own lives whenever they returned to their estates.

And then there were those who had seen their daughters abused and mistreated by men, even as they strove to be better husbands to their wives. Ones who had fallen in love with servants or villagers but known it was doomed before it began. People who were other than what they had been born as, and for all of them, I wanted to offer a hope that things didn't have to be as they were before.

As Welzes wanted to keep them, having the same power-hungry, misogynistic, selfish inclinations as the previous king.

As the court began to mutter among itself, reflecting on what we'd both promised them, I wandered over to where the two guards were still daring to hold onto my wildcat, their fingers digging into his shoulders and forearms as he strained against them.

"You can let go of my man now," I said, my tone making it clear that it wasn't a suggestion.

"I would expect you'd rather they didn't," drawled Welzes, and I seethed at the satisfaction in his voice as he relished getting to hurt me like this. How pleased he must have been to make Mathias bleed, knowing the pain would be felt twice over once I learned of it. "They're the only thing keeping him upright."

"Let." I met the gaze of one of the guards, then the other. "*Go.*"

They did. Perhaps they believed I'd win the lords' vote, or maybe they were hedging their bets and only following my order in the absence of direct contradiction from Welzes. Maybe they'd seen how close I was to taking their fucking heads for it.

Whatever the reason, they peeled their villainous fingers off my boy and stepped back, leaving him standing in a pool of tacky blood and wearing a similarly pissed off expression to mine.

With the manacles still weighing down his wrists and chained to the ones around his ankles, he couldn't embrace me, but we pressed our heads together, seeking and giving comfort and conscious of all the eyes on us.

"Hello, you," I murmured, cutting through the exclamations of surprise echoing around us as the court wondered at his healed injuries. Starling had come through for us, as usual.

"*Hola*," he whispered back. "I suppose you think you're terribly clever?"

"I suppose you think I'm going to free you from these shackles of yours?"

"On second thought," said Mat, "I think you're terribly clever too."

I laughed quietly, dipping a kiss to his cheek.

"Cast your vote!" Quintín Lago chirped, immediately bounding over to my side and dragging his husband with him. The older man grumbled good-naturedly but didn't resist.

As I opened my mouth to suggest this should be a *private* ballot to negate fears of retribution against any who supported the losing candidate, most of the crowd began to move, dispersing left and right to show their support to me or Welzes.

Lord de la Vega sidled my way. Lord Delgado, a friend of Navar's with lands laying further to the west, stomped over to stand with Welzes. Lord Martinez hurried to join them.

More nobles moved this way or that.

The few men who remained in the middle of the room, finding themselves left behind, gave tiny coughs or stretches as if to explain their delay and then quickly joined the two swelling clusters of noblemen. Only the women and servants hadn't moved, but when Lago stood on his toes to count the lords' numbers and declare the results of the vote, Isobella cleared her throat to draw our attention, preened like a damn cat when she got it, and drifted across the hall to my side with an elegance I was exceedingly envious of. The skirts of her dress swished in the resulting silence.

Welzes scoffed. "Women don't get to *vote*."

Martinez gave hearty, boisterous agreement. Even the elder Lord Lago made an assenting noise, likely as it didn't accord to the strict letter of the law, but at least he had the decency to do it quietly.

"Duke Welzes," Mathias called loudly over to the man, deliberately using his old title as if he'd already lost. Which, to be fair, he had. "Are you unable to count?"

Welzes' gaze flickered over the two groups of congregated men and he must have done the same calculations as Lago, for he quickly shook his head.

"If they must," he muttered, clearly torn between his opinions on the matter and his need to make up for his fewer votes. "And the commoners should too," he added quickly.

With those words, he offered me a challenging stare as if expecting me to protest. But I merely inclined my head, and a moment later there was a second flurry of movement from the remainder of the original crowd as they let their feet cast their votes. Women, servants, guards: all were equal in this fleeting moment, allowed to dictate their own future.

There were some who drifted Welzes' way. Probably more than I would have predicted, if I was being honest with myself, although I expected that despite my ambitious words there were still women here who would blindly follow their men as they'd been taught their whole lives to do, and men who would demand nothing less.

So perhaps not all of the votes were free from coercion, but each one who moved to Welzes' side of the throne room was someone I'd failed. Failed to show them what their lives could be like with the freedom and opportunity I offered, or failed in them already being too jaded or too greedy or too cruel to want it.

Yet the numbers were in my favour. As the crowd fell still, two thirds of the court stood on my side of the hall.

"It is decided," the elder Lord Lago declared, cocking his head as he gazed at me in thoughtful contemplation. "Renato Aratorre shall hold the Quarehian throne."

*

Chapter Forty-Nine

Mat

I hadn't expected Welzes to take the loss with good grace, so I wasn't surprised when he began to rant about it almost immediately, blaming everything from poor acoustics in the room such that those at the back hadn't *heard his speech properly,* to accusations of Ren apparently having spent the last several weeks not on the run, but in secret collusions with the court to dethrone him.

The prince rolled his eyes and gestured impatiently at someone. A moment later my shackles were unlocked, the chains noisily clattering down onto the tiles to form a grim pile at my feet.

"Of *course* they're going to vote for the arrant whore," Welzes was drawling to those still gathered around him, eyeing my lover with hateful distaste. "He's probably promised each man here that he'll spread his legs for them later."

"Just one man," Ren said mildly, but I could see the tension in the line of his mouth as he fussed over the state of my wrists, earnestly waving Starling over to us. She sauntered closer, the hair of her beard falling out before our very eyes, and offered a cheeky wink as she reached for my hands.

Several members of the court stared at Ren – and me, for the implication of his surprising admission clearly hadn't been lost on them – but it was Welzes who had his full attention. "I suggest you leave my palace and my country promptly, duke, before I learn everything you did to Nathanael and decide to repay it upon you tenfold."

Scoffing, the man brushed off invisible dust from his coat as he tried his best to look imperious. "As if I'd want to stay in this cesspit any longer. Come, Alondra," he snapped, and the woman faltered where she stood next to Isobella, her whole body going stiff when he beckoned her over.

Ren held up a hand. "My sister can stay."

"*Your* sister," Welzes hissed, a savage grin lighting up his face as he seized the opportunity his marriage gave him to hurt his enemy one last time, "is my wife. My property. She'll be returning home to Lukia, where I can promise you that she will pay for what she has cost me."

"A crown that isn't yours and never was?" Valeri asked with a snarl, ripping the gag from his mouth as soon as Ren waved a begrudging hand to order him freed as well. He got to his feet, angry and imposing. "A people who deserve better? You'll walk out of this room with nothing but your life, Welzes, and consider yourself fucking lucky."

It was remarkable restraint that both my lover and brother were showing in letting him live, but I supposed that cutting him down in cold blood or having him executed would be a dangerous move, politically speaking. There were clearly some Quarehians who preferred him as their ruler – although less than there had been before, as many who had voted for him had already strayed back over this way, either in resignation or disgust – and the man was a Lukian duke with the ear of its king. He could cause a lot of trouble for us.

Not that Ren seemed to give a shit. He offered a broad smirk as he meandered closer to Welzes, flicking his long dark hair carelessly over one shoulder. Despite the dried blood on his chin and the filth on his travelling clothes, he looked every inch an arrogant royal.

My arrogant royal.

"Alondra legally belongs to me," the duke sneered at him and the two men began to circle each other as they faced off. I stiffened as I noticed Welzes still carried Val's sword, yet Ren's own hands were bare and stuffed into his pockets. "You can't stop me from taking her."

"If she was married to a man," my prince agreed. "Only I'm fairly certain even Lukia isn't backwards enough to recognise marriages to beasts like yourself."

With his back now to me, I saw Welzes bristle. The blade in his hand lifted an inch and my brother cursed under his breath, moving closer to Ren as he noticed the same thing. I pulled out the knife I'd tucked at the small of my back before my capture, but shackled and with eyes always on me, I hadn't been able to reach it before now.

"What the *fuck* did you just call me?" Welzes demanded.

"Leave," Val cut in, directing a glare at Ren to instruct him to ease up. The prince just blinked back innocently, his long lashes framing those rich brown eyes. "We won't tell you again, Zidhan."

Welzes puffed out an irritated breath, but faced with an irate six-foot northerner, a court that had nearly all turned against him, and a wife who clearly wasn't moving, he knew he was beaten. He tossed the sword onto the tiles and headed for the doors, throwing me a filthy look as he passed by.

"Although," mused Ren loudly, "if you miss being Navar's puppet king and getting down on your knees for him whenever he demanded it, I could always-"

Welzes spun, his mouth stretched into a furious bellow of rage as he scooped the blade back up from the floor. Val darted in front of Ren, jaw set and already raising a borrowed sword to block the strike they both expected to land.

But Welzes wasn't aiming for Ren.

I saw the moment my prince's expression changed from triumph to horror as the duke swung the sword at my head instead.

*

Chapter Fifty

Ren

This wasn't supposed to be how it happened.

Welzes was meant to go for *me*. Letting him leave wasn't an option: I would not have my sister live in fear of him and his claim on her for the rest of her life, and as much as I could have arranged a quiet assassination on his return to Lukia, there was always the risk that something would go wrong. Goading people was as much my speciality as Mat's, and even in Jiron's absence it seemed there would always be a large, hulking warrior ready to protect my exquisite ass, today's in the form of a Temarian heir wielding a heavy sword with no more effort than I did a quill.

Piss Welzes off, make him attack me, pretend to be sad when he tragically got killed doing so. A simple plan that had gone so horrendously, unthinkably *wrong*.

"Nat!" I shrieked as the duke brought Velichkov's sword down on my lover, who suddenly seemed impossibly tiny and fragile in his shadow. My cry was echoed by his brother and Starling, and all three of us leapt forward as Mathias – my brave and beautiful and impossibly precious Mathias – stepped *into* the swing, moving closer to the man trying to kill him with the amount of idiocy only he could muster.

And then they were both tumbling to the ground, and a moment later Velichkov was hauling Welzes off his little brother, throwing the bastard down onto his back and readying the tip of his blade against his neck with a snarl.

Yet Welzes' eyes were already scrunched up in pain, the Mazekhstani sword falling from his limp fingers. Blood blossomed across his chest and bubbled up between his lips.

After frantically scouring Mathias' winded form and finding no injury, my gaze settled on his right hand where he clutched another of those damn knives of his. The blade dripped blood. It was small, only a few inches in length, but like the man himself its danger wasn't limited to its size.

AN OATH AND A PROMISE

"Mi cielo?" I whispered.

Mat uncurled himself from the floor, heaving in the breath he'd lost after Welzes had landed on him. He shot me a fierce glare, evidently as unimpressed about my terrible plan to provoke the duke as I was. Yet he didn't dare say anything out loud with the court's attention on us.

Fuck, he'd acted quickly. If my wildcat had been even a second slower, or less daring, Welzes might have killed *him*.

He let me pull him to his feet and into my arms, and we shared a brief, urgent kiss before looking back down at the man dying at our feet.

If this had been a ballad, Welzes would have uttered some poignant last words, I was sure. A threat, maybe, or last-minute repentance. Some prophetic bullshit.

But this wasn't fiction, which meant he entered the afterlife choking and coughing on his own blood, with the scent of piss tainting the air. Starling, who could have easily saved him in the seconds it took him to die, was busy examining her fingernails.

"Lukia won't be happy," Lord Hierro grunted, giving the corpse a nudge with the toe of his boot when it eventually fell still.

"That piece of shit just tried to kill a Temarian prince who is also a former ward of Mazekhstam and recognised royalty of Quareh," I said, clearing my throat when my voice emerged a little shaky. Mathias' arms around me tightened. "If Lukia isn't happy, it will have to take it up with the entirety of Riehse Eshan."

"Damn straight," Velichkov growled, swiping up his sword and clutching it possessively. I didn't miss the way he polished the hilt with the edge of his shirt before resheathing the blade, and grinned at the dramatic, contemptuous gesture. "Is that it? Or should we expect anyone else to try to kill either of you?"

"Don't be ridiculous, Val," Mathias said. He didn't let go of me, which I was wholeheartedly in support of. Perhaps I could implement a law where he was never allowed to stop touching me ever again. "This is Ren we're talking about. I'd be surprised if at least two more people don't attempt it by sunset, and I'll likely be one of them."

AN OATH AND A PROMISE

Velichkov eyed me. I winked at him and knowing he'd have a clear view, slid my hands down Mathias' back to cup his ass and give it a hard squeeze.

"Then expect me to be the second," the heir grouched in irritation as my lover hissed embarrassed curses in my ear, and he then turned to my sister with a deep bow. "Your Highness. If you ever need a reprieve from that impossible child you have the misfortune to call brother, you'll always be a welcome guest in Delzerce."

Alondra blinked at him in surprise. "I...may take you up on the offer, Prince Valeri," she said coyly. "I look forward to meeting that wife of yours."

I frowned as Velichkov ducked his head and muttered something incoherent. Had that been a fucking *blush* I'd seen on his normally stoic face? What the hell kind of plans did he have for my sister and his wife...oh. *Oh.*

Nope, I was not thinking about that. I was completely wrong, I had to be. Someone as honourable and uptight as Valeri Velichkov would not be propositioning my sister for a Blessed threesome minutes after her husband had been killed in front of her. Although it had sounded more like it was her who was propositioning *him*, and...

"Breathe, *dorogoi*," Mat murmured, running his fingers down my jaw and neck. I felt the slight pressure against my pulse, and although he didn't dare choke me out with so many eyes on us, the touch was enough to settle me. "Val's right. It's over. You won."

"We won," I said, and then raised my voice to be heard by everyone in the throne room. "I won't let you down. Any of you."

"We know, my king," Lord de la Vega said, a roguish, wry smile on his face, and there were nods and murmurs of agreement from the whole court.

"I'm still a prince until I'm crowned," I reminded them.

"Then for the love of Dios, God, and the Blessed Five," said Mathias, "someone get this man a fucking crown."

*

Chapter Fifty-One

Mat

Two days later, Ren was keeping his nerves at bay by playing with my hair, mussing it up with his fingers even though there was less than an hour to go until his coronation ceremony began. But even though I was well aware the asshole was doing his best to make me look like I'd just been fucked, I didn't have the heart to admonish him. Last time we'd been this close to his crowning, Welzes and Navar had branded him a traitor, and we both flinched every time there was a knock on the door in case similar poor fate found us again.

"Thanks for all your help, Star," I murmured, flashing a smile at the healer where she was curled up on the opposite lounge in the king's antechamber. We were in the Márosian palace, sunlight streaming through the windows and the soft scent of jasmine in the air.

She waved away my gratitude. "I did try to do you a favour by removing His Bitchiness' tongue permanently, but he seemed to have an issue with that."

I frowned at her. "*I* have an issue with that!"

"Right," Starling said, winking at me and pointedly dropping her gaze to my crotch. I immediately crossed my legs. "Would reduce his usefulness somewhat."

Ren snorted from where he was standing behind me, sliding his restless hands from my hair to my shoulders. "Please tell me my subjects value me for more than my ability to give head."

"*Well*," she began, drawing out the word and screwing up her face.

"Fuck you, Estrella."

The prince tugged on my shirt. I was wearing Temarian dress rather than Quarehian today as a way of showing the north's support for his coronation and subsequent rule. When he dislodged my collar from the perfect fold it had been in and unfastened the top three buttons of my shirt with deft fingers, I finally smacked his hands away. "Stop it. I am not walking in there looking like your fucking whore."

"Just a little bit," he whined. "And at least make sure to put a limp in your step. I have a reputation in bed to uphold, and it's decidedly difficult when you're the only one who gets to see it." He paused and gave a low chuckle. "Or *feel* it."

"*Nyet*. No."

"Two buttons?"

I sighed. "One."

He made a happy noise in my ear, fiddling with my shirt to show off the marks he'd left around my neck and throat last night. My brother was going to kill me when he noticed them.

"How's Dima?" I asked, mostly for the distraction that conversation offered.

Starling blew out a breath and shrugged. "The same he's been since we got here. The southern tower is tall enough for him not to be able to hear the minds of even the guards at its base, so he's happy as long as no one goes up there."

"And *is* anyone going up there?" Ren rested his chin on the top of my head, and I could imagine the disapproving look he was sending the healer's way. "Considering I ordered him to be left alone?"

"I thought he might be lonely," she said. Another shrug. "He wasn't."

It felt shitty exiling Dima to the top of a tower like a storybook princess, but Starling was right. He seemed to enjoy the solitude, and it granted the man significantly more home comforts than he'd had up on the mountain near Stavroyarsk. Even her visits as his healer weren't appreciated, and he'd straight up told me to fuck off when I'd ventured up there to say hello. No one else knew the identity of the strange man sequestered in the tower, and that was how we intended to keep it.

"Your Highness?"

I felt Ren tense where he was pressed against my back.

"What is it?" he asked carefully, and I glanced at the guard hovering in the open doorway to the antechamber where Parvan stood with a wary hand on the hilt of his sword. It was too early for Ren to be called to the ceremony...had something happened? If anyone else tried to come after my prince, I'd tear them to fucking pieces.

"It's Elías and Luis, my prince. And..." The guard faltered, biting his lip. "And Jiron."

We were out of the room before he'd finished speaking, tearing down the corridors and staircases with reckless abandon until we pulled up short outside the second receiving room. The door was closed but Luis and El stood before it in civilian clothes, snapping to attention as Ren drew close.

"Your Highness!"

They tried to bow. The prince and I tried to hug them. What followed was an awkward mess of limbs and soft laughs as the men attempted to maintain decorum and Ren playfully admonished them for failing to do so, while being the cause of it in how tightly he was embracing them.

"Jiron?" he asked.

The guards glanced at each other.

"When he didn't meet back up with us as we'd agreed," Luis began cautiously, glancing at the door, "we went looking for him. We...found him."

"Where?" My voice was quiet, barely a whisper, and it was drowned out by the dull thud of my heart.

"A rebel encampment in north Quareh," answered El. "Heavily guarded and well stocked. We were able to convince a few disgruntled locals to help clear it out, and Luis and I led the assault."

"Elías led it," Luis corrected. "I just went where he pointed me. Thankfully, that was at the throats of the fuckers holding Jiron."

Ren reached for the door handle.

"Your Highness, you should know...they had him for weeks," Elías said softly, his own voice wavering in a way that I'd never heard before. He blinked, and his mouth flattened into an agonised line. "The rebels had other Blessed in their ranks, and while he'd killed their tracker, they tortured him for your location until he was at the edge of death and then had their healer bring him back. Over and over again."

For *weeks*. Fucking hell.

AN OATH AND A PROMISE

The prince stared at El, not speaking. *Unable* to speak.

I lay a hand on his shoulder and he seemed to come back to himself, pressing down on the handle and stepping inside.

Jiron stood at the window with his back to us, his huge form comfortingly familiar in its shape and yet…wrong. His shoulders were hunched, his head was bowed, and his fingers were twisted and mangled where they hung at his sides.

"Jiron," Ren whispered.

The man turned. Amber eyes met ours, flickering between us without any recognition. His face was criss-crossed with thick lines: gruesomely scarred, evidencing either the limitations or the callousness of the rebels' healer.

Fuck. No.

"Jiron," Ren said again, and moved closer. Jiron frowned down at him, confused, and my soul screamed with the horror of him not knowing his oldest friend.

Yet the moment before the prince wrapped his arms around his waist, something seemed to flash across his face.

"My prince," Jiron rumbled, but even his normally soothing, deep voice was butchered into a rasp. "Are you alright?"

"Am *I* alright? Fuck, Jiron! You shouldn't have…" Ren hissed out a pained breath and smacked at the larger man's chest, making him arch an eyebrow as he gazed down at the prince. "Ow! I'm pissed at you! Why did you…why…why…"

He broke down into racking sobs and Jiron shuddered, gathering him closer and wrapping his huge arms around him. The guard's hands looked too fucked up to be capable of working properly, but if they caused him pain, he didn't show it.

Ren's legs gave out and they both sank to their knees on the floor, clutching at each other.

"I am sorry I could not be there for you, Your Highness."

Ren cursed at him some more through his tears. I felt sick.

We'd been wandering the continent while he was being *tortured*. By the

Blessed, Jiron had paid a heavy price for our freedom.

Starling inched closer and placed a sparking hand on the man's cheek, smoothing the skin and bending his ruined fingers back into place. He coughed violently and then flexed them, glancing up at her and murmuring his gratitude.

Jiron shot a fond look down at Ren, who returned it.

"Is…"

I didn't know how to ask it, but Star seemed to hear the question anyway.

"His body is now fully healed," she said quietly to me, withdrawing back to my side. "His mind is still a mess."

I couldn't breathe as I watched the prince and his guard touch each other reverently: little presses of fingertips to the other's jaw, arm, shoulder, like they were testing out this newness between them. Ren's hopeful yet sorrowful look. Jiron's flickers of confusion amid his adoration.

"You may say that," said El, coming to join us with his eyebrows raised, "but this is the best we've seen him since we got him out of there over a week ago. If Ren's mere presence can do this, there's *hope,* Your Highness. We will get Jiron back, I promise."

I nodded, swallowing down the lump in my throat that was making it hard to breathe and watching the men catch each other up on what they'd missed.

And then I saw the moment that Jiron reverted back to the silent, unresponsive state he'd been in when we'd entered the room, staring through Ren as if he wasn't even there. Then he flinched at something I couldn't see. Nothing could rouse him from that chilling detachment, not even Ren's soft little kisses and imaginative threats.

The prince rose to his feet and turned to us.

"Tell me you murdered the *fuck* out of them," he said to his guards, in what was little more than a snarl with syllables.

Elías inclined his head in confirmation, the faintest of grim smiles edging on his lips. "Some of them took hours to die," he told him quietly, and Ren growled out his approval.

"My prince?" The guard from earlier was back, nervously peering around the

AN OATH AND A PROMISE

door. Luis folded his huge arms. "They're ready for you in the throne room."

"Then they'll just have to wait until Jiron returns to us," Ren said. "Because the prick isn't missing my coronation. Mathias, two buttons, please."

*

Chapter Fifty-Two

Ren

I'd been prepared to wait hours, if necessary. Days, weeks, whatever it took.

But to the relief of those gathered, Jiron came back to himself within the quarter hour, and now stood proudly at the base of the wide dais with Elías, Luis, and Mat as I was crowned king of Quareh. It felt a little surreal when the heavy crown was placed on my head – as soon as I got chance, I was getting that shit swapped out for something lighter as I had done with the one I'd worn as prince – and I felt the weight of more than just the gold.

The lives of those we'd lost also settled on my shoulders.

Ademar, Altagracia.

Horacio and Laurita, my nephews Basilio and Félix.

Viento...nah, that one was just wishful thinking. The rat was still alive and kicking, as Mat had experienced firsthand when we'd ventured down to the Márosian palace stables this morning and he'd had his foot trodden on by the irate flaxen chestnut for not handing over the snacks quickly enough.

I saw Jiron relapse somewhere towards the end of the coronation, but to be fair, his wasn't the only face that had gone slackly blank by then. It was a long-ass ceremony, the bishop droning on about responsibility and honour until he had me entirely convinced that I was the wrong man for the job and was about to call Mathias up here in my stead – and then the crown was deposited onto my head and I guessed it was probably a little late for that.

But the deference that followed soothed both my mood and ego: waves of people bowing and curtsying as they tried to execute the gracious movements after two hours of losing both blood flow in their legs and the general will to live. Even Valeri Velichkov dipped his head my way, and the joy I felt at realising I *finally* outranked the heir to Temar buoyed me through the last few minutes of the bishop's speech. Yet it seemed he had begun to know me too well, as the bastard quietly slunk off with the rest of the guests spilling out of the throne room before I could abuse my newfound authority over him.

AN OATH AND A PROMISE

The hall emptied quickly, the lure of a coronation feast enticing even the most patriotic of my people out of the palace and into the gardens. Eventually there was only one man left in the room, his blue-grey eyes glittering as they gazed up at me where I was seated on the throne.

"Your Majesty?" one of my guards called from beyond the huge doorway at the far end of the hall. His voice echoed across the empty space.

"I'll be there in ten minutes," I said. I didn't take my eyes from Mathias.

"An hour," my lover corrected, holding my curious gaze. "Start the banquet without him."

The guard hesitated until I nodded, and then drew the heavy doors closed to seal the two of us inside. There was silence for a moment before Mat took two steps forward until he was standing directly at the foot of the dais. It was twice as high as the one in *la Cortina*, the throne far grander in turn.

"As the third prince of Temar," he murmured, "may I be the first to welcome you to the Quarehian throne, my king?"

The wicked look in his eye was making my mouth impossibly dry. I swallowed. "You...may."

Mathias' mouth twitched in amusement. He bowed to me, long and deep and formal.

But instead of straightening back up, he slowly dropped to one knee. Then a second.

I stopped breathing as Mat began to climb the marble steps up to the throne on his hands and knees. He moved carefully, precisely, knowing the value of what he was gifting me.

When he reached the top, he lifted his head and prowled closer, still staying down on all fours. *Dios mío*, watching my boy crawl to me was as arousing as fuck, especially when he was dressed like northern royalty.

Mathias' hands swept upwards from my ankles to my knees, his mouth following the trail a moment later as he peppered my bent leg with kisses. My bite mark on his neck, just visible beneath his shirt with its two undone buttons, quivered deliciously with the movement of his throat.

He shifted on the ground at my feet and winced.

AN OATH AND A PROMISE

I grinned, suddenly finding my words again. "Did that hurt your knees terribly?"

"You know it did, asshole," he pretended to grumble. "And now you're enjoying yourself even more, aren't you?"

"Your sacrifice to getting me hard is much appreciated," I told him with delight. My fingers clenched around the arms of the throne as he made me even more so by pressing his mouth to the bulge straining the seams of my trousers in a brief, almost chaste kiss. And then as I moaned for more, he climbed up to straddle my lap.

His knees brushed the seat of the throne, the first northerner to touch it in recorded history.

"You look tired, darling," Mathias said softly, his fingertip tracing a line under my eye.

I liked his smile. It was an expression he rarely made, but when he did, it was at me. The small, secretive little twitches of his gorgeous mouth had become full grins over the months I'd known him, and I savoured each one, memorising it to recall for later. Mat was usually so serious, often filled with anger or indignation, and while he looked adorable in any mood, a happy Mathias was something I was particularly fond of.

"Hmm," I agreed. "Someone kept me up all last night."

He gave me another of those fond smiles. "*Da.* My wrist still aches."

"Mine too." I pretended to flex it, but really it was just so I could settle my hand back down on his hip, enjoying the weight of him astride me. We hadn't *had* to write out all of the pardons by hand, but Mat had stubbornly insisted on it and it had felt strangely right that we suffer in some small way in trying to prevent the greater suffering of many more people. It had been deep in the small hours of the morning when we finally set down our quills, the hundreds of pardons ready to be issued to the various gaols holding those who had run afoul of the gender laws we were about to repeal, or wrongfully imprisoned for some other nonsense crime under my father's or Welzes' rules.

Mathias bent his head so he could press his lips to mine in featherlight, contented kisses. After everything that had happened, it seemed hard to believe that I got to have both him and the crown on my head, the one he was tracing reverently with his fingers as he slid his hands through my hair. But like the greedy bastard I was, I wanted more.

I wanted him as my husband.

"Nat?"

"Yes, Ren?"

"I know there's meant to be pomp and circumstance to this," I said awkwardly, "and asking you while I'm seated here as your king is probably not the best time to do it, but will you-"

"Will you marry me?" he murmured.

I froze.

"You absolute *prick!*" I hissed when I'd recovered, slapping his thigh hard enough for the crack to echo around the empty throne room. Mat frowned.

"You're generally meant to say yes," he pointed out. "Unless it's a no?"

"No?" I repeated, in disbelief that he would even suggest such a possibility.

"Oh," said Mathias, his mouth twisting downwards.

I spluttered. "No, that's not-"

"I understand, Ren." He patted my arm condescendingly and tried to slide from my lap, his knees not even unbent before I dragged him back to me and smothered him in kisses. He snickered, clearly unable to contain his amusement at the look of horror that must have passed over my face.

"No, you fucker, *yes!*"

He was laughing and squirming, half-heartedly trying to push me away as I nosed into his neck and licked at the marks I'd left with my teeth this morning as the ink dried on the last of the pardons.

"I was going to ask *you*," I growled into his skin, feeling him shiver against me.

"Yeah, well, you were taking too long."

"I was in the middle of the fucking question!" I protested.

"As I said," Mat teased, grabbing my crown and placing it on his own head as he'd done all those months ago when we were still a secret we'd had to keep hidden in the shadows. "Too long."

I dipped my hand beneath the hem of his shirt, scraping my fingernails over his ribs until he yelped. And then I did it again because he deserved all that shit and more.

"Let's try that again," I said, leaning back so I could enjoy the sight of him wearing Quareh's fucking crown. Mathias' cheeks were flushed, his eyes bright, and he watched me with a grin that spoke of mischief and exhilaration. "Nathanael Velichkov?"

"Yes, Your Majesty?" he asked.

"I'm going to marry the fuck out of you," I told him. "And you're going to let me. That's an order."

"Yes, Your Majesty."

*

Chapter Fifty-Three

Mat

Four months later

"Oh," Ren exclaimed happily from over my shoulder. "Velichkov is here!"

"I'll go and meet him at the gates, my king," said Luis, and I heard him leave the balcony, boots stomping on the tiles.

I sighed, leaning on the wall and resting my chin in my hands as I stared at the empty road.

"He'll come, *mi corazón*," Ren murmured to me, pressing a kiss to the back of my head.

"When?" I demanded, straightening up and beginning to pace the small balcony again, my eyes fixed on the horizon. The eastern tower of the Márosian palace provided an excellent view of any horses approaching the city, but that meant nothing when there *were* no fucking horses approaching the city. "Mila got here days ago, as did all my other brothers."

"Oh, I know," Ren said dryly. "Each one of them has tried to corner me for a 'talk'." He huffed out an indignant snort. "If I have to make *one more* impassioned speech about loving you more than I give a fuck about what excruciating torture they plan to inflict on me, I'll..."

I cocked my head without turning around.

"...explode with happiness," he finished carefully.

My mouth twitched in amusement, but I continued pacing. "Even your sister Mariana is here, Ren, and Onn is a lot further away than Delzerce."

"Nat," Ren said, slipping his arms around my waist and pulling me close. "Valeri will be here for the wedding."

"It's *tomorrow*," I hissed. Pressure settled in my chest, making it hard to breathe. "What if he doesn't intend to come? What if he can't accept me marrying you after all? What if-"

"Hush," my lover said, holding me tighter. But my restless energy chafed against my very skin. "Your brother will be here. If not, we'll defer until he is, even if I have to send El to kidnap him from his castle."

"Defer the wedding?" I was horrified. "Ren, we *can't*. There's the food, and the flowers, and-"

"I'm a king," he reminded me, kissing my neck now. "If I need to order the food to preserve itself and the flowers to remain fresh, they'll fucking well listen." I felt his shrug from where he was pressed against me. "Or I'll have it all thrown out and replace the lot. Who cares?"

I sagged in his arms.

"Your Majesty?" Luis was back, out of breath from the fifteen flights of stairs he'd scaled. "Prince Velichkov isn't…he hasn't arrived."

"Of course he has," Ren said. "I saw him walk through the gate myself. You must have returned up here too early."

"Apologies, my king. I'll go back to greet him."

"You do that," he agreed, and I glanced over my shoulder as Luis disappeared through the balcony door once more, the three gold bands on his collar flashing in the sunlight.

But my eyes were drawn to my husband-to-be and the white slash nestled among his ink black hair. Ren's mouth quirked into a grin.

"Finally, he notices."

I flushed. "Sorry." I plucked the white lock of hair away from Ren's head and stroked my thumb over it reverently. "How…?"

"Camila. She dyed it for me with some kind of soap they use to keep the linens white."

"That doesn't sound healthy for your hair," I admonished.

"Who cares about healthy?" Ren asked, rolling his eyes. "It's *pretty*."

I tried to give him an exasperated look but it quickly softened into a smile. I leaned in to press my lips against the lock of hair wrapped around my fingers, before using it to tug Ren closer. "It's gorgeous."

He preened.

AN OATH AND A PROMISE

"Your...Majesty. He still...wasn't there." Luis was nearly bent double this time, wheezing out the words.

"You're right, Luis," Ren said seriously. "That wasn't Valeri at all. I must have been mistaken. I'm terribly sorry for making you...oh, what's that?"

The guard squinted past us. "What?"

"That's him after all! What are the chances? Go and greet him at the gates, Luis."

"I don't see..."

"You wouldn't be questioning your king, would you?" Ren asked, injecting a note of hurt into his voice. "Because Prince Valeri is dismounting his horse as we speak, and if he thinks I don't respect him enough to send my best man to meet him..."

Luis snapped to attention. "On my way, sire."

I tried to shake my head in reprimand, only to find the king of Quareh plastered to my side, nosing his face into my cheek.

"Come," Ren murmured, running his tongue along the edge of my ear. "I wish to distract you."

I sighed. "That's not going to work."

He flicked my nose. "Shush. I only have one more night to ravish and ruin you before your husband gets his respectable hands on you, and I won't have you waste it with your surliness."

"So something quick and meaningless then?" I asked, feeling my mood lighten as it always did when we teased each other, and Ren gave me a mock offended look.

"You insult me."

"I try. What do you have in mind?"

My king hummed, looking thoughtful even though I knew him too well to be fooled. He'd had whatever it was he had planned in his head for a while, I was sure. "We've played with the-"

"Yes," I said hastily, feeling my cheeks colour. That had been...*interesting*.

"And all of the-"

"Yes." Fuck me, I hope no one had heard us that night. I didn't know how I'd possibly explain it.

Ren winced. "Although it didn't go so well when we tried the-"

I snorted in amusement at the memory of *that* particular disaster. It had proven to be a kink neither of us shared. "No."

"But there's something I've been too scared to do to you," he said awkwardly, "because I...I didn't want you to look at me differently."

I twisted around in his arms and kissed him. "*Ren.*"

"Fine, *mi amor.*" He tried again, barely murmuring the words against my lips. "I want it. Very badly. But I didn't know if you could take it or not, and I don't expect anything of you that you're not prepared to give."

"Then let's do it," I said.

"Are you sure, Mathias?"

"What's the worst that can happen? It's too much, and I safe word out."

Ren wet his lips.

"*Dorogoi,*" I said gently, cupping his chin in my hand. "Nothing you could do is going to make me leave you at that altar tomorrow. You know that, right?"

Ren exhaled slowly, and eventually nodded.

"It'll be rough," he whispered.

"It'll be *you,*" I answered. "I would say do your worst, but I know you wouldn't give me anything less."

Slipping his fingers through the loops of my belt, the king gave me a wicked grin that told me exactly where we were about to end up.

Naked and spent.

Keeping hold of me, he tugged me backwards through the balcony door. The possessive prick was forced to let go so we could safely descend the narrow stairs, but as soon as our boots met solid floors once more, he was waving off our guards, sending Luis back down to the gate with a single acidic word, and dragging me to his...to *our* rooms.

"Right," I said the moment he eagerly slammed the door behind us. "I suppose you want to do this slowly and gently?"

Ren gave a low, dangerous laugh before he leapt forward, curling his fingernails against my cheek. "I want to fuck you, Mathias, but first I want to make you hurt. Remove your clothes."

"Just like that?" I asked, trying to keep my voice level.

"*Clothes*, consort-to-be, or I'll tear them from you with my Blessed teeth. And as I won't allow you any others, it's going to make leaving this room later a hell of a lot of fun for me, and pure misery for you."

Ren began to dig his nails into my skin and I held up a hand, trying to remember how to breathe.

"Just...give me a second."

"*Ahora*, Nathanael, before your stalling gives me time to think of more things I wish to inflict on you."

"Fuck."

"Yes," Ren said, drawing the word out into a delighted hiss as he watched me hastily remove my shirt. I saw his smile slip from sweetness into pure predatory hunger.

I kicked off my boots and unbuckled my belt, glancing back up to find him with a length of rope already in his hand. The sight simultaneously made my stomach clench and my shoulders relax. From Ren's cruel smile, I'd somehow expected worse.

"Oh, it's coming," he promised me, clearly noticing the relief I'd been careless enough to let flash across my face, and I cursed under my breath.

And then he was pressed against me once more, tearing down my unbelted and unlaced trousers with one hand as he wrapped his other, fisted around the rope, around the back of my head to keep me in place.

The kiss was brutal; a clear show of his dominance, but the forcefulness just made it hotter as I surrendered my mouth to my king's and let him take what he needed. Saffron and citrus flooded my tongue, and I moaned at the glorious taste, chasing Ren's tongue as it threatened to withdraw.

"So fucking greedy," he chastised, finally pulling back with both hands pressed to my chest to separate us. But his voice was rough, his pupils dilated, and he seemed to be having trouble standing up straight.

Helping him would be the decent thing to do, and so I ran my palms down the edge of Ren's hips and around the curve of his ass, tugging him close. The feel of his clothing against my bare cock was both incredibly arousing and impossibly frustrating.

"Stop that," Ren breathed, not at all convincingly, and my mouth found his neck, kissing and nibbling my way up his throat.

Ren writhed against me and I let one of my hands wander across into the crack of his ass, tracing its shape through his trousers even as my other fought to undo his own belt so I could get at him properly. If I could just get my fingers on him, my king would fall apart under my hands as he always did, and I could ease Ren's sadistic mood with tenderness instead of pain-

"You're not escaping this, Mat," he warned, and then undermined his words with a long, helpless moan that was damn near a whimper. "You're just making it worse for yourself."

The belt loosened, and I nuzzled at his collarbone even before slipping both hands down to Ren's warmth. The hard heat of his cock found and nestled itself within the curve of my fingers, my left hand sliding down between his ass cheeks. Ren groaned.

"Hands off me, you bastard, or I'll tie them so tight you'll lose feeling."

I ignored him, needing just a few more seconds to win control, but the chance was denied to me when Ren's free hand shot up and yanked at my hair, pulling so hard that he almost tugged me over backwards. My grip loosened of its own accord, flying up to his wrist to try to relieve the pressure on my scalp.

His teeth nipped at my exposed throat, and I made a frustrated noise that caused Ren to do it again, harder.

"I almost had you!"

"I know," my king growled, giving me a shake. "And you'll see how fucking close you were in a moment, when you realise how hard I intend to punish you for it."

"Or we could get an early night's sleep," I suggested cheerfully and Ren snorted, twisting me around and using his grip on my hair to guide us towards the bed.

"If you think you're getting any sleep on the eve of our wedding, *mi gato montés*, you're not thinking straight." Heat rushed through me at how deep his voice had gone, the words like silken promise. "It seems I'll have to correct that. Hands."

Ren wanted, Ren got.

Sometimes.

I brought my hands behind me and snagged the line of his cock through his clothing, rewarded by a surprised intake of breath in my ear.

"You impossible asshole," Ren groaned, but he let them stay there for another second before catching my wrists. "Do you remember how this goes?"

I frowned. "Like Lago?" I asked uncomfortably, as Ren drew my arms above my head and bound my wrists with the rope around the horizontal bed post above us, just as he had done with the lord that night he forced me to watch as he took Lago and Isobella to bed in front of me. I certainly did not need – nor want – a reminder of that.

"No," he said, and bit into my bare shoulder, causing me to buck against the ropes that held me. He withdrew his teeth and kissed the wound before speaking again. "Like *you*."

Understanding hit me like a flood of cold water.

It'll be rough, he'd said.

Oh, fuck.

I twisted in the restraints, not hitched as high as Jiron had done to me that day which meant this time I had room to pivot, only to find Ren gazing hungrily at me. The man was damn near salivating.

"*Dorogoi*," I said, using the same tone I would when ordering a dog to sit. This was not negotiable. "You are not taking a belt to my back again."

"Of course not," Ren murmured, dragging his eyes up to meet mine. "I intend to use a crop on you today."

My lover crossed to his bedside table, and I realised that the longer length of rope hadn't been a kindness. Ren wanted me to see what he was doing.

His long fingers ran lovingly over everything inside the drawer. Fuck, half of the things in there I didn't recognise, and *none* of them looked like they belonged in a bedroom.

I stopped looking.

"Open those pretty eyes of yours, Mat," Ren warned, "or I'll get you much more acquainted with each and every one of these."

I scowled, but the threat was enough for me to obey. The prick hadn't even turned around.

"You're a depraved bastard, you know that?"

"It has been said." Ren plucked a black riding crop from the midst of the terrifying mass of objects, and shut the drawer with a deft flick of his hips. He shrugged and offered a broad grin. "Although mostly screamed."

"I'm not your plaything," I said.

I was, and we both knew it.

"Mmm," Ren agreed, stalking closer with a wicked expression. "Yet tonight, Nathanael, and every night after this, you're whatever I say you are."

He pressed his chest against mine, bringing our faces to within an inch of each other.

"And I say you're mine."

*

Chapter Fifty-Four

Ren

Mat shuddered at those words, so gloriously responsive and I hadn't even touched him. As my lover's eyes closed again, I didn't bother to remind him of my threat. I let the crop do that for me, dragging the leather end of it down across his parted lips.

His eyes snapped back open, that stormy grey-blue colour I loved so much. Fear and lust warred within their depths, and he muttered something uncomplimentary as he defiantly lifted his chin and stared me down.

Fuck, I loved this, all of it. From having him on display for me; arms stretched above his head, naked and trying to hide how he was trembling, to having wrapped the rope lovingly around his wrists with the anticipation of getting to see them laid raw by his struggles.

But there was still a tangled knot of terror in my chest that Mathias eased with his teasing smile and a playful kick aimed at my leg when I stood too close for too long. I hadn't been lying when I said I didn't know how he would take this, and it was all too new to him for him to have the answer either. But I trusted him to stop me if he couldn't – or if he didn't want to.

I idly inspected the crop, as if I hadn't already meticulously looked over every inch of it to ensure it wouldn't hurt him in any way I didn't intend. Welzes might have destroyed my toys during his brief stay in the palace but I didn't mind, loving the knowledge that the only flesh this new crop would ever mark was Mat's. My breathing shallowed as I imagined all the things I could do, the noises I could draw out of him, the patterns I could make on his skin...

"Let me show you what else I'm going to hit you with," I said, moving back towards the bedside table.

"No."

I paused. "No, you don't want me to hit you, or no, you want it to be a surprise?"

Mathias gave me a smile. It had teeth, and that told me everything I needed to know.

The latter, then.

"But you're going to bitch and moan about it anyway, aren't you?" I asked wryly.

"Naturally," he agreed, and then shifted in the ropes, rising up on his toes before planting his bare feet more firmly on the floor. My cock stirred at the mere promise of what was to come. "Alright. Let's get this over with."

Oh, my not-so-sweet nuisance of a brat. If he thought that was the way this was going to go down, he was *severely* mistaken.

This wasn't something Mat was going to be able to just obstinately endure for a minute or two and then get his own way. I was going to make him fucking feel it.

"Sure," I said conversationally. "Let's do that."

I stepped back into range and tried to turn him around with a hand on his bitten shoulder. The man resisted, *of fucking course*, so I let the crop fall lightly across his half hard cock.

That earned me a yelp, a snarled Mazekhstani curse, and a very promptly turned back.

I tried to hide my laugh at the clear indignance in his stance. If he let himself relax, he might find he enjoyed this to no end, but that wasn't the Nathanael Velichkov way. No, my wildcat would fight even blissful pleasure to his last breath.

"Mathias," I purred, pressing my mouth to the back of his neck and reaching around to give his cock two long, deep strokes. It came alive in my hand and Mat shuddered again as I trailed the crop across his stomach, letting him familiarise himself with its shape and texture.

"I promise I'll make this as good for you as it will be for me," I swore to the perfect, quivering northerner bound naked in front of me, and then added, "eventually."

Because Mat's inherent determination to resist meant it wouldn't be anything but painful in the beginning. There was nothing I could do about that but help him through it.

"Ren?"

"Yes, *mi cielo*?"

"Will you stop if I ask you to?" My lover's voice was quiet, trembling, but the way his cock stood hard and throbbing under my fingers told me that I wasn't imagining the slight note of excitement I could also detect.

I thought about his words, turning them over in my mind and dissecting the tone.

"No," I said, knowing I'd got it right when Mathias let out a soft little moan. Fuck, the man really was perfect. He was terrified of what was going to happen, but he also craved it, and I couldn't ask for more.

A good thing too, as I wasn't going to be able to hold out for much longer. I wanted my brat screaming, and I wanted it *now*.

I leaned in and caught Mat's chin, jerking his face towards me so I could be sure he'd register my next words. "Not unless you use your safe word," I said meaningfully, and he nodded.

I knew he would say it if he needed to, as he had two weeks ago when in the heat of the moment my taunting had drawn uncomfortably close to degradation. I'd spent the next couple of hours whispering reassurances and praise into his ear as I reminded him of everything I loved about him, delighted when we discovered that him exercising that trust had only heightened the enjoyment we took in our subsequent play.

"Please go slow-"

I cracked the crop hard across his ass before he could finish the ridiculous request. This wasn't like learning to ride a fucking horse. There was no *slow*, unless he wanted to be tickled with the damn thing.

Also a thought.

But not one I was in the mood for just now. I was all pent-up energy and ferocious cruelty, and the sound of Mathias' surprised yelp soothed everything that was loudly raging inside me.

Without another word, I delivered three more quick strikes to his thighs, ass, and back, causing Mat to twitch in the ropes as he cried out with each one. I ran a hand over the marks, gratified by the heat beneath my fingers, and even more so when he didn't tell me to stop.

His cock was already dripping, soaking in the pain and pleasure of the hits. I dragged my finger over the top of his alert, leaking crown, gathering the precum and then feeding it to him. He sucked my finger greedily, making such gorgeous noises as he did so.

Fuck. I found it so hard to hold back with this man, escalating things that I should have properly taken years to introduce him to, considering he'd never even been up close and personal with a cock until mine. From the occasional comments Mathias had made about his lovers back in Stavroyarsk, it was clear he'd never done anything beyond the plainest vanilla acts, and I was starting to discover the reasons why.

One, Mat was not bisexual. He'd slept with Zovisasha and Lilia because that was expected of him in the north and because he'd needed to find his release somehow, but pussies and tits were clearly not what he was interested in. Whenever we walked past couples in various states of undress around the palace, it was only the men who turned his head.

And two, he could endure anything, but only if he was pushed to do so. On his own initiative, he'd never dip a damn toe over the line, and that was a Blessed shame.

Which is why it was such a good thing that I had claim on him now. I wouldn't let Mathias settle for mediocrity when I could drag him, preferably kicking and screaming, to the heights of pleasure and beyond the limits of his imagination and any sense of decency. Pain brought him to life, spurring him into a vibrant, desperate, *beautiful* mess.

I rolled my shoulders and flicked the crop below the base of his spine several times in quick succession, landing the blows hard enough to draw more pained cries from his lips. On the fifth strike to the same place, Mat twisted in the ropes to prevent me from hurting him there further, just as I had expected him to do, and I offered a darkly delighted laugh as I took advantage of the new position to rain down hits across his chest, making sure to catch the leather against both of his nipples.

"*Blyat*, Ren!" Mat snarled, trying to pull away, but the rope wasn't long enough for him to escape. My – what was the word he'd used earlier? – my *plaything* had to remain where I'd put him, a toy all trussed up for me to torment, and my cock liked that. A lot.

I leant down and took one of his nipples into my mouth, grazing my teeth against the sensitised bud. My lover bucked against me but I held him in place, licking and biting and tugging it between my teeth. I knew the skin would be burning from the crop, agonising in its tenderness, and my rough, unceasing attentions to that same spot finally drew the anticipated scream from my boy's mouth.

But there were so many other delicious parts of him that I wanted to hurt, and seeing as Mat wasn't smart enough to turn back around when I finally, reluctantly, pulled my teeth away, I directed the crop across his still hard cock and underneath to his balls.

He danced backwards as far as the rope would let him, hissing out his indignation. I took pity on him and directed the next strikes across his inner thighs instead.

"Fuck off with that shit!" my brat yelled, and I grinned, giving him another hard swat.

Mat seemed to think that was unjustifiably cruel. But Mat was the one all tied up and helpless, so he could think what he liked and I could get off on ignoring him.

"Stop, damn you!" he demanded next, but he still didn't say the right word, so I had no intention of doing so.

"Does that hurt?" I asked.

"Yes!"

"Good," I told him, pleased. "Widen your stance."

Mat's glare could have melted steel. *"Poshel na khuy."*

Go fuck myself? Not very smart of you, dear consort.

Trying not to smile, I swapped the crop to my left hand so I could slap him – very lightly – across the face with my right. His head snapped to the side, more in surprise than force, but he brought his knee up as if determined to take me down with him.

I stepped back, narrowly avoiding the blow to my groin, and fixed him with a look.

"It seems you're enjoying this more than you're letting on if you're so desperate for further strikes," I warned, but Mat wasn't cowed.

"Do it," he spat, defiance sparking through his gaze, "and the moment I get free, you prick, I'll make you regret each one."

Oh, he never learned, did he? That was part of what made him so enjoyable to play with.

Half his body, usually so pale, was covered in hot, red marks, and yet my wildcat still bit. And would continue to bite until the very end, in that blissful moment when Mat finally submitted to me as he came.

I let the crop fall from my hand, and Mathias gave me a satisfied smirk as it hit the floor.

"Untie me," he said haughtily, raising his shoulders and grimacing through the discomfort it caused him, "and maybe I'll go easy on you."

I ducked my head to hide the way my lips twitched upwards. Mathias had a way of turning the serious into the humorous, of creating levity in the heavy. I was fretting about what beating him and letting myself be truly rough with him would mean for us and our relationship, and he was busy being a smart-ass.

"Don't go easy on me," I told him, pulling open the drawer to the bedside table once more. "For I don't intend to return the favour."

He never even got chance to see the cane before I laid it across his ass. Now *that* was a proper scream, startled and distressed. Dios, I liked the way Mat hurt for me.

But he'd practically been begging for it. It would have been rude to deny him.

I was lucky as all hell to have found *mi sol*, and luckier still that he allowed me this. I'd often thought on why my mind and body felt this burning need for domination in the bedroom, always reaching the conclusion that I wanted to reassert a control that my father and Moreno had stolen from me, and which being a royal necessarily cost when you acted in service to your people. Control, yes, but I also relished the sweet surrender that my partner – that *Mathias* – gave, and being wholly trusted to take him through to the other side, breaking him down and building him back up stronger than ever.

Mathias snarled, twisting furiously in the ropes. My wildcat was *pissed*.

"What the fuck was that?" he growled when he got his breath back.

I showed him.

"You are not hitting me with that!"

"I already did."

"Go back to the other one!"

"Maybe later," I drawled. "For now, I'd rather make you wish you hadn't mouthed off to me quite so much."

Mat cried out again with the second strike, a delicious noise that I felt through my groin.

On the third, he dropped his head and fucking whimpered.

And it was cock-hardening noises like those that made me undo my trousers with my other hand and free myself. Pre-cum gleamed at the tip, and it ached for friction. I gave it two strokes, the same as I had Mat, but it wasn't enough.

"Still with me, brat?" I tapped the cane lightly against his fingers where they were clenched into fists above his head, making him flinch.

He cursed me in his own language through panting, heaving breaths until I'd landed two more hard hits to his back and ass…and that was when he began to beg.

"Please," my northerner gasped as he thrashed in his ropes, his skin a pretty pink that would bruise ever so nicely. The muscles in his arms and legs glistened with sweat and exertion. "Please, Ren. Please stop."

When I peeked over his shoulder, his angry-looking, painfully hard cock reminded me what a fucking liar he always was.

Yet I paused, giving him the chance to put an end to all this if he wished.

That made him scowl.

"I'm not fucking safe wording!" Mat snarled in my face and I hummed, caning him again and enjoying listening to him howl before leaning in and tracing my fingers gently over the marks to memorise the feel of them.

While he liked less pain than some others I'd played with in the past, I was finding it surprisingly easy to adjust to his tolerances, as if my own desires had aligned themselves perfectly with his. What we were doing – teasing and tormenting him to the very edge of his endurance – was soothing the monster within me, and I wouldn't need to hurt him like this again for a while.

I laid my next strike across the back of his legs, rewarded by the way his voice was turning hoarse. I couldn't give him too much more. The skin was already raised and angry, and he'd have enough difficulties sitting for the next day or so as it was. I wasn't going hard with the cane, but it was thicker and less flexible than the crop, and was clearly hurting my lover so much more.

As it was meant to.

"Are you done yet?" Mathias gritted out, making his displeasure known in the stubborn set of his jaw.

Not even close, darling.

"I'll put the cane down," I promised, chuckling at the look of suspicious relief Mathias shot me. "*After* I've punished you for each act of disobedience you've shown me this afternoon."

Mat swallowed. "I thought this was about pleasure, not punishment?"

I grinned and peeled the sweaty strands of his hair away from his forehead so I could kiss it.

"It is pleasure," I said happily. "For me."

And for him, once he embraced it, but if I told him that he'd fight it. Obstinate prick.

"Now, tell me how you disobeyed me, Nathanael."

"Fuck you."

"Well, that's one," I said airily, and Mat sucked in a breath as he realised how easily he'd earn himself more marks.

And so my northerner stayed sullenly silent as I recounted each moment with perfect clarity, having intended to make him pay for them since the beginning.

"You didn't undress when I told you to. You kept your hands on me when I ordered you off. Twice. And you didn't *widen your fucking stance*," I chastised, kicking at Mat's ankles to force him to do so now, even though the crop had been long been discarded. He staggered, the rope biting at his elevated wrists, his pupils wide and dark. "That's five."

*

Chapter Fifty-Five

Mat

Ren turned back to the bedside table, and I stilled.

I couldn't take whatever else he pulled from that damned drawer – my mouth was already dry at the promise of five more strikes from the fucking cane and that calculated torment of his. Despite how close I'd come earlier to shifting the scene in my favour, he never lost his control when he was wielding it over me, delivering my agony with a precise level of care.

Ren's sexual cruelty was as intrinsic a part of him as his flirtatious ways and hidden thoughtfulness, and I'd known from the very beginning what giving into his attentions would mean. Being with him was more than a relationship: it was a complete surrender to the darker parts of human nature that I'd never expected myself to be drawn to.

But fuck, I was. Because for every act of roughness was a gentle kiss. Every cruel word was balanced with a sweet murmur, and every blow he'd ever landed on me, the type that brought heat and gratification to his gaze, was rewarded later with the softest of caresses.

And he'd be paying in gentleness for *this* particular session for a long fucking time.

But even if he didn't, that would be okay too. Because as much as every inch of me was hot and aching and burning and *fuck him to the depths of the continent* for the agony he'd delivered to my still tender nipples…that content look on his face, the tension draining from his body, his heavy, uneven breathing?

That was everything.

Already Ren looked far more relaxed than he had when we'd started, his shoulders looser and his smile shining through more freely. It had been a difficult few months establishing himself as Quareh's ruler and all the headaches that came with it: the gender law reform, the political pushback, the upholding of all the promises he'd made to win the crown. He'd only slept when I forced him to bed, only ate when Camila or I demanded it, and I'd even caught him the other day about to take citizen appearances with his hair unbrushed.

Ren. Unbrushed. *Hair.*

If he wanted this from me, I'd give it to him. I just didn't think, with the pain being so much more intense than anything we'd ever played with before, that I'd be able to enjoy it like he could.

And no Blessed wonder, considering all he probably had to endure was a sore wrist from being such a ruthless bastard to my back. And ass, and chest, and everywhere else he'd laid claim to me.

I frowned as he returned, unable to see what he'd palmed from the drawer. My imagination raced, and my breaths accelerated as the fear took over and-

"Nat," Ren said gently, and the way he was always mixing up my names with no regard for what he was calling me from one sentence to the next, pulled a breathless laugh from my raw throat.

"What's that?" I croaked out, thankful he'd calmed my breathing but fearing I would return to hyperventilating when he finally unclenched his fist to show me what he held.

But he didn't, just offering up a lazy smile instead.

"Nothing you need concern yourself with," the king said and laid the tip of the cane under my chin, forcing it up.

"I rather doubt that."

"I rather don't care. Eyes front."

I turned my head away before he did it for me, my ears straining for movement.

And even though I'd been expecting the stinging strike, it still came as a surprise as it landed across my ass and drew another snarled hiss from my lips. My hands twisted in the ropes.

"Uno," Ren said, counting the first blow, but he didn't land the second immediately.

There was a suspicious pause, and then the feeling of something pressing against my entrance made me jump.

"Relax, *mi amor*," Ren said from behind me, amusement in his voice. "I know,

that's like telling water not to be wet. But it's just my fingers. *This* time."

They were slick and cool, and he managed to slide one in as I exhaled at the realisation that all he'd been holding was oil.

A moan shuddered through me, my body already so sensitive and tender from everything he'd done to it, and the sensation of his finger inside me felt accentuated a hundred times over as he moved it in gentle, shallow strokes.

"*Mierda*, that feels perfect," Ren whispered, and I murmured my agreement despite the situation I found myself in.

"Would you like me to forget the cane and go straight to fucking you?" he offered.

"*Da.* Yes," I begged, but the king just gave a low, sly chuckle.

"I'm sure you would."

He moved deeper, the tip of his finger grazing against my prostate.

Pleasure built inside me, my cock dripping pre-cum onto the floor, and by the Blessed Five this was *heavenly*, and I could forget everything else that was going on as long as he didn't remove that finger-

And because he was fucking *Ren*, he removed it.

Another blaze of pain shot across my ass, the same ass that he'd been delivering such pleasure to a moment before, and the contradiction of it all took my breath away.

And then his hands were back on me, his finger restored to its rightful place, and I couldn't sort out what was nice and what was painful and what was good and what was bad and what was *please, stop* and what was *please, more*.

"*Dos.* That's it, Mat, take it."

He was deeper now, explorative and curious, and I moaned at the sensation as it lit me up from the inside. Ren pumped his hand twice before stealing it away once more, and I didn't even have time to brace myself before the third strike of the cane landed across the same fucking line as before.

"*Tres.* Good boy."

This time it was two fingers, and the soreness of my body both protested against and craved the thicker intrusion. I tossed my head back, pulling against the ropes that bound me, and Ren laughed in my ear as I chased his departing fingers.

The next blow drew another scream from my already chafed throat. It was too much, *too fucking much*, and it hurt but it also sang with such beautiful pleasure, and it didn't make sense why I wanted the touch of both his fingers and the cane, not when all it was capable of was delivering agony.

But this was *blissful* agony, all strangeness and sensation that rode the limit of my tolerance in an exquisite balance of pain and pleasure.

"Cuatro," he said. *Four.*

"You respond so well," Ren purred as he fucked me with his fingers some more. "It's almost a shame I have to keep pulling out."

"So don't," I pleaded, but he just hummed contemplatively against my neck.

"I can't hit you if my hand is in the way," he pointed out, quite reasonably and ever so unreasonably too, because I wanted his fingers and I wanted the cane and why couldn't I have both?

Wait. What did I want?

I didn't know and I didn't care. I just *wanted*.

"I know, *mi cielo*," Ren murmured, and fuck me, had I said that out loud?

"Next time we do this," he added, "I'll put something in here that you can keep in while I hit you, okay?"

I had no idea what the hell that meant, but the blissed-out fog he'd put me in meant it didn't really matter.

"Won't be a next time," I slurred, to remind him that even if he had me at his mercy now, he'd have to fight me all over again to make it happen a second time.

Maybe. Or I could give him the win for once, if he promised to make it feel like *this*.

Pleasure spiked, and it was only Ren's whispered *'cinco'* that made me realise he must have pulled out and delivered the final strike. That time, when the cane fell, I'd fallen with it, sinking into a fuzzy mindspace of no worry and no badness and no…thoughts at all.

I couldn't tell what was happening or when, and everything merged until pain and pleasure felt the same and fuck, if this is what my lover had been aiming to give me the whole time, then he really knew his shit.

Up became down and sideways became reality as the pressure on my wrists eased. Ren laid me on the bed, the blankets soft against my skin and yet excruciating where they rubbed against the welts he'd gifted me with, but when I thought about moving I found everything was far too floaty and happy to bother.

"Your skin is such a pretty red for me," Ren whispered reverently, running his fingertips along the lines he'd made on it. "So beautiful, Mathias."

A thick piece of hair had fallen free and framed one side of my king's face, the rest of it held back in a messy bun. He looked dishevelled and wild, but happy.

I reached for him, needing him closer. Closer than *touching*, closer than *close*, and he let out a soft little exhale in my ear as he settled himself between my legs and began to massage out the indentations the rope had left on my wrists.

When he reached down to take himself in hand, I expected to revert to our usual roughness. For him to impale me on his cock and fuck me hard, but when he slid himself home it was with those same slow, deliberate movements, accompanied by gentle neck kisses and affectionate murmurs.

Ren's gaze was unfocused and soft, and the feeling of him beginning to move against me was sweet perfection. I nuzzled my face into his.

Our hands met, fingers entwining as we sought solace in what we'd built together in a world that would have seen us ripped apart long ago. His foot traced along my bare leg. This was a leisurely indulgence, bringing pleasure to the act itself, and the sensation across my raw skin amplified every sensation.

And when our climaxes found both of us at once and I arched my back with a cry that was echoed by his, I finally let myself surrender, wholly and unequivocally, to King Renato Aratorre.

*

Chapter Fifty-Six

Ren

It was late afternoon by the time Mathias roused back to fretfulness from the mellow, contented state our play had put him into, recommencing the chewing of fingernails that were already bitten down to the quick. After I'd admonished him for ruining things that belonged to me, earning myself a disdainful eye roll that would have resulted in him going right back into my ropes if I hadn't been in such a light mood myself, I let him drag us back up to the top of the eastern tower.

We ascended quite a bit slower than we'd raced down the stairs hours before, Mat wincing with each movement, but the stubborn asshole predictably refused to concede defeat. Hearing his ragged little exhales with every step we took turned me on, knowing that hidden beneath his clothes was the unmistakeable evidence of what we'd done.

And what we'd done had been absolutely fucking fantastic. He'd never gone under as deeply before when we were playing, letting me bathe and feed and hold him for *hours* before his docile sweetness began to wear off, and even now, amidst the scowls, were soft little half-smiles sent my way that hinted at his happiness.

When we reached the rooftop balcony, I threaded my fingers through his. Mathias still looked floaty even as his eyes anxiously scanned the ground below.

"Luis?" I asked when I peered over the wall myself.

"Your Majesty," he said from behind me.

"Valeri Velichkov has arrived."

There was a noise like a grunting bull. I turned, one eyebrow raised, to find my guard's eyebrows drawn down, his fists clenched, and a mighty glower on his face.

"May I say something with the greatest of respect, my king?" Luis asked shortly.

AN OATH AND A PROMISE

"You may."

"*Fuck off,*" he growled.

I laughed. It may have taken him over a year in my service to stand up to me, but I couldn't deny he'd chosen to do it in style.

And also wholly unjustifiably.

Mat glanced over his shoulder at us, amusement tinging his own expression. "Val's *here,*" he said, and I heard the relief in his voice.

Luis levelled a glare on him.

"You can *also–*"

"He actually is."

"I refuse to fall for it again, Your Highness."

"Seriously, Luis," Mathias insisted earnestly, elbowing me to stop me chortling. "He's down at the gates right now."

Luis folded his arms and ignored us both. We waited patiently.

A couple of minutes later, Elías' voice echoed up the tower stairs.

"Luis!"

The guard snapped to attention. "Comandante?" he called back.

"Prince Valeri has arrived. Why aren't you there to greet him?"

Luis visibly paled, his eyes flickering between me and Mat as if he thought I'd order him punished right then and there. "Heading there now, sir. Sorry, sir." He took off hastily down the steps.

Snickering, my future husband and I followed him.

"Comandante," I acknowledged when we reached the bottom of the stairs, my eyes drawn, as they always were, to the rank embroidered onto El's coat.

He'd protested the appointment, of course, which made him perfect for the power the position bestowed on him, and then took to his duties with a quiet but fierce sincerity when I declared I wasn't going to listen to anything but glowing compliments sent in my direction, which meant I ignored everything Mathias said to me for the eight hours it took to forget I'd made such a decree.

AN OATH AND A PROMISE

There had been a mass resignation of guards upon the announcement, although if the men had hoped that would force their new king into changing his mind, it was utter stupidity on their part. All it did was relieve us of the burden of having to dismiss them ourselves. And I was proud of what El had managed to build from those who were left or had joined afterwards – including the influx of female candidates we'd received immediately after the abolition of the gender laws.

El nodded at me distractedly, running a hand through his hair. Trying to manage security in a palace filled with visitors from not just all three countries of Riehse Eshan but foreigners from off-continent, royals included, had to be a nightmare. I didn't envy him the responsibility. I'd have suggested he seize advantage of his new rank and all our tipsy guests to get himself laid, but he took his job far too seriously to properly abuse its perks the way I would have.

"Don't you think Elías looks sexy in his Comandante uniform?" I asked as he strode away, trying to watch him leave. Mat positioned himself to block my view of the man's pert ass.

"Not as sexy as you in your crown," he said coyly.

I grinned, suitably distracted. "Come here and say that again," I purred, dragging him closer by his shirt and reacquainting my tongue with his. It had gotten awfully lonely in the nine or so minutes since I'd last had the chance to kiss him, and even knowing I'd be marrying this gorgeous, amazing man tomorrow, it still felt a little surreal to be able to hold him in my arms without worrying about what anyone else might think.

"Nathanael."

I groaned into Mathias' mouth. "Big brothers should be seen and not heard," I complained, loudly enough for Valeri to hear as he marched down the corridor towards us with his huge wolf at his heels. "Particularly when they're so fucking late. Seriously, Velichkov, you about gave my boy heart palpitations arriving this close to the wedding."

"Sorry," he said, actually sounding contrite. A Dios-damned miracle.

The heir swooped forward to wrap Mat into a hug, and I tried to keep the savage glee from my expression as Mathias went white, his eyes widening and his mouth forming a silent *oh* as his brother pressed against the welted skin.

"I regret I did not arrive sooner," Valeri murmured, seemingly oblivious to my lover's discomfort. He drew back and held him by the shoulders, Mat's pained expression instantly lightening into a cheery beam before he could catch sight of it. "We had to travel slower with mother accompanying me."

Mat stilled, and I saw faint hope tug at his lips. "She's...here? You convinced her to come?"

Velichkov inclined his head. "Perhaps wait until tomorrow to speak to her, as she is resting. Her health is not what it was."

He turned and clapped me on the back, having long ago learned his lesson about trying to embrace me. I didn't know what was so *wrong* about being felt up – Mathias had once tried to explain the meaning of harassment to me, although I'd gotten distracted by the way his mouth was moving and that pretty, pesky tongue of his – but Velichkov acted as if I was a poisonous snake to be dealt with at arm's length. Naturally, I made sure to get closer than that as often as I could.

"Do you know what this means?" Mat asked with wonder, his eyes lighting up as he looked between us. "Every ruler of Rieshe Eshan in the same place for the first time in...decades! Over a century? Val, you did that!"

"*You* did, little brother. They are here for you."

My wildcat fidgeted, flushing and mumbling some shit about having nothing to do with it. As if *any* of this could have happened without him; the peace, the unity, the understanding. Did he still not realise how amazing he was?

It seemed I'd just have to spend the rest of our lives reminding him.

*

Chapter Fifty-Seven

Mat

"Nathanael," Valeri said warmly, patting the seat next to him in invitation. I paused in the doorway of the receiving room, eyeing the hard chair and trying not to wince at the reminder of how fucking sore my fiancé had left my ass.

"Thanks. But I...I'd rather stand."

"Oh, I bet you would," Ren drawled, looking as smug as fuck where he was leaning against the wall, ankles crossed loosely.

"Nat," Val repeated, frowning. "Sit down."

Mila eyed me suspiciously. I watched as her gaze shifted to my king in accusation and he winked at her, unable or unwilling to stop the shit-eating grin that slid across his face.

"Val," she murmured. "Leave it."

"I'm just offering my brother a God-damned seat!" Valeri protested. "Why the fuck am I the villain in-"

"*Trust me*," she said under her breath.

Ren's eyebrows rose in a way that told me he now found my sister even more interesting.

"Is everything ready for tomorrow?" I asked hurriedly, needing to distract them all – and me – from my sudden unwillingness to sit down. "The schedule, and the bishop-"

"Darling," Ren murmured, immediately at my side. He stroked his hand down my arm, the light touch soothing and grounding. "Everything's sorted. You've seen to that."

"I should check over it again," I insisted, but I was prevented from moving when he locked his other hand around the back of my neck. "Everything has to be perfect."

"Of course it will be perfect. You'll be there," he said, perfectly suave and yet ruining it with the smirk he shot me that said he *knew* how good he was. My brother pretended to gag.

"It's the first marriage between continental royals in more than two centuries," I reminded them all sharply, directing my glares at both men until they sobered, nodding in chastisement. "It's important that nothing goes wrong."

"And you're *sure* you want to do this?" my brother asked, although the question was half-hearted at best. He and Ren had become firm friends – begrudging ones, to be sure, and both vehemently denied such insulting accusations if voiced, but harder to deny were the hours they spent in each other's company on Val's regular visits to Máros.

"I would not be a Velichkov if I gave into the idea too easily," he added, teasing, and Mila snorted.

I groaned. "Don't I know it. I've already had the same conversation with Aleksi and Yiorgos. And they've apparently tried to intimidate Ren into calling the wedding off."

"Good," Val said, pleased, and I gave him a mock glare.

"I said *tried*."

"And I said *good*."

"Stop it," I admonished. "You should be happy for me."

"For you, my manipulative little brother who has the whole continent twisted around his finger?"

Ren laughed. Mila nodded. I blinked innocently at them all. "I have no idea what you're talking about."

"Bullshit you don't," Valeri retorted with an amused snort. "How are we supposed to enforce Temarian laws of sodomy when one of our own family is marrying another man? Couldn't you have at least *warned* us before accepting Aratorre's proposal?" He shook his head. "When his herald arrived in Delzerce with the news, mother had to make a pretty fucking hasty decision whether to disown you or support you, Nathanael."

I was surprised she'd chosen the latter. Did that mean there was something to salvage of our relationship after all?

"It wasn't Ren's herald," I said. "It was mine. I proposed to him."

Val closed his eyes and breathed deeply through his mouth. "Of *course* you did."

"Sooo," my king prompted, glancing hopefully between him and my sister. "If Queen Zora is here, does that mean Temar is abolishing its sodomy laws? I know an *excellent* legislator who does a damn fine job of both drafting repeal legislation and being a pestering ass until it goes through." Ren levelled a pointed look in my direction, unable to keep the affection from his expression.

"If that's your way of asking if you'll be allowed to share a bedchamber with my brother when you visit Delzerce, Aratorre, the answer is a permanent no," Val retorted instantly, and then softened. "But maybe. I'd like to speak to Panarina while she's here about changing the law in both northern countries simultaneously. That is, if she can make time for me." His tone turned wry. "It seems my little brothers are developing a habit for sneaking around with foreign royals."

I stared at him. "Yiorgos?"

Valeri snorted. "No, not Yiorgos. That man's a fucking idiot."

"Ah," I said. That only left my second oldest brother. "Aleksi."

"His wife died six years ago," he reminded us, "and he hasn't looked at another woman since. Except, apparently, Queen Astrid Panarina."

"Not that either of them will admit it," Mila added, and then shared a conspiratorial look with Ren that told me they'd both just made it their personal mission to extract those admissions – likely publicly – before this visit was over.

I wouldn't be betting against the two of them, even facing off with Astrid.

"I'm not sure I want to imagine a Riehse Eshan where all three king consorts are Velichkovs," mused Ren, pretending to shudder in horror. "The continent may just break apart with the weight of all that broody *scowling*."

"We don't brood," I said testily.

"At least I wouldn't be alone in my torment," he continued, ignoring me. "You'll all be sure to keep me and both queens on our toes."

AN OATH AND A PROMISE

"Prince Valeri?" Clementina had appeared behind me, the ring on her finger glinting in the candlelight as she curtsied to us all. Camila had proposed a month after I did, only their wedding hadn't required over a quarter year of planning...as she'd smugly reminded me the day they'd said yes to each other. "Queen Velichkova is asking for you."

Val pushed to his feet and followed the herald from the room.

"Oh, I almost forgot," he said, sticking his head back through the doorway and settling his frown on me and Ren. "Aksinia, our royal seer? She said that I had to tell you both *'well done'* and that it had *'worked out'*. Zero context. Mean anything, or is it her usual nonsense?"

"Yes," Ren said cheerfully, not elaborating. From his expression, I guessed it was less about him being an asshole and more about not wanting to explain Aksinia's part in his escape from my sibling's custody, or the terrifying prediction she'd made about the fate of the continent having rested on our shoulders.

In all honesty, I'd forgotten about that prophecy. Probably just as well, considering the stakes had already been high enough, but it didn't seem as far-fetched as it once had to imagine how imminent war and destruction had been if Ren and I hadn't done what we had. Not just unseating Welzes, but uniting Riehse Eshan and fixing some of its inequality and instability.

Not all of it: we couldn't work miracles, as much as Ren frequently liked to accuse me of trying, but I hoped that where we led, others would follow.

"Let me see," Mila coaxed. I frowned as she tugged at the hem of my shirt.

"See what?"

"What he did to you." She jerked her head at the king.

I offered her a blank expression. "I don't know what you're talking about."

"You're good at pretending, Nathanael," she said affably. "But the pain in your posture can't be hidden."

I set my jaw. "It's not what you think-"

"It's exactly what she thinks," Ren drawled, cocking his head. "What I'm trying to work out is which side of the whip she usually falls on. Reckon she takes it or gives it?"

By the Blessed, this was my fucking *sister* he was talking about.

"You *whipped* my little brother?" Mila demanded, slapping at his arm.

I choked and felt warmth flooding my cheeks. "No!"

"Of course not," agreed Ren, and I dared to hope he was showing discretion until I realised how futile such optimism was. "It was a crop and a cane."

"Ren!" I chastised, horrified. I buried my face in my hands, unable to look at my sister and wondering if a gruesome death would be preferable to having to face her ever again.

"The day before his fucking wedding?" said Mila from somewhere close, fury lacing her tone.

"Oh, is that what's happening?" Ren asked mildly. "I wondered why my palace was infested with you northerners."

"Nat?" my sister asked, more gently now.

"I'd like to never speak of this again, please," I wailed.

"Just tell me if you're alright."

I dropped my hands and scowled at her. "Of course I am. Now, if you'll both excuse me from this ridiculous conversation, I have six hundred and seventeen place settings to check over."

My lover pulled a face, fluttering a hand as if to shoo the mention of hard work away from him. "That sounds *horrendous,* darling. I'd help but it sounds like I'd only be getting in the way."

"That's okay," I said graciously. "I'm sure you'll be fine here alone with Mila and her knives."

"On second thoughts," Ren chirped, "there's nothing I'd rather do than inspect six hundred place settings."

"Six hundred and seventeen," I said.

*

Chapter Fifty-Eight

Ren

"*Finally*," I murmured as Mathias slipped into bed behind me, pulling the covers up over us both and gathering me into his arms with an ease of movement he hadn't had when I'd last seen him. "I thought you were *never* coming to bed."

"There was a problem with the flowers," he said sleepily, the words trailing off into a yawn. "And the rice. And then ten more things I had to do."

"Like stealing away all my pretty stripes?"

I pulled his arm more securely around me and tenderly kissed each of his fingers.

I loved how he tasted. How he smelled. How he *felt*, and fuck me, I was so in love with this man that sometimes it felt like I'd explode from it. How was I, a mere mortal, supposed to deal with something so huge and infinite as what I felt for him?

Mat pressed his face into my hair. I could feel him smiling against the back of my head. "Mmm."

"That healer chose your side as per fucking usual," I pretended to complain, and he laughed.

"I know you're the one who sent Starling in my direction a couple of hours ago, darling. Don't act so affronted when she did exactly what you expected her to do."

I'd reasoned he should probably be able to walk at his own wedding, even if I was planning on stealing that ability back off him immediately afterwards. Fucking him until he was limping was always immensely satisfying, in both the gratification of being able to affect and lay claim to him in such a visible way, as well as the inevitable grouching he'd give me afterwards for ruining what he wrongfully maintained was *his* body, but everyone knew belonged to the king of Quareh.

Oh, and the thought of marking him in a different way tomorrow, with a ring on his finger and a crown in his hair?

Dios, I could come from that thought alone.

I twisted around so we were facing each other. His eyes glittered in the moonlight filtering through the shutters, full of excitement and adoration despite the clear exhaustion written in the lines of his face.

"It's a shame your bruises are gone," I purred, all wicked smiles and vengeful kisses, "for I would have quite liked you to feel me tonight and tomorrow when we stand at the altar together. To know you're mine."

Mat slipped a hand down between us and wrapped it around my length, his warm, eager fingers making me gasp and throw back my head. "There's a solution for tonight, *moy dorogoi*."

"And tomorrow?" I asked, breathless.

"Ren," he whispered in my ear. "If you don't know that I'm yours tomorrow, then you're in the wrong fucking chapel."

*

AN OATH AND A PROMISE

Chapter Fifty-Nine

Mat

A sea of faces gazed at us expectantly, their features beginning to blur into each other, and this was only a *fraction* of our guests. Despite the Márosian palace chapel being much grander than the one in *la Cortina*, it still only fitted a small amount of those who would be attending the dinner and post-ceremony celebrations.

I swallowed, trying not to fidget under all the intent stares. Ren always said I wasn't very good at being the centre of attention, and I was beginning to suspect he'd been wildly under-exaggerating, because this was...fucking *horrible*.

The bishop was only halfway through his speech. I would know, having gone over it several times, but on paper it hadn't seemed *nearly* this long. What was I supposed to do while he spoke about commitment and cherishment for another three and a half pages?

One face among the crowd caught my eye. Val. He grinned broadly at me from the front row of seats, dipping his head and giving me a subtle gesture of encouragement from where he had his hands folded in his lap. My mother, seemingly as astute as ever despite her declining health, glanced sharply at him, but instead of then admonishing her heir, offered me a very slight smile of her own.

Before I could faint from the shock of it, I dragged my eyes further up the row. There was Petra, Valeri's wife, who had once counselled me against the exact thing I was doing now, but I only saw wistfulness in her expression. Yiorgos, my youngest brother, who looked like he might have fallen asleep, and Mila who gave him a brutal kick to his ankle to startle him back awake. Aleksi, who had somehow been saddled with keeping both his own children and Valeri's son quiet during the ceremony, but the sight of my nephew Zahari curled up in Astrid's arms, sticky fingers twisted in her immaculate dress and her not seeming to *care*, was too endearing for words. Across the row, Alondra – now an Aratorre once more – sat with Ren's other sister and her Onnish family.

AN OATH AND A PROMISE

My gaze drifted further back, deeper into the gathered crowd and resting on people I recognised. There was Lady Isobella, who shot me a sweetly poisonous look despite risking her own life to stand up for me that day in the throne room. When I'd confessed my confusion to Ren afterwards, he'd laughed and said that just because she wanted to cut off my balls and feed them to me, it didn't mean *she was a bad person, Mathias*. Then he'd proceeded to describe how she'd filled her father's estate with wounded and deformed animals to save them from the chopping block, until I found it hard to remember why I disliked her.

A couple of rows further back, blocking the view of the people seated behind him, was Jiron's massive form. He'd protested attending as a guest or wearing dress clothes instead of his guard uniform…right up until the blonde man bouncing in his seat at Jiron's side had asked him to, and then suddenly it wasn't even a question. Wyatt was a young Lukian with a ridiculously chipper personality and a bright grin on his face that I'd never once seen fail, and was one of those disgustingly and permanently *happy* people. The two of them were rarely found apart these days – Zovisasha could often be heard complaining that Wyatt missed his shifts in the gardens more often than he bothered to show up – but everyone knew that he was doing much more good in Jiron's company. The guard was still having…*difficulties* from the trauma he'd suffered, and his episodes were erratic enough that Ren had been forced to name Elías as Comandante in his stead, as much as I knew it had pained my king to do so. He ensured Jiron wanted for nothing, but what did money or luxury matter when the man's mind might never be truly whole again?

Swallowing, I glanced at the guards on duty, including Luis and El, who were standing to attention at the edge of the room. The bandings on the collars of their coats indicated whether they belong to the palace or mine and Ren's personal retinue, all Quarehian in ethnicity but for Parvan, yet he stood proudly among the men and women he now called colleagues. Parvan had served me these last few months without fuss, pleasingly defusing any hints of violence with a quiet word before it escalated into something worse, although I didn't think he'd been such a pacifist that night four months ago. Lord Martinez had seemingly fled *la Cortina* shortly after Welzes' death, only for his own bloated body to be fished out of the river downstream from the palace a few days later.

AN OATH AND A PROMISE

Parvan had only shrugged when I mentioned it, but Dima's ramblings around that time had made me decidedly suspicious that the Hearken had gotten a glimpse into the lord's head before he mysteriously disappeared, and wasn't that a Blessed coincidence, that a man as foul as Martinez should end up dead while my guard was loose and pissed off? I could only pity Dima for what he must have been exposed to in that prick's thoughts.

Martinez's widow was near the door, the noblewoman disregarding propriety to sit with commoners, among whom I recognised Consuela, Abril, Camila, and Clementina. Starling was close by, unwisely perched between Lilia and Zovisasha, and I wondered just how tempted the healer was to knock them both unconscious as they alternated between beaming in my direction and hissing what were assuredly insults at each other over Star's head.

The Lagos had found themselves a row of seats with Lord de la Vega, who had all been instrumental in rebuilding Algejón's infrastructure and trade ability, and there in the corner were the señoras Hernández, and near that pillar was-

A faint brush of knuckles against the back of my hand restored my attention to the only person in the room who really mattered in that moment. Ren's lips twisted into a fond smile as he glanced sideways at me through his eyelashes, looking coy and cute and irresistible in that irritating way he always did. It was hard to imagine, now, what my life had been like before he'd come barging into it with ransom claims and improper flirtations and that damn laugh of his.

My lover…my nearly *husband*, was demanding and inappropriate and clever and beautiful, and I was the luckiest fucking man on the continent for getting to call him mine.

How had I ever believed he didn't have a heart? It was *huge*, big enough for me and his family and his entire country, and he'd fight for all of us until his very last breath, as I would do for him. Ren may have been a contradiction in his tender savagery, his gentle sharpness, his insensible passion, but it was so perfectly him and I wouldn't change it for anything, not now I knew him.

And maybe that was the point. We'd grown up in a world where our nationalities defined us and set the course of our fates, and all we'd had to do to bridge the divides between what we were told we wanted and what we *actually* wanted, was to listen. Understand. And realise that while it might sometimes strike your heart against that of someone who was impossibly frustrating, devastatingly depraved, and had an ego the size of the fucking moon…love knew was it was doing.

Probably.

The bishop cleared his throat, having finally reached the end of his speech. My heart sped up until I could barely hear him over its noise, knowing exactly what was coming next.

"Do you, Nathanael Velichkov," he asked me, "third prince of Temar and honorary royal of Quareh, take Renato Aratorre to be your lawfully wedded husband?"

I looked at Ren.

He looked at me.

I shrugged.

"If I must."

Ren winked at me, mouthing exactly what he was going to do to me later for that *little display of public insolence, Mathias.*

The bishop faltered. "Uh, Prince Nathanael, I need you to say-"

"I do," I said, unable to stop the huge grin on my face as I spoke the fateful words. Ren's eyelashes fluttered, his throat delicately bobbing as he swallowed.

"And do you, Renato Aratorre, king of Quareh, take Nathanael Velichkov to be your lawfully wedded husband?"

Ren looked at me with such love in his eyes that I knew we'd be forever.

"Hell fucking yes I do."

***

THE END

AN OATH AND A PROMISE

But what about Jiron, I hear you ask?

His novella is on its way.

Visit www.adelaideblaike.com to sign up to my newsletter and receive a free, exclusive ebook copy of *A Guard and a Gardener* in late 2023.

AN OATH AND A PROMISE

ACKNOWLEDGEMENTS

I've been putting off writing these acknowledgements.

I cleaned the house. Started drafting the next book. Grabbed more snacks. And now I've run out of justifiable procrastination excuses and am sitting here in silence, fingers poised expectantly over the keyboard, knowing that all I need to do to get this book ready for publication is write the damn acknowledgements.

But that means it's over, right? The end of the end, and I'm not sure I'm ready for that.

Mat and Ren have held my heart for so long, and even though I know I can return to them anytime in the books already written, it won't be the same. They're not going to sarcastically drawl out the best comebacks into my head *just* as I'm finally drifting off to sleep. They're not going to bully their way to the forefront of my thoughts so that instead of whatever important thing I was meant to be doing, I'm scrawling down one of Ren's ridiculous plans that could have been five times simpler and ten times less fun.

But other characters are starting to take up space in my head, and they want their stories heard too. So it's a goodbye – at least a temporary one – to my two contrary princes and their long yet immensely gratifying journey.

A journey that I couldn't have travelled alone. I offer the usual gratitude to Ximena, Rian, and Diana and her partner for their assistance with my foreign languages and translations. My mother and sister for more out-of-context grammar queries. My husband for his patience and my daughter for her beautiful smiles that never fail to bring joy back into whatever terrible day I may have had.

A special thanks to Janice, admin and creator of the *Small but Mighty MM Romance Group,* for giving historical fantasy a chance, encouraging me to do my first ever release party with *Shadow,* and becoming one of the series' most vocally supportive readers. You have her to blame for Jiron's upcoming short story that is rapidly turning novella-length.

A happy birthday to Heather, and a thank you for all her kind messages!

As always, a huge appreciation for my beta and ARC readers, and also the support and love shown by the members of my Facebook group. You're all pretty amazing people, you know that?

And to you, dear reader, for your time. There are many, *many* books out there, and it makes me feel incredibly special that you were willing to read four of mine. I hope we meet again in a different set of adventures, in new and exciting worlds.

*Join **Adelaide Blaike's Blades** in the author's reader group on Facebook to discuss this book, get teasers from upcoming work, and stay up-to-date with the latest releases.*

AN OATH AND A PROMISE

A THRONE AND A CROWN

A Riehse Eshan Series novella

King Renato Aratorre is missing.

Mathias and his husband were meant to be enjoying their hard-won happily ever after. But with Ren disappearing without a trace and dangerous trouble brewing in every corner of the palace, the weight of the Quarehian crown falls on the shoulders of the northerner king consort.

To make matters worse, there's growing talk of the one thing that despite his best efforts, Mathias can never give to Ren and Quareh.

An heir.

A Throne and a Crown is a post-series novella set approximately a year after *An Oath and a Promise* finishes, and has its own HEA.

AN OATH AND A PROMISE

XERXES DESCENDANT

Book One of the House Epsilon Duology

With planet Earth in ruins and billions of people dead, Kyle Randall knows he's got it better than most. Even if the power goes out too often, he's never seen the sun, and the runes that keep the last of the great cities in the air are starting to fail.

Even if Kyle can't shake his attraction to his emotionally unavailable boss, the master of their lower city brothel who seems frustratingly determined to keep things *professional* between them.

And then there's the ex-client who wants revenge on Kyle, all the people mysteriously going missing, and whatever shady dealings are happening in the bowels of the city.

But that's all survivable, right?

Right?

The *House Epsilon Duology* is a futuristic fantasy MM romance featuring a boss/employee relationship, sunshine Dom + the competent bad-ass who subs for him, sex workers (portrayed in a positive light), floating cities, magic runes, plots and conspiracies, the usual levels of smut, kink, and banter, and ~~an unhealthy~~ a perfectly healthy amount of 1980s song references.

AN OATH AND A PROMISE

AN OATH AND A PROMISE

Made in the USA
Las Vegas, NV
18 February 2025

18351217R00243